BALANCED LUCK

TWISTED LUCK
BOOK EIGHT

MEL TODD

BAD ASH PUBLISHING

Bad Ash Publishing

86 Desmond Court

Powder Springs, GA 30127

www.badashpublishing.com

Publisher's Note: This is a work of fiction. Names, characters, places, and incidents are a product of the author's imagination. Locales and public names are sometimes used for atmospheric purposes. Any resemblance to actual people, living or dead, or to businesses, companies, events, institutions, or locales is completely coincidental.

Cover by Ampersand Books

Balanced Luck/ Mel Todd -- 1st ed.

Paper 5x8 ISBN 978-1-950287-32-1

Hardback 6x9 ISBN 978-1-950287-33-8

Audio ISBN 978-1-950287-35-2

Bad Ash Publishing

❀ Created with Vellum

There have been more rips opening. Creatures are poking out or escaping. What is the government going to do to protect us? Are we just supposed to accept this as normal? ~ Editorial Letters

CHAOS

The revelations in the council had not really changed anything. The next council meeting was set up for two days later. I'd spent my time talking to Jo and Sable and making sure they were safe. We were accelerating getting them into the Tudor house, but it wasn't going to be overnight.

I walked into the council meeting in what I'd started to think of as my "War Gear". Carelian decided to wear the harness and instead asked me to load it with treats, shears, and all manner of things. I didn't understand why he'd had this change of heart. I also couldn't figure out why he didn't clank when he padded behind me. Most of my questions disappeared as he sat there talking to someone and pulled a treat out of one bag, then pulled a file out of another small pouch, and the being's eyes, an Aralez in this case, widened. Carelian start pointing out things in the other bags, especially his bowl.

"Is he showing off his harness?" Citlali asked me from her chair. I'd left the chair of swords. It amused me and Citlali hadn't asked me to change it. The symbolism might be missed by some of the denizens, but for me it served as a reminder— this wasn't for fun.

"Yes," I said, watching the interaction and how more and more of the non-humanoid denizens were inching closer. "He asked me this morning but wouldn't say why his attitude has changed. And knowing the Cath like I do, I suspect there is something else besides the obvious going on."

Citlali and I watched for a long time. There was still time before the meeting was scheduled to start, and Shay had not shown up, though I expected him shortly. Dahli and Scott were coming with him and while Dahli seemed more straightforward than most familiars, she, like most of them, could open a rip to her realm.

"Kesis," Citlali said suddenly, her eyes still on Carelian. "Do you want a harness?"

Kesis, who'd been busy making sure her smoky gray fur was perfect, flicked an ear in the direction where Carelian was holding court. ~I would not be opposed to something simpler,~ she finally said, though she refused to actually look at him.

"Why did you never ask for one before?"

I ducked my head, expecting the answer about to come and I didn't want to make either of them feel like I was laughing at them.

~You never offered. Also, the ones I had seen always were things to control the animal. His provides him options. The thumbs are helpful but lacking them can be overcome.~ The disdain on thumbs had me fighting back a snort of laughter. It was the same disdain Jaz used when she really wanted something, but didn't want to let anyone know.

"Ah." Citlali fell silent. I went back to watching the political drama around us. People rippled and flowed in and around, with a heated atmosphere that I knew I was at the center of. The number of glances, glares, and smirks in my direction made that clear.

I should probably go mingle and get my opinions and needs clearly set, but it seemed like too much effort. Right now, I wanted to see what would happen. More than one denizen looked like they were about to start our way, then would glance at me and Citlali's chair and veer away. Or even more interestingly, go to talk to Carelian.

The constant opening of portals was a constant background pain, making me ignore the comings and goings completely.

"Morning, Cori," Shay said right behind me, and I flinched. I'd been too focused on the drama around us and forgot to keep an eye out for him.

I pushed my immediate fight response down—and when

3

had that become my first reaction—and smiled at him, Scott, and Dahli.

"Morning. You ready for this?"

Shay snorted as he pulled out his travel mug and settled into the chair that waited for him. "If I knew what this was, maybe. As it is, I've got bets as to what happens today."

"Oh?" I raised a brow. "Care to enlighten me?"

"Nope. Cause you'll change the circumstances if you know. Just be you." He smirked at me, and I narrowed my eyes at him, not impressed.

"Should I be worried?"

"No. I just have ideas as to what I think will happen and have a bet with Scott about it," he said with a dismissive wave. "Nothing major."

I looked over at Scott, who stood between Shay and the sword chair. "And what is the bet for?"

"Who cooks dinner tonight," Scott said with a laugh. "Personally, I hope he loses as his Japanese American fusion dishes are delicious."

I blinked, looking at the two of them. "You live with him now?" I knew it wasn't my business, but Scott was so much bigger than life that the question slipped out.

"Short-term stay with he and Sloane. They are just too cute, and it amuses me to be a foil. But I'm not good at staying in one place too long. Once this whole thing is done, Dahli and I will probably get back on the road."

The words bounced in my head. "Wait, Shay? You and Sloane are a couple?"

Shay looked at me, brow raised. "Yes? And?"

My mouth opened and closed, and I thought back to when I'd worked in the coffee shop. I'd seen him with more than one female date. But then there was Sloane, their behavior at

Sloane's house. "Huh. I mean nothing. I like Sloane, it just surprises me."

Shay shrugged. "He makes me happy, and for some reason he doesn't hate me. I'm not going to complain."

That made me giggle and feel like I was nineteen again. "Then yep you should stay with him. I would have strangled you."

Scott laughed, and I thought he was about to say something when a piercing whistle cut through the air and my brain. Who knew you could whistle in mindspeak? Once I'd quit wincing in pain, I searched for the maker of the sound even as everyone else fell silent and did the same thing, at least judging from rotating heads.

It didn't take long to figure it out as Tirsane stood in the middle of the circle, her head held high, and snakes slicked back into an undulating braid. Her hands were clasped in front of her and she just waited until most of the room had gone silent. She spoke aloud, but the same words were a soft echo in my mind. It felt odd.

"As there is no chair, there is no ability to call council to order. As we are trying to figure this out, all visitors be aware you have a voice as inhabitants of the realms. We seek nominations for the title of chair." She waited in the middle of the ring.

I scanned and noted groups of beings focused around central figures. Those had to be the groups that were going to nominate someone. I was proved correct in the next few seconds.

"I nominate Tirsane."

"I nominate Shiarissa." From the way the name was pronounced, I was pretty sure the naga had nominated herself.

~I nominate Jeorgaz.~

~I nominate Freya.~

~I nominate Zmaug.~ That voice I recognized and shot a

glance at Zmaug, who was glaring at Onyx lying next to her. I fought down a snicker.

~I nominate Cori Munroe.~

My spine went rigid at that comment, and I tried to place who said it, but there were too many moving beings to even have an idea of the culprit. Everyone fell silent after that, and I sighed. It really shouldn't have surprised me. It still did. I hoped that Salistra didn't pull any of her favors to the forefront.

After a minute, Tirsane spoke into the silence. "We have Tirsane, Shiarissa, Jeorgaz, Freya, Zmaug, and Cori Munroe. Are there any others?"

Again, there was silence though I heard lots of low-level mutters and the hum of communication in my mind that told me conversations were going on all around me.

"Very well. Let me hear seconds."

All of us but Shiarissa received a second, but that didn't narrow the field down much.

"Next step. Jeorgaz, are you willing to serve as a chair?" I had no idea what the flow for this was, but just the fact that I got asked made me feel better.

The crowd parted to show Jeorgaz, his feathers alive with flickering flames, sitting on a perch. For the first time I saw multiple other phoenixes with him. Given Brix's story, it meant they were all under a few thousand years old, but it gave me a sense of hope that there were more than just two. There was one in all the colors of blue, from a white blue to a black. Another had browns, but when the feathers moved I could see designs in iridescent blues and purples on the feathers. Yet another reminded me of cotton candy, all pastels and puffy as if it was so young its feathers hadn't completed coming in.

Jeorgaz turned his head to the others, and there was a sense of communication between them, then he faced Tirsane.

~I do not believe I best serve the realms by being chair. I

decline the opportunity.~ If there was emotion in his voice I couldn't read it, it just sounded like he was talking, not that something important was being decided.

Tirsane nodded. "Zmaug, are you willing to serve as chair?"

~Scorched ashes, no. I'd rather be thrown into the void than deal with you bunch of air brains.~ Zmaug's response was fast and hard, though I heard others besides me laughing. I found it hilarious that she attended most of the meetings but had no desire to be involved. Or maybe I didn't. Being an observer to all of this would be much more palatable than being in the middle of it.

Tirsane retained her implacable facade. "Freya?"

There was a long sigh, and a Valkyrie stepped forward. She was much older than Frej, though her skin was mostly wrinkle free. She had eyes that screamed her age, centuries not decades. Her wings were white where they joined to her body but went from that to all the ranges of grey to a black that called to the emptiness of the void. Her hair was the same type as Frej's, but it too had paled into a silver that almost out shined her armor.

"I will serve if elected."

Tirsane nodded. "I too will serve if elected." She pivoted to look at me. "Cori Munroe, will you serve?"

It took everything I had to not respond with an immediate "Fuck no", but instead I shook my head. "I do not believe being chair is the best use of my abilities."

Tirsane didn't smile, but her snakes bobbed at me, laughing. "Then the contenders are Tirsane of Spirit and Freya of Order." At her words, Freya moved out to stand next to her. "All beings of the realms have the opportunity to vote."

Behind her, out of the ground, rose two urns. One was covered with drawings or etchings of snakes, while the other was covered with similar designs of feathers. Next to them a large open bowl of pebbles appeared "Put a pebble in the one you desire to have as your new chair." With those words, Tirsane turned to talk to Frej in low tones and beings began to move toward the pebbles.

"Well, I don't have to cook tonight," Shay said with a grin in his voice.

I turned to look at him. "You bet they'd try to make me chair?"

"Yep. Though I didn't figure you'd take it, but I knew you'd be suggested." He looked around at the beings moving to vote. "I have to say I rather like their way of doing it. No speeches, fast and simple. It can take weeks or more for us to elect a majority chair in our political system. This speeds it up. Though I supposed it would be easy enough to cheat and win. Just have all your followers pick up two pebbles."

I snorted. "I bet you can't. But I wouldn't suggest trying."

"Who do you wish us to vote for?" Citlali asked, and I turned to her, my brow furrowed.

"Why are you asking me? You get to vote the way you want to vote." The idea of telling people how to vote made my skin crawl, but there was also the fact that I had no idea whom to vote for.

"Because you know the players better than I do and you might have a feel as to whom would be the best in this situation," she said, watching the beings drop pebbles in then move away.

I blinked, wondering if my eyes were tricking me because it looked like one urn was higher than the other.

"You've met Tirsane. I've never met Freya and other than her being named after a god from Norse mythology, I couldn't tell you much. But you need to vote your conscience and who you believe would be best in that role." I rose, partially to avoid the conversation, partially to vote, but mostly because way too many beings seemed interested in my answer.

There was an odd amount of space around me as I went through the line to get my pebble. Right before I got there, Carelian joined me and reached up to grab a polished stone as well.

"You can vote in this?" I asked, surprised, though Tirsane had said all beings.

~Any member of the realms that wishes to may, but they must come here. This will very probably take a few hours as until more than fifteen minutes has passed without a vote, it isn't closed.~ He was nonchalant as he dropped his vote in Tirsane's urn. I noticed they were actually placed on scales and you could see which was winning by how they balanced. For a minute I was amazed, but it occurred to me transforming stones to be exactly the same wasn't that hard and it made it easy to tell the leader.

Aware of too many eyes on me, I dropped my vote in Freya's urn then walked away. They had been close to equal when I went up with Tirsane in a slight lead. I didn't look back as I sank down in my chair. Citlali and Shay had gone up, though Scott and Dahli stood there.

"You two both get to vote also," I said with a small prompt from Carelian.

"We do?" He seemed surprised.

"You're here. You get to vote. Technically, I could go grab anyone from Earth I wanted to, and they could vote. Not worth it in this case, but it is interesting. If you care enough to come vote, you can."

Scott looked down at the big beast by his side. "You want to vote Dahli?"

~Yes. Dahli vote.~ They headed to vote, and I sat there and waited for the outcome, wondering what would change.

If you get an offer to go to the Library of Magic, take it. As far as I can figure out, Shay and Munroe are controlling access, but I've been there. It will blow your mind. If you are researching anything prior to the spread of Christianity, this is the place to go. They even have a room devoted to what was lost in the burning of the Alexandrian library. ~ Anonymous on the Emrys website

ORDER

Carelian was correct about the time. We had beings wander over, talk to us, leave. Esmere hung out for a while. Even Salistra wandered over so she and Esmere could exchange insults. Only Tirsane and Freya were not social, nor did they vote. I sent Carelian back to Earth to get food for us. Being a bit bitchy, I had him get pizza and lots of other stuff. I had no issue with bribes or other offers to help sway opinions.

When it was ready, Scott stepped into the rip to pick them up from the house. He also brought back fresh drinks for us, which improved my mood greatly. I'd needed some caffeine and no matter what I did, I couldn't magic up good tasting coffee or Coke. Water, yes, anything else, not really.

We sat there in the council chambers, filling it with the scent of cheese, tomato sauce, fresh baked bread, and meat. We had most of the chamber's attention while we ate. And when I set out a basket of pepperoni bites offering them to anyone who wanted them, a fist fight almost broke out. I was very clear about the meat, tomatoes, and wheat it was created with. Though from what I'd been able to discern about most denizens, they had food preferences, not real restrictions. Salistra had declared them "intriguing" giving me a hint as to what to bring next time to purchase her favor.

That stopped me and I tried to remember if there were any herbivores that I had seen as a denizen and not just an animal. Before I could figure out the answer, a bell chimed.

"A decision has been made. Freya is the new chair," Tirsane announced in clear tones. It was easy to see that the urn covered with wings was slightly lower than the one with hers. I let loose a silent sigh of relief. With that, Tirsane slithered back to her normal position in the ring of Spirit as moderate applause and cheers rippled through the room.

Freya stood there for a minute, then spread her wings wide. "I, Freya Odindotter, accept the position of chair for the Council of the Realms and all the duties that come with it." I could feel the pulse of magic and I saw a bracelet appear on her left arm. My mind flashed on something I'd never connected before. The ring Brix had worn on his right talon.

A hush fell as all eyes were on the woman and I watched just as closely. I knew nothing about her, so I had no idea if she was friendly or not to humans and me in particular.

"I call this council to order. Please clear the chambers." Her words rang with power, but I could hear the sound of another language. Tirsane had mentioned once that in the council chambers you always heard your mother tongue, but most denizens could speak at least one Earth language, otherwise they would mind speak, but here it was always in your language. A nice bit of magic I wish I could figure out. The effect probably involved Transform and Air or maybe Telepathy?

The huge group faded away, some to the upper gallery, but others just left, side stepping into wherever they had come from. I settled down and kept my eyes on the new head honcho. Maybe now things would change.

Freya stood, eyes sweeping around, and nodded when the only people down here were the lords and their advisors. Bane-yarl had showed up in the last hour, well aware of how long this took. He wasn't a fan of the pepperoni bites but enjoyed the spinach and feta breadsticks.

"The primary issue on the agenda, as far as I know it, are the rips from our realms to Earth and the danger Earth Lord Cori has stated is present from humans."

I almost choked on my soda. She'd managed to imply I was lying without saying it. I was impressed and offended at the same time.

"Does anyone have anything to offer?" She looked around, waiting.

~I say the Herald of Magic should be required to put forth her full effort to stopping the loss of magic before any more damage is done.~

Salistra again. But what was her game? I responded while still sitting in my lush chair.

"I have no issue doing that, if someone would tell me what effort should be put forth. I am the one who found the Library of Magic and we are getting ready to work on the information that is in there, but without any database or knowledge of what I'm looking for, it might take a while."

Freya nodded. "The full resources of the council are at your disposal. How shall we assist you?"

I didn't bother to repress my snort. "And what resources are those? Because prior to this the amount of assistance I've received has been minimal. I was the one that found the Library of Magic and we're trying to get information from there. I just haven't had time yet."

Freja cleared her throat. "I admit the resources we have are better focused on dealing damage or even destroying things than finding information lost centuries ago. However, the Valkyries and Order will not be seen as neglectful in this situation." There was a sharpness to her tone now. "The scrolls and edda's of the Valkyries are open to your perusal and I will offer up Frej to act as your liaison."

Frej glared at me, then rolled her eyes. It looked like someone was being punished for not helping sooner. I suspected bringing some mead would help with that. While I could piss everyone off and force them, being nice was much less effort.

"Spirit has been searching, but what records we have are all in memory stones and while those are available to the Herald, we are still reviewing them to see if any would have information to assist in this area." Tirsane's words didn't surprise me. She'd let me know all memory stones in Spirit were being rounded up and she and a few others capable of working them were going through them to see if there was anything on them that might be helpful, but it took a while to dig through. You couldn't assume one about weaving baskets didn't have something important later in the memory.

Esmere yawned, her sharp teeth catching the light in odd ways. ~Chaos looks, but other than some songs, most of our history is not recorded. The only possibility is bits of Chaos that have existed since the primordial times, but they must be addressed individually and it is not...~ She paused for a moment searching for a word. ~...expedient or comfortable even for those of Chaos.~

Those last words surprised me. Esmere had mentioned Bob was trying to help, but the word comfortable didn't make sense.

Freya turned her gaze to me, and I sighed marshalling my argument. "You know what we are doing. All I can say is keep looking because regardless of what Brix or the council believes, if I can't do it, your price will be higher than Earth's."

Freya tilted her head. "Would you explain that? I do not understand why you say that. You mentioned the weapons and they could do great amounts of damage, but why would we be at more risk?"

I heard Shay snort behind me, and I tried to figure out how to explain this.

"If I may?" Citlali asked. I sagged in relief and waved at her to continue. She turned to gaze to Zmaug and Onyx laying in the clearing watching through the torn down wall. "Zmaug, you are a mighty dragon. Are there many dragons or even other creatures mightier than you?"

Zmaug sat up a bit, preening. ~Not many. My mate, of course. There are a few great dragons that slumber that might be able to best me in battle. Otherwise I would say only Bob or the deep ones.~ She had a bit of arrogance in her response but overall it was actually well thought out. It also verified to me exactly where she was in the dragon hierarchy.

"How many humans do you think you could kill in five minutes?" Citlali asked, her voice idle, but she pulled out her phone. That confused me, as there was no signal here at all.

~Humans? At least 100 I would think.~ Zmaug sounded confused by the question which matched my own feelings.

"And how many denizens exist that you think could match you or even half of that?"

A wisp of smoke trailed up from Zmaug's nostril. ~Maybe a thousand, two at most. For those that are much less powerful than me, maybe ten or twenty thousand?~ This was said slowly and with a bit of fumbling with those numbers. I still just watched Citlali, trying to figure out the plan.

"Okay, let me suppose your numbers are low, and in fact there are a hundred thousand beings that are as mighty as you and could kill a hundred humans in five minutes."

I wanted to interrupt and mention guns, knives, grenades, all the other weapons humans had, but I kept my mouth shut and let Citlali run with it.

~I doubt there are that many with my levels of power, but if you say so.~ Zmaug's attention was firmly locked on Citlali, as was most of the chamber.

"Then a hundred people each for over a hundred thousand denizens?" Citlali prompted. Zmaug grunted in acceptance, giving Citlali time to type on her phone. "That would be ten million people that would die, if they attacked, or ten million to destroy all the very powerful denizens."

The chamber seemed to agree in principle, and I saw where she was going.

"That seems like a lot, but as Tirsane found out, to her surprise, Earth has over seven billion people. That means for every one of you that are as powerful as Zmaug, we have over seventy million people. Even if you could kill a thousand humans before you fell, we would still crush you."

The chamber had fallen silent as everyone registered that.

"Then there are our weapons," Shay contributed. "We have guns that can put a metal bullet through inch thick steel hundreds of yards away. People can get these and use them. And that is assuming none of us are mages. And there are a lot of us who are very, very capable of killing. We just don't."

The hush that fell over the chamber turned my insides cold, and I suspect I wasn't the only one.

"I see." Freya cleared her throat. "Does anyone else have anything to say?" Freya waited a minute, then continued. "If you find anything that is of assistance with these rips, I advise, for all our sakes, to get the information to the Earth Lords as quickly as possible." She looked around to make sure her message was understood. "Then I call this meeting to a close."

There was an odd burst of sound after she said that, as if everyone exhaled in relief that nothing more had happened. Beings came streaming from the gallery and the chatter from so many made the chamber feel like it had shrunk.

"I'm going to go talk to Freya. Can you go talk to Chaos? Just be careful asking Bob things. It won't talk if you don't ask direct questions. I take that as a kindness." They nodded. Bob just made human minds bleed.

I headed toward Order. Freya was an unknown quantity, and I wanted to see where she fell with the whole Herald crap.

"Cori?" Tirsane's' voice caught my attention, and I pivoted to go talk to her for a minute.

"Hey, Tirsane. You glad you didn't get selected?"

"Rather. The chair position has never interested me. I prefer to run my domain and make sure my charges are safe and as happy as possible within the limits of their own efforts." I nodded. The conversation between Tirsane and Marisol regarding social responsibility and the differing types of governances had been enlightening.

"I get that. To be honest," I said with a touch of guilt, "that was kind of why I didn't vote for you. I didn't want to lose my friend Tirsane when I had to deal with the Chair Tirsane."

Her smile widened. "Ah. That explains much. Many wondered about your choice, and it influenced many in how they voted."

I cringed. "Sorry."

"Do not be. That is the nature of the game. The weak follow the powerful."

"Ugh. I know, but still. So what's up?" I really did want to talk to Freya and I could show up to talk to Tirsane really at almost any time.

"I have been thinking about the issue we are facing," Tirsane started, her voice more serious than I'd ever heard, but what really had me worried were her snakes. They were in a bun at the back of her skull, hiding from me, from everyone. They'd never done that before.

"Did you come up with something?" I couldn't imagine what option she'd discovered to cause her snakes to hide.

"I believe so. I think it would be best if you killed me."

The Emergency Broadcast System will start issuing alerts for rips in the zip codes they occur. Make sure your smart phones and your car are set to display alerts from the EBS system. Your life and the lives of those you love may depend on it. ~ EBS PSA

SPIRIT

Her words acted like a wave of silence that rippled through the chamber. The silence becoming an effect that spread out until the sound had died away and everyone stared at us.

"What?" I managed not to screech the word, but my voice cracked, forcing it out. Carelian was at my side, and I buried my hand in his fur, seeking reassurance.

"I have gone over the options many times. I am unable to shut off this power funnel I created, and the realms are falling apart, risking all our lives. It seems to me if I am dead, then there will no longer be an issue." Her voice sounded calm and serene, but her snakes told me she wasn't so relaxed about this option.

I knew I didn't do well when I was surprised or upset. I knew I should probably walk away and think about this. I knew all of it. And I couldn't stop my mouth.

"Why would you ask me that? Why not ask someone else to kill you or even kill yourself?" I wanted to cry and scream. The idea of killing her, of a killing a friend, was like all of my worst nightmares coming together. I'd always been worried about accidentally killing someone, but to do it on purpose and to a friend. It would be a repeat of Stevie all over again, but this time with intent.

All the pizza we'd eaten threatened to return.

"I thought about killing myself. Salistra and I discussed that option. But I fear the risk is too great. If I died by any other means than that of the Herald, magic may still just funnel without any control. But the odds are greater that if you were the one to end my life, then Magic would take that as an end to our agreement."

The weight of everyone's attention was like a smothering blanket. I found myself frozen in place, even down to the fact that I struggled to breathe. Being attacked would have been a blessing compared to this. Fighting the entire council would have been easier.

"Cori, it really is the best option. I have sisters and others in Spirit that can act as the realm's central leader." She sounded like she was trying to reassure me. The words managed to crack the ice that locked me in place.

"And if you're wrong?" I finally managed to squeak out, each word forced past a throat so tight I could barely inhale. "If you are wrong and I kill a friend and it doesn't change?"

She shrugged. "Then we tried, and you keep on going. But if it works, then the problem is solved. The realms will go back as before."

"No." My voice was hard and flat. I leaned in. "If you presented with me any level of proof, any examples where this had worked, I might, MIGHT, have possibly considered it. But this? An idea? No." I bit out each word, fighting to keep from vomiting as I did. "I will never do it if it is a random possibility. I'll die first."

I looked around the chamber and the number of beings watching me with disapproval on their faces, as if they thought I should do what she asked, hit me like a whip.

"No." I managed to say one more time and then I side-stepped home. Running away from the attention, the looks, running to my safe space. Hamiada's warmth wrapped around me as I stood in the house, panting with stress and nausea. It was too quiet. The kids were with Marisol while Jo and Sable finished the house. Already things had started being moved over, and the lack of things was another knife across my heart.

I couldn't stand there. I had to know. I burst out the front door at a run, racing to the Tudor house down the street. It wasn't a long walk, maybe ten minutes at a light stroll. I ran, and it took forever.

The door was open, and I raced in. "JO!" My voice was a scream of need and emotions that threatened to destroy me. I had to know she was okay. I needed her. Sable. I'd go to the kids in a minute.

"Cori?" Jo stuck her head over the railing to look at me. "What's wrong?"

The years of love, support, just being my family had erased any walls or need to pretend to be strong. I raced up the stairs and threw myself at her.

Jo's arms wrapped around me, still strong, still my rock, and I shattered in her arms. "Cori, what happened?" She sank to the ground, pulling me softly wrapped in her arms. I felt Carelian appear next to me, his heat and purrs filling the area. A minute later, Sable appeared.

"Jo? Cori?" Her voice sounded confused and worried, but I couldn't stop crying. Images of me plunging a knife into Tirsane, or worse, just killing her and watching her drop dead. The idea of people cheering, thinking her sacrifice made everything okay, was almost worse. I panted with the effort to not vomit, even as I sobbed.

"I don't know. She's crying too hard to talk. Carelian, are the kids okay?"

~Yes. This has nothing to do with them.~

"Thank you. Sable, can you get some coffee and then we'll figure out what is going on." Jo sounded so calm and sure, the tension that had been in her voice fading as Carelian verified the children were okay. I should have thought of that, but I hadn't.

No one can cry forever and I rarely let myself cry. The smell of coffee helped me cut off my tears and focus on my breathing as I pulled away from Jo.

Sable handed me a mug of coffee and some tissues. I wiped

my eyes and nose and wrapped trembling fingers around the mug.

"Sorry about your shirt," I muttered, looking at Jo's soaked shirt. It had been an old tee, so not like I'd ruined a silk shirt or anything, but still.

Jo snorted. "Like I give a fuck. What is wrong?"

Sable sat on the floor with us. We created a small circle as Carelian wiggled his way over to put his head on my lap, purring. I pried my right hand off the mug and petted him.

"Tirsane asked me to kill her," I said, swallowing hard to keep the nausea down.

"What?" burst out from both of them, so in between sips of whiskey-laced coffee I explained everything. It tumbled out in a fast and disjointed manner. I think explaining it took longer than the actual event.

They both looked at me, though I stared mostly at the floor. I was still shaking just from the horrible images in my head and the odd sense of double betrayal. Betrayal that Tirsane thought I'd kill her and a betrayal that no one else protested.

"I don't understand," Sable said. She leaned over a bit to rest her hand on my leg. "I mean, I get why you're upset, but why would she think that her death is the answer?" She paused and signed. "No, I get that too, but why ask you like that?"

~It is not unheard of,~ Carelian said quietly. He'd been surprisingly silent this entire time.

"What do you mean?" Jo still had her right arm around me, while Carelian had his head and paw on my left. I felt surrounded by love and it was going a long way to making me feel much more secure.

~You treat us as humans. We aren't,~ he said with a sigh. ~Your stories of human sacrifices aren't stories to us, they are still part of our lives. There are many areas where if food gets scarce, the old are eaten. Granted, they are treated well, but it isn't uncommon for the old to ask someone they trust to take their life. To die for others is honored and expected when times get bad.~

"You've eaten other Cath?" Sable's voice was barely above a whisper, and I didn't blame her. I couldn't imagine butchering a Cath. The idea made it even harder to keep my lunch down. I didn't think I'd ever be able to eat pepperoni pizza again.

~No. That is one of the reasons Esmere is so popular a Lord. Since she took the position, the resources are well managed and there has never been a famine. All the beings that live in her realm are healthy and sleek. We lack for little in the way of food, water, or protection. Even the prey is happy and fat.~ There was a rumble of approval there. ~But if things went wrong, she would offer to die to fix it.~

"A sacrifice to Magic?" I asked, my voice still thick with tears.

~Yes,~ he said simply. ~But always it is voluntary. Magic is fickler than you can imagine, you've only ever been to stable realms and pockets. What else exists is beyond anything you've seen.~ His voice was calm.

"But if she's dead, where does she go? Isn't she functionally immortal?" Sable's question echoed my thoughts. Most of us believed in an afterlife. Magic was too wondrous for there to not be more, but there was little in the way of a widely established religion. It was hard to have faith when so many could do miracles. Buddhism was probably the most popular, as it worked well with the ideas of magic. It allowed you to become a better person while still doing miracles.

~Immortal?~ Carelian sounded shocked. ~No. Of all of us, only Bob is functionally immortal and even then, that aspect of him can be destroyed. Brix is older than I realized, but all of us can be killed. Gorgons simply age slowly. I believe if she lived to die of old age, she would slowly turn to stone, a statue of herself.~

"But why ask me?" I knew I was whining, but I didn't care. Why me?

~Magic. You are the Herald. A powerful quean. A tool of Magic. Who else should she ask?~ He sounded so matter of fact. I wanted to hit him, pound my fists on the ground and scream my refusal.

Instead, I managed to pull my hand from his head and wrap it around the coffee cup. I took a deep sip, letting the whiskey sink into me.

"I won't. I don't care. Maybe, maybe if she was desperately hurt, I could. Or if someone could offer me proof, absolute proof, I might consider it. But no, I won't." My heart hurt with every beat.

~And if both humans and denizens keep dying?~ His voice was soft, compassionate, and for the first time ever, I didn't want to see or hear him.

"No. I won't." I forced myself to my feet. "I need to see the kids." I just turned and headed down the stairs, the mug clutched in my hand so tightly that my hand ached.

"That sounds like a good idea," Jo said softly. They all followed me out of the house and down the street. The coffee was stone cold by the time we got to Marisol's, but I couldn't put it down. It gave me something to hold on to.

"Marisol, we're here," I called out as I walked in. The sound of kids in the kitchen drew me there. I turned to see them making drop cookies, smiles on their faces and the quetzos on the counter watching very carefully.

"Look! We're making cookies," Jaz declared, swinging the spoon around enough so that a bit of cookie batter flew off. Azul jumped up and caught it, eating it with every evidence of appreciation.

"I see that. You mind if I watch?"

Marisol darted a look at me and the somber Jo and Sable behind me.

"Sure, Momma Cori. You can taste them when they get out." Magne grinned as he spoke, and I leaned against the wall.

"I'll make us coffee," Jo said softly. Sable pulled me against her and Carelian rubbed his face on my leg.

~You are my quean. Always.~ He sounded sad, and I just ached wondering what else might be destroyed before I could fix it.

We stood there letting the kids yammer. I'd deal with this later. Right now, I needed to wrap my family around me.

CHAPTER

FOUR

When did Atlantis become hot again? And how can I get in on the research wagon? Are we talking fiction? Because we all know Atlantis wasn't real. Plato was trying to use it as an analogy and the documentation that would back it up has been lost to time. But really. I can read Greek, Hebrew, Babylonian, and a bit of Viking runes. What is going on? ~ Message on the Emrys Research Board

CHAOS

I t took me two days to get into a headspace where I could even begin to address the idea. With Stevie, I hadn't known what I was doing. Killing someone when fighting for my life was hard, but I could do it. But just kill a friend because of a possibility?

Monday morning, I found myself awake way too early. What was with this finally retiring and I never seemed to sleep in? It implied something very wrong with my mindset.

"I need to talk to her." I said the words out loud. Carelian had barely left my side the last two days, but also hadn't said much. This was one of those cultural things that I didn't know how to broach.

With my words as my driving force, I got up, showered and filled a travel mug with mocha. I needed the extra sweetness. Ten minutes later, I walked into Tirsane's grotto.

Another gorgon came out, one I'd never met before.

"You must be Cori?" she asked with a smile. Where Tirsane was an alabaster white that never seemed to tan, this one was the rich color of ground nutmeg. She also had slitted eyes and obsidian black teeth, but a friendly smile.

"Yes. Is Tirsane available to speak to me?" I had to talk to her, but I'd do everything to keep it as friends. We were still friends, I hoped.

"Yes, she is expecting you. If you want to sit, I'll fetch her." She waved over to the little seating area I'd been at before.

"Thank you." I headed there as Carelian went to peer at the small pond and the fish that darted one way and another as his shadow loomed over them.

"Do not eat my fish, Carelian. You have larger, much tastier options at home, I believe." Tirsane's voice reached us before I saw her. She came out from behind one of the walls.

~I was not going to, but chasing them is entertaining.~ He left off and came over to throw himself at the ground next to where I sat, and started grooming.

Tirsane had circles under her eyes, and, for the first time, she didn't look like someone perfect and untouchable. She sank into the chair across from me and peered at me with her alien eyes. Eyes that had become as dear to me as Jo's.

"I fear I have upset you. May I still call you friend?"

The words made my shoulders sag in relief. "As long as you wish to be mine."

A similar relief washed through her and we sat there in silence. It was broken by the other gorgon coming out carrying a tray with a kettle that still steamed and two cups.

"Here, I brought you drinks," she said with a soft smile, then disappeared as quietly as she had appeared.

"Ah. Stenia is thoughtful, as always," she murmured. "This is coffee from the area you call Greece. When we lived there long, long ago, it was a favorite and still is. I warn you, it is strong compared to what you drink." She poured some rich, dark brown liquid into each small cup. Not quite an espresso cup, but similar, and handed it to me.

Understanding the test and offering for what it was, I took the cup, sniffing first. Cinnamon, spices, a hint of sugar, wafted up to my nose. I took a sip and swallowed in delight. It was rich, thick, darkly sweet, and strong enough that only the Mexican coffee I made occasionally could stand up to it.

"Thank you, this is delicious."

We sat there quietly. I, at least, didn't know where to start.

"I did not mean to offend you with my request," Tirsane finally said softly. "It was meant to be an honor."

I shuddered at that and put the cup down, wrapping my hands back around my travel mug. It was made of stainless steel, so I didn't need to worry about cracking it with my grip.

"Carelian has tried to explain that. But from my point of view, a friend asked me to kill them because it might, possibly, maybe work. And I suppose, way deep down somewhere, it might be worth the price if it did work."

A smile started to grow on her face, but I raised my hand.

"But, the odds are very much pointing to the fact that it would not make any difference and I would be left having killed my friend. I will not do that." I sunk every bit of firmness into those words, even as my stomach roiled.

Her smile faded. "There is that."

"Are you really so anxious to die? Are you sick and see this as a better option?" I was grabbing at straws here and I knew it, but why would anyone be so ready to let themselves be killed?

"No. I just don't know how else to help," Tirsane admitted.

I looked up at the same blue sky with a diffuse light and caught the faces peering at us from the door to her home. All of them looked relieved in the second I had to register their presence before they hid again.

"Keep at the memory stones. I'll start going through mine. I'm headed from here to the Library to see how Cleo can help."

Tirsane nodded and her snakes twisted around, caressing her face, and giving little snake kisses on her cheeks. It told me at least deep down she hadn't wanted this, regardless of what she said.

"Would you like to come?"

Tirsane tilted her head. "Yes. I may not stay long, but I would like to get a library card so I can remember where it is."

I started to rise, but her raised hand stopped me. "Cori, it may get to a point there is no other option."

I stood slowly and looked at her. "It might. But I will have tried everything else, up to and including sacrificing my own life before I am willing to take the lives of my friends. So we had both better make sure there is another way to fix this."

She smiled, tinged with sadness. "I can but hope." She rose and Carelian opened a rip to the Library. We entered at the front steps and Tirsane gazed at it in wonder. "It is more than I had thought. I knew it existed when asked about it, but then it was gone. Vague ideas of what it should look like didn't begin to do it justice."

I smirked and waved to the door as I walked. "Let me introduce you to the librarian. You two have the same dress sense."

Tirsane gave me a funny look as we went up the stairs, so I expanded. "In that you don't wear anything, normally."

She started laughing as I pulled the door open and we went in. "Carelian, can you let Citlali and Shay know I'm here?"

He could talk to their familiars faster and was getting good at talking to Shay. Apparently, the more he was around my strange collection of friends, the more flexible his mind became.

Cleo sat behind the desk, checking books in, with a smile on her face. She looked up as we walked in and the smile grew wider, revealing her long, pointy canines.

"Cori Munroe. I have books for you based on your last requests." Her voice was friendly and even though the smile proved she was a carnivore, it also struck me as friendly.

"Thank you." After the revelation about her magic translating anything to a language I could read, I'd popped back asking for books on Atlantis or the disappearance of Magic. Out of a suspicion I'd also asked for anything on phoenixes. I waved at Tirsane. "She would like a library card."

"Wonderful. It has been so long since the Library was this popular." Her smile all but radiated happiness. "Cori, your books are in carousel 10. Please use the gloves provided. These are old and while I can repair most damage, humans are oily and some of those stains are troublesome."

I repressed a laugh and turned to look at Tirsane. "We are still friends. I just can't even process the idea of planning to kill someone that I care about. And I will do everything possible to make sure this is never a choice I have to make."

Tirsane dipped her head, the snakes still rather subdued. "I understand. Thank you."

With that I left, going toward the reading cubical. Carelian had still been following me, though his self-containment was extreme for him. The carousels were small little rooms with books, gloves, utensils for turning pages, and reading stands. It made sense, given how many beings didn't have hands like I did.

~Cori?~ he said before I reached cube ten. I stopped and looked at him.

He sat down and started to groom his paw, then stopped and looked at me. ~You know I think you are amazing.~

I shrugged, fighting not to hunch my shoulders. "Yeah."

~You are amazing exactly because of how you react and treat your friends. Anyone else would have been dismissive, rude, maybe even eager at the idea of killing a Lord. You got upset because a friend asked you to kill them. Would your reaction have been the same if it was Frej or Shiarassa?~

His gaze was so bright green I couldn't look away. "Yes. Though I wouldn't have been so upset. Annoyed, even disgusted that they would want it, but the situation wouldn't

31

have reminded me of Stevie dying. Of losing someone that I love."

~Ah. I do not think that occurred to most of us.~ His tail lashed as he looked at me. Something relatively unusual. Cath in general glanced at you, then kept scanning. They didn't like locking eyes as it made them unable to keep their eyes on their surroundings. ~Even after all these years, I still underestimate the cultural differences. And I think I hurt your feelings.~ These last words were said as if they were pried out of him.

I wrapped my arms around myself, wanting to feel wrapped in someone's arms. "Hurt? Maybe. Just the idea, the knowledge that you would think killing someone is something light and easy to do. It hurt. Why would you want me to be the one to do it?"

We stood there in that huge, empty library, the scents of dust and books a proper measure to the grief, conflicting emotions, and the vast gulf that seemed to lay between us.

~Ah.~ He closed his eyes, tail still twitching as we stood locked in this tableau of pain and love. ~On Earth, people that someone respected are often asked to give eulogies at their death? Like you did for Henri?~

"Sure. That is simply being asked to help honor their life." I didn't get where he was going.

~For us, once you are dead, your remains are returned to the realms if your people do not have other use of it. Either via fire, air, earth or water. It doesn't matter. We don't have grave-yards because even the bones are usually gone in a month. The world here is hungry and the flesh of those with magic is rich and tasty. It isn't the speaking after the fact that shows the honor, but asking to be the swift strike that ends the suffering. We don't have the medicine or other things you have. Here, if it is time for you to die, the one you respect the most is asked to deliver that blow, though often it is via magic. You trust they will do it with kindness, honor, and a minimum of pain. That is what Tirsane did publicly. She told the entire council that she respected you above all others and that she wished for you to be the one to end her life. Being Herald and the cause of all of this were just extra reasons. Mostly she said she loves you.~

I froze and played it over in my mind. "That is a strange way of saying you love someone."

~For you. How else do we show love other than offering someone our life?~ His voice was calm and measured.

I broke, again. I needed to get over this. But I moved over to him, dropping to my knees to wrap my arms around him. "Don't you dare ever ask that. You must be dying in extreme agony with no hope of a cure or solution." It was more of an order than I'd ever given him.

~But then you would? You would love me enough to set me free of this flesh?~

I hid my face in his coat but sighed. "Yes."

~Then you understand. And Cori, you have always and will always be my quean.~ It finally hit me that he wasn't calling me royalty, or he was, but more, he was saying he loved me beyond anything he could put words to.

I don't know how long we sat there before I pulled back, sniffing. The tears had only been a few and were easily dealt with. I stood, and we moved to number ten, my hand buried in his fur, needing to feel him. I pulled open the door and stopped. I had figured if I was lucky, I might get five or six books. Maybe ten. There had to be almost a hundred books in the cubical. The shelf rose up in the air and I could see titles spanning further than I could see. Gloves, a stand, and a notepad sat there, ready for me to grab the first book.

"We are going to need a bigger crew. A much bigger crew," I said, staring at the books.

Mages have floated in and out of government service from the time magic emerged. But when the United States faced World War I, there weren't enough soldiers to fight it. At this time, most mages had a level of cachet in America because the stories of magic users from the old days still created the idea of mages as more than human. In an effort to stem that and supply the war effort with men to fight, men who could use magic, President Woodrow Wilson signed the Mage Draft Act into law. The backlash sent many mages on the run, and soon after the Rogue Mage Division was created. ~ History of Magic

ORDER

I backed out of the cubical. "Did you remember to call Citlali?" I asked, staring at the door like it might explode.

~Yes, and Dahli let Scott know.~

"Would you get your mother and I'll get Baneyarl? Have Scott come as well," I said slowly.

~Baneyarl,~ I pinged softly, still staring at the cubical full of tomes and parchments.

~Yes, Cori?~ he responded after a moment.

~We have lots and lots and then more books to look at. Would you be available now?~ I was honestly worried it might take us years. As Tirsane had proved, it wouldn't be fast to go through; you could never tell what might have the information needed.

~Ah, Cleo found what we needed. Excellent. I will be there shortly.~

~Thanks,~ I said as I turned and headed back to the front desk. Tirsane was still talking to Cleo, though from their laughter and friendly demeanor, I figured they were talking about more than books.

They paused to smile at me as I walked up. "Have you reviewed all of them already, Cori?" Cleo asked.

"Uh, no. About that. Can you split them up into seven rooms? At least two that don't have humanoid hands?" I paused to count beings in my head quickly. "Unless you want to stay and help, Tirsane?"

"I will if you need me, but we still have hundreds of memory stones to go through. Why everyone thought their ancestors would want to know every detail of their day, I will never understand. I do prefer the teaching ones. They at least are direct and often have an index in them."

I laughed. "No, we'll figure it out. Thank you. And Tirsane," I said as she was about to slither off, "I love you too."

She froze, glanced at me, then Carelian. A soft smile spread across her face, then she moved out of the library. Cleo tilted her head and headed back to the cubes, humming softly.

A piece of my soul healed, and I reached out to pet Carelian. "Thank you," I said softly. He rubbed his cheek against me. Then the spikes of pain indicated incoming.

By the time everyone arrived, Cleo had returned. "The books you requested are split up from cubical three through ten. Remember, no food or drinks near the books and all the lighting is magically controlled. Use gloves or the provided utensils to turn pages. Most of you are magical enough to pull down a book without touching it. If you summon fire, I will skin you, tan your hide, and use it to repair the older books." Her words were flat and eyes cold. It wasn't a threat. It was a statement.

"Yes, ma'am," I replied automatically. She cast hard eyes over all of us. I think Esmere was the only one that didn't flinch under her glare.

With that, she flicked a tufted tail at us and headed back behind the desk.

"Come on, I'll show you." I led everyone to the cubes, though I kept number ten, hoping maybe we'd find something. "I was told the magic in here would enable us to read it, so if there are issues, go whine at Cleo, not me. I'm over being responsible for everything."

The humans laughed while the denizens just stared at me. I smirked and headed into my cubical and took a deep breath.

"You staying in here with me?" I asked Carelian. We'd learned a long time ago he could read but reading for pleasure or longer than a few minutes wasn't anything he enjoyed.

~I have little desire to leave you. You need to understand you are my quean and bad things happen when you are alone.~ He wiggled under the desk. I slipped off my shoes and put my feet on him. The slow rumble of a purr helped ground my world, and I pulled on the gloves. I reached for the first book and set it down on the stand carefully. At first, I was scared the magic didn't work, but then the text wriggled and the title appeared.

Minoan Legends

I started reading, noting anything that referred to Atlantis, magic, or a city island. It wasn't a long book, but by the end all I'd decided was that the Minoans had traded with Atlantis and not much else.

With a sigh, my body already hurting from sitting still, I reached for the next.

Treatise on Sea Fishing
Weaving Patterns
Trade Good Logs
Magic of the Ocean
Life on a Boat
Unexplained Phenomena

I sighed as I laid that one down. I'd broken down and started skimming, setting up looking for the word Atlantis and using Pattern to help me flip fast. So far, I'd had mentions of them. Oddly, the Weaving Patterns had talked about them the most with mentions of fibers, patterns, and styles that had come from Atlantis. But otherwise, I'd learned about fishing, boating, water spells, spells to call fish, and that olive oil had been highly prized, as well as salt and ambergris.

I'd had hopes for Phenomena, but there wasn't anything there except the mention of the storm in the middle of the ocean that lasted for a week and when it was over, the city nation of Atlantis had disappeared. But since there were no dates on any of these, it didn't do anything but confirm what I already knew, or at least supposed.

I reached for the next one and froze. *The True History of Atlantis* by Mera.

"This. This is what I remembered seeing in the Library when I was here. It was on a pedestal. I knew I'd seen something." I don't know if I was talking to myself or Carelian, but he answered.

~Does it have the answers you seek?~

"I don't know. I haven't opened it up yet. Kind of scared to. If it doesn't, what will?"

~There is so much information here. There may be something in the others. Surely no civilization could just disappear without some records.~

"One would think, but humans still aren't sure what happened to civilizations of the past. And what we do know, we tend to discount. We're only now starting to realize how extensive some of the civilizations in South America were." I stared at the book while I talked. "Okay, let's get to this."

With my breath held, I opened the book. Most of the older books didn't follow the same flow that I was used to. They simply said who wrote it and what it was called, then a paragraph of information. This one had an actual title page, then the next page was an author bio. I'd never seen that in what I'd been looking at.

I grew up on the shores of Atlantis. My world disappeared

when Atlantis did. *I will never stop grieving my people, but I don't want all they were to disappear.*

My hopes rose as I continued to read. It was more of a memoir than a history book, and I didn't skim. I read. It wasn't excellent fiction, there were awkward phrases and some sentences I had to read a few times to figure out. The magic translated exactly, it didn't fix sentence structure. Atlantean, or at least I assumed that was what this was, it could have been Greek, had a syntax that struck me as odd.

Run I beach flat sand water blue clear.

I figured it actually said - "I ran on a flat sandy beach near clear blue water." This made it slow going. It described a city from a girl's point of view. Talking about the decorations, the food, her family home, and my hopes started to drop. If she had left Atlantis in her teens or twenties, her observations, while interesting, wouldn't tell me what happened.

I kept going, laboring through the awkward, to me, phrasing. The last chapter finally had something that at least looked like it might be interesting. I needed feedback on what I read, so I reached out and pinged everyone.

~Yes?~ Shay said with a sense of startlement. The others sent me a questioning impression. It was like a mental version of Shay's thought.

~I have something I wanted you to hear, but I don't or can't take this book out of the cubical. Got a minute?~

The overall response was yes and so I read what I'd translated out of the book.

~Our high priest was selected today. Zenobia is a powerful mage, and she is so pretty all the boys talk about winning her hand. She is pretty, but I don't like her. She always has this sneer to her, like she thinks she's better than us. I mean, she is the high priest and the most powerful mage I've ever heard of, but she's not kind. I like Uriale better. She is kind. I wish she had been elected.~

~There is that, then pages later, this is one of the last things she writes.~ I sent the next part.

~We have phoenixes. They are so pretty. One of them gifted me a feather all the colors of fire. Zenobia talks to them all the time, but she reminds me of a merchant trying to sell something you don't need or want. But I have a pretty feather for my new dress. I wish we weren't leaving. The long sun day celebration is coming soon, and it is always the best. This year Zenobia said she would start including the phoenixes in the celebrations~

I cleared my throat, mentally and physically. Mindspeaking like that was an exhausting mental focus. ~That is one of the last things she says. Her next two are about her boat trip to a place with lots of big buildings and where women are supposed to walk behind their husband. She has opinions about that. Then she says two years later, all communication with Atlantis stopped. They apparently had regular letters back and forth, and they were gone. You think that means anything?~

There was a thoughtful silence in the mindspace as if everyone was humming under their breath.

Citlali spoke up first. ~Longest sun day is most likely the summer solstice. Most cultures have celebrated that and the winter solstice, longest and shortest days. It would make sense, but I don't know that it gives us new information.~

~True,~ I said. ~But it gives us some ideas. I might try to find Brix and ask him questions. I'm sure after thousands of years, some of the details have faded. If I can get him to talk to me.~ I didn't mention I was reluctant to cause him more pain, but if there was no other way. ~Anyone else find anything?~

~Mostly that it did exist, the fibers and weavings were impressive.~ Esmere put forth.

~Yeah, I got that too.~ I said with a wry tone. ~I now know more about weaving and fishing spells than I ever wanted.~

~I plan on utilizing those spells next deep sea fishing trip,~ Carelian said with a sense of expectation that made me smile.

~Anyone else?~ We had been at it for hours.

~Not yet,~ Scott admitted. ~But I still have at least a dozen or more books to go through.~

Everyone else said the same thing, including me. ~You want to break for some lunch, talk to Cleo, then get back to it?~ I was dying for coffee and a chance to stretch my legs. The suggestion was accepted eagerly, and I left the cubical to meet up with them.

At the front desk I smiled at Cleo. "Cleo, we're going to have a picnic out front." I ignored the surprised looks from everyone else. "Would you like to join us? It would give us a chance to ask you questions."

Cleo blinked at me. "Are you sure?"

"Of course. I assume you don't have any allergies, but prefer protein."

"Why, yes?" she said, sounding confused.

"Great! I'll go get us food." I turned to look at the bemused crew behind me. "If you'll get an area outside set up as a picnic area, I'll be back in about fifteen."

Citlali started to laugh. "They should have called you Sirocco Cori. You change everything with the ease of a storm."

I shrugged. "What? Everyone needs lunch. You all put too much weight on things. You'll set up a picnic area?" I wanted to make sure as the area right outside the Library was rather bland and dusty.

"Yes, Cori. Go," Shay said with a laugh. I sidestepped home, then called two delis and placed orders to pick up ASAP. I grabbed the car and hit the local grocery store, grabbing their sushi, chips, potato salad, and disposable plates and utensils.

Then I headed to the delis. It took almost an hour all told, but when I returned—it took me two trips—a marvel awaited me.

Now there was a lawn of grass, a large tree that looked like a willow, tables, chairs, and some blankets to lie on. Cleo sat under the tree, looking around with amazement.

"This looks wonderful," I gushed, smiling wide as I set down the food. We all fell to it and talked about what we'd found, asking Cleo questions. At the end of the day, we still didn't have answers, but my ring of friends had grown stronger and I couldn't argue about that.

Does anyone know an ancient Babylonia treat recipe? Would have to be at least four thousand years old. I want to make a treat for Cleo, but finding a recipe that would remind her of home seems impossible. Anyone? -> Response: I've got one for a Mesopotamian *mersu* she might like. DM me. ~ Message on private Library Board on Emerys forums

SPIRIT

T he next few days were torn between spending time in the library and responding to calls for help shutting rips. They were happening multiple times a day, but so far, the really big ones were only once every other day.

The difference was they grabbed me for the really big ones, the other ones multiple mages could close. But it was still a lot. My brain hurt from parsing language into English. My offerings were dangerously short. I'd used up all my saved ones, trying to do it as cheaply as possible, but I was still running out.

My hair was at my ears, my nails down to the quick, and I hadn't needed to worry about my period as I was raking my uterus of offerable material too often. If I knew how to excise my appendix, I might have. The temptation to have it removed so I could use it was there, but preservatives tended to ruin the ability to offer flesh. Yes, mages tried weird things at times.

I couldn't handle another day at the Library and it was the middle of the week, so I was curled up in my study flipping through James' journals. I still had years of stuff to go through. Jeorgaz admitted he didn't know all the stuff James had done, so I couldn't make any assumptions. Mostly, I just needed the quiet.

My phone rang, and I smiled. Kris. We hadn't talked since Christmas.

"Hey, baby brother. How are you?"

"Cori, it's bad." His words were grief stricken and exhausted.

"WHAT?!" I jerked straight up, my relaxation forgotten as adrenaline slammed into me and I was ready to go.

"There was a rip. Things got out, but we closed it." He said the words with a heaviness that told me what was coming.

"Who?" I asked, my chest hurting for my baby brother.

"Laura and Peter."

I closed my eyes. Peter had been his roommate since he went to college. Laura had been the girl he'd been flirting with. Last I heard, they weren't dating, but he was interested. They were going slow wanting to make sure there was more than lust between them.

"Carelian," I said.

~Going now.~ He knew, and I didn't have to ask.

"Kris, come home now. I'll be waiting." It wasn't a question, it was a need for both of us.

"Thanks, Cori. I don't know what to do. Give me ten." He hung up without anything else and I headed downstairs, prepping coffee with lots of Baileys.

Kris lost his roommate and the girl he liked. Carelian's bringing him home. I sent it to the group chat of Jo, Sable, and me. Then I sent another similar one to Marisol.

I'll be over shortly with soup. I have my chicken soup in the freezer, Marisol responded almost instantly.

I can't leave right now. Will be home soon as possible, Sable sent. Jo just said she was going to pick up the kids, instead of letting them do their after-school program, then she'd be home. They normally got out at two in the afternoon, but they both had sports stuff afterward. It wasn't formal, mostly it just helped them wear off some of their seemingly inexhaustible energy.

I felt the spike as Carelian came back and headed out into the hall from the kitchen to see Kris standing in the transport corner, his face gray and pain etched on his face. He had a duffle bag in one hand and the other buried in Carelian's fur.

"Kris," I murmured and opened my arms. He was in them, holding on as he started to sob. I just held him. Kris had me by a good four inches, as he was about five foot ten. At twenty-six he was still lanky, but muscled as he was a runner. His hair, the same brown as mine, was in long braids that normally hit him mid-back. Today his hair was fly-away and at his shoulder blades. Considering I'd seen him less than three weeks ago at Christmas, losing that much offering told me a lot.

I just let him cry until he was ready to pull back. "You want some coffee? I've got the fire going in the sunroom."

Swallowing, his nose and eyes red, he nodded. "Let me hit the bathroom. I'll meet you there."

I went and grabbed the coffee, his almost white with the Irish cream, and headed into the sunroom. He dropped into one of the chairs as he got there and reached for the coffee with shaking hands. His tattoo on his temple seemed as faded and gray as he was. His blue, green, and gold looked like the brightness had been drained out of it.

I didn't speak until he'd had a chance to drink some of the coffee. He looked up at me with dark eyes that showed the grief still wrapped inside.

"You want to talk about it?" I didn't want to pry. I hated to talk about things to this day, but he wasn't me.

He nodded his head jerkily, but didn't talk immediately.

"Marisol will probably be here in a few with her chicken soup. Sable and Jo will be home as soon as they can, but it'll still be another hour or two. Do you want to tell me now, or wait until everyone is here?"

He blinked at me, then drank some more coffee. I just let him process it. If what happened was as bad as I feared, there was no need to rush him. The images were probably seared into his soul.

"I want to tell you, I need to talk about it. But I don't think I can tell it twice. Can I wait?" His voice was rough, and I figured it was both from screaming and crying.

"Of course." The front door opened. "In here, Marisol," I called out. She came in and pulled Kris into another hug. A better one than mine, to be honest, she had more experience in giving them.

"I'm going to place an order for takeout, and have Jo pick it up, okay? I don't think any of us will be up for cooking." Kris nodded, and Marisol flashed me a smile.

"Kris, I brought some soup. You probably need something now. It will still be hours until dinner." Marisol had looked him over carefully and I didn't disagree that hot food was a good option.

"Please?" He croaked, and we set off on our separate things, while Carelian lay at his feet, purring, letting him know he wasn't alone. I ordered food, gave Sable a grocery list, and made sure there was food for the quetzos. The kids would be good for him. Their open love could go a long way to healing wounds. I wasn't surprised to come back to find him curled up on the floor lying alongside Carelian sleeping, the mug of soup empty next to him. I just let him be.

~Thank you,~ I sent to Carelian.

~He is hurting,~ Carelian sent back to me just as quietly. Kris was as open as me to hearing mind speak.

~Grief takes all forms.~ I replied, and Carelian just purred. I headed into the kitchen finding Marisol there, putting the extra soup into containers for later.

"He's asleep holding onto Carelian," I explained as I helped set the table for dinner later. This way it would be done.

"Good. He needs it. Did he tell you what happened?" she asked, her eyes dark with worry. Marisol had adopted Kris the way she'd pulled me and Sable into the Guzman family. There were so many days I'd thought of changing my name to Guzman because they had been more of my family than the Munroe's had been.

"Just that it was a rip. The rest is relatively obvious, but I'll let him talk." A burn started in my chest. This could all be laid at my feet, and I hated that I still didn't have an answer.

She nodded, and we spent the next few hours letting him sleep, while we cleaned and talked in the sitting room, not wanting to disturb him sleeping in the sunroom. Jo texted she was on the way home when Kris called out from the room.

"Cori?" There was a note of worry in his voice that caused a wince of empathy.

I rose and headed that direction to find him standing at the door to the sunroom. Carelian was stretching behind him.

"Hey. Sable is bringing home dinner and Jo and the kids will be home in a bit. Need anything?"

He looked pale and his brown eyes were lifeless. "Maybe?"

I walked over and hugged him, resting my head on his chest. "Anything. You know this. Come on." I could hear the car pulling into the driveway and knew in a minute there would be two bundles of energy, which would do him good.

I pulled away as I heard the front door opening and stepped aside.

"Unka Kris," was shouted as soon as the door opened, and the twin terrors aimed right for him. He smiled as he hugged them and listened to their babble about school. They were excellent for distracting. He was dragged up with them to be re-introduced to the quetzo's, because they would have forgotten him since Christmas per Jaz, and hear about their day.

Sable followed not a minute later, giving me a wink as she carried in food. "Convinced work I needed to come home early."

I grinned at her. "Excellent. Kris is upstairs with the terrors. I'm sure he will be down soon."

"Do you want me to take the kids to my house while you talk to Kris?" Marisol offered, her voice quiet.

I glanced at Jo and Sable, who looked torn. I sighed, knowing we needed to make this decision together. "I think they should hear. Rips can happen anywhere and I'd rather they understand all the bad things that can happen. It might give them nightmares, but at least then they won't talk about it being cool, which they've already started to do about the one at the zoo."

Sable grimaced, and Jo nodded. "Agreed. I'll deal with nightmares rather than them thinking it was harmless."

Marisol shrugged and I couldn't tell if she agreed with us or not.

"Okay, I'll put the food on the table. We can get the eating out of the way and then hear his story," I said, heading to the kitchen with the carryout packages. Carelian paced with me as we moved out of hearing range.

"Is he okay?" I asked, my voice soft.

~He is wounded in his heart, but being here will help. He didn't say much, but moaned a bit while he slept.~

I nodded as I pulled food out of the bags. "Would it help for me to invite any others?"

Carelian licked his paw while he thought. ~I do not believe so. There is nothing they could do to change it, so it is best it stays just family.~

Marisol had embraced Kris as a member of the family, just like me. I didn't know if he even spoke to his parents anymore, and I didn't pry. It would only stir up old wounds.

Jo and Sable changed clothes while the twins had Kris occupied, then came in to get all of us drinks. Ten minutes later, Sable called up the stairs. "Dinner."

The stampede back down included two small dragons, two hyper kids, and one rather frazzled adult. Kris had lost the shell-shocked look and now just looked overwhelmed. The twins dropped his hands as they darted to their places.

Kris stared at us. "How do you handle that? They are exhausting."

We all snickered, including Marisol. "Lots of practice," Jo said with a smile. "Come on. Let's get you fed."

We all settled down, the adults with stronger drinks available, the kids excited to have their uncle back, though even they seemed to sense he was sad as they kept up a nonstop babble that was funny but didn't require much input from the adults.

After we had been served and the first rush of hunger sated, I looked at him with a sad smile, my hands around my wine glass.

"You ready to talk now?"

The rips that are appearing worldwide have a pattern to them, I believe. I'm looking for more information from other countries, I have the US under control. If you have any information please send it to arachenaspet@ gmail.com. All information will be kept confidential. ~ Post on multiple boards

CHAOS

HE GLANCED AT THE KIDS, but we nodded. Kris cleared this throat, focusing more on the plate than us.

"Everyone knows about the rips. I mean the news talks about it non-stop. But half the time it's like 'ho-hum another rip' as if it's a tornado that wandered by or it's 'the world is ending'. There's nothing consistent. The school has set up procedures, but I mean, it's like an earthquake drill. They never happen."

His laugh was bitter and if I'd been sitting next to him, I'd have probably reached over to hug him. Instead, Jaz leaned over, and Azul crawled down her arm to wrap her tail around Kris's neck.

"Thank you," he whispered to Jaz as he petted Azul's tail. Kris swallowed and continued. "They've been using the air-raid siren system, but a rip occurs so fast and if you're where it appears the alarms don't do much good." He scrubbed at his face, blinking back tears. "The three of us were in one of the open areas. It was about lunchtime, and we'd been talking after class. Peter was going to head back to the apartment, while Laura wanted to get some food before our next class."

He fell silent again, and we just waited. It didn't need to come out fast.

"We had fifteen minutes, so we got up to head out and I felt a needle jab into my brain, hard. For a second, I wondered if Carelian had come to get me, but his rips are more like pinpricks. I feel them, but not enough to react or care. This one made me stumble, it hurt so bad. Then Laura started cussing. I turned and I saw the rip. It was vertical from the ground up and it was in front of the campus library, so the distortion stood out really obvious as part of the building was missing."

Both kids were as mesmerized as the adults, everyone wanting to hear what happened.

"The sirens started going off about then, but we were supposed to head to the library, which the rip was in front of. Peter said we should just head to the dorms, and we were going to, when things started coming out of it. They were like walking plants with open mouth things, like a Venus fly trap mouth. But then they had these fist-like things that looked like a mace? I mean, it had lots of points on it." Kris fell silent and waved his hand away. "I guess it doesn't matter what it looked like."

~It sounds like a Kudya. They are predatory plants with limited mobility,~ Carelian said with a careful tone. ~They are deadly.~

"Yeah. We found that out the hard way. About that time people were running around and screaming. We grabbed our stuff. We weren't really thinking and text-books are expensive."

There were unconscious grunts of agreements from me, Jo, and Sable. I'd have grabbed them too, to be honest.

"We were trying to figure out which way to go, when one of them got closer and screeched." He sighed and reached for the rum and Coke we'd made for him. "I know everyone says plants can't make sounds, but these things screeched, and it was loud enough it startled us, badly. Laura fell. I stopped to help her up." He took a sip, though I suspected he wanted to drain a bottle's worth of rum to ease the pain. "And then these thorn things came flying out of its fists. They looked like darts. I dropped to the ground, and they missed me, but Laura was trying to stand, and they hit her. Peter had turned to see what was delaying us and they flew right into him."

His face lost what little color he'd gained back over the day, and I wanted to tell him to stop, not to tell us, but I knew he needed to expel it from his mind. The twins were hanging on every word and the quetzos had curled up tight in their arms, though they watched Kris with dark eyes as well.

"Laura screamed. I've never heard a sound like that, and she didn't quit screaming until she did. I mean—she was screaming and writhing. From every thorn that had hit her, black lines were spreading outward so fast I couldn't believe it. And her screams. Then she just stopped. All of her stopped. She was dead. I had her in my arms and she was just gone. I turned when I heard Peter stop screaming too to see him in a motionless lump on the ground as well."

"Oh Kris," Marisol murmured. I had my hand around the wine glass wishing desperately it would lessen or erase the pain, but I knew it wouldn't do anything to make this easier. For any of us.

"I lost it. I'm strong in Soul, pale in Relativity and Psychic. Such useless skills."

His words were bitter, and I made a note to teach him about the Soul Pull, though I didn't know if it would have made any difference in this situation.

"I'd already cast Lady Luck, but it didn't really help, or it kept me alive. I don't know what to say. I remember screaming and I grabbed the rip and yanked it closed. It cost so much, but I didn't care. Nothing really mattered. That act focused the plants on me, and they started shuffling my direction. I tried something weird." He took a deep breath and a bigger sip of his drink.

"Biology. We've been studying bio-electrical impulses in plants. How they are there, just almost unnoticeable. Well, I took my own bio-electrical energies and slammed them into the plants. I fried their systems."

"Kris, you could have died," Sable gasped, her dark skin had a gray undertone to it.

"I didn't care," he said flatly. "And I thought I might have succeeded as doing that knocked me out. I was woken by someone cracking smelling salts under my nose. There were police and response units everywhere. Two others had been killed by the darts. They'd found me holding Laura, with Peter not fifteen feet from us. The plants were dead, and they verified

I'd closed the rips." He shrugged, avoiding our eyes. "Hours of questions, triage, and then they sent me home, and I'm here."

We fell quiet, not sure what to say or do.

"Do Laura and Peter's parents know?" Marisol asked that quietly, and I was horrified that I hadn't thought about that.

"Yeah. The cops said they'd been notified," he said, his voice a low flat line. "They also said they'd died so fast that basically the second that dart hit them, they were dead. Nothing could have saved them."

I should have managed to stop this. My brother shouldn't be here grieving because I can't do my job.

~They were right. Kudya are only fought by naga or dragons. Their poison darts will kill almost everything else. The naga are immune and unless they hit a dragon's eye or tongue, the darts bounce off. You are not to blame.~ Carelian tried to be reassuring, but his words didn't really help much.

The kids had migrated to laps during this story, even if they were getting a bit too big—Magne was in Jo's lap, while Jaz was in Sable's. The kids were holding on like limpets, and the quetzo's were mimicking them, wrapping around them in a similar way.

"Kris," I said softly, getting his attention. "There is nothing I can say that will make it better. You are not to blame, and you can stay as long as you need. I think we all need a good night's sleep. Do you have a preference?" I didn't know what he wanted or what would be better for him.

He sighed. "I don't want to be alone. Can... can I sleep here?" His apartment in the garage was still there, clean and ready, but I could understand not wanting that distance right now.

I nodded, trying to figure out how to get him a bed. I could let him sleep in mine or I could sleep in the sunroom with a few blankets.

Hamiada stepped into the room out of the walls. Today her hair was all barren twigs, but with the hint of green at the ends. Winter with the hope of spring. There were days I wondered if she read minds, or maybe the house was just that attuned to us. "Kris, I sorrow for your loss." She looked at us, as if seeking permission. "If you want, I can turn the old nursery into a room for him for a few nights. It would just need blankets and a mattress."

Smiles lit up most of our faces. "Hamiada, that would be perfect. I loved that room," Kris said with a smile.

She nodded and trailed a hand over his cheek. "I do not intentionally listen to you, but emotions are hard to ignore, so I heard. I sorrow for you. Follow me."

I glanced at the others, then shrugged and got up, the rest trailing me to where Hamiada stood in the entry hall. We lurked in the space between the dining room and entryway. She turned once, and a door appeared between the door to Sable and Jo's room and the hall powder room. "I thought it might be best to not have it open into their bedroom. I do not believe you need instant access?"

We all laughed. When the nursery had been created, there were two doors, one to my room on the second floor and one to Jo and Sable's on the first. It made nursing and childcare easy. But he didn't need to be changed in the middle of the night.

"No, I think I'm good with just one door," Kris said with a muted smile.

Hamiada floated on a toe. "I do not have a mattress. The one in the garage apartment?"

"I'll get it," Jo said immediately. "If you'll get the room ready, I'll grab it."

"I'll help. That queen is too unwieldy by itself," Sable put in.

"Do you want to grab some clothes, Kris?" I asked watching him.

He flinched at the idea. "No. There's some old stuff in the apartment. I'll just wear that or maybe go to Walmart."

I understood the flinch. Peter would be everywhere in that apartment. "Okay. Hamiada, is the room ready to look at?"

"Yes, she said. "Let me know if you need something else." With that said, she faded back into the wall.

"You two put the dishes in the sink." Jo gave hard looks at the twins who had followed into the hall. "We'll clean up the rest in a bit."

"Yes, Momma." They chorus and started the whirlwind of twenty trips to put things in the sink. They weren't coordinated about it, but they could do it just fine.

I smiled and took Kris's arm. "Let's go look. I'd almost forgotten about this room."

Together we stepped into the hall and the new door that sat there. It made no sense logically—even a closet couldn't have fit in that space—but when we opened it, the room spread before us. Larger than it had been for the twins, a bed frame of curved branches awaited in the center of the room. A chest of drawers sat on one side, and the closet. This time, there was no door to my room. The trees on the walls were still there, and a squirrel scampered across the branches. A bird whirling in the sky caught my eye.

"Ah, I had forgotten about that," I said mildly, watching the hawk circle.

"Forgot what?" Kris asked. He leaned against me a bit, even though he was taller than me.

I cast a glance at him, then shrugged. "We had a baby shower for the twins and had an unexpected guest. As an apology for disrupting the event, she gave the twins two feathers from her Thunderbird."

"That sounds cool," he said, but his voice was doubtful.

"It was, but that wasn't the big aspect. Each of the feathers grants access to the AIN." My mind was spinning, but I still didn't see any way it would change the current situation.

"Ah. That is cool. You mentioned there was a new representative?" He seemed interested as we looked at the room.

"Yeah. She's interesting. If I get a chance, I'll introduce you."

"Hey, a little help out here!" Jo called from the front door. We left the room with me glancing once more at the hawk circling up above us and a shudder ran through me.

CHAPTER

EIGHT

With more rips happening and first responders being pulled to deal with them, the increase in deaths due to fires and other natural disasters has spiked. Nationwide, the request for more personnel has increased, but it takes time to get people trained. The question is how many more people will die because our first line of defense is busy with rips? ~CNN Talking Head

ORDER

Regardless of my desire to wrap everyone in bubble wrap and put them in stasis where they'd be safe, Kris headed back to school after staying through the weekend. He said he couldn't miss that much school and staying here, while safe, didn't change anything.

It hurt so much to let him go, but he knew he could come back if he needed. Though he said he'd prefer the room back in the garage—the house was too noisy. It was said with a laugh and hugs for everyone.

I was back at the Library with Shay, Citlali, Baneyarl, Scott, and three merlins who had responded to Shay's ad. They were almost catatonic with joy when he'd brought them in, and they were proving invaluable when it came to slogging through all the books Cleo found for us.

And it was a slog. There were so many books and sometimes it was just a note here or there. But one of the merlins loved doing research and papers. I think his name was Sveethani, but I'd only been introduced once and the only things I could really remember were the yellow and red tattoo with blinding white teeth and eyes that were so wide with excitement that I was worried he was stoned. But he was taking everything we found each day and entering it all in a database on his laptop. He had one that worked just fine, though he couldn't charge it.

The fact that the light in the realms was enough for plants to photosynthesize, but not charge a solar battery was an interesting side note, but nothing I had any time to worry about. Instead, I read. Then I read more. But out of all the books Cleo found, none of them were really helpful. We found more information about Atlantis, Zendia, and the disappearance of the continent. That part was still a low-level argument. Had it been a continent or an island? I didn't care, but it kept the researchers entertained.

~Cori?~ Hamiada's voice pulled me out of a snooze-worthy discussion on trade routes from about 500 BC. The writer must have been Greek, and the stilted information made me want to curl up under the desk with Carelian and fall asleep.

~Yes?~ I yawned trying to fight off the boredom.

~Stephen Alixant is on the phone. He says he needs you.~

~Okay. Ask him to hold. Two minutes.~

I felt her assent as I rose. "Duty Calls. Come on." Carelian rose, stretching like me. It took us a minute to get outside. The area we'd created had become more expansive as others had added to it, creating a beautiful area out front that was perfect for getting some fresh air, sitting and talking, or having lunch. He opened a rip to the house, and I stepped through to my cell phone laying there, screen on.

"Hey, what's up?" I suspected it would be bad news but getting out of the Library felt good. At the rate I was reading my eyes were going to revolt.

"I need you," Stephen said, his voice hoarse. "I've been leaning on the emergency response groups from schools and Houses, but this one is huge. Three merlins haven't been able to close it. Can you get there?"

He'd been seriously trying to not use me, but if it was too big, I was the only one and I'd managed to keep my fear at bay.

"Yep. Location?"

"Right above the St. Louis Arch. It's visible from the ground."

I frowned. "That's pretty high up. Is it causing issues?" If the rips were not causing issues, usually you just ignored them. If nothing was coming out, a watch was set on it, and we let it be. They all had closed so far. The longest time had been two days, but nothing had ever appeared except some dust.

"You could say that. Water. Fish and water. While the fish themselves aren't dangerous out of their element, they make that marlin look like a goldfish. It's the water that is the issue. St. Louis is flooding and already the infrastructure is cracking as nothing had been built for this level of water."

~Fish? Excellent. We can replace our dwindling stores.~ Carelian's eyes were dilated with excitement at the idea. I rolled mine. We still had at least a hundred pounds of fish left, but we'd gotten a lot of milage from the fish and stasis meant we didn't need to worry about it spoiling or getting freezer burn.

"Okay. Give me a few."

"Just hurry. This one is getting out of control quickly." He hung up with that and I opened my pack to pull out Carelian's harness. He stepped into it without argument, and I already had everything else I needed in the bag. It'd become habit.

"Can you find St. Louis?" Neither of us had been there before.

~Big silver arch thing?~ he verified.

"Yes."

~Hmm.~ He opened a rip to the crossroads place and when I'd stepped through, closed the rip behind me. He took a minute, then raked across the air and a rip opened. ~This is it,~ he said after he'd peered through it and stepped out of the crossroads.

"Wait, you sure?" I asked as I followed and was instantly in over a foot of water. "Never mind," I muttered as I looked around. People were abandoning vehicles that were starting to float down rivers that had previously been streets. I moved out of the shadow of the arch to look up. Somehow Carelian had brought us right underneath it. Water cascaded down either side, creating a stunning waterfall effect over the sides of the arch with a roar of sound that matched the sound at Niagara

Falls. If it had been planned, people would have come to stare at it, but up above the arch there was a gash in reality letting water and other things tumble out.

As I watched, a fish the size of a large dog wiggled down the arch and hit the rising water with a slap, wiggling out and then away.

~Fish. We need to get them. This will be great.~ Carelian's tail was lashing as he crouched, ready to pounce as a fish was swimming toward him, almost too big for the amount of water on the ground.

"Not now. Help me close, then you can go fishing," I replied, staring up at the rip. When we'd closed the Niagara Falls rip, we'd stopped the water first with the riverbed. This one I didn't have the option. I'd have to close it without seeing where the water was flowing from. With the rip I'd fought to close in the ocean, there had been water on both sides of it. That meant there wasn't much flow to resist closing. It had been almost equalized by the time I sealed it. Here, though the force of water was a major consideration. I stared at it, thinking fast.

"Carelian, if I can hold the water back, can you close the rip by yourself?"

He'd given up watching the fish and looked up at the rip. ~No. It is not one of mine and that is larger than I can handle alone.~

It was extremely difficult to run two magic spells at the same time. I'd done it occasionally, but usually little things like having fire and water dance for me. There was no way to control this level of water, and if it was an ocean or a lake, waiting for it to drain would be deadly. So I needed to block it. I cycled through everything I'd learned in school, but most options weren't feasible.

"Oh, this is going to hurt." I'd had to scrape my uterus less than two weeks ago, so I didn't think I had enough to offer quite yet. I'd offer my eggs, but that was almost always an all-or-nothing offering. I didn't think I had enough hair and offering up my top layer of dermis meant days of looking like a lobster and being uncomfortable. I sighed and dug the sealed scalpel out of my pants pocket. There were multiple scalpels stashed in the pocket.

~Must you?~ he asked, staring at it, ears back.

"It's easier than you biting me. Plus, this you can heal. Anything else I'm going to run out. I can lose blood without risking myself."

I hope.

There was always a risk of losing too much blood, but I didn't think this rip would require that much.

He lashed his tail but didn't say anything else as I drew the blade along my left inner forearm. Slashing my palm was stupid as it made it difficult to do anything else with that hand. A long slice down my forearm, not too deep, bled copious amounts of blood, yet I could still use that arm.

With blood flowing, I offered to Air. I pushed a hurricane toward the rip, pushing back the water. Air thought this was great fun and went at it, but I needed a lot of Air and the Arch above me began to sway.

I wonder what wind speed that's rated for.

I didn't really have a choice and if I had to choose between taking down a famous object and something like that kraken getting into downtown St. Louis, I'd demolish the arch.

The arch whipped back and forth above my head as the winds rose. The advantage to this was once it got going, it didn't stop immediately. Air liked being a storm. I'd run the risk of it staying here and storming when done, but that was the price for this level of effort. I twisted my arm sharply to cause more blood to flow out, ignoring the spike of pain. A huge clang sounded somewhere around us, but I didn't pay any attention. The rip and the water had it all.

~Do not offer too much,~ Carelian cautioned.

"If I'm not dead, it isn't too much," I snapped back. Sweat was running down my face as I pushed the water back. The storm attacked it and I had to lean against the arch, so I didn't get knocked over from the force of the winds, Carelian leaning against me to help with the stability. If this kept up, I'd have to sit, risking the water swirling around my knees.

"Now," I muttered, talking mostly to myself as I grabbed the feeling of the rip and fought to close it. The howling wind turned my hair into sharp slashes, releasing more blood from my skin, which I used ruthlessly. I used wind to slow the flow enough that I could pull the rip together. Inch by inch I struggled to seal the break in reality. I slid down the Arch, water hitting me at my shoulders, my back pressed against the solid structure. The creaking above me caused momentary spurts of worry, but I ignored it and focused on my job—closing the rip. I had to trust the engineers had done theirs. Already the storm was lessening, so I offered up more blood, urine, and the tips of all my nails to whip it into an even greater frenzy.

Cars were being pushed down the streets by the wind that whistled by me, laughing in gleeful destruction as I pressed it into the much smaller rip. The Arch waved back and forth so hard it was moving me. I watched the surrounding buildings sway with the force of the wind. Deep staccato snaps vibrated through my bones.

"Now, Carelian, help!" I leaned everything I had into a hard push with the wind howling around me like a dervish. The water rushed around, threatening to overwhelm me, even as I began to shiver from cold. My arm stung as water and dirt got into it, but I had to get that rip closed.

I felt his extra push of magic as I forced the rip to close.

With a sudden give it snapped together and I collapsed forward into Carelian, whose weight held me in place. The water lashed at me as I let the request to Air fade. There was a huge ominous creak above me and I glanced up, my heart still pounding from the exertion.

A huge piece of metal plummeted down toward us like a plow share into the ground.

~CORI!~

Reports of rips in most every country have been rising. Europe as a whole is reporting over a hundred a day, but the minor ones are easily closed by any Spirit mage in the vicinity. The larger areas are having more problems with rips that are large and often difficult to shut. Each country is approaching it differently but they are managing. The Draft Board is rumored to be sending people to the various countries to look at their techniques and see if they are things the US can duplicate. ~ CNN Mage Focus

SPIRIT

Water washed over my face as something pulled at me. I tried to figure it out. I realized my backpack was being pulled through the water and me with it. I'd remembered to strap it on tight before I'd stepped through. My paranoia was paying off. My attention wavered and black started to creep in around the edges of my mind again.

~Cori?~ Carelian's voice poked me over and over again as water kept splashing on my face. It pushed back the darkness, and I forced myself to grip tight to that mental familiarity.

I tried to take a deep breath and choked as more water splashed into my face.

~Quit breathing in water. You aren't a fish.~

My head lifted up out of water and I groaned as my body shivered with cold. I could hear voices yelling in the distance. I reached up and my fingers snagged on his harness, giving me something to hold on to.

~Help is coming.~

My body was pulled onto something sloping upward.

~My mage needs help here.~ There was a sharp tone to his voice, and I groaned as the words cut into my already tender psyche. My head throbbed in time with my heart. I didn't want to open my eyes, suspecting that it would hurt. On the bright side though, I didn't hear the roar of the water coming out of the rip nor the wind howling.

"Nice kitty," I heard someone say, and I choked on a laugh that ended in a whimper.

~I am not your kitty.~ Carelian's voice was acid and I moaned a bit at the sharpness in my mind. The next words were more moderated, but still sounded like he was pushing and snapping off each word. ~She was hit by a piece of metal and needs help.~ I heard a groan of metal underneath us as he moved away from me. His warmth moved away, and I tried to turn to follow it, but my body rebelled.

"Alixant," I muttered, wanting to cry, but that seemed like too much work.

~I know. Contacting Alixant now.~ His voice reassured me and I relaxed.

"Ma'am, I'm a firefighter. Can you tell me what happened?" The voice sounded competent, and I dared to open my eyes. Pain lashed in and I shut them immediately.

I hate being right.

"Not sure. Closed a rip, something fell at us. Last I remember." I could hear the creaking of their jumpsuits and the splash of water as they moved around me. Where was I? Taking a deep breath, I dared to open my eyes again to milder slashes of pain through my eyeballs.

The city loomed ahead from the clearing I was in, and I could see people wading out. Two men stood in front of me in SLFD uniforms, one with blue eyes and pale skin, the other dark eyes with light brown skin. I took a breath and practiced breathing as my eyes shut again.

"Fraid I need you to open those. Need to check for a concussion," one of them said. I forced my eyes open, only to flinch from the light, whimper as the flinching caused more pain, and start to slide off what I was sitting on.

"Nooope, let's not do that." Arms pulled me back up and then phantom hands did a thorough inspection. The goose egg on my forehead made its presence known when they prodded at it. Talking as they did so, letting me know what wasn't wrong.

Through slitted lids that really wanted to stay closed, I realized Carelian had pulled me through the water up onto the hood of a Porsche, whose nose was just at the water line. The men weren't panicking, and they hadn't said anything to stress me out.

"Smart cat," I murmured.

~I will have you know I am at genius level for humans. Alixant is swamped. Sends his thanks and says he has officers headed this way from the local office.~ Carelian paused, and I heard him speak in that overly clear manner. ~Is she hurt? Details if you would.~

The men glanced at each other, shrugged, and addressed him. "Not obviously. Besides the various cuts and bruises, her pupils are equal and reactive. She might have a mild concussion. But overall, she's damn lucky she didn't drown or get badly hurt. That sign could have cut her in half." He was putting a bandage on my arm as he spoke, making sure it was clean, which elicited a hiss from me, but I didn't argue. They continued the check over while Carelian watched closely.

~Good,~ Carelian murmured when they were done. There was a strange sigh from him. ~Do you have any skin glue or a wrap with you?~

"Sure. Why?" I forced myself to sit up at that. I needed to know why as well.

~The sign clipped my tail and cut off the tip. It is annoying stinging in this water. I do not wish to take the time right now to heal it.~

"What?" I jerked up, trying to reach for him, and I cried out as my body protested.

~Cori, it is a literal flesh wound. I would just prefer for it to not ooze blood until I am free to deal with it.~

I forced myself to watch as one of the firefighters took the tail. "Yeah, I can help. This is going to burn, but I want to clean it first."

~Go ahead.~ The words were long suffering. But Carelian only hissed, not moving his tail as they cleaned and sealed it.

"You were right, only a minor wound, but I imagine it was stinging with the crap in this water." The firefighters looked at us. "You two okay to stay here? There are other people trapped and for the moment, you're safe."

They sounded conflicted, but I waved them away. "I'll be fine. People are coming to get me. I'm not moving, and the water is going down."

"Okay. We're headed out." With that, they were splashing away through water that had fallen to the tops of their boots as opposed to their knees.

~Don't move. I need to kill a few things.~ Carelian hissed.

I opened my mouth, then shut it. Carelian did not handle me being hurt any better than I handled him being hurt. He needed to express his emotions before we went any further.

"Go. I won't move." I'd barely finished the words before he sprang off the car and grabbed a fish that was flopping by. His teeth grabbed it on either side, then he did something weird and threw it in the air, cutting the reality underneath it. It fell in and disappeared. He repeated that over and over. Hard vicious attacks where he threw his whole weight on the creatures, then threw them into another place.

I might have felt sorrier for the fish, except all of them fought back with spines, wicked teeth, and thrashing that knocked him around. A long keening cry of glee cut through the air as he spied a huge thing struggling in the shallower and shallower water. It had to be at least fifteen feet long and three feet tall. It didn't have a spike like a marlin, but instead had barbs along its spine that retracted and extended. Carelian avoided all of them to reach underneath and flip it. It had to have weighed four or five hundred pounds, but he flipped it like a toddler flipping a toy car.

The water sprayed around it as it tried to right itself, but Carelian moved in and gutted it in a fluid move. Another few slices and the creature quit moving. He slashed to create a rip, then Carelian sunk his teeth into it and pulled it out of my current reality.

Before I had a chance to panic, he walked back out and sealed it behind us. He shook himself, water fluffing away from him. Then, tail still held high out of the water, he padded on back to me.

"Feel better?" I asked. I didn't, really. My body ached, my arm hurt, and I just wanted to sleep.

~Yes. And I restocked the larder. Those are true delicacies; they would also make excellent bribes. Few ever get to taste those.~ He jumped up on the hood, looking me over. ~You need to get home.~

"I know. But let's wait for the officers, then you can get us home. I don't think I have the strength to do much besides stagger to my feet." If I was being honest, I didn't know that I had that much strength. His narrowed eyes told me he thought the same.

Before I had a chance to argue, sirens came toward us. I was overly familiar with ambulance, fire, and police. This wasn't any of those. A minute later, a Hummer with lights and sirens came around the corner. Two men jumped out and headed right toward us.

"And there is the calvary," I said with a sigh. I struggled to sit up and almost slid off the hood. The two men raced over to me.

"Merlin Munroe. Are you okay?"

~Does she look okay?~ Carelian hissed. It was obvious he still didn't have his worry under control. I lifted my arm to pet him and hissed out in pain as everything hurt.

"Yes sir. Come on, ma'am, we've got water and can get you back to the office where we have some supplies."

"Yeah," I said. I tried to rise, and all I managed to do was start sliding off the hood.

~Cori,~ Carelian growled in my mind and I couldn't help it, I flinched. Everything hurt, I was struggling with a headache that was about to break my skull open. His voice dropped to a whisper. ~Be careful my quean, I can not lose you.~

The men at least reacted and a moment later one of them, obviously stronger than I would have expected, was carrying me bridal style to the hummer. He gently set me in, buckled me, and then, to my relief, wrapped an emergency blanket around me. I'd started to shiver, and all I wanted was a hot bath in clean water.

Carelian jumped into the back next to me. He lay down on the seat, being careful not to bump me and let his head spread across me. Exercising his strange brand of healing, he licked at my wounds helping them to close. ~I should have done this immediately. I was not taking good care of my quean.~ There was a level of shame in his voice that worried me.

"You can lick the cuts and bruises, but it won't do much for the pulled muscles, headache, or just exhaustion. Let's give a quick report, then go home." I stopped for a minute, then sighed. "And can you let Marisol know I need her? There is no way I can get my clothes off by myself and I need food. Lots of hot food, but I just can't." I hated asking for help like this, and being in so much pain and so tired made it harder and I had to fight not to cry. Instead, I clamped my eyes closed and just focused on breathing.

~I'll take care of it,~ he whispered. The rest of the drive to the FBI offices, he licked and healed me. But while the little pains started to heal, it didn't touch the rest of my body, the exhaustion, or the headache.

They got me into a warm office, offered me hot coffee, and one of the guys handed me two pills. "These are just ibuprofen, ma'am. We have an office bottle. Do you want them?"

I nodded, managing not to sob in relief as I swallowed them with the coffee. It was horrible coffee, but it was hot, and the caffeine helped with my exhaustion. They had me in an office, in a comfortable chair with my feet up. Then they brought in a screen and Stephen popped up on it.

"Cori, you look like shit. Are you okay?" He leaned forward, eyes darting over the screen inspecting me.

"I'm alive. Not sure what else to say. Most of my wounds are minor." I pointed down to where Carelian was licking my arm, where I'd sliced it to do offerings. "So I'll be healed. I'm just down about a pint and have a probable light concussion. I need sleep, food, and my bed."

He closed his eyes, and I noted his hair had more streaks of gray than it had a few months ago.

"I'm glad you're okay. But I take it that couldn't have been handled by anyone else?"

I wiggled my hand. "If you'd had a merlin with Air and maybe someone really practiced with non-organic and transform, plus a Spirit Merlin, maybe."

He seemed to pale a bit more at that. Or maybe I was just tired.

"Why?"

I explained about the needing to hold the water back to

stop the flow so I could close the rip. By the time I was done, he looked as exhausted as I felt.

"That isn't good. How often could this happen?" We both turned to look at Carelian, who had most of my arm healed.

~Each of the realms has water, oceans, but they are only a small part of the realms, not like Earth. It should be uncommon, but...~ He trailed off and laid his head on my legs. ~This whole thing isn't exactly normal, so my information is likely inaccurate.~

I rubbed his ears. "What he said. All I can do is keep looking. We have lots of people looking for information, but I just can't say if I know anything."

"I get it. Let me know if you need help. Can you come see me...in two days? I'd like to go over some data with you and see if you have any other ideas."

He'd been about to say tomorrow, and I was glad he hadn't.

"Yes. I'll see you then. Now I'm going home."

"Take care, Cori." The screen went black, and I looked at the two agents.

"If you don't need me, I'm going home."

"Yes, ma'am. Where can we take you?" They looked eager and worried.

A laugh escaped me. "Don't worry about it." I struggled to my feet. "Carelian?"

He opened a portal to the house, and I could see Marisol standing there with Hamiada. The two steps it took to walk into the rip and out were all the energy I had. Hamiada caught me with strength that surprised me, though really, I should have expected it. Then they put me to bed, fed me, and dumped vitamins and painkillers into me. I slept for fourteen hours.

Confidential Memo: To Director Alixant

Stephen – I don't know what you're playing at but the woman that just left my office looks like a resident of a refugee camp. Why is she out here dealing with rips? What is going on that hasn't been filtered down to the rank and file? Bottom line, what aren't you telling us? I thought the situation was being managed? That isn't being managed if you are driving young women to their deaths to protect us. What needs to happen and how can I help? Call me if you can't talk about this on official channels. Sincerely Head Special Agent St. Louis ~ FBI Email System

CHAOS

The next day I did nothing but eat and doze. But as exhausted as I was, I bounced back quickly. Which meant Wednesday morning I sidestepped to DC and Alixant's office. This time no one gave me or Carelian any flack. We both got out badges and walked in. I looked out of place wearing cargo pants, hiking boots, my backpack, and Carelian in his harness, but I didn't care. Both of us had decided it was better safe than sorry.

We strode through the building toward Stephen's office, an odd sight among all the suits. The door was open, so I poked my head in to see him behind his desk, typing. He was in shirt-sleeves and no tie. What I hadn't noticed two days ago was his hair was barely at his collar, meaning he'd been offering as much as I had.

"Stephen," I said as I walked in. Carelian followed to rub his head on Stephan's outstretched hand when he saw us.

"You look better," he commented, rubbing Carelian's ears.

"That is good, though I still want to sleep for a week. I'm still exhausted." I sank down into the chair. Carelian set himself against the window, curling up in loaf pose, just watching us. He'd been overly quiet and almost hovering. I let him.

"You did a good job in St. Louis, no matter how much

77

people are screaming," he said as he saved something on his laptop, then closed the lid.

"And what are they screaming about?" I asked, not really surprised. It seemed the politicians were always upset about something.

"Well, up until now, the Arch had been rated for wind speeds up to 150 miles per hour. You verified it can stand up to 225 mph. But the other things, not so much." I might have cared more if he wasn't fighting a smirk as he talked.

Maybe. My worry level over some of this stuff was nonexistent.

"Huh. Good to know. But do you know what hit me?" Carelian hadn't been able to tell me, and I just hadn't been in any condition to figure it out.

"That would be the other damage." His smirk faded. "Your winds grabbed one of the highway signs and ripped it off. It hit the Arch and bent. As far as we can tell, when you stopped the wind, the sign fell right toward you. Lucky for all of us, it only clipped you. If it had fallen a bit differently, both of you might have died."

"Oh," I murmured and glanced over at Carelian. He was still curled up, paws under him, tail mostly healed.

"Anything else?"

He sighed. "Five people dead, but at least three of them were due to stupidity. The others just got caught up in the water before they could get off the street and drowned, but they were dead before you even got there."

I nodded a bit. "And the stupidity ones?"

He groaned. "Some college jocks, and yes I'm using the term disparagingly, saw the fish and thought it'd be fun to go get some." Carelian snorted at this. "Well, they didn't realize these fish were like fighting bulls when the water was past their knees. They died of wounds and were at least partially eaten before the water drained off enough for the fish to die. Speaking of which, what do we do with the fish? They were collected and put in cold trailers until I could speak to you."

I lifted my hands and pointed to Carelian. "Talk to him. He was the one that was excited."

Stephen looked at Carelian with an arched brow.

~They are delicious both as sushi and cooked. The large ones are more like swordfish, the smaller ones are closer to salmon or tuna. In many ways, they are even healthier than your fish as our waters have almost zero pollution.~ He didn't open his eyes as he spoke, just stayed curled up.

"Huh. Okay. The food kitchens will be delighted to get them then." He flipped open the laptop and typed a quick note.

"So what now?" I watched him, waiting.

Stephen glanced at his watch. "That depends on you. There is no way you can be the only person to close rips. As it is, I'm trying very hard to keep you as the emergency option, but even so, I can tell you are getting short on offerings." He gave a pointed glance at my hair and the pink line on my arm. "I've got Charles, the OMO director, Department of Defense people, the head of the Draft board, a senator, and one of my deputy directors meeting here in a few minutes to talk options. I'd like you to sit in and hear about what we've got outlined and see if you can think of any other options."

I sighed. My enthusiasm was low, but I couldn't keep doing this. What was going on in other countries if I was having this many issues? How were they closing things? "Will there be updates as to what is going on in other countries too? Because if I keep this up, I'm going to be tapped out."

"There is supposed to be. Mostly from the OMO standpoint that doesn't have the diplomatic hassles I have trying to elicit that information from other countries." He frowned. "Though of late, Japan has been amazingly helpful."

A small slice of pain at losing Hishatio sliced through me. It would have been nice to have his help or insight with this.

"I can meet with them. Now?" My enthusiasm was lacking, but not meeting with them made my life harder.

He paused to check something on his computer. "It looks like the Senator, OMO representatives and the Draft chair are here. The others haven't arrived yet. But they've got twenty minutes before the scheduled time."

"Get me some coffee and I'll agree. And something to eat with calories." I was dangerously low on energy and calories. Food and heat with the wonder that was caffeine sounded great.

Alixant grinned, the smile lifting some of the exhaustion off his face. "I can do that. Let me get you situated in the conference room, and I'll run down to our cafeteria. They actually make good food and have a little coffee shop for us government stooges."

I laughed and pushed myself to my feet, swaying a tiny bit. Carelian was there and his warmth, plus the fact that his back was about at hip level gave me stability. "How's Indira?" I asked as we headed to the elevators.

"Tired as you. She's been on a bunch of the emergency response teams, but with so many rips the people we have are getting better at closing them. I swear I'm only reaching out to you when multiple people have failed. I need to work on getting teams together that are targeted for different types of rips." The elevator doors closed and whisked us upward.

"Different types?" My brain wasn't tracking, and I leaned against the elevator wall.

"One for creatures that attack, one for water, one for the Chaos things. It seems like you need different skill sets for each. Unless you're Cori Munroe." The doors slid open, and he waved me out.

"Ha, ha. But you're not wrong. The biggest problem with this one was volume of water and that I couldn't affect the water at all. For Niagara we pulled up the riverbed to block the flow of water. I couldn't even see this bottom to do anything. But hopefully this sort of thing will be rare." I frowned. "How many water areas are there in the realms, Carelian?"

His tail tapped me as we walked. ~A few. But only two great seas. The rest are smaller rivers or streams. Any lake we have would have emptied in minutes.~ He stopped mid pace. ~Wait.~

I stopped immediately. Stephen a step later.

"Carelian?" Stephen asked, looking around.

~The conference room is ahead?~

Stephen looked down the hall of doors. "Yes. Number one. It's the largest with room for about fifteen people."

~The ones in there are talking about Cori and mages. I think you should hear. I will talk for them. Two of them are men but their voices are similar, the other is a woman.~ Carelian was talking rapidly in my mind. From Stephen's attention, I figured he was also getting this. ~Listen, I'll try to copy their voices, but it might be confusing.~

His mental tone changed and voices pinged in my head. I closed my eyes to listen, and I leaned against the wall to help support myself. The blood loss still had me woozy.

It started with a man's voice. "I thought we had already agreed about how to handle her. Everything is in process."

"I still say we just need to reactivate all the merlins. We can't keep this up otherwise."

"Are you insane? Do you understand the voting block we are talking about? The number of merlins that are retired and having nothing to do but meddle is insane. If we didn't have laws keeping them out of office, they'd be running the place. Keeping them fat and happy is the only way to go. If we do this, it has to be specific merlins, troublemakers, powerful ones, the ones that the others can say 'see, that person is an outlier, it won't happen to me.' Because if they think they might be affected they will react."

"I know. Why do you think we're reactivating Munroe? She's always been a wild card, but over the last few years I'd hoped she'd had her teeth pulled and wasn't going to be an issue. But now with her bouncing everywhere, saving the day, she's becoming an issue. People are taking notice."

"Maybe." This was the woman's voice. The other two I just lumped together as men. "But either way, the rips are becoming a problem. It doesn't matter to a certain extent what we do with her. At some point, she'll get killed doing this. At that point we will have a merlin martyr. Then we can use what is left of her to our heart's content."

"You think it'll be that easy?"

The woman again. "Did you see what was left of her after St. Louis? Unless something drastic changes, she'll be dead, and we'll have her example to manipulate the masses with. At this point, it's a best-case scenario. She's too powerful."

"Please, she's a double merlin, not Merlin. Plus, she's a young woman with two kids. That makes her easily manipulated. Imply the children might be in danger and she'll do anything to protect them." The amount of scorn in the man's voice made me wince. The question was, did he realize I'd also destroy anyone that threatened to harm them? Ice had started to form in my veins. I usually went into rage like fire, quick, hot, then done. Today I was too tired and too pissed off for my temper to be that simple.

"They should be here soon. We should discuss it later. Dinner tonight? Del Mar?"

Carelian quit translating and looked at the two of us. Alixant was grey, his jaw locked, and fists clenched.

"I swear Cori, I knew nothing about this. I am so sorry." His voice made me flinch back at the pain in it.

"I didn't think you did. But it implies a lot. I wonder if I can use it." My voice remained calm and cool, but my hands shook as I sank them into Carelian's fur.

"Well, I already know what I'm doing."

His voice was so grim I jerked my eyes up to meet his.

"Don't do anything stupid, Stephen."

"It won't be stupid, I promise. It is probably something I've needed to do for a while. What about you?"

My smile had no humor in it and in the back of my mind there was a growl, but if it was mine or Carelian's I couldn't have told you.

"I'll deal with it. Do we go in now or wait another minute?"

~I hear Charles. He is coming up the elevator with others.~ Carelian's comment was almost too neutral, and I knew there was a risk those people in the room might find themselves very dead. I didn't have it in me to care. If he eliminated a threat to me and mine I wouldn't care. And trying to capture him would be impossible.

Stephen and I nodded to each other and flipped the conversation to dinner plans later this month until the others arrived. Charles smiled as he saw us and Arachena poked out of the hoodie and waved her palps at me, then went back in. Even to this day, her spider-like body tended to freak people out.

The two others with Charles were Alixant's deputy, Daniel Chambers, and the Department of Defense liaison, Chloe King. Chloe was a Spirit archmage, strong in Soul, which made total sense.

Alixant was better at the fake smile than I was. Mine felt brittle around the edges. We all headed to the conference room. From the way he was acting either Carelian had given him a warning or Charles sensed something was up. He kept glancing at the two of us, but I didn't say a thing as we entered the room.

The two men and the woman turned out to be OMO director Brian Harrison, Draft Board Head Oliver Martin, and Senator Heather Perry.

We all got seated after the introductions. Before anyone could say anything, Oliver Martin turned to look at me. "Merlin Corisande Munroe, per the power vested in me by the FEMA Emergency Mage Activation Executive Order passed a week ago, I am reactivating your draft."

It is stated as a truism that magic appeared in the 1850s, but that isn't necessarily accurate. There were mages, usually hedgies, that peppered both history and the remoter places on Earth. But about 1850 people started talking about their "emergence" and a coordinated study between Yale, King's College London, and Harvard was created. Oddly, none of the people running the study were mages. This is the basis for where the OMO emerged along with how they tested and measured mage talents, as well as the ranking levels. In the ten years of the study more than five thousand mages were tested. ~History of Magic

ORDER

"And I quit," Stephen said in the exact same tone.

"What?" The word burst out of everyone's mouth at the same time, including mine. I knew the attack of reactivating me was supposed to throw me off balance, but Stephen's comment derailed my planned reaction.

"Excuse me?" Senator Parry said, staring at him.

"I've decided that I no longer have the patience or energy to deal with political maneuvering and this is literally the final straw."

"Shit, Stephen," Daniel whispered, his face white. I could see the workload dropping on his shoulders and he was terrified.

There was an odd silence around the table then Oliver cleared his throat. "Regardless, the reactivation of your draft is started, Merlin Munroe."

The comment pulled me back on track, though I'd be talking to Stephen as soon as this was done. "I am well aware of that and will wait for the contract to be delivered to me, but I want to make you aware of a few things." I leaned forward, my casual clothes a sharp contrast to the suits everyone else wore. Carelian sat next to me, his head peering over the table with ease.

Senator Parry smirked at me. "Oh, and what would that be?"

"I am perilously close to the Wandering Mage Act limits. And if you threaten my family to force me to go past what I willingly offer, there will be consequences. Don't push me." My rage was like a sword of ice, and I had to fight not to show them exactly how much danger they were in.

The three of them went white and darted glances at each other, but I wasn't about to explain.

"I won't martyr myself for you, nor will I do anything to keep this quiet. I am sure the House boards, and I have friends in quite a few houses, would be delighted to share this information."

At this point both Charles and Chloe were leaning in, eyes narrowed, and Arachena had slipped out to stand on Charles' shoulder.

"And that would be?" the OMO Director said slowly, though of the three of them, he was the least at risk. The OMO was an associated agency like the UN, not one controlled by any government.

"That the US government doesn't want the retired merlins, all mages really, who are fat and happy to get upset and realize that they could change everything and anything if they knew exactly how badly they are being manipulated?" I smiled the entire time, my face aching, my voice perfectly calm.

"Oh, really?" Chloe said in a hard voice, her eyes not moving from the original three. "I am sure my House would love some more details on this. Could you elaborate?"

"Well, if they reactivate everyone, those merlins might get upset. So instead, they are going to use me, after they manage to get me killed, of course, as the whip and the carrot. Isn't that correct? Show what can happen to you if you don't toe the line?

While simultaneously praising me and holding me up as the example of a patriotic mage?"

Charles pulled out his laptop and started typing. His speed always surprised me. He'd told me once he typed about 100 words a minute—I was lucky to get thirty-five.

"What are you doing?" Senator Parry snapped out, her eyes like claws. I might have been more impressed, but when you were exposed to claws from the Cath not much measured up.

"I'm calling up the boards for three of the houses. I was bored and offered to take over managing the forums for them. I'm creating a pinned post that anyone logging in should be able to see. And while that is getting prepped, I'm pulling up the numbers of retired merlins and what districts they are in. Another few minutes and I should be able to have a post that details who the representative and senator for each district is, so they know, and I'm highlighting yours, Senator Parry. I'll make sure they all know exactly what you are in favor of." He didn't slow down as he typed.

"Cori, can you verify what she said?" This was from Chloe who had a poker face that didn't quit, but I could feel the rage in her soul.

I paused for a minute, wanting to give Carelian credit, but in this situation, it would actually hurt our case, not help it. "Yes, I can. She said, quote 'Did you see what was left of her after St. Louis? Unless something drastic changes, she'll be dead, and we'll have something to manipulate the masses with. At this point, it is a best-case scenario. She's too powerful.' Then they argued about me being a double merlin, not the actual Merlin."

And letting my secret slip about that wasn't what I wanted to do. I petted Carelian in mute apology, though I knew he didn't care at all. The three had gone even whiter.

"You have no proof," the senator stammered.

"You mean, do I have recordings or other evidence? No," I said calmly. "But as anyone with a modicum of Truth sense would know, I wasn't lying, and you are. It's a moot point." I just smiled, all teeth.

"Excellent. Let me see. I have the data and the reports and just for fun I'm linking each elected official's voting record to the post. Oh, and because I can see the questions in your eyes, I took over the tech support for the Elemental, Emrys, and Hallows. I'm sure the house of Spirit will be very interested as they are the group being drained the hardest trying to close rips." His smile was as friendly as mine and with Arachena perched on his shoulder, he resembled an avenging spirit.

From the paleness of Parry and Oliver Martin, I was pretty sure they realized their careers were over. And if she wasn't dismissed by the end of the week, I'd be surprised.

"Not all mages are as stupid as you think," I said mildly. "We understand the controls around us, though we don't always agree. But if you turn us into cannon fodder, we have nothing to lose by rebelling. And if that comes to pass, there are many details you are completely unaware of." Anger was making me reckless, and I tried to keep it down.

I should ask permission.

~Carelian, can you ask Kesis or Citlali, may I publicly state that the AIN is my friend and will have my back?~ The plan brewing in my mind was audacious and could bite me. But if she said yes, the possibilities were endless.

~Yes,~ he whispered as I watched everyone stare at us.

"Are you trying to get me to rescind your draft?" Oliver Martin asked, a bead of sweat forming on his brow.

"No. I figure I've been doing the same thing the draft would have had me do. Now you have to deal with anything I do or injuries I cause and you're also on the hook for all my medical needs." I shrugged as I was already planning on some massages billed to them. "Besides, it lets me prove exactly what the Draft office will do." I turned my head to glance at Charles. "Would you do me a favor and add that to the pinned post? Give them the date and time Merlin Cori Munroe was recalled to serve as an example."

His fingers were still flying. "On it. And so far, the posts have had over a thousand views. You might want to check your email, Senator." Charles was as calm as I was, though his rapid typing implied he was implementing something. Either way the people here were about to pay a high price for their actions.

Her hands shook as she picked up the phone and started scrolling, her skin leeching of color as she looked.

"I think you forget, Senator," Alixant said, his voice silky, "just how many mages are big contributors to political offices."

~She says yes. It plays well into their current plans.~

Just who was Citlali? Either way, it didn't matter and let me prove I had a much bigger stick than they had ever suspected. "Now that you see the folly of your ways, I have one more piece of information to provide you." I swear they all tensed watching me. "The AIN are friends of mine and will back any choice I make."

If I had gotten up and slapped them, I'm not sure their reactions could have been any more stark. Through all of this, Brian Harrison had been the least affected, but at that comment he went gray.

"You are speaking with the AIN?" He stuttered the words out.

"Yes. I have friends that I see regularly. There is much about them no one knows." I leaned forward a bit more. "So many more areas than what you know of."

He swallowed hard, his Adam's apple bobbing as he digested that news.

I let that lay there long enough for me to get my thoughts in order. "Now that all the posturing is done and I've proven my reach is much bigger than you thought, as far as I see it, you have multiple problems. You need a new Magical Crimes Director. Good luck finding anyone even half as good as Stephen was. And the fact that I did so many favors for him is gone. Now everything will go through official channels, or I won't respond to the request." I needed to be careful here. The idea of not helping if I could save lives would make the lie clear, but then politicians couldn't be mages.

The realization slammed through me like a lightning bolt. None of them were mages, so they didn't know when people were lying. Most people didn't lie in their day to day lives as even pale Psychic hedgies could truth tell. I filed that far back in my mind.

With an effort of will, I pulled myself back to the conversation at hand. "You need to come up with better ways to alert people to the rips and respond. And finally, we need to figure out other ways to respond because no matter if you put a gun to my head, I'm almost tapped out." Carelian growled at that, pulling the attention of everyone in the room. "Oh yes, about that. I promise you, if you threaten or hurt my children, my partners, or any of my family as a way to get at or control me, you will find out first-hand what I did with the nuke in D.C." My voice changed from friendly to flat and hard and I leaned forward, the smile gone. "I'll grab you and drop you in the realm and you can die there. If you're lucky, it will be fast. If not, you'll have to see if you die of radiation poisoning or dehydration first. And I won't spend a second feeling sorry."

At that, everyone in the room looked at me. Chloe, Daniel Chambers, and Stephen with something that resembled surprise and respect. Charles just nodded, a corner of his mouth tilting up in a grin.

The silence stretched as I just sat there scratching Carelian's ears as they stared at each other and their phones.

Finally, Stephen's deputy, Daniel, broke the tense stalemate. "Stephen, can I talk you into at least giving us two weeks?" He sounded like he would beg.

Stephen stared at the people assembled. His jaw clenched and I could tell he really wanted to just walk out, but the man I knew would never be able to leave with it in this situation.

"I will work until this situation is resolved. But I want to make it very clear the second it is over, I'm done. I will be going to my boss after this meeting, making it clear that if there is a single incident of political interference in my job, I will walk. And you will not be able to find me. No more. I expect you to take this back to your peers. Make it very clear I'm done. If they want someone else in this position, please feel free, but anything else other than a replacement will see me walk. Am I understood?"

All of them nodded, looking wary. From the constant vibrating of their phones, I guessed there was a storm brewing, and I didn't care.

We spent the next two hours hammering out what they would bring back for vote, changes to implement in their own offices, how to prioritize the rips, and a promise of budget for the Magical Crimes division under emergency spending. I was assigned a controller and given a special as needed duty position. They'd have everything to me in the next day or so.

Charles provided numbers that removed what little joy I'd found in the proceedings. Once again, I'd lost control of my life, plus I never did get my coffee and food.

CHAPTER
TWELVE

T he Trail of Tears is one of the most horrific things the American government did, and it (as well as the power of magic) resulted in the formation of the AIN and their separation from the rest of the world. While the area around their walls has been mapped in detail, there is no concrete information as to what the land behind those walls looks like. It is estimated to contain twenty-three thousand square miles and is broken up/surrounded by various states: Washington, South Dakota, Nebraska, New York, Utah, Texas, Colorado, Arizona, New Mexico, and Oklahoma

SPIRIT

I went home shaking with low blood sugar and exhaustion.

~You need to eat and get some sleep,~ Carelian scolded as he walked next to me, ready to brace me if I fell.

"I know." I stared around the house. The kids were in school, Jo and Sable at work. I desperately required calories and all I wanted to do was crumble in a ball and cry. The Draft had been bad the first year, and even later it had never been fun, but it hadn't been horrible. Now I suspected it would be horrible. I had to get food in me and rest. I wouldn't have time soon.

My legs wouldn't move, and I just stood there, swaying. There was food in the fridge. I just needed to go get it.

Walk. You can do this. Walk. Microwave. Easy.

The words went through my mind, and I nodded to myself knowing what I needed to do, but I didn't move.

A low growl with a pinprick of pain grabbed my attention, but by the time I could focus, Carelian was gone.

Oh.

I stood there swaying, trying to convince myself to move. The jarring sound of the doorbell wrenched me out of my inability to move. Habit dragged me to the door via ingrained responses. You answered the door when someone was there.

I pulled it open, and a delivery driver stood there, a package in his hand. "Special delivery. Cori Munroe?"

My head bobbed almost without my conscious effort.

"Excellent. Here you go." He shoved it at me, and I took it. He grinned and raced back to his truck. The package said Draft office.

They moved fast. Or they had planned this before they even got there.

That idea seemed more likely. I stood there, package in one hand, door held in the other, and I stared at the street.

"Cori?"

Marisol's voice had me turning to look at her, then back at the street. Had she come in and I missed it?

"Oh, you are in a bad shape. Come on." Her warm voice and hands wrapped me up and took over. I was never so glad in my life to give up control. Soon enough she had me in the sunroom, the fire going, a cup of tortilla soup in my hand, tortillas to dip, hot tea, and a bottle of electrolyte replacement.

The shaking stopped as I ate, the heat and calories helping to smooth me out. But I still felt like all my energy had disappeared.

At some point, the bowl was emptied and taken from me. Another tortilla with cream cheese, sugar, and cinnamon was placed in my hand, rolled up.

"Eat." Marisol sat down across from me, worry on her face.

The sugar and cinnamon helped pull me into an awareness. "Thank you. I take it Carelian went to get you."

"Yes. He said you were overloaded and exhausted. That might have been an understatement. Are you better now?"

"No. But I don't have a choice." The food was getting my brain to work, and I started compiling the lists of things I needed to do. First was dealing with the Library, then with the Draft. "Can I lean on you a bit more to help me with some stuff?"

"Oh Cori. Always. How can I help?" Her warm eyes smiled at me, and I wanted to just fall into her arms and let her do it all. Unfortunately, that wasn't an option.

"Carelian, I need Citlali, Esmere, and Shay. We need to get the Library research off of me for the most part. I have a book I'd like to read. So...." I sighed. There was nothing I wanted so much as to put this off, but if I dealt with it now, I could move on.

"Never mind. Can you ask them to meet me at the Library?"

Carelian tilted his head. ~Shay and Esmere are there now.

Citlali is headed there. But you should rest.~ He growled at me softly and I put my hand on his head, trying not to laugh. Or maybe it was sob.

"I know. But food helped." I smiled at Marisol. "If I can get a few more of these, I'm thinking I can get to the library and back in under two hours. Then I'll pass out, I promise." I held up the tortilla wrap in my hand and she nodded with pursed lips.

Carelian actively growled and bit my hand, not even breaking the skin, but his teeth pressing against me. ~You will rest soon. I will not lose my quean and I will stop you if you try to use any magic. You are too exhausted.~

I popped the last bite of the tortilla roll in my mouth, then touched his nose with my free hand. "I know. But I can't quit now. Would your quean quit?"

He dropped my hand with an agitated swish of his tail. ~No. But you will not use magic.~

I simply nodded, not wanting to commit to anything. My life didn't seem to allow for absolutes anymore.

I sat there for another fifteen minutes sipping the tea and then I forced myself to get with it. I guzzled down the remaining electrolyte drink and stood. I slipped my pack back on and looked at Carelian. "Would you do the path, please?" At this point even using the smallest bit of magic both would annoy him and might make it so that I didn't have what I needed at the worst time.

His tail lashed, but he opened a rip and I could see a glimpse of the library beyond.

"Cori, remember we love you and don't want to lose you." Marisol's comment caught me unaware and, in a rush, I remembered the veiled threats toward my family. I didn't want to leave them, but if it was a choice between my life and theirs, there wasn't a choice.

"I know. I'm trying, I promise." She handed me a bag with the extra roll ups, and I stepped through.

The calm of the library seemed jarring when compared to the chaos in my mind. I sighed and headed up the steps. Once inside, I headed directly for Cleo.

"Herald," she said with a nod. "How may I assist you today?" She seemed happier and almost glowed with satisfaction. I could hear the sounds of people in the library, and I swear there was a giggle or two of glee that came from the stacks. Not a sex giggle, but the 'oh shit look what I found' giggle. Right then, I wanted to be that person, but not today.

"There is a book I've been trying to find time to read, but other things keep popping up. Can I check out a book?" I didn't know if she allowed that and some of them were so old that I was worried about touching them. But the worst she could say was no.

"Not exactly. We can't risk losing any of the volumes." I sagged a bit, but I had expected that answer. "But if you bring the book in question to me, I will show you how it works."

"Oh, okay." I perked up a bit at that and turned, planning on heading to my regular carousel where my books still were, but the others were waiting for me when I turned around.

"Cori. You look like shit. What happened?" Shay's words were blunt and even though Carelian growled, I couldn't help but laugh a bit. He was never anything but blunt with me. It would have been better if he'd been less accommodating with the other councilors, but it was getting better.

"Rips into one of the realm's oceans. It was... difficult."

Esmere cocked her head, looking at me. ~Water from our realm? That is interesting.~

~It was not pleasant. But I did get many fish.~ Carelian preened a bit as Esmere's eyes lit up.

~Oh?~ She said it a bit coyly, and I realized I really needed to try these fish if they were that valuable a commodity.

~The spine backs, razor fins, sweet flesh, and two others.~ He licked his muzzle, and I rolled my eyes.

"If we are done talking about food, I've been reactivated."

Shay paled, but Citlali and the denizens just stared at me uncomprehendingly.

"Shit. Really? How did they justify it?" Shay asked, his fingers twitching.

"Emergency Executive Order. I don't think it is going to be widespread, but it is there."

"What is reactivated?" Citlali asked, a frown on her face.

I quickly explained everything, and I could see the anger gathering in everyone. "Look, I get it, but it doesn't really change anything about what I was doing, just makes it more formal and less a favor to a friend." I took a minute to expand on the information that had been shared. At this point I'd gathered an audience. The other mages we'd brought in to help research, denizens, even Cleo had come over to listen.

Quickly I covered the boards, notes, who was involved, and the threats. Most of the mages we'd pulled in were merlins and all of them had at least twenty years on me. They were not happy about this.

"I get that you aren't happy, but I can't change it. If you don't like it, tell people, contact your movers and shakers, but right now I need to free up my time. I can't be here. I need to be on Earth dealing with things and I am so perilously close to being out of offerings, it isn't good. The worst part is because I've had to be in all these different places, they know Carelian can find where we need to go and they are going to leverage it hard. I'm the perfect agent. But it means they are most likely going to start looking at other mages with familiars to see if they can do the same thing. So be warned." This I said to everyone, and I could see as people started to realize the long-term consequences of my abilities being so public.

"Citlali, I used the AIN as a club. I don't know if this is going to bite me or not, but hopefully they'll slow down in their plans to roll over me."

The tall woman shrugged, her silvery hair waving down her back. "Don't worry about it. The plans have already been set in motion and our people have reached out to contact your government, Australia, and China. There are some upsets coming soon. It will not be an issue and as we regard you as a friend of the Nation, it only supports our plans."

"Good. So keep it up. I don't know how to stop what is going on and I'm not sure what else to do to stop this, but the rips are becoming more dangerous." I looked at them. "And my skills aren't best served here."

For a moment, the knowledge that my skills at research and biology had never been used to their full potential hurt, but now it just didn't matter.

"We got this. You need to work on eating as much as you can. But one of the archmages over here had an idea about offerings she wanted to talk to you about," Shay said, waving at a petite woman.

"Okay. Anything else?"

There were shakes of heads, lots of dark looks and more than one headed home with the assistance of other mages or their familiars. I went to talk to the mage Shelia. While nothing she told me was earth-shattering, it did give me some ideas on how to offer even more effectively, mixing blood and other offerings. At this point even a five percent increase could make a huge difference.

I headed back home two hours later after verifying with Citlali and Shay I would be available if they needed me. Either via their familiars, or Sloanes' or by cellphone. When I got back,

I opened the package that had been delivered and found wrapped up there the next phase of my life. A phone, a small notebook with names and numbers, a contract with the rates and on-call status, and a picture and name of my handler.

Forcing down the desire to cry, I put it away to deal with in the morning and headed to see the kids and Jo and Sable. They'd be moving soon, and I planned on enjoying the time with them now. Before I needed to make sure they were safe from me and the trouble that followed.

THIRTEEN

Which is more devastating: a rip or Merlin Cori? That is the question on everyone's minds today in the aftermath of the St. Louis Water Attack. The water that poured out on St. Louis put people at risk and the creatures that came with it surely did, but at the end of the day it was just water that ended up in the river. But Merlin Munroe called winds that did widespread damage and risked making buildings safety hazards. If this is the sort of help offered by the government, should we be finding other options? ~ New Yorker Editorial

CHAOS

I didn't have time to investigate the phone and the documents the next morning before it was ringing. "Yes," I mumbled as I staggered downstairs with the phone in one hand. I headed for the coffee machine. Today was shaping up to be a pot day.

"Merlin Munroe, we need you. We have a level four rip." That was one of the good things about the meeting.

With the OMO and Charles there, we had hammered out levels of severity for the rips. The little ones, like what I would practice with, were level one. Ones where creatures smaller than a cat, house cat not Cath, could slip through were a two. Threes were mid-sized with creatures slipping out, but nothing pushing against them. Fours were active with chaos tentacles poking out. These level fours required two mages, one to deal with the tentacles, usually Air to handle lightning, while the other focused on closing the rip. Five. Well, fives were large amounts of water, a huge rip, or immediate public danger.

"No," I said as I set the phone on the counter with the speaker on.

Per the agreement with the draft office, I was to only be called for class five rips. And I really hoped they weren't more often than once a week.

"You need to head to- what do you mean no?" The voice was male and youngish, though until I finished waking up it could have been a teenager and I just wasn't paying enough attention.

"I mean no. Level five is what you call me for. I don't have the offerings to mess with anything that anyone else can handle."

"But, they said, I was told, you need to go," the young man sputtered on the other end of the line, and I just loaded up the coffeemaker. Extra cinnamon today, that might help. There would be sugar in this cup. Lots of sugar.

"Too bad. Level five or nothing. And who are you?" I peered at the phone through barely cracked eyes, the lights in the kitchen were horrible in the morning, way too bright, we really needed to put in dimming bulbs.

"Stanley, ma'am." I blinked, trying to remember the name on the sheet. It hadn't been that, it had been a female name. The coffee began to brew, and I resisted the urge to lean my head against the refrigerator.

The name popped into my mind. "Yolanda somebody is supposed to be the only person contacting me." Well, her or Stephen, but not this Stanley.

"They just told me to call you and tell you to fix it," he stammered, and I shrugged, not that anyone could see but me.

"No." With that, I hung up. The clock displayed five-thirty, and I bit back a whimper. It wasn't worth going back to bed, and since I was up, I might as well make food for people. With a sigh, I pulled out bacon, eggs, and chopped up potatoes. That had been a life saver we figured out a long time ago. Zap the potatoes in the microwave for about five minutes, then chop up. They would cook up quickly in a pan and tasted great.

~Why are you awake?~ Carelian sat in the entry to the kitchen, yawning, his teeth looking like daggers.

"Stupid phone. Someone got ahold of my number already. I

said no." I didn't talk to him so much as the stove that held a pan that I was about to put bacon in.

~Smart quean,~ he commented. ~Could you grab me a bowl of fish?~

I nodded, pulling down the bowl. Then opened the cupboard to the stasis field. He and Jo had spent some time while I recovered processing fish. And there were stacks of it chopped up and ready to go. I grabbed a handful and dropped it in the bowl for him. Carelian was perfectly capable of grabbing the fish himself, but we all preferred him eating it out of the bowl. Especially Hamiada. She did not like rotting fish blood on her floors.

I put the bowl on the bar counter, and he jumped up into his seat and put some hot sauce on the fish before tossing it in his mouth. Hot sauce on sushi just never clicked right in my mind.

The bacon was about done, and I threw the potatoes in the grease as Jo walked in.

"You're up early. Decided you are missing us already?"

"Yes, that's it," I said. My hands were wrapped around the coffee as I let the steam wreath my face. "Coffee is made, extra cinnamon."

"Yum. So why are you up?"

"Stupid phone call. I said no." I took out the bacon and stirred the potatoes. Another minute and I'd cook the eggs. "Scrambled or fried?" Those were the only two options when I was the one cooking.

"Oh, fried two each for me and Sable, but scramble two for the kids. I'll make their burritos."

We worked in companionable silence. "You know you can come over in the mornings. You are never blocked from the house," Jo said into the silence, and I started as my mind had been on trying to get more protein and vitamins into my body and process it faster.

"I know," I said, looking at her.

"Hamiada said the door should be done next week. To both places. *Mami*'s house and ours will have doors for you. You just need to decide where to put the doors." She didn't look at me while she talked, and I leaned over and kissed her cheek.

"You could live on the other side of the world, and you would still be the woman I love best in the world. Promise." My words were honest, and I just hoped I'd live long enough to see the kids become the awesome adults I knew they would be.

Jo laughed, the momentary sober mood vanishing. "Not the being?"

"Well, that blasted Cath sitting over there has a pretty hard hold on my heart. Then there's my brother, the kids, Sable that are all kinds of tied to my heart. So, nope. I love you more than any other woman on the face of the earth."

She laughed and kissed my forehead. "And I love you more than any other merlin." We both started laughing at that as I cooked eggs. The kids came tramping down the stairs followed by Sable. We ate, laughing and talking about school and work. The mood stayed buoyant until they left, and I headed upstairs.

Carelian followed me, laying across my bed and taking most of it. ~I will sleep. You should too.~

"Nah, I need to take a shower and get dressed. I also want to run to the store and get some more energy bars. I'm not eating them often enough in the field."

He yawned again and closed his eyes.

I'd managed to get showered and dried off when Hamiada called out from the bedroom.

"Cori, this device is ringing."

With a sigh I walked out, still naked, giving her a smile and a nod. "Thank you. I'll take it."

She beamed at me. "Don't forget to give me where you want the doors."

"I won't," I said as I answered. "Yes?"

"Cori Munroe? This is Yolanda Rigalio. I'm your handler. I hear you refused an assignment this morning." The voice was arch and vaguely imperious. My heart sank as I realized this would be an adversarial relationship. How far did I want to push this? The answer came in a flash. All the way. I was tired of all of this, and I was literally bleeding myself dry trying to help.

"One minute." I reached for my coffee cup, took a sip and grabbed underwear and a tank bra to pull on. Then I sat on my bed and picked up the phone again. It had been much longer than a minute, close to three, and I didn't care.

"Okay," I said, ready to deal with the hand Magic had dealt me.

"You will not make me wait." Her voice snarled out at me. "I expect instant response when I call. You are-" I hung up.

"This is going to be a long day, and I forgot to get the book I wanted from Cleo. When this is done, do you want to swing over to the Library? Then we can head to the store?"

~Fine,~ he murmured, still mostly asleep. The phone rang again.

"This is Cori," I answered.

"You hung up on me. How dare you!" her voice was a screech of outrage and I hung up again.

"How long do you think I'll have to keep doing this?" I headed over to find pants and socks. If I needed to run, I'd rather have clothes on.

~Twice more.~

He was wrong. It was three times. And each time I just hung up. The fourth time someone else was on the other end —Stephen.

"Morning Cori. Causing problems already?"

"Me? I'm not doing anything. I'm just setting boundaries and they won't be crossed." By this point, I was back downstairs, refilling my coffee and planning the day. Library, then home. This weekend was going to be the official moving day, and I didn't know if I was ready.

"You are a draftee and will listen when I talk," Yolanda snapped at me, and I sighed. Before I could respond, Stephen cut in.

"Yolanda here is a former manager of one of the rogue mage teams. She is used to dealing with a rougher crowd." Stephen sounded like he was trying to be cajoling, but mostly I heard exasperation.

"And you talk to them like that and you're still alive?" I had a hard time imagining anyone talking to Scott like that, but maybe that was just me.

"They are responsible for following my instructions." Her voice was rapidly getting on my nerves.

"Awesome. Well, here is how it will go. I will speak to you and only you. You will let me know, politely, where the rip is and what is going on. I will say no if I feel that I don't have the ability to deal with it at that time."

She started to sputter, and I cut her off. "I am well aware that I have been reactivated as the martyr to the cause, and at this point, most other US mages are aware of it as well. I have been making offerings of blood because I am so low on genetic material. Do not push this because I have very little patience at this point. If you yell at me, if you start demanding, if you call me names, I will hang up. Do you understand?" I was standing in the middle of the kitchen, still in socks, sipping coffee.

"Yolanda, she isn't kidding. She will give everything she has, but if you treat her like a misbehaving animal, she'll walk away. She doesn't bite, she simply leaves."

I could hear the sputters on the other end and almost laughed. "She can't do that. She's been reactivated. She'll be killed if she doesn't listen."

Stephen cleared his throat, and I could hear him trying to figure out how to phrase this. "That is true. But here is the hard truth, right now she is the only mage who can solo close class five rips. If she is killed, if she vanishes, our country is in a load of hurt. So, explain to me exactly how threatening to kill her is going to motivate her at all."

My previous bosses would have never done this, and I made a mental note to ping Scott when this was done. I had questions.

There was a long silence on the phone. "Miss Munroe. Is it true you said no to a call earlier?" Her voice was overly formal, and I preferred it that way.

"Yes. It was for a class four rip, and multiple mages can close that. I am to be called only for class five and above."

She cleared her throat but continued in the same formal tone. "Very well. That has been noted. I will be your only contact. Is this the best number to reach you?"

"Yes. It will almost always be answered, but if I am not available, someone else may answer it and I will get back to you as soon as possible."

Her voice sharpened. "And why would you not be available, or it not be answered?"

I would have preferred if she wasn't so snide in her tone, but I answered it. "If I am in the realms, I leave the phone here as there is no service there. Usually, I will be contacted in one to five minutes. If I am in the middle of closing a rip, I am unable to answer." All I could do was hope they never called during a council meeting, but perhaps Freya was more forgiving than Brix had been.

Her voice sounded reluctant, but she responded. "That is

valid. I will contact you when you are needed." She dropped off the line and I sighed, knowing Stephen was still on there.

"Are you sure you don't want to grab Indira and just run away to Fiji or something?"

He laughed. "I am very sure I do. But I'm hoping this can get solved before I bail. Have you made any headway?"

"No. And I'm running out of things to try," I admitted. "I'll keep you posted."

We hung up, and I refreshed my coffee.

CHAPTER

FOURTEEN

Mage Reactivated – for the first time in almost fifty years a mage who has fulfilled their draft has been reactivated and this time it is the merlin with the mostest Merlin Munroe. You read that right. Even though prior to now she has been responding to rips and closing them, she now has to do it as she is back under government control. The question of the day is going to be can we trust the government to manage Merlin Munroe correctly or will they squander such a precious resource.

~ Magical Daily News

ORDER

With Carelian following me, I darted into the Library. I wanted that book. With all the hub-bub yesterday I'd gotten sidetracked.

"Cleo, you said there was a way for me to get a book that I could take home?"

"Yes. Do you have the book?" she asked, looking down at me. I was always surprised by her size. Her head was about the size of my torso. It just seemed like I was looking up, even when I looked right at her.

"One minute." I darted to the carousel and brought back The Evolution and Life of Phoenixes by L.Brash. "This one, please."

"Ah. What do you know of the being that wrote this?" Cleo smiled as she gazed at it.

"Nothing?" That surprised me. Why would I know about an author who wrote a book thousands of years ago?

"Ah. All of us have heard the story Brix told. This is the child of Brix and Shera. Brash - a blending of their names. That was more common centuries ago." She picked the book up and set it in one half of a wooden box that was divided into two pieces. In the second half of the box, she grabbed a stack of parchment and set it inside. "This will take a few minutes." She stared at the box, her brows furrowed.

"What are you going to do?" This fascinated me. The magic

of the Library was interesting enough, but I hadn't seen Cleo use much magic.

"I am from the realm of Order." I had assumed she was a Spirit creature, but then what did I know? "This allows me to see all the text and pattern. Then I duplicate it on the paper here. It is not permanent, as the ink is prone to fading. But it will last a year or two and if it is damaged, the original isn't affected." As she talked, I could see the pages rustling slightly.

I reviewed in my head how Pattern and Replicate worked and if she merged Create Pattern with it. This didn't seem impossible to do, other than... My mind trailed off. "Doesn't that mean you have to have the entire book in your mind to duplicate it?"

"Yes. I have to pull the full content of it into my mind, then rebuild it. It is not difficult, only requires mental effort, control, and minimal offering. The Library helps to a great extent." A minute later, the copy of my book lay there, and she handed it to me. "Here you go. Let me know if you need anything else."

I shook my head, a bit shocked, and headed home. I dropped the book off in my study and headed to the store. By the time I was done, the cart was full of electrolyte replacement drink, pre-natal vitamins, protein bars, and frozen smoothie mixes. I got home and put it all away. I really needed to raise my calorie content by a lot. Already I'd lost weight that I didn't need to lose.

Wishing I dared change into leggings and a t-shirt, I made myself a high protein and caloric smoothie. Arguing with government officials had burned off the calories I'd eaten at breakfast. With a sigh, I curled up in my study to start to read while sipping on the smoothie.

I'd gotten to the end of the first chapter, which explained his life and gave me a different view of Brix and Shera, when the blasted phone rang. If I could have sent lasers out of my eyes, the phone would have been a melted slag.

"Yes?" My voice wasn't curt, but it sure wasn't friendly.

"Level 5 in Northern California," Yolanda said, not even bothering with any small talk. "Near something called the Sutter Buttes. Tentacles and large creatures coming out. Three dead. Team on the way, but you can get there and shut it. They'll deal with the creatures if needed."

I was up and moving. Grabbing my bag and taking the minute to get Carelian into his harness.

"I need a more specific location. Where near the Buttes? Which side?" I snapped out as I drained the smoothie. I'd be trying the new method the mage had suggested. Hair and a touch of blood. My hand brushed against the pocket I kept scalpels in. They were there, waiting for me.

"South side, near the base of the foothills. They sent me a picture. It is obvious enough that if you're in the vicinity, you should be able to see it easily." Her voice was calm and professional. That I could handle.

"Got it." I hung up and looked at Carelian. "You know where that is?"

He and I had hiked in most of the mountains in the US. Someday we were hoping for the Alps and Himalayas, but it wouldn't be now.

~I believe so. But I may need to open multiple rips from the cross roads and see if we are close.~

"Go." I set the cup down on the desk and stepped through the rip he'd created to the gray barren pocket realm he called the crossroads. He sealed it behind us and then he sat there, tail swinging back and forth as he opened a rip. California, he knew relatively well. He'd gotten better at finding places over the years. He hated planes that much and hated me being on them just as much. I knew he'd been exploring across the country when I was busy with other stuff and right at that moment, I wanted to hug him in gratitude. Otherwise, this would be much more difficult.

~I have it.~ The rip widened, and he leapt through it.

I followed and halted, looking at the gash across the mountains. The Buttes were a tiny mountain range in the middle of California between the Coastal Range and the Sierra Nevada. Normally, they were rounded mounds that weren't overly impressive when compared to the mountains on either side. They were beige colored with rocks and trees, nothing exciting.

That wasn't so today. A gash ripped along the base. It was longer than any I'd ever seen. At least a mile long with thin questing tentacles flickering out of it. To my mind it looked like they were tasting, testing things, then pulling back and thinking. There were also creatures slipping out on either side. Large, fur covered, but they resembled bison more than any predator I'd seen.

"Do you know what those are?" I was already digging out the scalpel and pulling up my shirt.

~Bitualas. They aren't particularly dangerous, but they are omnivores like your bears, just with hooves and horns. They don't have a fear response, as even Cath struggle to take them down. Their inherent magic is all armor and solidity. The biggest problem is their shit.~

"Huh?" That distracted me for a minute and the scalpel slipped, making a much deeper cut than I'd intended. I hissed in pain, ignoring his snarl.

~Do not do that.~ Worry and frustration laced his tone and if I could I would have petted him and assured him it was okay.

"I know. Go on. Their shit?" I reached for Air and started slamming lighting into the tentacles.

His tail lashed and he glared at me. ~It is toxic and can befoul water and soil. They are roamers because they poison the land behind him. Most caretakers kill them as soon as they arrive. Their flesh is sweet, but their organs are toxic to most creatures, which means they aren't hunted to extinction as they should be.~

"I swear I'll never understand some of the creatures magic creates."

He didn't answer, just watched. I focused on the rip, trying to pull it closed as soon as I'd chased most of the tentacles back. Most of these rips were stubborn, and I had to fight to get them closed. This one wasn't as bad as most. The problem was its length. Up until now, I think the biggest one had been a few hundred feet. This was a mile. I'd get part of it closed, the tentacles would come back, I'd have to stop and slam them with lightning to get them to go back, while their pressure would undo some of what I had done.

It felt like the phrase "two steps forward, one step back" because that was what it was. It took me over an hour. Carelian stayed with me, watching the Bitualas. They were content to graze where they were right now, which meant at least they weren't moving away. From my quick view, I didn't see any running water, but I'd need to remember to call in a hazmat team to deal with their shit.

I was too tired to even think at this point. All I could focus on was my task. The rip was almost closed when Carelian warned me mages were coming. My head nodded as I fought. All the blood and at this point I'd given up and just used up the rest of my hair, leaving my skull shiny, naked, and cold. I only had about ten feet left when they arrived.

"Hey, we're here from Yuba College. How can we help?" a young man who seemed way too excited, asked.

"One second," I muttered and twisted my arm, getting a bit more blood out as I sealed the rip. My knees buckled, and I slumped to the ground. Maybe I should start bringing a camp chair with me.

"Lady, you okay?"

"No, but I'll live." I focused on him but once again exhaustion battered at me. Magic took genetic offerings, but using it, directing it the way I was took my own energy and I felt like I'd run a marathon. "Okay, see the big beasties? They are like bison, but their shit is toxic. Round them up, slaughter them, or get another mage to open a rip into Chaos, though killing them might be kinder. Then get a HazMat team here to collect all their shit. It can kill the local flora and fauna and we don't want that."

"Ooh, new biologicals? I bet the biology department would love to take a look at them," someone else said. I craned my head a bit to see a few other people there, but I didn't even care enough to do more than register multiples.

"Fine, just be aware their internal organs might be toxic, poisonous, something like that. You have the rest of this?" I knew to get home I had to stand. Nothing had ever seemed so daunting. But I didn't have a choice, I had to stand.

"Yep, thanks ma'am. We'll take it from here." One of the youngsters spoke, and it amused me that I was thinking of them as young. When had I gotten old?

I forced myself to my feet, wobbling a bit as I stood there. "Carelian, would you?"

He glared at me, but opened a rip to home, and I stumbled through it to lean against the wall. This looked like a good place to fall.

~What I wouldn't give for a human musculature and skeletal structure right now.~ His voice came to me as a mutter, something I wasn't really supposed to hear. I just held onto the wall, preventing myself from sliding down it only by the knowledge that I would have to stand back up or crawl somewhere stopping me. That sounded much more difficult.

~Hamiada, could you assist, please?~ His voice this time was more soothing and less annoyed.

"Ah, she is not doing well." Hamiada stood next to me, a puzzled look on her face. "This is not healthy for mortals."

~No it is not,~ Carelian agreed. ~Would you assist me in getting her into bed and making some food? Carrying trays is not my forte.~

"Of course. Come on." Strong wooden arms slipped underneath me and lifted me easily. "Though I am not sure of this new hairstyle. I think you looked better with it longer."

I found the strength to run my hand over my now bald pate. She was right, I liked it better long. There had to be some stocking caps somewhere. The random thoughts continued as she carried me up the stairs with surprising smoothness and put me on the bed. My shoes were removed before she moved me back into the bed to sleep.

~We will bring food and liquid. You will drink,~ Carelian ordered. I nodded and closed my eyes, letting my mind slip away.

CHAPTER

FIFTEEN

Senator Heather Perry's meteoric rise seems to be crashing. Without any explanation, the senator has been removed from two committees and even her own party is refusing to work with her. The only public comment from her office has been, "She is choosing to focus on her constituents at this time." However, there have been various notices on house boards about her efforts to force mages into something much closer to slavery than draft service. ~CNN

SPIRIT

T kept changing the ring tone on the phone. I needed to find a piece of music I hated and make it the ring tone. A piece that was rarely played. Already I was developing a traumatic response to the phone jangling.

It had been four weeks, and I'd gone out five times. All of them required everything I could come up with. My period saved me at least one of the times, stripping my uterus for some powerful offerings. Magic seemed to delight in any offering that related to fertility. I rarely talked to anyone anymore and if I wasn't out dealing with closing tears, I was sleeping or eating.

I'd lost another fifteen pounds. Weight I needed, but I couldn't eat enough to put it back on. My nails were gone to the quick, feet and hands, and I didn't have many fat stores left. My skin was shining and bright red as I had offered up the external layer of dermis more than once.

I was curled up in bed, shivering, starving, exhausted, and wide-awake all the same time. Carelian had curled up around me, his purr interrupted by soft snarls. He wasn't really asleep, just holding me and keeping me warm. The snarls tended to match when I was wracked by a whole-body shiver.

"Dinner's ready, Cori," Jo said from the doorway. "You've got visitors."

I lifted my head and nodded. I had stubble, mainly because what was growing back wasn't enough to even begin to offer with. I was wearing a soft green silk cap. It amazed me how cold your neck and ears got when you had no hair.

"Anyone I actually want to see?" I asked as I pried myself from bed.

"Actually, yes. So come on. Loaded baked potato soup, steamed vegetables, and some fish. And yes, everything is cut up for you." My hands had been shaking so much lately that the effort of cutting food was almost more than I could handle. The odds were the soup was a calorie laden glorious creation that she'd make sure I ate every bit.

"Kay, I'll be down in a minute." I rose and went into the bathroom, wanting to pee before I went downstairs. The mirror told me truths I didn't want to see as I washed my hands. The last few weeks of nonstop either reading, closing rips, or writing reports had done me no favors. I'd never been gorgeous like Jo or Sable, but now I resembled a victim of some horrible disease. My skin had a sallow grey tone to it. There were circles under my eyes, my hair was a stubbled grime on my skull, and you could see my collarbones and ribs—if I pulled up my shirt. I really looked like I should be in bed with someone waiting on me hand and foot.

I laughed to myself I as I headed down the stairs. I'd seen cancer patients that looked better than me. But I didn't know what else to do. The book by L. Brash had been fascinating, but while the author had referenced the disappearance of Atlantis and death of his mother, it hadn't felt like someone mourning, more like someone listing off a famous person that had died. Was the family dynamic normal to phoenix families? Maybe normal to Brix? Or was there something else?

I sighed as I turned toward the dining room. For all I knew the book had been edited and that editor had stripped it of emotions.

The food smelled good, and I moved in, expecting to see Marisol, or maybe Shay, Sloane, and Scott. I jerked to a stop as Indira and Stephen looked up.

"Fuck me. Cori, what happened?" The words burst out of Stephen's mouth, while Indira just covered her mouth with her hand, her eyes wide in horror.

I tried to remember the last time he'd seen me. After thinking about it, I realized it would have been when they reactivated me. I hated video calls lately, so I'd been avoiding them. That meant he last saw me when I was about twenty-five pounds heavier, had hair to my shoulders, and didn't look like a zombie.

"Hey. Just doing my job." I looked around for the kids. They'd been super worried about Momma Cori and I didn't know what to tell them. "Where are the twins?" I forced myself to eat dinner with everyone. I was missing too much of their lives and unless I couldn't move, I was having dinner with them.

"I sent them to have dinner with Marisol. They took their dragons with them," Sable said with a smile. "This is about you."

My legs trembled when I let them fold. I needed a day or two of not closing rips. I didn't know how much longer I could go on.

"Cori, why haven't you used the Wandering Mage Act to stop going and closing rips?" Indira sounded pained as she sat on my left. Carelian had moved over the last week and rather than sitting across from me and was seated next to me, his tail in my lap.

"Because I can still do it. They said they don't have anyone else." I wanted to cry with exhaustion. Worry still coated the back of my mind that I wouldn't have anything to offer in an emergency.

I still have all my toes and fingers. There are still options.

Part of me suspected I should be worried about thoughts like that, but that required more energy than I had.

"Cori, you are past what you can do." Stephen's voice was gruff as he stared at me. I turned my head to avoid his gaze. "And they are getting better. They have teams in multiple areas that are at worst 30 minutes away. Most of the rips aren't so bad that a half hour makes a difference. You need to say no."

"And when she tells me fine, she'll order my death?" I tried to make it a joke, but the fierceness on every face at the table surprised me.

"Tell them to try it. They won't have a government left if they dare. It is supposed to be the stick, not a reality. We haven't ordered anyone killed for refusing their assignment while in the draft for years. That isn't the normal flow." Stephen's voice was thick with anger. "If they try that, I'll destroy the department from the inside out. No one should be offering this much. We need your skills, not your life."

I ducked my head and felt the roughness of Carelian's tongue on the back of my hand. He'd licked me to heal so often lately, he'd joked he was becoming a connoisseur of my blood.

"I'll see. I just..." my voice trailed off as I tried to figure out what to say. I'd noticed more and more, that in the moment of fighting the rips I could think clearly. The rest of the time, I moved in a fog. Even the words I read lately took multiple times to register. I tightened my fist around my fork, using the pain to push away any need to cry.

"Cori, if I have to, I'll knock you out, I will. Or worse, I'll ask Esmere to come sit on you." Jo's voice was harsh. "Have any of them even seen you since this started?"

She filled a bowl full of soup and set it in front of me as she talked. "And yes, you are going to eat every bite of that, plus the fish. And I have a rare steak in cube form for snacks for you later. And ice cream." Her voice sounded a bit panicked, and I felt myself shrinking away even more.

"Sorry. I'll eat more." I brought a spoon of soup to my mouth, concentrating on that action, and it wasn't until I slurped it down that I realized no one was talking. I lifted my head to see Jo and Sable, hands clasped on the table, silent tears on their faces as they watched me. Indira had both hands clasped in front of her, hiding her mouth as she watched me with glittering eyes. Stephen just sat silent, but the guilt I saw in his eyes matched mine at not being able to do it all.

"I need to say no?" I said into the silence, stirring the soup quietly.

"Yes. Unless it is a level 6 and they have zero mages, and people are dying, you need to say no," Stephen ground out. He sighed and his shoulders dropped a bit more. "The rips are happening more frequently than we can handle, but if you die, we've gotten bigger problems."

"Freya," Sable snapped. "Carelian, can you ask Esmere to ping me?" Both Sable and Jo could respond to mindspeak, but neither could initiate it, especially with a denizen that wasn't there.

~Yes?~ he said, a questioning lilt to the response. A moment later, another voice rang in our minds.

~Carelian says there is an issue?~ The curious voice of Esmere made me wince. She wasn't modulating as well as normal and it hurt. Just one more bit of pain. My arm barely hurt anymore when I sliced it.

~Esmere, can you call Freya and ask her to come to our house immediately?~ Sable's voice was clipped and forceful as she focused on each word. For me the mental speech had become almost automatic, but not for them.

~There may be a cost involved in it,~ Esmere warned.

~If you want your herald alive in the next week, someone had better pay it.~ Sable's voice snapped out and I could feel Esmere's surprise.

~Should I come?~

~If it will help you get Freya here, fine.~ Sable paused. ~And besides, you are always welcome, you know that.~

A slice of pain and then the giant emerald green cat walked out of the hallway into the dining room and froze.

~By the void, what has happened? I saw you not three

weeks ago. You were tired and thin, but not this. What is going on?~

All of them launched into explanations, even Carelian adding bits to explain why I looked like the zombie I felt like. I just focused on eating soup. I had no idea what Sable was thinking and as long as I could eat food and not have to make any decisions I was going to go with that.

~Stupid humans,~ hissed through my mind. ~Yes, I will get her. This will have no cost. Though I do not know what you think she can do.~ Esmere's tail lashed back and forth, a sure sign of her agitation.

"I know, but I have an idea," Sable said, her jaw set.

I wanted to protest, but mostly I just stayed silent and kept eating. The rich carb and fat laden soup tasted delicious. Even though I looked like a starvation victim, I wasn't, so my stomach had no issues with me filling it full of food.

Esmere looked at me and hissed. Then she was gone. They all kept looking at me, then Indira spoke. "What plan do you have?"

SIXTEEN

"Dispatch, we have another rip in progress at 3rd and Main. Over."

"Understood Baker 3. Can you provide more information? Over."

"Big rip in the space time continuum? I'm not sure what you want me to say, Dispatch. It's a rip, no one is dead yet, so can we get it closed? Over."

~ Viral transcript of a radio call from a police officer to Dispatch

CHAOS

"It's more of an idea. Cori comes home and tells us about the meetings and what the problems are." Sable shrugged, but her facial expression wasn't casual. "From what I gather, the denizens aren't super creative and don't really think outside the box. Cori needs some time to heal and rest up. That means the magic needs to be used, so it isn't bursting out at the seams. I'm going to give them something to do with the excess." Sable cut a piece of fish off and moaned in pleasure as she put it in her mouth and chewed. "Carelian, you were correct. This is delicious."

~Told you.~ He still watched me eat more than ate himself.

A minute later, I heard a ping. ~Freya is with me.~ Then a slash of pain and the two of them walked in. Freya was looking around the house with an inquiring look. Her wings were not in evidence, but she still had an aura about her that drew everyone's attention.

I watched her and saw the second she registered my presence. Her eyes widened and her face went immobile.

"Are you dying? Have you brought me here to claim you?" Her question brought the room to a halt.

I choked. "I don't think so. Wow, I look that bad?"

"Yes," half the room chimed. I sighed and put more soup in my mouth.

"If not, then what requires my presence?" She looked at all of us, her eyes pale but somehow seeing more than I was comfortable with.

Sable spoke up. "That would be me. You're the chair, right? The person who says what gets done in the realms?"

Freya let a quick laugh slip out. "I doubt anyone can claim that, but I am the one that can guide and focus efforts. Why?"

Sable focused on the Valkyrie, and I blinked at the set of her shoulders and jaw. Of the two of them, Sable tended to roll with the flow, but when she decided to be stubborn, it was like pulling someone out who was stuck in quicksand.

"From what Cori says, the magic is overflowing, and that flooding is why we are having troubles. Why she looks like that. Too many mages are dying because the realms can't absorb the magic." They weren't questions, but she waited for an answer.

Freya nodded. "Yes. That is why we need the Herald to figure out how to stop this."

I swear half the room ground their teeth at that and I almost laughed. Instead, I kept eating. I was full, but right now every calorie I got in was important as my body was burning through them faster than was healthy.

Sable glared at Freya. "Well, if she can't get some recuperation time, she's going to die before that happens, and then we are all fucked."

Another choked laugh slipped out at that, but Sable didn't glance my way. Carelian leaned against me, a soft rumble, and I knew he was congratulating himself on smart queans.

"Sable, do you have a suggestion?" Freya didn't sound confrontational, which was better than Brix would have been.

"Yes, actually. I assume you've seen the pocket realm Cori created to hold the nuke?"

Freya swallowed hard but nodded, her eyes drifting to me too often.

"Excellent. Duplicate it. Make as many pocket realms as you can, empty and barren of magic, and have Tirsane dump the magic in there. Why stick to the existing ones? Create new areas and just dump. Have the other Lords do the same thing anywhere the magic is pooling and looks like it might break through."

The room went silent, and Esmere and Freya stared at Sable, then turned to look at each other.

"Would that work?" Freya asked, focused on Esmere, whose tail had frozen.

~It might. We wouldn't be able to control what it would create, but it would absorb a lot of magic.~ Esmere sounded thoughtful.

Sable sighed. "Do you have anything to lose by trying it?"

"No, actually," Freya admitted. "We usually only have tiny pocket realms managed by the being living there, or larger ones run by various lords. There are pathways that connect them, or the ability to step through. Each realm has solid lands, but I am unaware of realms being created and allowed to run wild."

Sable rolled her eyes. "How do you think they were created in the first place? Create new places. See what happens. Give Magic something to do."

"I've always known Sable was brilliant, Jo. But now I'm wondering how I might steal her away from you," Indira said with a smile. "That is an idea I've never thought of."

"Cori created one and sealed it off. So why not do it with lots? The magic can be dumped in it, then let to do its own thing," Sable said. "Later, if you need, the pocket realms can be connected or not."

"Will you ask Tirsane? I will contact Salistra," Freya said, looking at Esmere.

~Yes. Then I will convince Bob. One way or another.~ An odd determination vibrated in Esmere's voice, and her eyes locked on mine.

"I'm okay, you know," I tried to reassure the Cath.

~No, you are not. And I have zero desire to deal with a grieving child. Besides, my goddaughter would miss you greatly.~ With that comment, she turned and headed into the hall, disappearing around the corner.

Freya nodded to the table. "Thank you for the idea. I will

report as soon as we know anything. But it will not change anything immediately."

"I know," Sable said, her shoulders relaxing. "But if it helps, it could give us the time we need to figure this out."

Freya nodded. "Be well, Cori Munroe. Magic still has need of you." With a flash of her wings, she vanished, leaving us there.

Stephen looked at all of us and sighed. "Now what I can't figure out is: did Cori corrupt you into her chaotic ways? Or did she draw you to her as your energies match?"

"Oh, they've always been like this. They're just sneakier than I am," I said before either Jo or Sable could respond. "First, they make you think they are sweet and innocent. Trust me, they aren't."

"Nope, we aren't. Which also means you need to say no to the next couple calls Cori. You are too weak." Jo stared at me, her eyes worried, and I crumpled a bit.

"And the cost?"

Jo snorted. "Not as high as it will be if you die on the next call or the one after that. They have lots of mages. How are the other countries handling it? They don't have you, so we, and by we, I mean the United States, need to quit using you as the one size fits all solution. If they can do it, we can."

"This is true," Stephen said. "But most countries aren't as big as we are."

"Bullshit," Sable snapped. "Cixi knows Cori. Ask her. Ask Russia. Ask Brazil. If they aren't all dealing with the same issues, then something else is going on. But if they are, what are they doing?"

Stephen shrugged as we all looked at him. "I don't know. I can push a bit more for that information, but that is assuming anyone knows it."

Sable rolled her eyes. "Really?" She pulled out her phone

and started typing. "Here it is. I've got five news stories about what France is doing, Spain, and England. China is, as always, mysterious. It looks like France and Spain have pulled out individual army units and have them stationed every twenty miles with motorcycles. It means they can get anywhere in about 15 minutes. They also say they have rapid response teams in all subway hubs. They are using six mages per team to shut them down. Why aren't we doing that?" Her voice didn't give any leeway, and she glared at Stephen.

He heaved a sigh, one hand rubbing his temple, marring the merlin symbols etched there. "We are, or at least we are trying," Stephen stated. "Trains don't work well outside places with defined subway systems. Cars only work if they can get through the traffic, and helicopters aren't practical if it is a dense city area or remote area. Teleporting is damn rare, and Cori is the only mage I've heard of that can do it easily and that isn't publicized. We've asked all the mages to talk to their familiars because Carelian has highlighted just how powerful they are, something we'd mostly ignored. And by we, I mean the government and law enforcement. Merlin only knows what the OMO thinks. If you have any ideas please share them, because I've created groups from students, the societies, and all current draftees, but closing rips isn't something we train many mages to do and look at how much it is taking from her to close them." He waved his hand at me and cringed. "Most other mages are good for one, maybe two, and they are out of offerings." His voice had gotten sharper and more depressed as he spoke. "So please give me an idea to prevent killing someone I love."

Those last words acted like a bomb in the room, and we all stared at the table.

"Well, fuck," Sable muttered.

"I need time to regenerate. If they can create some realms, maybe I'll get a bit of peace," I said quietly. I'd eaten as much as

I could, but I'd grab more later. I was eating nonstop, but it still wasn't enough.

Sable's mouth pressed into a thin line. "Can you teach others to close rips? Those that aren't Spirit mages?"

"No," I said.

~Yes,~ said Carelian.

The entire table stared at him. "What do you mean, yes?" Indira's voice was quiet.

~You can be taught, but the price is very, very high, even with a focus. Maybe you might be able to close one or two large rips. Spirit has a direct path to how the realms form, so they can close it easier.~ His ears laid back. ~Think of it like learning to play a musical instrument, but you are deaf. You can learn, but it is always mechanical.~

"So not really feasible?" Indira clarified, the minute hope that had sprung up fading.

"Wait," I said slowly. "Can all Spirit denizens close rips?"

~If they are mages, I believe so.~

"How far do the powers of the Herald stretch?" All my attention was on him as my mind wandered to a possibility.

A quick flick upward of his ears, then back down. ~Not that far. You would need to pay.~

I sagged as everyone stared at me.

"Feel like enlightening the rest of us?" Jo had the same frown she'd worn most of the evening. I knew she wanted to wrap me in bubble wrap. I wish she could have.

"Denizens need payment for favors or services. And while I can pay a lot, I'm not sure what the US could pay them. From what I see, gold or money wouldn't mean much. But I was thinking if we could get realm denizens to step here to close rips, it might work."

"Hmm," Stephen said, his eyes narrowing. "It is possible,

but you are the only one I've ever heard of that talks to them regularly."

I snorted. "I might be the only mage, but as far as I know, almost all the familiars keep in touch with family and friends. They could ask, but the prices might be ones we don't expect."

"Like?" Sable was watching me, curiosity writ on her face.

"Future favors, prized possessions, doing something for them, up to and including killing someone. And I don't know how difficult closing the rips is for them. It could be anything from a token to something you aren't willing to pay."

Stephen snorted. "What wouldn't someone be willing to pay?" He sounded dismissive, and I turned to stare at him.

"Your firstborn child?" My voice was mild, but I wasn't teasing.

The room stilled as they looked at me, then at Carelian.

"Oh," someone whispered softly.

"That might be a price too high. Not to mention if word got out that they might be willing to do things for us..." he trailed off.

"Exactly. It might devolve into a djinn situation." I paused and focused on my familiar. "Carelian, are there djinn?" I asked worriedly. That one hadn't crossed my mind.

~Yes, but not in the way you think. They don't grant wishes, they are high level Air creatures that prefer to live in confined spaces. When someone is unlucky enough to break into their house, they often toy with them. Granting "wishes" in the worst way possible, then enjoying the suffering. They find it amusing. Be aware they are genderless, they are air, there is no gender the way mammals think of it. They enjoy emotional and physical chaos - though they are of Order.~

Stephen rested his elbows on the table, head in his hands. "Just once, I'd like something to be easy."

"Me too," I said, fighting not to whine. "I'm headed to bed. Hopefully, Freya and Esmere will get back to us soon."

There were hugs all around and I climbed the stairs to my room slowly, Carelian at my side the entire way. I could sense them watching me, but I didn't let on, I just made it to the top, then staggered into my bedroom. Taking off my clothes was too much effort, so I collapsed on top, curling around Carelian, and I fell asleep.

"Scott, of all the things in the movie and stories after your explosive entry into the mainstream, what was the one thing everyone got wrong."

"Well, Darla, it would have to be that I had a familiar. I'd never been that lucky. I have one now, in the form of Dahli whose mage died. At the mall, the creature they thought was my familiar was just a stuffed dog I'd purchased for my niece. But the image with the legs sticking out looked so realistic I couldn't convince the reporters it had been a stuffed animal." ~ Special Interview with Scott Randolph the Mage Hunter, whose life the Rescue of Stranthorn was based on.

ORDER

My phone, my tether and leash, rang, pulling up from sleep. It took me a minute to find it—Carelian was not willing to move. His warmth made sleep possible. I seemed to always be cold lately. His warmth both kept me from shivering and comforted me. I also slept better, wrapped around him and breathing in the odor that was uniquely Carelian. It was a mixture of blood, cinnamon, and cat. It probably should have smelled awful, but it was my favorite scent in the world.

It took me two tries to sit up, and I managed to answer the phone. "Yes?"

"Merlin Munroe. We have a class five rip in Sacramento, California, located near Morse Rd. How soon can you get there?" Yolanda's voice was clipped, and she could have been an automated message.

I tried to stand up, but I was shaking.

~Cori, no. The cost is too great. I will not lose my quean.~ His voice was soft, but unyielding.

"I can't." The words slipped out like a sigh.

"Excuse me? That wasn't a request, it was an order. We need you there."

"The cost is too great," I said, every word feeling like a failure. If I'd had the energy I would have cried. Instead, I sank back into the bed.

Yolanda snarled. "You will be arrested for dereliction of duty. This is not acceptable."

~Enough,~ Carelian snarled in my mind. He reached over and delicately shut off the phone with an extended finger. ~Alixant. Where is this woman named Yolanda?~

~Huh? Oh she's here in DC, why?~ Stephen sounded as confused as I was.

~She is threatening my quean. Where is she?~ There was an oddly compelling tone to Carelian's voice.

~You can't kill her,~ Stephen warned.

~Yes, I can. But I will not at this time. But I will show her.~

~Carelian,~ Stephen said, trying to sound stern, but he'd been as worried as everyone else with my appearance yesterday. ~Don't do anything reckless.~

~Why not? It seems to be the only thing humans take into account. Address.~

Stephen rattled it off. Carelian broke the connection.

"What are you going to do with that?" I knew he could use maps and had seen him on the computer once or twice but hadn't followed up on it.

~You'll see. Lay here.~ He stepped into a rip with a flash of pain. I shook my head and contemplated food and coffee. The clock said seven in the morning. I needed both, but stairs seemed impossible at this point, so I just laid back down, my eyes drifting shut.

"AAAIIII!" A blood-curdling scream jerked me out of my doze, and I sat up, staring at the door. A moment later, a woman wrenched open the door and rushed in. Her entire attention was on the opening as Carelian stalked in snarling, his tail lashing, fur puffed up, and teeth on full display. Even knowing he'd never hurt me, the sight of him caused my heart rate to kick up and I had to fight not to panic.

"What do you want from me?" Her voice was trembling and scared.

I examined her. She wore dark blue designer jeans and a light knit top in a cream color. Her heritage had to be mixed Pan-Asian with long dark hair twisted into a chignon on the nape of her neck and light brown skin that looked too pale against her hair. She was at least mid-thirties and a healthy weight. Something I wasn't.

~Look at her. Does she look like she can afford to give any more? Look like she can do your bidding?~ Carelian's silky voice implied imminent death, and I shuddered.

She whirled to look at me, her eyes scanning and dismissing me with a shudder. "I don't know who she is. Why am I here?" I should have felt sympathy. She was obviously terrified. But I couldn't find the energy.

"I recognize you," I said softly. I'd managed to sit up and my legs hung off the bed. I was still dressed in the clothes I'd worn last night, a t-shirt and sweats. They hung on me, making me look even gaunter than I actually was.

She turned and stared at me. "No, I don't know you."

"Really? I thought you'd recognize the woman you've been ordering around." Maybe I was too sarcastic, but then again, she'd just threatened to have me arrested, which rarely went well.

Yolanda went still, then reached into her pocket and pulled out her phone. She tapped it multiple times, then stopped. She held it up, staring at it, then me multiple times.

Carelian had sat down between her and the door. I could see she wasn't a mage. Most government employees left after their draft was done.

She kept looking back and forth between her phone and

me. "What happened to you, Merlin Munroe?" Her voice was sharp, but this time there was worry too. "The last images I have from you were only a month ago, and you were hale and healthy at that time."

"You've been sending me to close rips, more than I easily could. This is how much I've offered." I waved a hand up and down my body feeling like a sideshow freak.

"That isn't po-possible," she stuttered. "You look like you are half dead."

A choked-out laugh was my only answer.

"But, but, I was told you would complain and try to get out of your duty. That it was easy for you." She babbled out her protest as she stared at me.

"You were used. They want me as a martyr," I said, not surprised by her response. "But I need some time to heal. There has to be some other way. I just can't right now. I need at least a week, if not more."

She finally stopped shaking and glanced back at Carelian. "You sent him to terrify me?" A bit of the sneer and contempt was back in her voice.

~No. I went to gather you because you were putting my quean in danger. That could not be allowed. The only way to convince you was to show you. You would never have come willingly, so I forced you.~ He laid back his ears and bared his teeth to her.

She opened her mouth to protest, then looked back at me. Her eyes hardened and narrowed as she processed what she saw.

"Mages are spoiled, pampered, and avoid doing real work if they can." It was a statement. "And I am not well liked as I'm too brusque, don't tolerate social bullshit, and have no patience for pampered princesses. This is something well known and most people that are placed under my purview are slackers."

I blinked at her. Right now, I didn't feel anything like a pampered princess. I felt more like Cinderella before the ball. Abused and covered in cinders. "Do I look like I've been slacking?"

"No," she admitted. "This means someone is manipulating me as you are not someone that needs threats." She had regained some of her color, making her look less like a victim and more human. "I dislike that as much as I feel mages are spoiled."

"That is your prerogative." I didn't have the energy to be snarky. "But I need down time. Otherwise, when you really need me, I won't be able to help."

Yolanda hadn't moved, but she didn't seem like she was in fear for her life anymore. That didn't mean she looked happy.

"It is obvious you can't do much more until you heal up. I'll push back. Unless something is apocalyptic, I won't be calling you, but you must do everything you can to heal."

I nodded. It wasn't like I wanted to feel this way. Already, the idea of food sounded excellent.

"However, the incident with your cat will not happen again." Every word was bitten off as she stared at me.

I started to chuckle, then cough, as the amount of energy was too much.

"What is so funny?" she snapped.

"That you think I have any say in his behaviors," I managed to say between coughs. This being run down was exhausting.

She glared at me, then squeaked and jumped back as Carelian walked by, his tail lashing out to strike the back of her legs.

~I will do whatever I feel is needed to protect my quean. You will not ask her to do things that will put her at risk. She is too valuable to squander over property or people's fears.~ He sat by my feet, facing her, letting his heat wash into me. ~Do not forget, I have no qualms about killing or eating those that threaten me or mine.~

She lost what little color she'd managed to get back. "We don't respond to threats."

~I have no reason to make threats. I am simply giving you a piece of advice. Humans don't understand they aren't the most dangerous creatures out there. They will learn otherwise.~

The smart thing to do would have been to scold him, flinch back, or even apologize. Instead, I laid my head on his head and smiled at Yolanda.

"I'm sure you have information you want to provide your superiors." The temptation to make her find her own way home nibbled at my brain, but the desire to have her gone was stronger. "Carelian, would you please open a path back to where you found her?"

He sniffed but rose up and stared at her. ~Follow me.~

Yolanda gave me a hard glare, but it was lacking power as she flinched as she took in my appearance. Without another word, she disappeared out of the door. I felt a slash signifying a tiny rip as I laid back down. I knew I should get up and eat, but right now, that seemed like way too much effort.

A few minutes later, Carelian was peering down at me. ~You have not died, correct?~

That managed to get a laugh out of me. "No, I haven't died. Just tired. I need to eat. Is there a way to get me healthier faster?"

He tilted his head, tail lashing back and forth like a live wire. ~No. You are not sick or injured, you are low on resources. I shall fix.~

"Raw fish is not an answer," I called after him. Sushi was fine, but not in the quantities he wanted to eat it.

~No. I shall ask Hamiada to help me get soup for you. Make sure you are in a position suitable for eating when I return. You need calories and rest. Now that the woman has been dealt with, you will have a chance to rest.~

I stiffened with sudden worry. "Please tell me you didn't kill her." I raised my voice a bit as he'd already headed downstairs.

~Silly quean. If I had killed her, I would have brought you her head as proof of conquest. She still lives but hopefully with the correct appreciation for your health now.~

I decided to interpret that as un-maimed as well. Any other way to translate that would add a load of guilt on me I didn't need. My eyes closed of their own volition.

The scent of potato soup and the feeling of being stared at pulled me out of my drowse. I opened my eyes to see Hamiada staring at me, a tray in her hand.

"Carelian says you are not dying. You look like you are dying." Her hair was lush with leaves today and I smiled.

"No. I might look like it, but I'm not." I scooted up, and she set the tray down. Potato soup, chunks of steak, and hot tea were on it. "Thank you."

"You must eat and get healthy. It is not a good look for you to be so thin. My sister-daughters need their guardian to be able to protect them." With that, she turned and float out of the room, as Carelian padded in.

~Good. Eat. Then sleep. You need padding. You are too bony.~

I chuckled and ate, relieved that I'd have a few days to recover.

EIGHTEEN

Over the last few months, we've become accustomed to rips and even have memes about them. But this is a new one. A rip occurred in the small town of Marysville right inside a bank. This rip was a water one that was filling the building with water. When the responding mage team showed up, they were a bit over zealous in pulling concrete up to block the water and instead ripped out the bank vault causing money to come flying out all over the street. As you can see in this video the reactions to the rain of money were amusing. Bank officials have said that the majority of the money has been returned, the mage—whose name is being withheld—has apologized.

~ KTVZ News Station

SPIRIT

It had been three days since Yolanda was dragged to the house. I'd spent all of them eating, sleeping, and going on walks between my house and the Tudor. It was enough to keep my muscles limber, but not wear me out too much. The remodeling on the house was almost done, and I feared seeing them leave.

I'd asked Hamiada to set the door next to the study door. If anyone looked at it, you'd think it was for a small closet or something. Per Carelian's request, the handle was a lever type, not a doorknob. If you lifted up you went to the Tudor house, if you pushed down it took you to Marisol's. If the walk between the houses became too much, I cheated and used the tunnel to get home. It felt like sidestepping to me, but smoother. Jo said stepping with me was like riding a Tilt-A-Whirl carnival ride. This was going through a rotating door. Needless to say, no one complained about Hamiada's tunnels.

Everyone was at work, and I was curled up in bed, watching the news with Carelian. It amused me that for once even I couldn't detect a bias in the reporting. Everyone was using the same words for the rips. And the government had failed in getting them swept into the past like they did with most magical incidents. There were too many, and it was happening too often.

But from what I could see on the news, they were mostly smaller rips, and the response teams were getting faster. Stephen had taken to heart Sable cussing him out, and the OMO had sponsored a strategy meeting for next week, to come up with methods to react.

"BREAKING NEWS" flashed across the bottom of the TV screen and yanked me out of my stupor. "This just in: both Russia and China have launched missiles into planar rips appearing in their territories. In both cases, creatures were seen to be slipping out of the rips that were only a few feet off the ground. China is broadcasting the footage of it now." The news caster faded away to be replaced with footage of people in uniform aiming a big missile on a movable base, then ducking and covering their heads. It flew out of the cradle faster than the eye could track, disappearing into the rip between realms.

I had to remember to breathe as I watched it disappear. If you stood and looked into a rip, a random one, it never made sense, a jumble of scents, colors, shapes that your mind struggled to categorize. It could make people go crazy. But to a static place, like the crossroads, it was like looking in a window. I had no idea what to expect.

The gout of flames and smoke that appeared but a scant second later seemed appropriate, but somehow ominous. What had the missile hit? The worst part, or maybe it was the best part, the rip rippled and closed. I kept my fingers crossed that was because a mage had closed it, but I had a very bad feeling that wasn't the case.

"I should get dressed," I said, forcing myself to stand and head to the closet.

~Why?~ Carelian raised his head to look at me. The last week or so he'd all but laid on me, grumbling every time I did anything but the minimum. It was both sweet as all get out and twice as annoying.

"Because I strongly suspect an emergency council meeting will be called here shortly." Somehow, I didn't think any of us were going to be lucky enough to have that missile land somewhere unnoticed. I'd gotten my cargo pants on, though I'd had to tighten the belt by three notches, and a tank top, which hung on me more than I liked, when Freya's voice rang in my head.

~Emergency Council meeting in fifteen minutes. All lords are required to attend.~ I sighed and kept dressing.

"See. Come on. I want to make sure I take food with me." I steeled myself to take the backpack. A month ago, the twenty pounds it usually weighed wasn't an issue. But today it was. I managed to get downstairs and load it full of food and caffeine. Then I double checked his harness and took my tumbler in my hand. I had Mexican coffee, but this one had ice cream, protein powder, and electrolytes in it. Churro ice cream in Mexican coffee was awesome. It also hid the taste of the protein powder.

The backpack felt like it weighed a ton, but I needed to push myself and make sure I didn't lose my muscle tone. Carelian opened the portal, and we slowly walked through. The noise slammed into me almost as a physical force and I staggered, grabbing onto Carelian for balance. I'd never heard it this noisy. I stayed in the shadows where Carelian preferred to enter and watched.

Everyone was shouting, roaring, or creating noise to the point it just came across as a wash of energy. If I could figure out how to use that as fuel for my magic, I would have never run out of magic to use.

"Carelian, can you catch what they are talking about?" I could hear mindspeak not directed at me as an off to the side whisper. But pulling it into clarity wasn't something I could do. Carelian, on the other hand, did it without thinking.

~They are talking about the attacks. It hit Order and Chaos

and one of the areas was populated.~ He sounded somber, and I rubbed his ears.

"I'm getting stronger. We'll figure out how to fix this."

He didn't say anything, but his flattened out ears and still tail told me how unhappy he was. We made our way to the Earth circle. I could tell as beings caught sight of me. There was a soft ripple of silence as more and more turned to look at me.

Tirsane was making her way over even as I settled into my club chair, the noise half of what it had been.

"Cori, what is wrong? Are you injured?" Her voice held more worry than I'd ever heard. All of her snakes were twisting around themselves, hissing at me. Their tongues flicked at the air as if trying to find an enemy that didn't exist.

"I've just been doing too many offerings trying to close rips. It is getting bad out there. Did Esmere talk to you?" I took a mouthful of coffee. The richness helped, but at the rate I was pulling in calories I always felt slightly overfull. But I needed to keep it up.

"Yes. We were going to see what could be done. I need to get rid of some of the excess magic soon."

I looked a bit closer at her and she was glowing a bit. I nodded and started to ask about Spirit closing rips, when Shay, Scott, Citlali, and Kesis showed up.

"Cori? What the actual fuck?" Shay blurted, when I turned to look at him. "What happened?"

Citlali looked just as concerned, and Kesis made the smallest whine. Scott scanned me slowly, and I felt exposed under his gaze.

I stuttered a bit, trying to answer. "I, I well... just they've been calling me a lot. They put a woman, Yolanda, from Rogue Mages to manage me."

Scott sucked air in through his teeth and I gave him a side

eye glance. I'd never remembered to talk to him about her attitude. I really needed to do that. Maybe after the council meeting.

"That level of magic is not sustainable," Citlali said very carefully.

"Don't worry about being polite. I look like shit. I've said no. And we have some other things in play to see if they will work." I drank some more coffee, already needing another nap. How had I been still moving?

"Good. Because I've seen dead people that looked healthier," she said bluntly, and I managed a chuckle.

"Okay, back to one of the things in play." I pivoted my head to look at Tirsane. She was watching me with an odd look in her eyes and all the snakes were staring at me, too. As if on cue, the one in my arm wriggled and I fought not to gag. Feeling something wriggle under your skin is not conducive to keeping food in your stomach.

"Tirsane, can any of your denizens close rips?"

She tilted her head. The snakes stayed looking at me as if her head hadn't moved, which was just odd. After a minute, she responded. "Yes. We can close any we make. Just like most sentient denizens can."

Now that was a bit of information that I hadn't had before, but in retrospect, it made sense. I started to follow up on if denizens from her realm would be able to close rips on our side. But Freya called the meeting to order. Tirsane nodded at me and moved back over to the Spirit ring.

I sighed and settled in as the others took their chairs, with many cautious looks at me.

"Earlier today, some of the weapons Lord Munroe warned us about came through a tear and landed in the realms." Freya's voice rang with power, and I noted she didn't care if there were spectators still on the floor. Or this was just more important than caring about observing the formalities.

A hush spread through the chambers like ink across a tissue. Beings clustered together, seeking support from others of their realm. The largest was hanging around Salistra, which didn't tell me much except that Order had probably been affected.

"There were two that we have tracked, though perhaps Earth can tell me if there were more?" Freya turned her gray eyes toward me.

I shook my head. "I can research, but right now I don't know. At this point, you know more than I do."

There was an ugly ripple through the room. "Are you saying Earth doesn't remain aware of what goes on in their realm?" This came from Shiarissa in a low hiss and I could feel answering anger.

"I got this Cori," Citlali said quickly as she stood. "I believe you misunderstand how Earth works. It is huge. Shiarissa, if you went from one end of the Chaos realm to the other, diving into all the pockets, how many days would it take you?"

Everyone paused and looked at her, then back at the naga.

The naga shrugged tossing her hair behind her. "Multiple weeks, maybe as much as two months, though there would be areas I wouldn't visit."

Citlali's question had derailed them, and I let her run with it. Even those that visited Earth regularly still viewed it as a series of pocket realms, not the immense amount of land it was.

"Ah - there is the problem. If you walked around just the widest part of Earth in a straight line with no detours, assuming most of it wasn't under water, it would take an adult almost a full year of walking without rest. Earth is huge. You've heard us talk about the population. That population only resides on land and our world is 70% water. There is no way any one person or three or a hundred could be aware of everything going on."

There was a ripple of discontent but they didn't argue though I didn't think any of them, even Carelian, truly comprehended how big and populous Earth was.

"One landed in Chaos. Is there a report of damages?" Freya directed her question to the Chaos ring. Bob, Shiarissa, and Esmere were there, though Bob was oddly jelly like.

~There are none to speak of,~ Esmere said. She had been sitting in her Egyptian cat pose, unmoved by Shiarissa's posturing. ~It went into a wild area of Chaos. There is damage, but no worse than a herd of Bitualas' going through.~

"Good. Order?" Freya turned to stare at the Order group, Salistra in the lead, her tail thrashing. I mentally braced myself. This would hurt.

~My people were attacked, hurt. There were groves damaged, at least three of those under my charge were killed by the explosion. Now the chemicals and debris poison the area around the crater. I demand the Herald stop these intrusions, immediately.~

Every word sliced into my brain like a knife and I held my head in my hands, aware of the worried looks from Citlali and Shay. When she stopped talking, I lifted my head and stared at her.

"Tell me how." I didn't say anything else. What else could I say?

Salistra screamed, a horsey scream that cut through my thoughts and felt like a physical blow. ~I am tempted to call in all my debts, Herald. You will make this stop and protect magic.~

The threat lay in the air, and it felt like the world was holding their breath, waiting for a fight, anger, fear, something.

I shrugged. "Call them in. There is nothing I can do that I

am not doing. If you know of something I can do, you will need to tell me. And if you make me default on the debts and choose to take my life—" I paused and smiled, all teeth, no humor "—then you can deal with the problem yourself."

CHAPTER

NINETEEN

Dennis Strictfield has been declared a Rogue Mage. Convicted in absentia of murder in the 1st degree, grand theft, embezzlement, and conspiracy to commit murder, a writ of execution has been issued in his name. Per the powers granted to me by the State of Texas, I authorize the Mage Hunters to find and eliminate this person. ~ Live feed on CNN Mage Focus

CHAOS

"What would you have done if she followed through on the threat and took your life?" Citlali asked after the meeting. We were in the sunroom, with hot drinks and food for me. She and Shay had wanted to talk after to make sure I was okay. I had asked Tirsane if she could come too. Scott had headed home saying he wanted to check on something and would ping me at a later point.

"Die, I guess?" I sighed. "I had no belief she would do that. They are all scared, and, for some reason, they all believe it is my responsibility or fate to save them. It makes them oddly narrow minded."

"No, Salistra would never waste a pawn so easily," Tirsane said. She wore a dark red hoodie today, with a pocket in the front, and it went down to about a foot past her waist. If there hadn't been snakes peeking out of the hood, you would have thought she was an emo kid wearing her dad's hoodie.

"What happens if they call you again, Cori?" Shay asked. He'd barely taken his eyes off me since we stepped back into the house, courtesy of Carelian.

"I decide if I can go. I've lost so much weight that even using tricks of fertile material to supplement, I'm struggling. But my handler knows, so hopefully that will help." That might have been a lie, but at this point, hoping for the best was all I had.

~I made sure she knew if my quean died because of their misuse, her death would be but the first in a long string of them,~ Carelian said as he gnawed on a bone while seated at my feet. Kesis was curled up next to Citlali on the loveseat, nose tucked under her tail.

"Carelian," I said, shocked. "You were supposed to take her home."

~I did. I also made the consequences of you becoming a

martyr very clear. They are all too used to posturing. I don't posture.~ His tone sounded like he was trying to spit out the words.

I just rubbed his head. I knew how he felt, but I didn't think that would be helpful in the long run. But at the same time, Yolanda hadn't called. I was going to take what I could get.

"Okay all of that aside, Tirsane. You said your denizens can close rips." I focused on her, trying to keep my thought process clear. Lately, anything that distracted me was liable to make me forget what I was thinking about.

"Yes, it is part of our inherent magic," she said, sipping on some tea.

I took another drink of my hot chocolate. Everything was as calorie laden as it could be, and I still wasn't putting on weight fast enough. "If I called you or one of your sisters or one of the other lords, could you close a rip that is on this side?"

She pulled back, looking at me and then the others. "Call us here, to Earth, to close the rips?"

"Yes. They are so big and powerful we can't, so I thought maybe Spirit creatures could close them." I was watching her carefully, but the snakes told me more than her facial expressions did. They were twisting back-and-forth hissing at each other softly, questioning, then going to talk to another snake. It was like they were comparing information.

"I can not answer that. I have no memory of a rip ever being closed from the Earth side that was not made by closer. For instance, I opened a portal here and closed it when I arrived. But I don't know if it would be easy or hard for me to close things opened by others."

"Carelian? Would you?" I smiled at him, taking in more hot chocolate. I was stuffed, but I knew I needed to keep feeding my body.

~As you wish.~ Carelian yawned and a rip about six inches

wide appeared. It was pointed to the neutral crossroad he used. As safe a space as any to open to.

"Ah, the crossroads. I had not been aware that was still being used. In my youth, many of us used that to visit other areas." She tilted her head, the snakes bouncing up and down, one of them opening its mouth and hissing as something vaporized from it. The rip closed with a bit of hesitation.

"An interesting test of my abilities. Yes. I can close that. The cost is not high."

"If I may," Citlali asked, "do you need offerings to magic, like we do?"

"Yes and no. Anything I do in the realms or for my realm comes from Magic herself. The extra that has been loaded into me has made my realm more abundant than it has been in recent memory. If I wish for something for myself, here on Earth, it is an offering. For that, a drop of venom from one of my snakes." Tirsane reached up and scratched under a chin that was offered. It was the same snake I'd seen hissing.

"Does that go for most of your... people?" I didn't know how else to put it. They weren't her subjects, slaves, congregation, or even populace. They were the ones that lived in Spirit, and she worked to keep Spirit safe for them.

"Those that chose the magic path, yes. But there are many in Spirit that never bothered to learn," she said quietly, her eyes dark as she watched me.

"How many do you think might be able to?" I was desperate at this point and reaching. As much as the population of Earth slipped away from them, the population of beings and magic users in the realms slipped away from me. I wasn't sure they actually knew how many beings were in their realms. Maybe just the ones with magic.

"Maybe a few thousand. It varies from year to year. Though with all the magic that has been poured into the realm, there should be more in a few years." She tilted her head watching me. The snakes had tied themselves behind her and were peeking out. "Cori, are you looking for me to come and close rips?"

"Yes. I can't keep up. And some of the bigger ones are dangerous. I understand there might be costs, but at this point I don't care." My exhaustion killed my desire to be polite. "If I have to ask as the Herald, I will. If I need or order or demand, I will. But I need to get some help with the rips."

She settled back in the chair, seeming to curl up a bit tighter to herself. "I am willing to try as an experiment. It would do me some good to see if my magic is up to what Magic herself is doing. Call me and I will come for my own amusement. After that, we can discuss."

I nodded, a bit relieved. "Good, because after this, if I can get a few more pounds on me, I'm going to go talk to Bob."

All of them started looking at me. "Are you sure? Why not Esmere?" Shay was staring at me, even Carelian had jerked his head around to stare at me.

"Because it is the oldest being and there might be memories floating in that mess that can give me information. Otherwise, we might all die, and I'm assuming that isn't what anyone likes." I was getting snippy.

"Cori? You here?" Jo's voice rang through the house. I glanced at my watch. Only noon on a Wednesday and she was home early.

"I'm in here, Jo," I called. A minute later Jo came breezed in, her braids slapping against her ass as she stopped.

"Hey, didn't know we were having a party. Citlali, Tirsane, nice to see you. Shay - you're still you." She grinned at him, showing no insult meant.

He, for his part, just waved his hand at her and drank his coffee.

"It's all done. They are leaving today," she all but crowed at me.

I blinked, trying to figure out what she was talking about. "Who?" For a minute I was scared I'd really missed something important.

"The flooring contractors. They are finished; the painters finished last week. It's done. Everything is ready for us!" The joy that leaked out of her face made it impossible for me to respond any other way than to match it.

"Woot! That is awesome. So, this weekend?" I knew they'd been ready to move but wanted the house as perfect as possible.

"Yep. You guys want to see?" Jo wiggled her eyebrows up and down as she grinned. "Everyone is invited. We can take the door."

"Door?" Citlali and Tirsane said, a bit confused.

"Yep. Come on." Jo all but pulled me up out of the chair, but gently at that. "And she figured out a new trick with the stairs for you. We've been worried about them once you're alone."

"Oh?" The stairs were becoming an issue, but I still took them, trying to make sure even though I was weak I was still functional. I knew all too well what could happen if you stayed too sedentary.

"Yep. We talk about you, you know." She smiled as she wrapped her arm around my waist, both loving and supporting.

"You do, huh?" I leaned into her and ignored the looks of amusement on everyone else's face. Jo would never be shy about showing her love for me, and it was one of my greatest joys.

"Yeppers. And Hamiada and Marisol are in on it. Just because we are moving out, you aren't ever going to be alone." Her tone was still teasing as she took me to the stairs.

"Why does that sound like a threat?" Citlali asked, and I laughed as I glanced behind us. We were the head of a little parade. Carelian was behind me, followed by Tirsane, Citlali, and Shay. Kesis was at the very back and I swear she was laughing as she watched us.

"Because it is," I said, with my lips twitching. "Oh well, it means I probably won't starve to death. On my cooking alone I might."

"Pfft, you've gotten much better. I think you're up to twenty recipes." Jo had walked me to the base of the stairs, and I bit back a sigh, looking at them. "Go ahead, step onto the first one."

I let go of her to grab the railing and took the first step and almost fell as the stair started to move upward. "What?" I grabbed tight onto the railing, which luckily moved up too. I turned to stare down as I rose up.

Jo laughed at the base of the stairs. "I showed her escalators, and she didn't see any reason why she couldn't do that. Especially as she was very adamant that she didn't want your blood everywhere if you fell and got hurt. Something about 'stains badly'." The twitch of humor was still there as the stair I was on stopped at the top.

I released my death grip and walked forward with a smile. I could climb them but then I'd stand at the top catching my breath. "That is wonderful. Hamiada, thank you."

Hamiada stepped out of the wall at my words. "You like? Good. Having you die would be unpleasant. I rather enjoy you and your life. Most other mages aren't as accepting as you." She didn't look at any of the other mages as she spoke. "My daughters should wake later this year, so when they are stronger, I will show them the wonders of HGTV."

I choked back a laugh. Of all the shows for Hamiada to get addicted to, that had been the one. She kept trying different things and already had a new list of materials she wanted so she could incorporate new stuff. It was entertaining.

"I'm sure we'll look forward to it." I glanced back to Jo. "So, show me the house." I'd been over regularly, but the last week I'd been stuck here mostly, so I was looking forward to the final show, even if I wasn't looking forward to the emptiness.

Jo bounded up the stairs and went to the door between the study door and the staircase. She lifted the handle and waved her hand. "Please, come and see our new home."

I walked in first and the rest followed. The house was everything she had ever dreamed of, and I could see touches of Sable at every corner. I wanted to cry for her happiness, but instead I just smiled and knew I had to make sure this wasn't destroyed.

CHAPTER

TWENTY

In 1948, Congress changed the law to make all mages serve a draft term regardless of gender and tied it into mandatory education. World War II had taught them that the better educated a mage was, the more effective a weapon they could be. At the same time, the Draft Board was established to help keep track and make sure all mages served their four years. ~ History of Magic

ORDER

T spent the rest of the week and the weekend supervising and keeping the kids busy packing stuff. Jo and Sable used the door to carry boxes of stuff almost from one room to another. Magne and Jaz each had their own laundry basket. They would carry it to their room, fill it up, then drag it back to the door. From there they dragged it to their room. I kept watch, mostly just walking the few feet back and forth.

The Tudor house had multiple levels—a basement, ground floor, and second floor—and they had decided the best place to put the door was on the second level. That house wouldn't be able to do fancy tricks like the escalator until Zelinka was awake and grown. But the kids' bedroom was on the second level. Hamiada mentioned she could move it, but for now I'd just make sure someone could help me downstairs, or we could move it at a future date.

The kids were delighted that they each got their own bedroom, a playroom, and a bathroom that was theirs. They were less delighted about having to clean up their bathrooms, but life was very tough. By Sunday night everything was moved, and they just needed to clean the rooms left behind. We were turning the kids' room back into a guest room, but I had no idea what to do with Jo and Sable's. It was a great bedroom, and I was tempted to move downstairs, but refused. This weakness was temporary, and I wouldn't give in like that.

Kris came home for the celebration dinner in the Tudor. So, we had Marisol, Kris, Jaz, Magne, Carelian, Hamiada, and myself. Jo had pestered Hamiada about something to eat until she admitted that a plant food nutrient drink would be nice. At the dinner, which was steak as we were all starting to get sick of fish—even Carelian—she had her own glass of nutrients.

We were giggling as she sprouted flowers, then leaves. It seemed this was like getting a dryad high. If nothing else, I knew an excellent gift now if I needed something from any of the dryads. We'd made it to dessert, Sable had made a baked Alaska, when a ring tone shattered the good mood.

"Bodies Hit the Floor? Really?" Sable asked with a snicker.

"It seemed appropriate," I muttered as I dug into the pocket of my pants for that phone. I hated carrying two, but I didn't want these calls to corrupt my regular phone.

"This is Munroe," I said, trying to keep the exhaustion out of my voice.

"We have a class five rip, really it's a six, but the scale doesn't go that high." Yolanda didn't bother with niceties. Her voice sounded exhausted. "I've already sent three groups. They all failed and wiped out their available offerings. The problem is we've got lava coming in. We need it closed." She took a deep breath. "It's headed to an oil refinery and if we don't stop it before it hits that..." Her voice trailed off, the implications clear.

I stood. "Send me the address. I'll be there shortly." I hung up before she could say anything else. "I have to go. Carelian, can you go grab stuff while I'm headed up the stairs?"

~You are still not that strong,~ he warned as he rose, looking at me.

"I know, but I've got almost an inch of hair, I've gained five pounds, and I can lose a pint of blood with no risk. Besides, I still have eggs, some nails, and skin. I'm also calling Tirsane as soon as we get there. If nothing else she can carry back a message to the council on just how drastic these are." I'd addressed Carelian, but everyone else was listening in. The kids' faces were the ones that hurt the worst.

"Momma Cori? Are you going to hurt yourself again?" Jaz asked as Carelian bounded up the stairs. Kris rose as I stepped toward them.

"Yes, no? I'll be okay, but I have to go close a rip before it gets worse." I hugged them both tight as they rushed me. "I'm coming back. This is my job." Pulling away from their dark eyes physically hurt, but I didn't have a choice.

"I'll come with." Kris stood next to me, and I'll admit I was willing to use him to get up the stairs.

"No. Help me get home, then you stay here. I'll let everyone know if anything happens."

Marisol had jumped up the second the phone rang and raced to the kitchen. As I reached the top of the stairs, she raced up them to meet us. It was sad that a woman in her late sixties was in better shape than I was. This was ridiculous.

"Here Cori, you'll need fuel." She handed me a cooler lunch bag. "There is meat, cheese, honey sticks, and some boiled eggs. With Tajin. Your favorite."

"You've been planning for this haven't you?" I said, peering into the bag. There was no way she'd created all this in two minutes.

"Yep. We knew this would happen again, so we made sure we had supplies ready for you. Slip it in your backpack." She smiled and kissed my cheek. "Come back to us."

My throat caught, and I forced a smile and stepped through the doorway. Carelian waited with my backpack, his harness already on. I ran my hand over his head. "Let me grab some liquid and I'm ready." Kris frowned at me, but he went back to the others. I needed to know they were safe and frankly, these houses were safe. Worst case, Hamiada could pull them into her pocket realm.

The stairs took me downstairs and I grabbed my water bottle, some electrolyte packages, and a protein drink. With everything in the pack and it on my back, I pulled up my phone and looked at the address.

"It's in Texas. Can you find it?" I showed him the map, and he stared at it. I still had no idea how his ability and maps worked. He'd tried to explain, but it made no sense. Something about how places and people had feels. He knew the general layout of the United States to figure out most places, but then he could zero in to where he wanted by feel. He'd heard Yolanda's voice often and had her feel. That was why, when he learned the general area she was in, he could step into her home.

If he was a serial killer or a stalker, it would be terrifying. I also didn't talk much about his ability to find people. If anyone thought about it too much most mages with familiars would be in deep trouble.

~Yes. Lava should also be easy to find.~ He pulled open the rip to the crossroads, and I stepped through. A minute later, he was pulling open another portal to a place of heat and smoke.

"Either that is it, or you took us to the wrong area."

~Hawaii is the next closest active lava field, and that is a huge difference from here, though I'm more than willing to go there instead.~ I laughed and shook my head. He huffed a sigh and stepped out with me. We fell silent looking at the scene. It was like looking at a really good movie CGI. A river of magma slowly fell out of the sky, dripping down into globs. It piled, then started to flow towards a series of huge tanks. Fire trucks, police, ambulances, and any number of other responders were rushing around. I looked and saw a small group of bedraggled mages over in one section, slightly apart from the rest of the insanity.

Moving slowly, I weaved through, no one stopping me, mainly because the lava had everyone's attention. "Hey," I said when I got close. "I'm Munroe. Can you tell me what you've tried?"

There were six people there, all bald, with shiny skin and an exhausted look on their faces. One of the women, dark skin in jeans and a tank top, looked at me and laughed a bit hysterically. "You have less to offer than we did. We're all going to die." She choked off the laugh when someone else put their hand on her shoulder.

"Merlin," another man said. He probably had red hair from his eyebrows, the rest of him was pink from offering and the heat. "We've tried in two sets, offering everything we had, and most of us had hair down to our waists. The lava is too heavy. We can't stop it from flowing and we can't close it while it flows."

I nodded and looked around. There were tanks that lined the river, the magma was dropping into the space between. The only reason everything hadn't blown up already was it solidified as it fell. But the more that accumulated the warmer it remained and therefore more liquid. I kept scanning and a glimmer to my right and a ship gave me hope.

"Is that a river over there or just a pond?" I asked, pointed toward the glimmer.

"Outlet to the Gulf of Mexico," someone replied.

I heaved a sigh of relief. "Okay. If you have anything left, can you pull heat from the magma flowing toward the tanks and sink it into the river? That is enough water that it should be able to absorb a lot of heat before there is any risk to the ecosystem."

There was a murmur of argument, and I held my hand up. "I'm not saying my thermodynamics math is spot on, but flat out, pulling out enough heat or energy for the liquid rock to quit moving and dumping it into the river is a thousand times safer ecologically speaking than letting it hit the oil storage and all that catches on fire or blows. Am I wrong?"

"No. I've got some to spare for that." The voices at this point were a jumbled mess, and I gave up trying to even decipher gender.

"Here," I said, reaching into my pocket and bringing out a few scalpels. "Don't be afraid to use blood. You'll be amazed at how far it goes. Women, if your uterine lining is thick, you can use that too." I didn't even have the energy to roll my eyes at the disgusted faces a few of them made.

"I'm going to see if I can get someone to help me close this." I had barely moved since I got close to the group. Someone in a suit ran over and started to shout at us. "Someone deal with him. I don't have the energy. And if he gets in my way, Carelian, disable him." The loud snarl that Carelian let loose sounded like a chainsaw. The area went quiet as everyone turned to stare.

"Oh, better," I murmured and pinged Tirsane. ~You ready to try your experiment?~

~Already? Yes, I can. I might bring Stenia with me. She had mentioned being curious.~

~K, Carelian will open a portal. It's hot here.~ That was an understatement. Texas was in a warm spell for February and with the magma way too close, I was already sweating under my light jacket.

~Excellent. We are coming.~ I swayed a bit as I waited. One of the scalpels remained clinched in my hand. Blood was easier to replace at this point. Carelian opened a tear in reality and two gorgons slithered out. I knew Tirsane could appear to be twenty feet tall, but today she seemed her normal size of about six feet, though just lifting up on her coils she could easily get to eight. Her sister behind her gave me a chance to compare them for the first time.

Tirsane had over a dozen snakes on her head. They'd never held still long enough for me to count them, all different types. Stenia, by contrast, had about six thicker ones that reminded me of constrictors. Even her scales were different. They held more patterns than the consistent green of Tirsane's. She had blue eyes with the same white pupils and a more aquiline nose.

They were looking around as Carelian sealed the rip behind them.

Screams of terror burst up behind us, and I really wished I had an easy way to silence them. I could have removed the Air, but that tended to kill people, a bit overboard for this situation. And doing a general KO wasn't worth the scolding I'd get afterward.

"This is most interesting. What are these?" Tirsane asked, looking around and gesturing at the huge tanks.

"We store oil in those," I said and pointed to the magma making its way toward them. "As you can imagine, having that hit them would be very bad."

Both of their eyes widened as they looked at all the tanks and how much oil they would change. "You use this much oil?"

I laughed. "It's complicated. This is only one of dozens, if not hundreds around the world. But for right now, can we focus on the rip?"

They turned and spied the rip, and they blinked as their faces went to immobile, remote beauty.

"This might be more challenging than I had anticipated," Tirsane said, looking at the fall of glowing magma.

I would have felt better if she didn't sound worried.

CHAPTER

TWENTY-ONE

A sheep farm in Australia has reported that a new species of goat has appeared in their sheep herds. There is photographic evidence, but the second anyone gets close to any of them, they flee. At this point, he has decided to let them be as the loss of sheep due to wildlife, dingoes, snakes, and such, seems to have completely stopped. The goats are aggressive to any threat. He figures until it's time for the sheep to come in to be sheared he isn't going to worry about it. Some things from the rips aren't deadly. ~CNN Mage Focus

SPIRIT

"Challenge or not, we need to get it closed quickly. I've got people trying to slow down the flow, but it won't be enough." My voice was rough, and I hated how wobbly I felt.

"So I see," Tirsane said, still shocked by the sights surrounding her. She looked up and her jade green eyes narrowed on the rip. All the snakes on her head stood up in a corona around her, hissing as they focused on it too.

Stenia watched the rip, her six snakes coiled on top of her head, facing the rip.

I had my eyes locked on it and I saw the rip move a tiny bit. My heart sped up, excited, and I glanced at Tirsane and all the hope drained out. She was sweating and her snakes were contracted into coils, more separate from each other than I'd ever seen. Her labored breath added to the picture, and I knew this was going to go badly.

Another fraction, and then she sagged. Her own body structure, the coiled serpent's tail, prevented her from falling. "This, this is what you've been closing?" she gasped out, her chest heaving.

"Pretty much. This one is going to be ugly though. I'm taking it that you can't close it?"

"No, not at all."

I sighed and went through the options. My best bet was a

strong Chaos mage with fire as their primary. The world had better appreciate the sacrifices I was making.

~Zmaug? I need your help. I will owe you a favor,~ I pinged the dragon and hoped she would be willing and able.

~A favor? Now that is interesting. What is it you need?~ Her voice was amused and lazy.

~Can you suck heat out of actively flowing lava, large amounts, and create a dam so I can close a rip?~

~Interesting question. I have never tried before. What do you trade?~ All the denizens had been blunter since they figured out I'd been oblivious. It was both a relief and annoying.

~A favor from me that does not cost anyone else,~ I replied easily. This much I knew I could do and most of the time the favors were smaller things. What I was asking shouldn't be for something huge. I hoped.

~Ah, a favor from the Herald. Why not? Where are you?~ I sent her the image of where we stood—well, the large empty space to the left of where we were.

~Coming,~ she murmured in my mind as pain sliced through my head. She walked out of the rip to a chorus of screams and people running away. I sighed as I saw a few people reach for the weapons on their hips.

"I asked her here to help stop this. If you can't behave, I'll knock you all out." I used Air to carry my voice—that amount of offering was barely noticeable. It brought home how difficult closing the rips were. "Tirsane, any more luck on creating those barren pocket realms?" I asked as I watched people closely. I really wasn't worried about Zmaug if they fired on her. What her response would be concerned me.

"I was going to do it tomorrow, but trying to close that rip has drained me and I barely moved it." She sounded defeated. I, on the other hand, perked up.

"Really? Huh. So, if I have you come to spend the energy on closing rips from the magic, will it balance out?"

"Maybe." Tirsane sounded doubtful. "Lately it feels like magic oozes out of me, like sweat. No matter how hard I try to contain it, magic is leaking out. All the realms are bursting at the seams, so while they might slow down, I fear the ruptures are becoming more common."

That dashed any hope I had. Sighing, I pushed it away and looked at Zmaug. "Can you get that to stop flowing?" I pointed at the magma oozing out of the tear in the sky.

~ Yes. But then the opening will be blocked,~ she said. Zmaug sat in the clearing basking in the heat while the rest of us were sweating. Stenia had even created a fan to keep a breeze going on her face.

It was a measure of how serious the situation was that few people were paying any attention to the nudity of the gorgons.

"I know. But if you can get it to dam up past the opening, I should be able to shatter the cooling rock and close the rip. At least that is my thought." I'd been running ideas through and honestly, the only other one I could come up with involved figuring out where the rip was. My mind stuttered to a halt. "Do you happen to know where that lava is coming from? Could you get to the other side and stop it? Are you even hurt by lava?" It was a valid question. I knew she could breathe fire if she wanted.

~Yes, lava can hurt me.~ Zmaug stretched out her neck, head pointed to the rip. ~No. I see no skylight and scent nothing beside heat. I would suspect it is inside an active volcano.~

My shoulders sagged. "Oh well, I figured I'd ask. So, heat?"

~I can not absorb that much. Where do you want it dumped?~

I pointed to the river. "Spread it out if you can. I'd rather not cause another ecological disaster while trying to prevent one."

Zmaug glanced at me and snorted. Then she turned to stare at the wall of molten substance pouring through. It began to slow, then solidify while off to my right a steam began to rise from the water. That was more heat than I'd expected. Nothing I could do about it now.

As it turned solid, I mixed Break Pattern and Open to cause chunks of it to fall. The ground shook as they hit, but not enough to worry me. Besides, Texas tended to be pretty geologically stable—I thought. Either way, I kept going. Zmaug started to glow and the red scales became brighter as she worked.

What is she offering?

The thought flitted through my mind and disappeared as I focused on the lava stone that was hanging in midair.

It took fifteen minutes of whittling away at it while Zmaug glowed and the water steamed. The area was still full of noise, lights, cars, sirens, and water, but around us people were quiet as they watched us work.

"Stop for a second. I think I have it broken off behind the rip," I panted as I spoke. The offerings weren't large to do this, but there had been many, and I was back to being bald again. I'd sunk down to the ground at some point and leaned against Tirsane's coils while Carelian braced me from the side.

I tested the rip learning its price. With a sigh, I sliced my arm, blood instantly welling up. Carelian gave a low rumble of displeasure, but I ignored it and offered it up. The rip resisted, but the force that had been holding it open was gone. With a pop, it snapped closed.

The release of tension rocked me back a bit, and I was glad for the coils behind me.

"It is always like this?" Tirsane asked as I greedily drank from my protein drink.

"Like what?" I managed after draining the bottle.

"The people, the difficulty, you offering blood?" Her tone was too neutral even as Carelian began to lick my arm.

"People not usually. The other yes. I don't have anything else to offer. Hair is gone again, nails are to the quick, and I offer up the top layer of dermis so often I should never get wrinkles. Why?" I didn't bother looking at her. It would have taken too much effort.

"The cost to you is much greater than I would have guessed. Even seeing you so worn and ancient." Tirsane sounded more contemplative than upset.

I choked back a laugh at that comment and let her continue.

"I believe we may be wrong about what needs to be done, but we have no other path and Magic has said you are the answer."

"Explain that to me. Why do you say that?"

"Well..." she trailed off, and I looked up to see her looking at the gathered crowd. Their expressions were a mix of wonder, horror, astonishment, worship, and fear. It made my skin crawl.

"Yes, perhaps not here. Zmaug, you good?" I knew I should be more formal with the dragon, but frankly I didn't have the energy.

~I am well, though that was more than I have ever processed. My scales will glow for weeks. Perhaps Onyx would be interested in a mating flight and another nest of hatchlings.~

I stared at her. "Wha?" The comment was so unlike her and Stenia began to snicker.

~Yesssss, a mating flight, a fight, new eggs. I shall go. Don't forget the favor you owe, Herald.~ She turned and sliced the air, and reality rippled. With a wave of her tail that barely missed multiple people, including me, she walked in and disappeared.

"What just happened?" I asked, staring at the empty space and the ground that seemed to have fused into glass.

"Processing all that heat has stirred up her hormones. I do hope Onyx is ready for what is headed his way." Tirsane's voice was oh so prim, but I saw the twitch at the corner of her mouth.

"Are you telling me processing heat and dumping it made her horny?" I blurted, ignoring everyone staring at us.

"Horny?" Tirsane considered it and laughed. "Yes, hornier than a herd of unicorns. I expect a clutch of eggs in the near future."

People were beginning to inch toward us, and I had no energy to deal with them. I pulled out the annoying phone, not mine the other one, and called Yolanda.

"Yes?" Her voice was anxious, and I looked at how close the cooling lava had come to the tanks. Too close, but it was cooling so the tanks should be safe.

"It's done. Nothing exploded. Clean up will be a bitch, but it is moving cold lava, magma, whatever it is called when it quits moving, not anything else. Maybe they can create a new market for pumice stones?" I stared blearily at the pile of still steaming rock. "Or weird art?"

"Thank Merlin. Are you okay?" she asked next.

"I'm back down to blood, but I pulled in help. Still, I'll need another week and you've got to get these people to start thinking outside the box. Don't you have any mavericks that are always in trouble because they don't think straight?"

"I did. Their names were Cori Munroe, O'Shaungessy Sato, and Scott Randolph. You're the only one still in play for the most part."

I groaned and thumped my head back on Tirsane. "Whatever. I'm headed home and yes, before you start reading the reports, there were two gorgons and one dragon. No one died. No one was turned to stone. Nothing blew up. Bye."

My finger hit the disconnect button before she could respond. "My place?" I managed to push myself up. This had been much easier. Honestly, someone else could have closed this if they had approached it correctly. The overly direct scientific approach to problems that all magic users were taught was creating this problem. And it wasn't one I could fix. But seriously, they needed people who could think outside the box, not just follow the plan.

"Whoa," I wobbled and almost fell over as I'd been paying too much attention to my internal thoughts than where I was walking.

~Careful. Here, step in.~ Carelian nudged me forward, and I saw the welcoming brown of the house. I wobbled in, making sure to move so I wouldn't block the others coming after me. I made a beeline to the fridge, grabbed another protein drink and stood there with the door open, as I drank. Only after that was gone did I slide the backpack off and get some water. I was parched and still needed calories. I'd work on drinking the water, but what food? Oh, yes, the cooler bag.

I turned after getting a full glass of water to look at the two gorgons staring at me. "What?"

"You are the strangest being, Cori Munroe," Tirsane said mildly. Stenia, meanwhile, was looking around with wide eyes.

"Only to you," I countered. I reached down and pulled out the cooler bag Marisol had given me. The protein drink helped, but I wanted real food.

~You are very strange my quean. That might be why I chose you. Now go sit. Talk.~ He chivied me toward the sunroom, the fireplace, and my chair.

CHAPTER

TWENTY-TWO

AIN, or the American Indian Nation, remains shrouded in secrecy. Everyone knows the story of how they seceded from the nation, but the ramifications of that are still murky. There are areas that planes can not fly, roads have to detour across, and entire swaths of land are unavailable. The United States has been trying since 1901 to reassert communications with the people inside. We have no knowledge of what their lives are like, though we have various reasons to believe they are alive in there. The question becomes, when the walls come down, what will happen then? ~CNN Mage Focus

CHAOS

I kicked off shoes and my jacket, grabbed the blanket sitting there, and curled up. Logs lay in the fireplace, ready to go. Carelian scratched them, and they burst into flame. Another odd way he could use his magic. Whatever. I'd worry about it after I solved all this.

The two gorgons looked around, uncertainty on their faces, and they were shivering.

"Sit, or curl. There are blankets. Feel free to use them." I waved at the chairs and blankets that were there. We all loved the fireplace, but Hamiada was not a big fan, hence the only one was here in the room exposed to the outside. Something she could cut off and destroy at a moment's notice if the fire threatened her. But that did mean in February it was still cool, hence the blankets.

It took them a minute, and I felt like a horrible hostess, but standing and getting them tea or snacks wasn't really possible right now and it wasn't Hamiada's job to be my servant. I had my cooler bag and already the eggs were calling my name.

"Carelian, can you grab a plate and put some of the prepped sushi on a tray for them?" The idea flicked through my mind.

He stopped mid-stretch, heaved a sigh, and left the room. He came back a minute later walking on three legs with a large platter full of pieces of fish, something he despised. It meant I was more exhausted than I thought. Or he was more worried than I realized.

~Here,~ he said, setting it down on a low table, then he went back to find a seat by the fire.

"If you need something to drink, please feel free to get anything you want in the kitchen. There's water, wine, or you can make tea? I'm just too tired right now." I sipped on my water, trying to remember the topic. Oh yes. Magic.

"I am fine," Tirsane murmured. Stenia shook her head, but she was looking around at everything.

"First time here?" I didn't want to say 'the mortal world'. That sounded way too much like it was something out of a movie.

"Yes. Tirsane traveled more when she was younger, but I never did."

There were so many questions I wanted to ask, but I let them go. Maybe someday, if I survived this.

"Tirsane, what do you mean Magic Marked me?" I drank more water, feeling the dryness start to fade. I had an internal mantra, chanting to myself to heal and grow. Then I pulled out an egg and sprinkled the seasoning on it, my mouth watering for the flavors.

Tirsane had pulled a blanket, a pink and purple one that Jaz loved, up to her shoulders and the snakes kept trying to get their heads under the blanket. It was adorable.

She snuggled in tighter, a frown on her face. "It is like there is a glow to you. No, that isn't right." She furrowed her brows harder, trying to think. I just let her as I got trying to explain things there weren't words for.

"Have you ever met someone and just known they were powerful? That the way they moved or held themselves meant they were someone to take notice of?"

I nodded at that. Stephen was that way. Even when I wanted to strangle him, he had that aura of power and command that few people could resist.

"You have that with magic. You radiate power, yet there isn't the arrogance of myself or Salistra. You exist yet are so solid it is like we know we can lean on you because you can't move." Tirsane sighed, trying to figure out how to explain.

"When I look at you, I feel safe knowing you will rescue me, that Magic will never reject your pleas." Stenia's comment pulled both my attention and Tirsane's to her. She flushed, but continued. "Your magic is so solid that I want to bask in your presence."

~You are a quean. It is why I chose you. You are a quean that attracted other queans.~ Carelian didn't move from where he'd laid down in front of the fire. His ruby coat reflected the light from the flames.

"Quean. You've always called me that. It isn't 'queen', it's 'quean'. Why?" This was something I'd tried to get him to explain before—maybe this time he would.

"Ah yes. You are a quean, and magic is part of your power." Tirsane's eyes lit up, and she smiled, making her beauty expand. "That was the word I was looking for."

"That tells me nothing. What is quean?" I was exasperated but at the same time it was starting to make sense. Except why would they think I was that person or that powerful?

~Quean is a leader, someone that puts her pack before anything else. You put everyone before you. You will do anything, be anything to protect and save the ones you love, and you love everyone. You don't know how to hate. Even the parents who turned from you, you don't hate. You are a quean. You created a family with Jo and Sable, molding them into equal queans by your very existence.~ His voice rumbled through my mind and heart as he sent feelings too. Pride. Honor. Sacrifice.

I didn't know if I should be horrified, scared, or honored.

"Please tell me you don't see me as some sort of god?" That much I knew I didn't want.

Tirsane laughed. "No. Not even a prophet. By your rules, I am a demigod in that my realm is mine, just as Esmere's is hers. You are a lightning rod that magic is pulled to, but you can control the strikes. You are change. You are a quean, no matter how much you've never believed that about yourself."

I sighed, sprinkled another egg with Tajin and popped it into my mouth, letting the sharp citric acid and salt burst on my tastebuds.

"It still doesn't make sense, but I get the feeling I'm still Cori Catastrophe."

Tirsane shrugged. "I would think blessed by Janus is a better way to look at it. Change is always scary and over-whelming. You are just the one that causes us to change. Look at me." Her voice had moved to an attitude of abstract thought.

"What do you mean?"

Tirsane rubbed her nose a bit before speaking. "Just your presence, the way you treat everyone, has made me softer, more willing to try new things. It has been a long time since I left my grotto for more than meetings or to deal with idiots like how you first met me. I can't remember the last time I visited anyone besides another lord before you entered my life. Now I have been to Earth more times than I can think, I have had visitors to my grotto, even my sister has emerged. Esmere is calmer and softer than I remember her being in a long time. You trusted us with your children." She paused and the snakes peppered kisses over her chin and neck in an act of reassurance. "If you had meant ill will, I fear what the results might have been. Your presence, your queanness has changed even Salistra."

"But that is good?" I felt off balance and grabbed a cheese stick out of the bag, peeling off the plastic to take a bite.

"It is change. Cori, I have been alive about 1500 of your years. In my youth, I visited what you now call Greece and Italy. I turned anyone who annoyed me to stone and never thought about it. I quit bothering to visit about a thousand years ago. I stayed happy in my own little world. Nothing has changed for almost a thousand years. And then you appear." She waved her hand to take in the house and everything. "Now, everything has changed."

Stenia smiled and looked at her sister. "You are more fun now. You were in danger of going to statue. Now you have energy and excitement. I prefer this."

Tirsane grinned, her obsidian teeth the shock they always were. "Me too. So, there you go, Cori. You are marked by Magic and we see it or feel it or know it. It just is."

They hadn't really answered my question, but they had. I knew Jo and I were going to be best friends the first day I met her, and apparently so had she. I'd known who to steer away from sometimes before they said anything. Maybe it was all the same thing: a feeling, a presence. I laughed to myself as I realized I was using the same words as they were.

"Then I guess that is that. Though it doesn't help with the rips. Which way will be better to deal with the excess magic? Trying to close rips or the pocket realms?" Another egg was calling to me, but I'd need to nap soon. That had required energy, both the magic and dealing with people.

"Trying to close the rip was draining. It never occurred to me they could be that difficult to close. How did you figure out how to close it?" She was back to frowning at me.

"Oh, fighting with the two, no, three water ones I've run

into helped. It is much easier to shut if you don't have a flow keeping it open. I knew that lava becomes solid if it gets cold. I just didn't have enough offerings to do that and close it, especially if there was more than I could see. I figured Zmaug as a dragon would work well with fire. I was right." I snorted in amusement at a memory. "Though maybe I should have charged her for the aphrodisiac I apparently gave her. But with the flow stopped and broken off, I managed to close it. It still wasn't cheap, but less costly than I feared."

"I would have spent all my energy trying to close it, never thinking to stop the flow first. See, the Herald," Tirsane said with a teasing smile.

"No, just more experienced at thinking outside the box, which is something they have got to start doing. I'm seeing downsides to only formal magic education."

"Oh?" Stenia said, looking interested, and I wondered if they or any of the other denizens would be interested in our education system. They felt Magic more than ordered it. But— assuming the laws of physics were still followed—knowing how things worked might make magic easier for them too.

"Yes. By law, as soon as we emerge, we go to school to be educated. I was educated outside of that and had to work before I was pulled into that system. I think having to make ends meet made me more open to options." I shook my head. "It doesn't matter, but it might become a problem if I can't figure out how to stop this."

"Ah. Are there books?" It was a subtle hinting request from her and Stenia and I smirked.

"Sure. I'll get you some, in trade for some of the grappa I was offered previously. I think it would make an excellent present for friends." I was pretty sure Stephen would enjoy trying something so different.

Stenia's face lit up, and I realized she was almost as beautiful as Tirsane, just in a different way. "Done. I make a lot of the grappa, so I can make some for you and put it in pretty bottles."

"Deal. Just give me a week or two. I need to order them. But right now...crap!" I stared Carelian, worried that I'd caused my partners stress. "Carelian, please let Jo and everyone know I'm home safe. I didn't tell them." Guilt wracked me as I tried to unwind the blankets from me and stand up. They were probably freaking out. It was thoughtless of me.

He laid stretched out by the fire. ~I let them know as soon as we stepped back home. Hamiada knows as well. All is good. I told them you had visitors and then you would be taking a nap.~ His ear twitched toward me. ~And I believe it is time for you to do that.~

I sagged as the stress evaporated. "Probably. Thank you for trying, Tirsane. I'll need to keep working on it."

"It was an interesting change of pace. I shall practice to see if there is something I didn't do correctly." Tirsane nodded at me and rose, letting the blanket fall back down to the dismay of her snakes.

"I could roam the realm and look for rips from our side?" Stenia said as I was trying to get up. "It might be easier and maybe I can close them before they become an issue?"

I wobbled as I stood and looked at her. "That would be a great help and would provide some relief if you manage to close any. Please let me know."

They both nodded and slipped out to go home. I headed up to my bed, barely managing to take off my shoes and pants before I crawled in. Two weeks hadn't been enough, but I had a bad feeling it wasn't going to get much better.

TWENTY-THREE

As more and more mages are being pushed to their breaking points to close rips, the question arises of familiars and what happens when a mage dies. We know from anecdotal stories that their grief is real and as devastating as losing a spouse. However, they rarely are seen after the death. It isn't known if they go back to the realms or if they, like so many animals, go somewhere to die alone. ~ Magic Explained

ORDER

Thehouse felt empty without the kids and the queztos and I missed the sound of the car pulling up and knowing I was about to be invaded. It meant I headed over to the Tudor house in the evenings and Marisol fell into a pattern of joining me for lunch at least three times a week. She'd been making friends and was developing a social life, of which all the Guzman's were delighted. Carelian took her back to Georgia when she requested, which was really only about once a month.

Carelian spent all his time coddling me. I put on ten pounds in two weeks and had almost reached a point where I felt like I could walk down the street without issue. I'd decided to start taking the long way to the Tudor house. It would help me build up my strength again.

It was early afternoon, and I was contemplating a nap. Those had gone a long way to helping me get back up to where I needed to be. Shay gave me regular updates on the Library, but while everyone was looking, there wasn't much about Atlantis. I began to suspect they had had their own library and when the island or continent was destroyed, so was that knowledge.

An idea had been glimmering at the edge of my mind but I'd not been able to get it to come into clarity. It seemed like every time I was about to put pieces together, I'd get distracted. It was harder and harder to keep myself on task. I really hoped at some point that would change. I missed the old purpose-driven Cori.

~Herald, I call in your favor!~ The words blared through my mind filled with panic and anger. I reeled back in my chair as I tried to deal with the assault on my mind.

~Zmaug? What is wrong?~ The mental voice had been so

anguished I wasn't sure it was her.

~Yess,~ the response was a snarl of anger and fear. I found myself standing and heading to my room. This wouldn't be good.

~What is wrong? What do you need?~ I let the stairs carry me up and started pulling on my "adventuring" clothes. It had become a uniform at this point. Carelian stood next to me. His tail lashed back and forth as we waited for her response. It came slower than I expected, and I had managed to get dressed before she responded.

~Tiantang is hurt. He will not come home. His mage is in a rage, and he is frantic. You must protect him. He cares too much about that human.~ She spit out that last word like it was foul, and I wondered what had happened between her and Cixi.

~I will go there. Any other information?~ I put Carelian's harness in my pack and then headed downstairs for my food supplies. The odds were low I would need them, but I worked very hard not to make assumptions. For now, his harness shouldn't be needed.

Another long delay, then her voice snarling in my mind. ~No. And I can not go there. I am too full of eggs, and I will not risk them.~ The level of anguish in her voice surprised me. The familial relationships in the realms weren't consistent. Another thing I didn't understand.

~Congratulations?~ I managed to send that without laughing. It seemed Tirsane had been correct.

~Thank you.~ There was the tiniest lessening of anger with that. ~But go to my son. This fulfills the favor you owe me. Make sure he is well.~

~I will.~ My response was immediate. I would have gone regardless of the favor. Tiantang was my friend too.

~Let me know,~ Zmaug replied, this time a bit less frantic.

~Yes,~ I agreed and turned to Carelian. "Can you find him?"

~Always. He is a friend.~ He studied me but nodded. ~You look better but not hale. I miss hiking with you.~

I sighed and rubbed an ear. "Me too." I ran over everything in my mind and sighed. "I'm ready. You?"

He didn't answer, just opened a rip, and we stepped through into the crossroads. The entrance sealed and a moment later, another rip appeared. He went through first and I followed into bedlam. Soldiers, mages, civilians were running around screaming, and I could see Tiantang laying on the ground of the courtyard we were in. Even from here I could see the gouge in his side and the blood leaking.

"Shit," I whispered and headed to him. I managed to get within three feet of him when soldiers and mages jumped in front of me, hands or weapons up and pointed at me. I froze. "Carelian?"

~This is the mage friend of Cixi. I am a friend of Tiantang. Let us through.~ The power of his voice stunned me slightly, and I had to shake my head to get past the effects. They looked at me, then him, and one of them, a man in a uniform with lots of ribbons, said something so rapid it sounded like a string of discordant music.

~Yes. Let us through.~

~Peace, they are here for me,~ Tiantang's voice was a pale shadow of his normal exuberance. Something in it made people move, and I headed toward him, dropping to my knees—not at all gracefully—at this side.

"Tiantang, what happened?"

~Carelian, can you fetch Cixi, please?~ The dragon's voice whispered across my mind.

Carelian snarled and turned to me. ~Do you have enough offering to sidestep if there is an attack? If you don't have time to draw blood?~

I blinked at that and assessed. Sidestepping wasn't expensive, but I was low. My hair had grown out though, and it was enough for me to do that. "Yes."

~You flee if anyone attacks you.~ His words were harsh as he turned back to Tiantang. ~You owe me.~ He jumped before I'd finished processing the words, disappearing.

The dragon barely moved. ~Yes, more than I can pay.~ I did a quick assessment on him. Tiantang was more snake-like than his mother, though I'd been assured by multiple people their anatomy was closer to a long lizard. His mustache tentacles were covered with blood, and lay drooped against his face, the brown red jarring against his pure red scales.

"I'm going to look at your wound. It's going to hurt." I couldn't even think of a way to make it not hurt, so I didn't bother. From behind his left front arm to a foot from his back leg, a gash ran down the length of his body. Organs and bone were visible as it gaped open.

"Shit, shit, shit," was a litany under my breath. The only good thing I could see was that none of the organs looked ruptured, but the blood loss wasn't good.

"Tell me what happened." I had basic first aid in my bag, but stitching up a wound of this size, I needed a mage, and I needed someone to follow my orders. Making a list in my head about what I needed, I dug out gloves as Tiantang began to whisper in my mind.

~There was a tear to the wilds of Chaos. Creatures came swarming in and were killing people. The mages were trying to get here in time, but I couldn't let people die. This is my land, my home.~ The weight of the words sunk down into my mind and I understood how he felt. Though I felt it for this planet.

My guilt at not doing enough sank a bit deeper. I needed to think outside the box. I pressed his organs back into his body, ignoring his high cries. It had to hurt like hell, and there wasn't anything else I could do.

"Then what happened?" I encouraged him to talk. It would distract him. I moved and straightened, hoping Cixi would get here soon.

~I attacked, I killed many.~ There was a bit of pride in his voice at that. ~But there were dozens. They swarmed on me. They ran on two legs with long tails, feathers, beaks, and sharp claws. So many that I couldn't move quick enough. They were susceptible to the guns. I was down and the army protected me. But it took them longer than I could hold off as they closed the rip. Our mages are strong.~

The description made me lift my head and look around, trying to see what he meant. There, laying about forty feet away, was a creature that, for all the world looked like a dinosaur. I squinted, hoping I was seeing things.

"It looks like a velociraptor mixed with a rooster?" I tried to think about what it could be, but nothing jumped to mind. It was a monster. I left it at that.

~The pain became too great, and I collapsed. How did you know?~

"Because your mother sent me. She is not happy and would be here, but she said she was too full of eggs."

Tiantang's tail twitched. ~She has bred? That is wonderful. She had refused since my disappearance. I'll be a sibling.~ The amount of joy in that had me glancing at his head out of the corner of my eyes. Maybe I was making more of a change than I should have.

I had everything in and had created staples of flesh to hold it together, but if I was going to do more, I'd need my blood. I'd spent what little I had. This whole situation made me respect and understand better the "what if" attitudes of older mages. I seemed to live in the "what if" world and could never have enough offerings.

A slash of pain and then Carelian was there. ~You are uninjured?~ His immediate question made me smile.

"I haven't moved, and they have all just been watching me since Tiantang said something."

"Tiantang!" The shout came from my right and I looked over to see Cixi, collapsed next to his head, a stream of words rushing out as she petted him.

~She did not want to come, believing that I was lying. Her anger is potent.~

I snorted. "Too bad. If she wants Tiantang to live, she'd better listen to me, because he is losing a lot of blood." I'd been trying to seal off the leaking arteries, but I was just about out. "Will you translate for me?"

~Yes,~ he said without hesitation.

~Yes, she will listen, I will make her.~ The weak voice of Tiantang floated through my mind, too faint, too weak.

"Okay. Cixi, I need you. I'm going to guide you through sealing up this wound. You have enough pattern to pull it off, but you need to get over here and listen to me."

The translations were like hearing a soft echo of her words. I could hear them in my mind and ears. It was oddly disorienting, but I pushed through it. I refused to lose a friend. Worst case, I'd have Carelian bite me. He could help with the healing, but I needed the structure put back together first.

"You, this is all your fault. If you had never consorted with the monsters in the other realms, this wouldn't be happening." The acid in her voice was impressive. I didn't care.

"That is actually a possibility but somehow I think something else would have happened. Right now, if you want Tiantang to live, you need to get over here and follow my instructions."

"I am the empress. I do not listen to mages that think they are better than me." She spat out the words, but her hand trembled as she petted his head.

"Then he dies. Come help me save him. Because if he dies, your empire will crumble."

~Listen to her my flower. She has been a good friend. Your pride and fear are blocking you. Learn from her.~ Tiantang's voice was smooth, cajoling, and way more adult than I'd ever heard from him. Did everyone in my life have multiple personalities?

"You promise you are trying to save him?" She rose, staring at me. All the uniformed people around us knelt as she stood there, her robes declaring her rank.

"I promise."

She stared at me for a long time. Seconds ticked by and I felt his heartbeat struggling.

Something in her face crumbled, and she rushed over to me. "Show me what to do." Cixi was about a decade older than me, so she was in her late forties, I thought. Her smooth skin gave no hint as to her age. Part of me wondered if Tiantang was the only person she could love and trust in her life.

The idea of living like that, always being a political puppet and wondering what someone wanted sounded exhausting. The love I received was something I never took for granted, and I needed to tell them that more often.

"Okay, I'm going to hold this skin together. Reach in with Pattern and see the cells that have been torn asunder. I want you to find them and start to repair. As you go, there will be blood vessels broken and leaking. Connect them again, removing any blocks as you go. It doesn't have to be good, just sealed." We worked slowly to put Tiantang together while around us a tempest of activity swirled as people rushed to clean up the dead creatures and the aftermath of the rip. The entire time Carelian prowled around us, snarling at anyone who dared to get too close.

TWENTY-FOUR

The autopsies of three of the realm creatures have been compared. While they are related to earthen creatures, the differences are startling. Larger brain cavities in all, comparable frontal lobes, and brain weight comparable to dolphins. The few nonmammalian creatures have a distributed nervous system that has synapse speeds five times faster than any earth analog. ~ Presentation to Biological Studies Symposium

SPIRIT

T t took us a solid hour to repair the laceration down Tiantang's side. Carelian licked the wound as we closed it, the odd healing of the Cath kicking in. I monitored Tiantang's heartbeat and asked Cixi to get him water. She snapped out words that Carelian didn't bother to translate and minutes later water was set in front of the dragon's snout.

We talked as we worked, slowly and carefully. And I got a better picture of the woman. I shouldn't have refused her back at the beginning. She had wanted to be friends, and I avoided the effort, scared of getting drawn into more political games. In hindsight, that was stupid. If I had, maybe this would all be different.

Are we all this stupid when we are young?

Food and drink were brought to us. It took a long time, not because Cixi didn't try or that she was resistant, but she didn't have my training and I don't believe she'd ever seen a wound before. Plus, there was trying to explain some concepts. Even though communication between Tiantang and Carelian was almost seamless, not all words translated. Epidermis, cellular structure, and cell regeneration took a bit of back and forth to make sure the concepts were communicated clearly.

Night had fallen, and they had lamps up around us by the time we finished. I'd kept track. The wound down Tiantang's side had been nine feet long and went up and down as he had writhed trying to get away from the monsters. Carelian had informed me they were cockatrices and were definitely different from basilisks.

~I have done all I can. He should heal. A bite from Tirsane's snakes would be helpful though.~ Carelian sat next to me, and his whiskers drooped, displaying exhaustion as bad as my own.

That stopped me. I could ask. She would come. At this point it wasn't a secret, but that would be granting a favor.

"Cixi, there is someone I could ask to come help, but it would cost me a favor." Every time I said her name, everyone around me bristled, but I just ignored them.

"A favor?" Her eyes narrowed at me. She wore kohl around them, so they looked dangerous, brooding. "How big of a favor?"

"Very big," I said. In some ways Cixi understood this better than I did, the idea of bartering for assistance. It still felt wrong. I wasn't perfect by a long run and the number of times I had resentment at having to stop and help someone when I was in the middle of things at work or home was endless. But I did it because you helped people. That attitude was always why I would have never made a good cop.

She tilted her head and looked at her sick familiar. I was sure Tiantang would live, only because the denizens didn't seem susceptible to our bacteria. If he had been a human, we would have needed IVs full of antibiotics.

"Could I provide the favor or pay the cost?"

"No clue. I can ask. What would you provide?" We sat there on the ground, soaked in blood, our clothes covered with blood, dirt and sweat. My bald head gleamed in the lights they had set up around us, and I'm sure the pictures had already made it to the press by now. I'd have to deal with that later.

She bit her lip and thought. "Who is the person?"

"A gorgon. Her name is Tirsane." I'd given up and leaned back on Carelian. I knew I should go home, but standing up seemed like a lot of work, so I'd lay here a bit.

"Ah, yes. She has been mentioned much in my security briefings."

I arched an eyebrow at that. I hadn't offered them away yet. Being the subject of security briefings didn't really surprise me, but Tirsane? The subject wasn't worth worrying about at this point.

"Yes. I have a silk scarf woven by hand by the great Chinese artist - Jen Li Sung. It is an image of Tiantang, the dragon of China. It is one of a kind and cost thousands."

"Do you have a picture of it?"

She pulled out a phone and flipped through her pictures. It took her a long time. Finally, she held the phone out to me. There was a scarf that had to be six feet long and woven in brilliant silk colors. Tiantang flowed across it as if alive, his brilliant reds popping against the pale blue background. I'd have framed it and hung it on the wall as a work of art.

"I can ask. One moment." She nodded and went back to petting her familiar, who lay quietly just breathing. He wasn't asleep, and I didn't know if that was good or bad.

~Tirsane? Cixi, the Empress of China, wishes to know if you would trade some healing bites for this?" I sent an image of the scarf. ~It is very valuable and unique.~

There was a mental sound of curiosity. ~You never fail to provide unique challenges. Tell her yes. Will you bring me?~

~I'll ask Carelian. Thank you Tirsane.~ I levered myself up to sitting. "Carelian, can you go get Tirsane, please?" I looked at Cixi. "Let everyone know that a friend is coming through. She is a gorgon. They are not to shoot or react. I will not be pleased if any of them try to hurt my friend." I layered those words with every ounce of steel I had.

Carelian sighed as he stood and stretched. ~Some day you and I shall have a quiet life of woodland hunts and long sleeps.~ He licked the side of my face and I smiled. ~Cixi. She is powerful. Do not threaten her.~ He stepped into a rip and was done before she could react.

She stared at me, then called out in a loud voice, giving sharp orders and people responded to her words. I had no idea what she said but the results were obvious as everyone pulled back and turned around facing outward. That wasn't a bad option.

A minute later, Tirsane came out, much warier than she had been at the oil refinery. She turned, watching around her, her face trembling on the edge of the creature she could be. But everyone kept their backs to us and Cixi stood slowly. I watched her inspect Tirsane and kept my mouth shut.

"You are more beautiful than the reports suggested. The mythology called you a monster." Her words weren't accusatory, more questioning.

"The past is mostly written by men. They fear what they do not understand." Tirsane arched a brow at the woman, treating her as equal.

That made a smile break across Cixi's face. "Yes, they do. I do not have the scarf with me." A flicker of worry crossed her face.

"I trust you will have it delivered to me," Tirsane said simply. Cixi sagged a bit at that and waved at Tiantang.

"Can you help?"

"Yes. But it will look like I am hurting him."

I snickered, remembering when she had to help Carelian after an explosion. I almost lost it. Warning someone was a very good idea.

"Very well." Cixi nodded and moved to Tiantang's head, gently petting it. He'd fallen unconscious a minute ago, and I had no idea how badly we'd hurt him. Yet one more thing I'd never had the time to study—how to create painkillers in a body for surgery.

Tirsane ran her fingers along his side and down the bloody sections. We'd sealed the skin, but the job would leave a nasty scar.

She leaned down and two snakes struck out and bit him, pumping their venom into him.

"That should help. It will not make a miracle recovery, but that should allow his body to heal faster. I also added a pain killer."

Indeed, his body relaxed. "Thank you. I couldn't figure out how to do that."

Cixi also looked relieved, though she was much more inscrutable than I would ever be. "He will be better?"

"Yes. I'd say he should be able to move in a few hours. One venom was a pain killer, the other concentrated nutrients with blood replenishment chemicals. You did a good job putting his hide back together. If there is no damage to the internal organs, I see no reason he shouldn't be fine. We tend to heal fast." Tirsane smiled gently at Cixi.

"Thank you, honored one. I will get the scarf to Cori as soon as I can." Cixi darted a glance at me, checking if that was okay.

I nodded. "That works. Tirsane, I'll let you know when I have it. Then we can decide how to get it to you."

Tirsane nodded regally, obviously not worried about her payment. It made me wonder how many denizens had dozens of favors owed to them or that they owed to others that were simply never collected on. I glanced at my arm and the two favors still left Salistra and the three Tirsane owed me. Such a frustrating system.

"Be well." She turned, and a rip opened, waiting for her, and she slithered into it.

Cixi started to slump but caught herself and straightened. She shouted out to the people around to get a tent and blankets for the dragon of China. People exploded into action, and she turned to me.

The woman who'd spent the last hour helping me heal her

familiar was gone. In her stead was the Empress of China. I bit back a sigh. Cixi I could almost like. The Empress was a pain.

"Merlin Munroe, I thank you for your assistance with the Dragon of China. You and your familiar were instrumental in saving his life. How can I repay your assistance?" Her tone was overly formal, and her hands were tucked in her sleeves, making her appear even more constrained.

I opened my mouth to spew some bullshit about being honored to assist and that no payment was needed. I stopped as I looked around.

"Empress, as you may know I am trying to find the source of these tears and stop them." Her eyes narrowed as she focused on me. The personnel that had gathered near her snapped their attention to me as well. Apparently, they had not known. "I would like to know how you have been managing to close the tears. As you can see, I have exhausted myself fighting them." I ran a hand over my bald scalp and then put it back down to find Carelian waiting there.

She blinked rapidly, glancing at Carelian then me. It took what seemed like forever before she responded. "We have teams of five. Two are Spirit Mages that work in concert. They each take an end of the rip and start closing it. The other three either eliminate the forces holding it open or creatures emerging. We have also found that throwing grenades into the openings helps to make them easier to close. The explosion seems to destabilize the force keeping it open."

That bit of information was new. "And the missiles?"

"Those are used when there are creatures like these coming out." She waved at the dead denizens around us. "Or the rip is higher than we can easily reach. Any that are above thirty meters we use various ordinances."

I could see a man in a soldier uniform with what I took to

be high-ranking marks on his collar wincing as she spoke, but he didn't stop her.

"Thank you. That information is very interesting." I paused trying to figure out how to phrase my next sentence. "I would request that the use of missiles be carefully monitored. One of the last sets that was sent in, though I know not if it was from China or Russia, landed in a populated area and killed a few denizens. The rips are small localized events and if the missile continues to fly much past ten feet, it is past what is creating the opening."

She looked at me, then her general. He switched his eyes back and forth between me and Tiantang.

"Understood," he finally snapped out through clenched teeth.

"Thank you for that information, Merlin Munroe. We shall take that into consideration. Once again, thank you for your assistance." With that last word, she turned her back on me.

My head was throbbing. I wanted my chair and hot chocolate. "Home please?" My hands rubbed on his head. He'd been only quiet the entire time.

~Yes,~ was his only comment as we stepped through the rip he made back into the house.

CHAPTER

TWENTY-FIVE

As the rips between our plane and the others increase, the responses to these incursions are becoming more vital. China uses five-man teams stationed every hundred miles in densely populated areas, while Russia has multiple strike teams made up of mages and their own Hunters. But some of the worst rips have taken up to twenty mages to control. We rely on one woman and from the news snapshots of her, she is becoming increasingly frail and worn. The United States will need to start replicating China and Russia soon or the death toll is going to increase. ~ CNN Report

CHAOS

I'd spent enough energy on Tiantang that I crashed almost the moment we got home. The only thing I did was let Zmaug know her son was fine. Her reply was "Excellent" then she hung up on me. Who knows what that meant?

Wednesday, I was looking at all the research the various mages had come up with from the Library and it was all fascinating. But none of it gave me any ideas. They talked about mentions of Atlantean religious practices, how one and three were considered special numbers, that phoenixes appear all through history and cultures, but they are only mentioned as "wondrous, magical creatures".

Nothing about rips or how to stop or repair them. I sat in my study, remnants of breakfast by my side and Carelian grooming himself in the window seat. Everyone seemed to be sure I'd starve to death by myself, so the refrigerator and freezer were full of calorie laden meals that I just needed to throw in the microwave.

If I'd been in any other condition, I might have protested. Maybe. The food was much better than what I'd have made for myself. But given the current situation, I was just grateful. If this ever stopped, I'd have to be careful because I'd be gaining weight like crazy.

I forced my mind back to the topic at hand, which was — I didn't have any information.

"I think it's time," I said out loud even as I cringed just thinking about how much this was going to hurt.

~For?~ Carelian asked. ~I think a walk would be good. The weather is nice.~ He had stopped to peer out the window, and he wasn't wrong.

"Well, a walk will be part of it, but I need to go talk to Bob."

Carelian whipped his head around to stare at me. ~No,~ he snarled, his ears back and tail slashing back and forth.

"Yes. There isn't any place else left. I need to talk to him. See if somewhere in the pieces of him is the information I need. If you can think of anyone else, I'll gladly ask them first." I stared at him, open to anything.

He fiercely groomed his claws for a minute before sighing and sliding the claws back in. ~Very well. But you must have support waiting for you to get back here.~

I didn't argue. I knew that I'd be coming back in bad condition. "I agree. Let's go talk to Marisol."

~Mmm, tamales,~ he replied as he rolled off the window seat, stretching.

"Is that what she is cooking?"

~Yes. I can smell it from here.~

I rolled my eyes and got dressed. He slipped into his harness, and I double checked it. I might need to be holding onto it by the time we got back here. If not worse.

Ready for a trip to the realms, I went to the door and pushed the handle down, then pulled it open. I stepped forward into the grayness and out into the hall in the craftsman that Marisol lived in.

"Marisol?" I called out as I headed to the kitchen. I could hear her in there and, indeed, it smelled of tamales.

"In here, Cori." She was in the kitchen wrapping them in corn husks as I walked in.

"What's all this for?" I said looking at the literal piles of tamales. There had to be close to a hundred.

"Don't you remember? Angelique's *quinceañera* is this weekend. I'm prepping so we can heat them up later." She handed an unwrapped cooked one to Carelian, who took it and blew on it.

"Ah, yes." That note was on my calendar. "Would you be able to stop and help me in an hour or so?"

"Of course, *mi hija*. Why wouldn't I?" She shot me a look and I marveled once more at how much more alive she was than she had been a year ago. Moving here had been good for her.

"I need to talk to Bob. The odds are I'm going to be coming back in bad shape. I'll need some help. I'll be asking Hamiada as well." I hated asking for help, but I just had a feeling this was going to be worse than normal.

"What do you mean, bad shape?" She looked at me, worried, as she stopped wrapping the tamales.

"You have time. But I mean probably screaming migraine, bleeding from the nose, and exhausted. I could be wrong, and come back just fine."

"Why on Earth would that happen?" Her eyes were wide as she looked at me, her brows furrowed.

"Talking to Bob is difficult. But I have to. It's getting worse."

She stood there indecisive, then started taking off her apron. "Then I'll come with you."

I held up my hand. "You can't or you'll be worse off than me. Just come when Carelian calls?"

"You sure?" I nodded, trying to look less exhausted than I felt. "Then I'll be there. Just be careful, Cori.

"I will." I left before I could say anymore, though there were two fresh tamales in my hand, and I noted Carelian had already inhaled the one she'd handed him. The handle went up, and I walked back into the house.

"Hamiada?" I called out.

"Of course, I will. When I feel the doorway here, I will be available to assist." She spoke as she stepped out of the wall.

"Huh?" It took me a second. "Oh, you heard?"

"Yes. I am well connected, and I pay a modicum of attention when the door is used. I enjoy the connection to my daughters." She spun slightly. Today flowers coated her body, and her hair was green twigs.

"Thank you. We'd better get going. I don't think it will take more than an hour or two. I hope." I didn't mention that I hoped I'd have the energy to get home. It didn't matter, Carelian would get me home.

I trusted him.

"Carelian, do you know where to go?" He didn't look at me. His ears were back, and his tail snapped like a live wire, but he opened a rip and walked in. I followed and found us at the crossroads. He closed the entry behind us and stared at me.

~We are going to the heart of Chaos. Walk slowly and if I tell you to stop, do it. Do not touch anything. Much of Chaos is unamicable to human life.~

The urge to tease him, to make it all a joke, pulled at me, but I pushed it down and nodded. "Got it."

He stared at me for a long time, then turned and opened another entry and walked through. I followed. It took me a minute to get my bearings. It felt like a primordial jungle. Something you'd see in a movie about dinosaurs. The wetness clung to me, and it was almost hard to breathe. There was green, red, yellow, orange bursting from every corner. Where there weren't green leaves, there were flowers or other plant life displaying a variety of hues.

"This is pretty. This is where Bob lives?"

~No. This is the center of Chaos. Hello Cori.~ Esmere's voice filled my mind, and I turned to see her green form emerge from the jungle. I'd always wondered why she was green. It was such an odd color especially for a creature that lived on the plains. But now watching her in this primordial space, the color suddenly made sense.

"Hey. I take it Carelian told you?"

~Yes. Is there a reason you didn't ask me for this?~ She didn't sound hurt, just curious.

"You have asked as much as you can, but I need to be there and follow up with the answers, ask different questions. I know you have tried, but Bob is the oldest sentient being anyone knows of. I need to ask him directly."

We walked down a trail as Esmere thought. If I was in a movie, I'd expect the heavy tread of a dinosaur about to appear behind us. Instead, there was just so much life and not one of the creatures I saw matched any Earth creature I knew of.

There were birds, lizards, snakes, rodents—but different. Sometimes the differences were cute, other times they were scary. None of them ran at our approach. If anything, I'd say they followed us, watching me as much as I watched them.

~You are correct that he is the oldest and I have asked. This shall be interesting. But Cori?~ She pushed a bit on that last word and I glanced back to look at her . ~Don't push too hard. You could die.~

The matter-of-fact words shook me more than I expected, and a shiver ran down my spine. "I know. But I need, we need this information."

~So be it,~ she murmured softly. That didn't make me feel

any better, but I couldn't send anyone else and as much as I loved Esmere, I didn't know what to tell her besides what she'd already asked.

Instead, I admired the scenery, the diffuse light cast shade everywhere, but it wasn't a creepy darkness, it just felt old. It made me feel like an interloper in a world where I was never meant to belong. My hand trailed along Carelian's back. His tail tapped the back of my leg in reassurance.

The path we followed got narrower and narrower until we were in a single file. The trees became darker, the air was like breathing in a sauna, and the scent had moved from woody and mossy to fetid and sharp. Sweat trickled down the back of my neck to under my shirt. The lack of hair made it easier and harder. The sweat ran, didn't collect to make me cold or hot, but it also meant it traced down the skin, a constant tickling distraction.

Carelian stepped to the side, and I frowned, but I took the two extra steps and found myself in a clearing. If we had been on Earth, I would have sworn a meteor had landed here eons ago, creating this area. The clearing was almost perfectly circular and in the center of it was a deep, dark pool. Moss in variations of green covered the ground to the pool. I looked around, but other than the plants surrounding the area, it was just a deep pool.

After spending two minutes scanning the clearing, looking for something or someone, I gave up and looked at the two cats. "So?"

~Bob will be here shortly,~ Esmere replied sitting on the opposite side of me. My mind was involved with the imagery of me standing there with two huge cats sitting on either side of me, when the pool began to bulge.

"Oh," I muttered. For some reason, I'd assumed it was water. Now that I looked at it, I realized it wasn't dark water, it was the same stuff Chaos tentacles were made out of. That Bob was. It rippled and bobbed up and down until at the edge nearest us, a blob began to grow. It oozed out toward us, but kept growing up and up, until Bob was the same shape and size I'd seen at the SEC games and at the house, when I'd been challenged as the Herald. Bob was big, scary, unknown, and it took concerted effort not to flee.

~Yes?~

I caught my breath and breathed through the pain. I had to do this. I'd spent the last few days thinking about this and creating my questions. I couldn't afford to ask anything frivolous. It might kill me.

"Bob, thank you for being willing to answer my questions. I've been told you have caches of memories that go back to when magic first came into existence, maybe further. Can you go through them and see if you have any that relate to Atlantis? If so, do any of those memories show anything about the Undoing?"

I crossed my fingers. The first question was a yes or no. If I could keep them to yes or no questions, this wouldn't be too bad.

~Yes. Maybe.~

Each word was like a knife jabbing into my brain. The "Maybe" didn't help. I'd have to figure out what the maybe encompassed.

"Does it involve Zendia or the phoenixes?"

~No.~

That didn't help. I braced myself. "What does it involve?"

~Atlantis. The creation was witnessed, as was the destruction. Magic sundered and snapped its bounds. It involved the sacrifice of three. Remember that. To rebind three will once again require sacrifice. What was taken without choice must be repaired with choice. There is no work around available.~

Every word sliced into me. My knees buckled. The tickling on both sides of my head annoyed me, but I pushed it away.

"How? Where?"

~It will be revealed when you are ready and willing to sacrifice. Magic must grow more to be ready. You must be ready. The sacrifices must be ready.~ Its words were more advanced than usual, but that meant every syllable felt like a razor through my mind and psyche.

The mossy ground bit into my knees and I sluggishly realized at some point I'd crumpled. Carelian was holding me up with a low, continuous growl. Esmere was on the other side, but while I could sense her, turning my head to look wasn't that important.

"I won't kill anyone," I bit out, staring at the blob.

~Then the worlds will rip each other apart. You are the herald. If you do not bring in the new era everything will be destroyed.~

The last words floated across my brain as my body gave up and I sank into darkness to the sound of a Cath snarling.

CHAPTER

TWENTY-SIX

Evelyn Crane is the most decorated Mage Hunter in America. With over 350 confirmed take downs she is considered one of the most accomplished hunters in history. She died this past week at the age of 85. No reason for death is given but she died by herself and never married. A great Hunter has left us. ~CNN Mage Focus

---

ORDER

"**M**mm?" I whimpered as I moved my head. I felt like I'd been drinking all day and then decided to top it off with more. I'd heard people talk about hangovers where death seemed preferable. But I rarely drank.

"Cori?" a voice said softly.

A whimper slipped out as I turned my head toward the voice.

"Can you open your eyes?" The voice was familiar, tender, and oh so soft.

Eyes, I had eyes. It took me a minute to remember how to open them. But I managed, squinting at the low light. Marisol came into focus and I managed to smile at her.

"Ah, there you are. Good. Do you want some water?"

The question seemed silly. I wasn't thirsty, was I? I tried to swallow and winced as my throat cracked. At that point, I realized my mouth felt like the parched desert. I managed a tiny nod, even that making my head pound harder.

"Here you go." She put a straw in front of me and I sucked in cool water. Nothing had ever felt so good. Another few sips and I was exhausted and trying not to cry in pain.

"Are you in pain?" she asked. I realized my eyes were closed. It took me a minute to remember how to reopen them. Another tiny nod and she did something outside my vision. "There, the meds should kick in shortly."

That made no sense.

I looked around for pills and saw that my arms had tubes coming out of them. Was I supposed to have tubes coming out of my arms? With great effort, I managed to look at one of them as a wave of soothing warmth spread from my arm up to my mind. The agony faded, and I smiled and closed my eyes falling into sleep again.

This time a warm body and a rumbling purr guided me into

consciousness. I opened my eyes, squinting to see Sable seated in a chair next to me, her feet up and a book in her hands.

"Sable?" The word came out as a croak, and she almost threw the book she started so hard.

"Cori, you're back. Are you in pain?" I thought about that for a long moment.

"No?" Again, my voice sounded like I hadn't spoken in years.

"Here, drink some water." Another straw and water and it coated my throat relieving the dryness. Just that bit of water helped me feel better.

I lay back looking around. I was in my room. Sable next to me. Heavy curtains were pulled across the windows. I had IVs in my arms. Carelian lay next to me, still purring. I petted him, that hand not restrained by tubes.

"What?"

"Hmmm, you sure you're ready to talk?" Sable was running her hand up and down my leg as she watched me.

I nodded and sobbed as my head exploded in pain.

"No, I don't think so." She reached up and this time I watched her fiddle with an IV bag. "This will help. I'll see you in the morning. You'll probably feel better then."

Warmth spread up my arm and wrapped around the maces battering into my brain. I sighed and closed my eyes.

My eyes opened as noise in the room pulled me up. This time the room was full of sunlight and a woman in scrubs walked back and forth. Jo was standing there in the doorway.

"I think she is going to be fine. She's responded appropriately, her familiar isn't overly stressed. The biggest question is removing the liquids and catheter." The medical person was talking to Jo.

"She'll hate that, but let's leave it until tomorrow. We'll have to work to get her back to full strength." Jo looked my direction and must have seen me watching. "Hey Cori, how are you feeling?"

I blinked and moved my head around. It didn't explode. I wiggled my fingers, toes, and shoulders. I was achy and stiff, but not in pain. "Better?" It was a whisper, but I answered.

"Yeah, definitely better." She moved over to sit by me as the nurse, at least I assumed that was what she was, wrote things into a table. "So, think you're going to stay awake this time?"

I blinked, but the overwhelming exhaustion wasn't there. "I think so? What happened?" My hand kept petting Carelian, his warmth and rumble making me feel safe.

"What do you remember?" she countered watching, and I got the feeling it was more than an idle question.

I frowned, trying to answer the question. Images flooded my mind. "Bob. Went to talk to Bob. Got answers I didn't like. That I would need to sacrifice three for the realms." I frowned, trying to remember. "I can't remember anything after that."

Jo seemed to sag back. "Good. Then you really haven't forgotten anything. Carelian and Esmere got you back here, unconscious, bleeding from eyes, nose, ears. Your pupils were nonreactive. Contacted Stephen and he got medical personnel out here. Apparently, this happens occasionally when a mage has offered too much. They got you set up here with meds, saline, and catheter."

I wrinkled my nose at that and instinctively wiggled my hips.

Ugh, that's why I feel weird.

"Better than us trying to use a bed pan. I figure we can leave that in another day until we get real food into you. You were about to get a feeding tube if you'd gone much longer. You don't have fat reserves at this point."

At the word food, my body seemed to wake up and my stomach grumbled. Jo laughed and patted my arm. "*Mami* is making some broth and tortilla for you. You'll need to go slow, but I figure as soon as you need to do more than urinate, it will be a good time to get the catheter out and see if you can walk."

"Not enthused at that, but not letting me get dehydrated is a good idea. How long?" I glanced at the light coming in. It was at least early afternoon.

"It's Saturday."

I jerked my head to look at her, worried. "I've been unconscious for three days?" We'd gone to see Bob on Wednesday.

"Meh, mostly. You came around for a few minutes Friday afternoon, then late Friday night. That told us you'd probably be up sometime today. Hence why we had everyone here."

"Ah. So Carelian, is this where you go 'I told you so?'." I tried to keep my voice a teasing level, but I did feel like he was going to lord it over it.

"Don't expect him to talk to you for a while," Jo said as she got off the bed.

"Why?" I darted a look at her, worried that I'd missed something.

"He said the mental speak hurt you too much. Until you can talk to him without a twinge of pain, his words might hurt you." She had a sympathetic look, but the fact that she wasn't reassuring me told me I'd be without his voice in my mind for a bit.

~Carelian?~ I tried and choked on air as my brain caught on fire. It felt like my brain was covered with paper cuts and I'd just poured hand sanitizer on it.

"And that is why no mind speak. You need pain killers?" She frowned, leaning forward and watching me.

I forced myself to breathe through the pain, my heart ratcheting up and down. "Maybe?" I kept panting as I tried to get the pain to fade.

"Here." She handed me some pills and a glass of water. "A

bit less powerful than the IV version, but they are going to pull that after you get some food."

I took them gratefully, then laid back, eyes closed, and practiced breathing. If this didn't start to fade, I might be asking for the IV version.

"You lay there. Going down to get you some food. I hope what you got from Bob was worth it. It's been.... bad."

I cracked one eye open, but she was gone before I managed. Bad? What did that mean? I looked around for my phone. I found it, but laid back, letting the pain wash through me over and over. It would be a bit before I tried that again. My hand remained buried in Carelian's fur.

The next things I knew, Jo was shaking me as Sable walked in with a tray. They helped me sit up and talked about the kids while I ate. The chicken soup, while not her normal stew-like consistency, was delicious. Add in homemade tortillas, I ate slowly but I ate all of it.

When I finally finished and I realized the pain had faded, I looked at them. "Okay, what does bad mean?"

They glanced at me, then shrugged. "Multiple rips." Jo said. "They are struggling to get them closed. The information you passed on from China is helping, but they are reluctant to give grenades out to civilians."

Sable picked up. "There have been multiple creatures slipping out. Thursday, there was even a pack of Cath, but that one Carelian took care of the second Stephen called us. He went over there and from the news reports, it was like watching a mom tear into her kids. They were all slinking back into the portal, and it closed from the other side."

I smiled at that and petted him faster. "Good job."

"That was an easy one, though. There've been a lot of casualties." Jo's voice was grim, and she reached out to hold Sable's hand. "They are reactivating anyone with a strong Soul. They are struggling to keep up."

I wanted to reach out and ask Freya about the pocket realms, but the memory of the pain stopped me. "Carelian, are they not doing the pocket realms yet?"

There was a whisper of talk and just having it around me seared like I'd held myself too close to a flame. Without intending to I flinched back from the virtual fire.

"Oh yeah, no mental talk for you for a while," Jo said, frowning at me. "But he said it is starting this week. And that Esmere tore into the Cath that came over. They knew better."

"Ah." I felt my energy ebbing, and I leaned back. The soup was all gone and most of the tortillas. "Anything else that I need to know?"

Sable shrugged. "Kids miss you, have cards for you, and even the dragons were checking you out regularly. Stephen said he'd call tonight."

I managed to nod, but sleepiness was nibbling at my brain.

"Go to sleep, Cori." Jo rose up, taking the tray and dropping a kiss on my forehead. Darkness dragged me back down.

I opened my eyes to see the dim light through the window. A mug of something hot sat next to me and Carelian was gone. That loss ached through me, and I looked around for him. "Carelian?" Panic started to set in for some reason. I struggled, trying to get up. The IV was gone, but the catheter was still there.

"Cori?" Jo stuck her head in. "Hamiada said you were up."

"Where's Carelian?" I asked, almost in a panic.

"Deep breaths." She moved over and took my hand. "He went to get Stephen. They'll be here shortly." She handed the mug to me. "Drink and I'll get you a washcloth. Not like you need to brush your hair."

I relaxed when I felt the slash in my mind of a rip. Jo had

helped me brush my teeth and gave me a quick sponge bath. We both agreed tomorrow I'd get a real bath. She'd just tucked me back in bed when Carelian came bounding up the stairs. He stuck his face in my hands and I rubbed and scratched, fighting back tears. Not being able to talk to him hurt more than I expected.

"Silly Cath. You left and I didn't know where you were." He licked my hand and jumped up on the bed, pressing against me as he purred.

"I'm not sure if you look better or look like shit."

I looked up to see Stephen in the doorway.

"I look like better shit?" I offered.

He laughed as he came in and took the chair near my bed. "They sent me pics when you got home. You looked like you'd been beaten. We were worried. Indira sent over some pita bread and *meghli*. She swears she put enough spices to help your blood."

I grinned. Her *meghli* was delicious and mild enough I could probably eat it. "Sounds good. Now, what's the bad news?"

"What? A friend can't come by to see you?"

I just lifted an eyebrow at him, my hand still buried in Carelian's fur.

Stephen sighed and the attitude of happy humor faded. "The senate committee on the rips wants to see you."

"Why me? I'm not on any of the boards. I avoid politics." That worried me. Yes, I was powerful and often a target, but I avoided politics more than most.

"You're the face of it, especially after China."

I'd been right about the pictures. They spread like wildfire. And everyone talked about me. "When?"

"Next Monday. You think you'll be ready?" He looked worried and glanced at the catheter bag still hanging off the bed.

"If not, I'll go in pushed in a wheelchair. Get me a driver, though. I can't really afford to sidestep."

He nodded, and we fell into talking about plans and ideas about the rips and what they were trying on the other side. And with every breath, I missed Carelian's comments even as he laid by my side.

TWENTY-SEVEN

News from Australia: thirty dead as the result of a rip that released multiple creatures resembling Komodo dragons but smaller and faster. Their bites, however, killed within minutes. It took a squad from the military to shoot them before mages could get close enough to close the rip. Calls for a reworking of the gun laws in the Territories given this incident. ~ CNN

SPIRIT

I took a glorious bath Sunday night after the embarrassment of getting the catheter out. Then came a solid week of physical therapy. While I could walk and the escalator stairs kept me from becoming overly exhausted, the plan still was to push me into the committee room in a wheelchair. If we were lucky it might provide me with some sympathy to play on.

I managed to get dressed by myself. Jo had decided she was going with me, as she refused to let me go anywhere that far away alone.

"You sure? This is a stupid reason to miss work."

"Meh," she waved my argument away. "They like me. I have vacation time and my partner is the famous Cori Munroe. I don't think you understand the amount of cache that gives me." She sounded bitter.

"Jo?" Worry raced through me and I stumbled to a halt.

"Huh?" She turned and saw my face. "Cori. You are famous. We get flack every so often. Lesbians are one thing, but poly? Most people get curious. Then you are you. The woman I love, and I can't imagine not having in my life. But trying to explain our life?" She threw her hands up, laughing. "How do I tell them the terror, the joy, the wonder, the worry it is made up of?"

I looked at her hard and saw the worry lines by her eyes and if I wasn't wrong, there was a trace of silver at her roots.

"Jo?" I reached for her and was terrified when she wrapped around me, holding me tight, a sob escaping.

"I thought you were going to die. You can't die. You can't," she sobbed into my shoulder. My arms locked around her and Carelian leaned against us purring.

~I will not let my quean die. Any of my queans.~ Carelian said in a near whisper and a smile spread across my face.

"I heard him, and it didn't hurt." It was a teeny lie. Jo didn't have Spirit, neither did Carelian, so I let it be. It ached a tiny bit. And I was more than willing to suffer that to hear him again.

She hugged me even tighter, and I sighed. "Jo, I can't lose you, and if I could do anything to let someone else deal with this crap, I would. But," my voice cracked. "If I don't do this, I might lose you, Sable, the kids. I'll throw myself into lava before I'll let anything happen to you. You need to be there for those two amazing children. I'm expendable." I kept my voice low, but I meant every word. Of all of them, I was the one that we could lose.

"None of us are expendable," she snapped, pulling back. "None of us. Do you hear that? I'll do whatever is needed for all of us to die in our beds of old age." She looked like she might start yelling at me.

I lifted my hand to cradle her face. "I know. But sometimes, the price of whatever means you don't get to die in bed."

Her lips thinned and her hands hurt on my arms. After a moment, she closed her eyes. "I know," she whispered.

"Which means we need to get to D.C. so I can deal with elected idiots."

Jo snorted and pulled away. "Yes. And I get a front-row seat." A car pulled up as we spoke, and I arched a brow. It wasn't a sedan, no, this was a limo. A man and a woman got out of the front seat and walked around to us.

"Merlin Munroe, Archmage Guzman. We are your drivers and assistants today. There is a wheelchair in the back for when you arrive. Let us assist you." The man spoke even as the woman was opening the door.

Before I had a chance to even come up with questions, we were all ensconced in the car and it was pulling away. Carelian lounged next to me, his head on my lap. Jo sat opposite watching me with a quirk of a smile on her face.

"At least they are taking us to the inquisition in style," she said.

The window between us rolled down, and the woman turned to look at us. "There is a private plane waiting for us, and there will be another driver waiting for you in DC. We will be at the airport in twenty minutes. There are snacks and drinks in the refrigerator. Please feel free to help yourself. If you need anything, hit the intercom button located in the panel to Merlin Munroe's left."

With that Jo and I were effectively isolated. I started laughing and a moment later she joined me, the stress of earlier, not bleeding off, but changing.

"Only you, Cori," Jo finally said as she dug in the refrigerator. "They've got soda, water, bubbly water, cheese, boiled eggs, and mini bottles of champagne."

"Well, absolutely not the champagne. With as hard as my body is struggling to process everything, I'd probably be tipsy as can be by the time we arrived there." I took the full sugar soda she gave me.

"Oh, I don't know. Drunk Cori chewing out a room full of senators would be hilarious." She kept digging through the cupboards. "Hey Carelian, they even have kibble for you."

He huffed. ~I am not that hungry, thank you.~

"You've gotten spoiled," I said. The fresh fish had made him picky. Though we did still add kibble once a day. It had nutrients the fish didn't, and he knew it.

~Yes. It is how I should be. A spoiled, pampered, dangerous creature.~ He rubbed his head on my leg a bit, then went back to dozing.

The transfer to the plane was just as quick. Even Carelian tolerated the plane ride, mostly because he refused to be away from me. The flight only took ninety minutes, and we were plied with snacks again. I didn't know if they treated everyone that way or if they were that desperate to keep us happy.

Jo and I spent the flight just talking. It had been a while since we had this much time alone. We talked about how much she loved the house, the kids, and that they would be in first grade this fall. But mostly we just talked.

We landed at the Regan airport and people were waiting for us once again. They got us into the next car, another limo with again two drivers, a male and female, just as quickly and efficiently as the first set. We were in the back and told it would be about forty minutes to get to Capitol Hill.

Jo and I just snickered at all the five-star treatment. "We need more date nights," she said suddenly, staring at me. "I don't know why I didn't realize that before."

"Okay. They are my kids too. Leave them to my tender mercies more often." I shrugged. It wasn't like I didn't enjoy the kids and I didn't regard it as babysitting. They were mine as much as theirs.

"No, I mean us. I mean you and Sable. Sable and I get our date nights twice a month, but you don't." Her eyes were direct and excited. "But we don't get date nights with you."

"What are you talking about?" She'd lost me. I kept petting Carelian, reveling in having him back in my mind again. His silence had hurt more than Bob's words.

"I love you. Sable loves you. You are a part of us, but we've been forgetting to date you. Sable and I remember to still date each other, but this has been missing." She waved her hand around the inside of the limo. "Just us. I didn't realize how much I missed getting you to myself. We need to do that. Give you and Sable date nights. Give the three of us time to spend adult time with each other. I've missed you and this is something I can fix."

Warmth spread through me, and I smiled, ducking my

head, then looking back up at her. "I agree. I've missed this too and I don't think I realized it. So, when this is all over?"

"No," Jo said instantly. "Now. While this is going on. We spend too much time waiting until something is resolved or dealt with or whatever. No. I'm not willing to wait because I almost lost you. I want it all now." She looked at me. "Cori, you were just this side of being put in the hospital. But since the only thing you needed was rest, pain killers, and nutrients, they let you stay. I could have lost you. I'm not willing to lose any more time with you. With any of you."

I leaned my head back against the seat, looking up at the ceiling and fighting back tears. I'd put on a touch of makeup, and I didn't want it to run. When I thought I'd be able to not start crying, I looked down at her. "I would really like that."

"Good," she said and started her furious typing on the phone. "Okay done. I have reservations for the four of us Friday at a restaurant. Sanchez is going to come over and do a movie night with the kids in the media room. And we are going out to dinner, even if you have to be pushed in a wheelchair."

"Four?" I wondered what I'd missed.

Jo snorted. "Yes four. Did you forget your boyfriend? He's laying on you."

~I am not her boyfriend. I am her focus. She is my quean.~

"Fine. Your focus. He is as much your partner as we are, and I'd never think to exclude him." She reached out and tapped his tail with her foot. "He'd shed all over my clothes."

I laughed, a simple happy laugh, and for the first time in a very, very long time I wished I was interested in sex. The idea of being loved by her and Sable made me smile. But they loved me as I was and maybe that was better.

"We are arriving now," the driver said, and I looked up to see the buildings of Washington around us. Time had flown as we talked and repaired tears in our relationship neither of us had even seen.

The limo pulled into a parking garage and the two drivers-- or handlers--had us out and me in a wheelchair with smooth efficiency. Before I knew it, I was being pushed through the halls of the senate. People stopped to stare at us as we were escorted through. Jo, as always, was amazing to look at in black pumps, dark gray slacks, a vivid burgundy blouse, and a matching gray jacket.

I was dressed up, but the clothes hung on me. I wore black leggings, ankle-high boots, a tunic in green and burgundy, and then a long black cardigan. If I stood up, the cardigan and tunic almost hit my knees. I still looked a bit disheveled, but that was because everything hung on me. It had looked much nicer when I was about thirty pounds heavier. Carelian stalked next to me for all the world death on four paws. Between the two of them I'd have looked too.

We were scanned, badged, and then escorted into a large room. At the front there was a long curved piece of furniture that looked like a judge's bench for at least fifteen people. Behind it was a gallery where even more people could sit. A small table sat in front of the curved area with room for four people. I was looking around as they wheeled me in and almost choked with surprise and worry when they placed me at the table and Jo in the chairs behind me. It was still relatively empty, leaving me looking around in confusion.

"What is going on?" I stared at the female driver that had just placed me here.

"This is where I was told to deliver you, ma'am. I'll be waiting for you outside when done." She nodded at me and was gone.

I craned my neck to stare at Jo, who just shrugged. It was

nice to know she was as confused as I was. Carelian prowled around the table, then went underneath it.

~I shall stay here for a while. Let others think you are alone. This smells of a trap.~

"I think you might be right." I fought back a sigh. I'd been ordered to appear for a senate committee hearing, but other than saying it was about rip response, there hadn't been any other information. Stephen let me know he'd been summoned too but didn't have any other information.

I spent my time people watching, and it was confusing. The upper gallery, obviously for people to watch the proceedings, had a stream of people coming in. They held things in their hands, and I saw at least three people with large stuffed cats.

"Jo, look." I nodded up to the gallery. "What is all that?"

Jo turned around to look, her brow wrinkling as she studied the people packing the gallery. "Oh, it's your fans."

"My what?" I stared at her, not sure what she was talking about.

"Cori, do you ever check social media?" Jo gave me an exasperated look.

"No? I mean, if I'm not working, I use my free time to go hiking or read the journals. I don't even remember if I have an account for most of them." I didn't mention I hated that everyone was fixated on looks or sex or conspiracy theories. Spending time with Carelian was much more fun.

Jo gave a small laugh and shook her head. "Well, those are your fans probably here to see you. I'm sure this was publicized, so they would have found out about it."

"Do I need to do anything?" I kept watching as the group of people kept growing and were glancing down at me. The gasps when they saw me and instant chatter with their associates told me all the conversation was about me.

"Wave? Otherwise, don't worry about it." Jo didn't seem to find this odd, but it made my skin crawl.

I kept glancing at them, when someone else approached the table I was at.

"Oh good, you're here." Yolanda's voice interrupted my musing. "I hope you are ready for the questions they'll aks," she fussed, putting her phone and a notebook on the other end of the table from where I was.

"And what would those be?"

"About the Herald of Magic and why you haven't solved this problem yet. Not to mention the problems with closing rips." She sneered at me as she settled down in her seat.

A cold, churning pool of acid started up in my stomach. "Herald of Magic?" I said slowly. I tried to think. Had that ever been said in public? Around people we didn't trust? For the life of me, I couldn't think of anything or anyone that would have spread that. Besides which, who would have taken a comment about me being the Herald of Magic seriously?

I stewed in a mix of worry and confusion until Stephen showed up. He settled in next to me. "You still look like a torture victim. Though seeing you out of the bed is an improvement."

"Yeah, well, helping Tiantang and then talking to Bob really did knock me for a loop. You have any more information about this?"

"Not really. It seems to have come about suddenly, and I have no idea what caused it," he admitted. He had his laptop and a notebook with pens on the table. "We'll just have to see what happens."

The fourth person in our little group was the military general that had been at a surprise symposium last year. The one I'd been yanked from when Hishatio had not showed up to a council meeting.

He nodded at us with a grunt, then sat down, looking very stiff.

"This is going to be a fun meeting, isn't it?" I asked softly.

"Only if your definition of fun is having teeth pulled without Novocain," Stephen replied back. I snickered while we waited for the rest of the hearing committee to be assembled.

CHAPTER

TWENTY-EIGHT

All bands with Spirit mages need to be reviewed for spells laden into the music, declares a music reviewer. Sparky Adams swears that has to be a level of persuasion magic or some sort of compulsion. "There is no way 'Don't Worry, Be Zappy' could be as popular as it is without magic being involved. Even my daughter likes it and she hates everything." Mr. Adams is calling for a review of the laws about mages and music. ~ CNN Mage Focus

CHAOS

We must have been earlier than I thought, or people didn't move as fast as I expected. What I found fascinating was neither Stephen nor Yolanda asked me where Carelian was. I could feel him rumbling under my feet, and it kept me anchored and less anxious than I would have been otherwise.

It also meant we didn't get the constant freak out that newcomers seemed to have around him. Idiots. If they understood what he could and would do, they would have been attempting to bribe him non-stop.

I'd watched the round bench fill up with people. None of them mages, of course. The only mage I could see was the person recording this, a type of court reporter per Alixant.

~I'm going to move a bit. Stay there, but I'd like to see the others with me, without craning my neck,~ I told Carelian. I maneuvered the wheelchair so I was at a slight angle. It let me see at least some expressions and body language of other victims up here with me.

A podium stood off to one side and two people stood there. They were mages. Based on the tattoos, the one dressed in a dark navy suit was a Spirit mage strong in Soul. I'd lay money that was a truth senser, but then how did the elected officials get away with all the lying they did?

When it seemed like no more people were streaming in, though a quick glance behind me revealed a gallery packed like sardines, one of the mages stepped up to the podium.

"Attention. This investigative hearing is being called to order." He went through a bunch of formal things, such as having us swear to answer all questions to the best of our ability. Listing all the senators peering down at us with expressions ranging from curiosity to disdain. After completing all the formalities, the man spoke again from the podium. "The Chair for this hearing is Senator John Williams. Begin your opening statements." He stood at the podium, waiting.

The man in the middle of the curved station was in his sixties, with reading glasses, thinning gray hair, and a florid face. He needed to watch his drinking, given the number of broken capillaries alongside his nose and spreading across his cheeks.

"This is an investigative hearing into the tears occurring between the magical planes and Earth. As well as the dismal response to it. First, we call on Stephen Alixant to explain." He looked up, his eyes locked on Alixant.

I had to fight with my internal desires. The idea of rolling my eyes and storming out poked at me. But right now, I'd get a lot more goodwill using honey instead of vinegar. I wasn't ready to become public enemy number one. I also didn't know how long I'd be able to control my tongue.

"Senator," Stephen said, his voice a cool rebuke to the sneer that had been present in the Senators. "What would you like me to explain?"

"Exactly why you haven't stopped these rips from appearing," the senator snapped, and I caught the flicker of surprise on Stephen's face.

"Because that is something I don't have any ability to do."

Every eye on that bench darted to the man in navy who nodded once. Frowns creased multiple brows.

Senator Williams glared at him. "You have mages in the draft at your disposal. You have the military at your disposal. You have the right to reactivate any mage you want. You are telling me you still don't have the tools you need to stop these rips?"

"That is what I am telling you." Stephen kept his voice

neutral, but I could see his knuckles whitening around the pen in his hand.

The Senator flipped through some paperwork in front of him. "Interesting. General Stone. You had reported that other countries are firing missiles into these rips and it appears to be working. Why aren't we?"

The general's spine stiffened. "Senator. We have been investigating that, but unless the rip occurs in a place where we have that type of equipment, it isn't feasible. We haven't had a land war in literally centuries, and we don't have the same variety of offensive weapons. Those that we do have are not as mobile as you might expect. Even something like tanks only exist in about five bases in the United States. While we can deploy them, tanks don't move very fast and are gas hogs. Unless the rip occurs within a range of about thirty miles, by the time we could get equipment in position, either the rip has closed, been closed, or the casualties would be so high that waiting for us would have been a mistake. The possibility of aircraft is there, but targeting doesn't work on a rip, just the general area, and if we are off by even a degree we would be destroying civilian homes or cities."

He spoke every word in a hard, flat voice and I had the feeling he'd been getting hit with this a lot. I almost felt sorry for him.

"I see. You are saying our military isn't responsive enough?" He sneered at us, peering over his readers. I got the image of a teacher peering down at a recalcitrant child. My temper bubbled.

"No. I am saying our military is not designed for waging battles in this manner. We are adapting as fast as we can, but no matter what, especially given the process funding requires, we are looking at one to two years to implement the capabilities you are suggesting and then another year to get them stationed in multiple areas. Even then, some areas are not easily accessible to the reactive weapons you are talking about. Though we are working on getting more of our smaller squads outfitted with grenade launchers, given the information that was relayed to us last week."

The bench exploded into murmurs as people covered their microphones and talked to each other. After a full minute of chattering to other people, Senator Williams turned and looked back up at us. "Then that leaves us with the mages. Director Alixant and Deputy Rigalio. Have the mages not been working as they are expected to?"

Neither Stephen nor Yolanda looked at each other, but I could see their bodies twitch as they wanted to conference to make sure their answers coincided.

When neither of them spoke first, Stephen gave off a barely audible sigh and leaned forward. "We are working to increase our effectiveness. While we have multiple mages, our rapid response teams have managed to close most level 4 and lower rips in under thirty minutes. Research wise, we haven't learned much that we didn't already know. The only stable rips have always been the ones at Area 51 and the OMO has that information locked down. Deputy Rigalio is the coordinator for the level 5 rips. She ensures the most powerful groups get to those to close them. She has priority levels and determines who to activate and how to get them there."

There were a few scoffs that traveled past the little wall, but the man in the middle didn't glance up, still staring down. Something caught my eye, and I turned. There, at the far side of the curved station, in the row of seats behind the people at the front, was Senator Perry. Most of the glare she focused on our little table was centered on Stephen and me. I frowned. I'd almost forgotten about her and the debacle of reactivating me. It surprised me she was still here. But not that much. I hadn't bothered to pay any attention to the fallout of that meeting. I'd been busy dealing with more important things than her.

"I see. And how has that been going, Deputy Rigalio?" He lifted his head to give her a look. I got the feeling he was expecting her to be trembling.

To my delight, and it made me like her much more, she arched an eyebrow. "It has been going about how we expected. Do you want numbers?"

The senator frowned. "What do you mean 'how we expected'?"

Yolanda shrugged. "We knew sending mages to deal with events for which they had no training, were something most of that population had never encountered, and would have unique challenges every time, would result in a large number of failures. It has resulted in these closure rates." She paused to glance at her paper. "65% of them were closed by the first team to respond. 25% required two teams. 10% required three teams. The last 10% were all closed by the various emergency response teams."

A toothy smile crossed his face, and I watched as most of the people in the gallery behind him leaned forward like sharks scenting blood in the water.

"Ah yes, your response team. Let's talk about it. What is the team and who comprises it?"

"I have five groups. Most of them are merlins that volunteered to be reactivated. They are positioned in major cities across the United States. We use helicopters or small jets to respond to level 5 rips for most of them." She was calm, but at this point I was waiting for what would come.

I should have brought food to eat.

"Really? You said most. Who doesn't that include?"

I could see Yolanda sigh.

"Merlin Cori Munroe is a last resort that is sent out on rips

that have resisted multiple teams or where danger is imminent." Her voice remained cool and collected, but I could see
the tension in her shoulders.

"I see. If she is so good at closing rips, why aren't you
sending her to all of them?"

I could see her getting ready to walk through all of it and
the problems that involved. But I'd been thinking about this,
and I'd always thought this hearing was a modern-day witch
hunt since the moment I heard the word Herald called out. All
of this struck me as ridiculous and wasted time and energy I
literally did not have. Not if I was going to be capable of pulling
a miracle out of my ass later.

So I answered. "Because I refused." The sound of my words
acted like a silencing spell. I had to fight not to laugh as half the
place went still in shock. Maybe it was my arrogance or what I
said.

Senator Williams turned his supercilious look toward me. "I
see. And you are this merlin?"

"Last time I checked." I just smiled, as if none of this bothered me. In truth, it didn't. Nothing they did could measure up
to talking to Bob.

*I really need to get better criteria in my life for what qualifies as
stressful.*

"I believe your draft was reactivated, and yet you are
denying orders from your superior officer?" His smooth voice
tried hard to convey reasonability.

"No. I'm informing the deputy when I have surpassed my
ability to close rips without there being a cost beyond what I
am willing to offer." I knew my bald head had some people's
attention, but the cardigan and the wheelchair hid most of the
physical damage. I wasn't even sure the people in front of me
realized I was in a wheelchair. Table drapes mostly covered my
legs. But I knew the fan section in the gallery behind me was all

too aware. Jo had been whispering updates from my fan pages. She followed all of them, apparently.

Another person leaned forward to their microphone. A woman. They had introduced everyone at the beginning, but I'd glazed over on the names. Just too many to remember, and I didn't care.

"Does this mean you are too good to be a little uncomfortable to save lives, property, infrastructure?" Her voice was snide.

"How much is a five-foot six-inch woman supposed to weigh?" I countered.

"What?" She looked at me, her brows furrowed.

"I believe the Army has five-six at around 145 pounds for a woman." With a soft grunt, I pushed the wheelchair back from the table and stood up. I pulled off the cardigan and put it on the chair. Then, my eyes still locked on the gaggle of idiots, I walked around the desk. "I currently weigh about 109 pounds. I've resorted to offering up blood for the last few times I've been called. I've stripped my hair, my nails, my skin. When I'm healthier, I strip my uterine lining, but I've offered so much my period has stopped. I've even offered eggs. Right now, I refuse unless there is imminent danger to lives, because if what I have left to offer is squandered and I'm rendered incapable, then something tragic might occur. You have other options."

Everyone in the room hung on my words, their eyes locked on my all too gaunt form.

"Cori, Cori, Cori!" A low chant filled the room behind me, and I could see people flicking their eyes up to the public gallery behind me. I just enjoyed the feeling of not being hated by everyone.

"And here I thought you were powerful. The herald of magic." Senator Williams managed not to sound contemptuous—barely.

"I am powerful. I'm also smart about how I use my powers. The other mages are getting better. Learning to approach the problems differently." I turned to sit back down.

"And the herald of magic?"

I stiffened but continued to sit back down in the wheelchair. After I was comfortable, I looked up at them. "What about it?"

"Are you the herald?" The words were soft, waiting. I checked out the responses from other senators. Most of them seemed clueless based on the confused looks they gave him. The truth senser stared at me, waiting.

"That is what others have called me," I said after a few seconds.

A minute nod. It was an interesting set up. I wondered if he was there when they were only talking among themselves. The desire to see if they employed a truth senser in the senate chambers made my fingers twitch, but I just watched them.

"Are you the herald?" The attack came out like an accusation.

I tilted my head and shrugged. "If I am or not, many believe that I am. So, I'm not sure it matters."

He sneered down at me. "I don't believe for a second you are some magical savior sent to fix this, but if you are this herald, why haven't you fixed this issue?"

At this rate I'd be having this conversation in my dreams. "Because I don't know how. If I did, it would already be fixed."

"You got this, Cori. We believe in you! You can do it!"

I twitched, trying not to turn around and stare at whomever was back there yelling this. It was quickly becoming a chant. "We believe in Cori!" More than one senator was watching them with a vaguely horrified look on their face. I still didn't know what to think.

"Try harder," another senator snapped.

My temper began to simmer. "What do you think I'm doing? Did you actually look at me? I'm at the point where I can't walk."

"The penalties for refusing the draft are harsh," someone commented.

"Yeah. You might kill me. If I continue like I've been, I'm dead anyhow. Would you like to try another threat?"

My anger was spiking hard, and I was starting to wonder if I'd make it through this without losing it. Only the fact that I was so low in offering prevented me from doing something really flashy and showy.

"We can hold you in contempt," he warned.

"Go for it. That means I'm in jail and won't be at your beck and call to close rips. Can you handle the outcry?" I fired back, not missing a beat.

"Leave her alone! Can't you see she's trying? What are you doing? We don't see you out there trying to deal with this!"

The noise behind me was incredible, and I managed to keep the smirk off my face, but it was hard.

"This isn't a game!" Senator Williams roared. Though at me or at them, that part was a tossup. "Our constituents are being killed. Buildings destroyed."

"Profits derailed, contributors threatening not to finance your election campaign, and people realizing you don't actually do anything," I responded. Half the people in the room were staring at me, even Stephen.

"Young woman," someone older and in a horrible suit started to snarl.

"No," I said and raised a hand. "I am risking death every time I go out. I am trying very hard to stop all of this. If I am or am not the herald, I am still a mage trying my best to do what is right. You can't threaten me into trying harder. You can't offer anything to help me do this and you have zero idea what is involved in closing these rips."

They spluttered and looked at each other. I sighed. Behind me people were stomping their feet and shouting, "Let her be," over and over. The noise was loud enough I just wanted to cover my ears.

"Order. If we do not get order, this hearing will be closed."

"Let her be, let her be, let her be!" The chant was all I could hear, and I didn't know if I should laugh or groan.

"Merlin Munroe," the senator roared out over the noise of my fans. I tilted my head as if I was listening to him. "You will figure out how to deal with these rips and resolve them."

I sighed, though it was lost in the racket my fans were making. "And if I don't?"

He glared at me. I just smiled. "Hearing is closed!" His bellow barely made it over the stomping and chanting of the viewing gallery. Their chant had changed a bit.

"Let the Herald be! Let the Herald be! Let the Herald be!" Between that, the fact that none of us they were trying to interrogate even blinked at their questions, there was a large subsection of senators that looked about ready to blow a gasket.

~Carelian, want to show off a little?~

~Always.~

~Open a rip in the middle. Make it showy.~

I turned and beckoned Jo to me. "Just push through the rip. Trust me."

She arched a brow but shrugged. Carelian came out from under the table and my watchers went crazy. The screams for my Cath made their attention to me seem like nothing. And the bribery. They were yelling and offering him so much stuff to come be their familiar. If he could be permanently bought, that might have swayed him.

A large rip opened up with the accompanying jab in my mind. Rather than his normal ones, which were usually just tall enough for me if I ducked a bit going through, this one was huge, hitting the ceiling, flaring at the edges with magic. Everyone screamed, fear this time.

I waved to the people behind me, and Jo pushed me into it amid the pandemonium. I caught a glimpse of Stephen caught between rolling his eyes and coming with us. I just laughed to myself and let Jo push me home.

CHAPTER

TWENTY-NINE

Thank you everyone that showed up to support the Marvelous Cori against the government that is trying to cut her down. We strongly believe our presence in the room helped them see how much we support her. As a reminder, you are not to send presents to her—she has stated often that she doesn't need anything and would prefer we support other charities. This week's Walk with Carelian is being done to support the food bank in Albany. Sign-ups are available on the website. See you soon! ~ Email from the Marvelous Cori Fan Group

ORDER

J o and Sable entertained themselves by reading me blurbs and comments from the fan pages every time they saw me. I just groaned, but I paid a bit more attention to my fan pages and the comments on them.

I, for one, still couldn't figure out the comments about me being the Herald. Not to mention trying to deduce who might have told the government that tidbit, much less who they would have believed. The bright side of all of this was the social media and news backlash had been severe. Pictures of me working with Zmaug to stop the lava flow, the aftermath of St. Louis with some camera images of me struggling, and a few that hadn't been as drastic received millions of shares. My public email address had so many emails the server overloaded. I got more random gifts than I knew what to do with. In reality, all I wanted to do was go hide.

A week had passed since the senate hearing. I was finally walking from my house to the Tudor house without being exhausted by the time I reached it and I'd gained five pounds. I still received regular updates from Shay regarding the Library, but no one had found any answers.

On the bright side, Tirsane and the others started creating barren pocket realms to dump magic into. It had the side effect of pulling magic from oversaturated areas. In the last four days, only two rips were reported, which helped lower my stress levels. But I knew it wouldn't last forever. From what Citlali said, creating the barren pocket realms took a significant effort. It had taken two days before any of the lords had regained consciousness. Or at least with Chaos it had been two days before Bob responded to anyone. Tirsane didn't rouse for three days. That meant they wouldn't be able to create them very often.

It left me still with no direction and that was enough to drive me crazy. I'd taken to reviewing James' notebooks, looking for something wild and crazy to try. So far, nothing had jumped out at me.

~Cori, are you free? There are beings that wish to speak with you.~ Carelian's voice pulled me out of my fugue state. I'd been just staring at the journal in my hands, sorting through ideas of something else crazy to do.

"Sure." I closed the book and craned my head to see him standing in the office doorway. "What's up?"

~Not here. Come?~

I rose and slipped on shoes. "Do I need to change clothes?"

~No. This is just a discussion. There should not be any action required.~

I stared at him for a minute, then shrugged. "Sure." He opened a rip and stepped through. I followed him to an area that seemed familiar.

"Isn't this the area in Order where they were offering children to Magic?" That was why I owed Salistra so many favors. Even now, I winced when I thought about my arrogance. When I heard "offered to Magic", I assumed sacrifice. In reality, it had been closer to a baptism. I needed to learn more from my own mistakes.

~Yes. Come.~ He led me through the portal of stone into the plaza. The altar was gone, and it remained the same with paving stones and walls, but this time it brimmed with creatures. I almost tripped over my own feet looking at the gathered beings. I'd never seen such a variety in one place.

~Here, sit.~ Carelian guided me to a bench on a small dais. I fell onto the bench, still staring. There were Chitterians, Aralez, barghest like Dahli, a few Cath, smaller felines, phoenix, quetzo's. A variety of beings that I struggled to wrap my head around. I frowned, sure I'd seen Elsba. But the mass of fur, feather, and scales didn't stay still long enough for me to be sure.

~She is here. Settle down.~ Carelian's voice rang in my mind, and I winced. But the constant movement slowed.

"What is going on?" I asked as I looked out at the sea of creatures. There had to be a few thousand here, maybe more. I couldn't make out the various types of beings that I could sense.

A familiar figure flew up from the milling beings and then over to me, landing on the steps to the dais.

"Jeorgaz," I said, smiling, though I still had no idea what was going on.

~Cori. Carelian, thank you.~ The phoenix nodded to Carelian who had taken up a pose next to me, ensuring he was close enough to me to react, but not so close that it might hamper him from moving. Though what he thought he needed to protect me from, I had no idea.

All of their eyes were locked on me and I had to fight not to shift under the weight of their stares. "So, what's up?"

Jeorgaz flapped his wings and a perch rose out of the stone. ~Much better.~ He gazed out at the sea of creatures, then back at me. ~Cori Munroe, I am sure this is a surprise, but we need to talk to you.~

I tensed up at the use of my full name and managed to not glance over at Carelian. "Okay. Who is we?" I could see all the beings here, but that didn't really tell me anything and the variety was astonishing. There were so many more types than I even knew the names for.

Jeorgaz waved his wing to encompass the area. ~We are some of the familiars for humans. We gathered to here to talk to you.~

I stared again at the sea of creatures and nodded even as I didn't look away from them. "Talk to me about what?"

Please don't let there be another problem I need to solve.

I whispered that in my mind as Jeorgaz puffed up, then settled back down.

~We have tried to warn the council for years that humans possess the capability to damage the realms, but compared to most of the council members, the majority of us are what you would regard as fragile or low magic.~

I couldn't help it. My eyes darted to Carelian. Once he'd passed about five months old, no one could have called him fragile.

Jeorgaz warbled out a laugh. ~No, not the Cath, or the Aralez, or even the barghest. But me? A Chitterian? The quetzo's? All of them are easy to damage or kill, especially if attacked by our humans. And we all know that consistency when it comes to humans is not the norm.~

I bobbed my head in agreement. I'd been on enough 911 calls to know something could go from simple to insane in a split second.

~The lords should have reacted and been prepared for what humanity could do but know that we believe and are all too aware of the devastation humans can cause.~

I wanted to wrap them all in hugs. "It's okay. They did not want to believe me either. Some people you need to just let them learn the hard way." It felt good to know others had known this was possible. But it didn't really change anything.

~It is our fault the humans know you are the herald.~ Jeorgaz sounded oddly formal.

"What? How?"

~I am speaking for many, but some of us told our humans that the herald was coming. That the Herald of Magic would save us and stop the rips. Most did not believe us, but some did, and their reactions were not what we would have expected. They panicked and went to your governments and eventually it made it up to the blind ones, starting all this.~ His feathers drooped as he talked, and his fiery colors dimmed.

"Ah," I said, a light coming on. "Someone or multiple some-one's told them about the Herald and that it was me and one of them was a bigger jerk than they realized and let the senate and others know. That at least makes sense. I couldn't figure it out." Now it was my turn to sag a bit. That puzzle had been driving me crazy .

~You are not angry at us?~ The words contained a strange hum as if multiple creatures were sending it simultaneously but unwilling to directly say it to me.

"No. Why would I be mad? People are idiots and even if someone told their mage thinking something would happen, it wasn't anything they could control. Besides it isn't a secret, it just isn't anything most humans would believe. They would laugh and assume you were talking in hyperbole or that you had misunderstood. I mean, I'm almost more impressed any of the mages took you seriously."

~It is an issue. Many of our mages assume we are no more intelligent than children. You are different.~ Jeorgaz was almost humming as he spoke.

I rolled my eyes. "Nope, I just treat people like people. It isn't that hard. So, is that all?" Finding out this helped a bit, but it didn't change anything in the long run and I didn't know what they wanted from me.

~They wanted you to know that if you need them, you can call on them. They will bring mages to you or other things you might need.~

That had me jerking upright. "Wait all of you can open rips home, right? Can you do it to the crossroads and then to another focus or to me?"

Jeorgaz turned to look at the sea of creatures and the background hum intensified to an almost physical level. I turned my head to look at Carelian, who had his ears down and eyes slitted.

"Carelian, are you okay?" I scratched the top of his head as I waited for an answer.

~Yes. They are loud and discordant.~ His reply was curt, but he sent an image of kids screaming in a play area. I managed to stifle my laugh.

~The consensus is yes. Not all of us, but most could. It is the biggest thing we have always hidden from mages. Humans do not react well to discovering that we can do that.~ The words were weighted oddly, and my memory flashed to what he was implying.

"Ah. No, I believe you are right. If they are not someone you can trust implicitly, you should not let them know. And I'm not talking trust them with your life, but everyone's." I bit my lip a bit and started to talk, thinking out loud. "What I would need is to know what mage is available with a familiar that Carelian could grab, but no. There are too many, too many countries. I can't take them from other places. I'm still worried about the cost to other countries." I fell silent, thinking it all through. My hand still petting Carelian as it kept me grounded and calm.

I took a deep breath, then sighed. "I thank you for the offer and if I can think of anything I will ask, but right now the risks are too great for too little value. I would say help your mages as much as possible so that they can close the rips quickly. Let others know if you see something that works better or if there are new dangers we should prepare for. Mostly just try to help. There are people fighting this globally, not just me. If you can share info that others can learn...." I trailed off and grinned as it occurred to me. "That's it. You can share information regardless of language or political barriers. Share information." My grin got even larger. "Arachena, are you here?"

The Chitterian bounced across heads until she reached the steps. ~Yes.~

"You are a pattern weaver. Help Charles create new patterns. Gather all the information from the familiars and let Charles use it, process it. That will help more than anything else ever could. Information.~

There were excited sounds, and it reminded me of people being told how they could assist in an emergency.

"One other question," I said as something else occurred to me. "If you know of anything regarding how the Undoing happened or where we might look, please let me know. I have zero idea what to do next and even the Library isn't helping."

There was another chitter of response, then the familiars started to disappear one by one.

"Thank you Jeorgaz. Let me know of anything or if they need something." I paused. "Do you have the ability to leave your mage if they hurt you? I mean familiars in general."

Carelian, Jeorgaz, and Arachena all seemed to avoid looking at me. Arachena's way of doing that was the oddest, as she turned completely around, her eyes all facing away from me.

"What?" Fear wrapped me. Would something bad happen to Carelian? No, we'd talked about this. So what was it?

~You can,~ Carelian said, though he wouldn't look at me. ~But it is a great mark of shame and failure. That you have poor judgement. It is unlikely any other denizen will ever trust you again. Many would rather die than return with people knowing they left their mage, no matter how bad the abuse.~

I stared at them, then asked, "So why don't they kill them? I mean their mage would be dead, they could return home, and there is no way for human authorities to find them, much less punish them. And I don't see how any other denizen would know that is how the mage died."

All three of them whipped around to stare at me. Horrified is an odd expression on a cat and a bird. Arachena just curled up with all her legs under her and rocked.

~Kill our mage? My quean?~ Carelian sounded like he was choking.

"What, it never occurred to any of you? Humans can be awful. If a familiar found themselves in a bad place, why not kill the mage and then go home, the mage having tragically died?" I wasn't sure what the issue was. A familiar couldn't press charges against their mage in either world. If they had to protect themselves, why not make sure that person couldn't hurt anyone else ever again?

They sputtered at me, unable to even form coherent responses. I shook my head. "I'm just saying, if leaving a mage is that bad, and the abuse makes leaving the mage the only option, why not kill that mage?" I rubbed my temples. "I can't believe I'm condoning murder, but I don't know of any recourse a familiar has. Just saying it is an option."

None of them reacted, and I sighed. "Come on, Carelian. We should go and I need to call Charles and warn him about the deluge of data about to hit him."

In 1963, President Kennedy set up Executive Order 11119 requiring all merlin level mages to serve a decade. This was sparked by outcries by other mages who were running themselves dry to do what a merlin could do without a thought. There was a push that if you were that powerful you owed society more time. Kennedy agreed and signed the Executive order. ~ History of Magic

SPIRIT

The familiars refused to talk about the idea of killing their mage. Given their reactions, I was relieved I hadn't said it to the familiars that had gathered to speak to me. But I wondered what or if things would change. The blind spots we all had amazed me sometimes. Though I had my own collection of them.

Charles was ecstatic about the amount of data he was getting. He promised to let me know when he had any information. I reminded him to let Stephen know if new techniques appeared that were working elsewhere. Other than that, I sat and ate and tried to figure out what to do.

"I need to go into a rip," I said while Carelian and I were in my study. There were books piled around me. I'd read the one from Brashera twice, and while the book held interesting tidbits, he talked very little about his parents.

~You go into rips all the time.~ Carelian was making sure his pelt was perfect.

"I know, but I need to go into one of the tears that are forming spontaneously. See if I can close it from the other side."

He stilled, ears flicking back, then forward. ~That is exceedingly dangerous.~

"Maybe. But I'm thinking if I can get Shay and Citlali to come with me, we can explore it. See if there is evidence as to what caused the rip. Maybe new insights for closing them." I'd figured since doing it from the outside wasn't working well, maybe from the inside would.

He went back to grooming without responding.

"Is that a yes? Will you help?" Carelian would refuse to do something if he thought I would be at too much risk, and this might be pushing his comfort levels. Unfortunately, I didn't see much else I could try.

~Depends. If lava is involved, absolutely not. We are not salamanders or djinn.~ His voice was hard.

"Agreed. Only one where I'm pretty sure we will survive. I'm not trying to get myself killed. I just want to see if we can do something from the other side a bit easier."

He shifted to his hind leg which I was going to take as tacit agreement. I checked the time. It was still early. Hopefully both of them were still at home.

I called Citlali first. "Hello Cori," she said in her calm tones. The woman should record books to help you meditate. Her voice was that soothing. "Is there an issue?"

"Always, you know that. Let me grab Shay? That way, I only need to discuss this once."

I put her on hold and called Shay. "I'm still drinking my coffee. I do not deal with emergencies prior to my first cup."

I couldn't help the chuckle as I agreed with him. "No emergencies. Let me pull in Citlali." A moment later, they were both on the call. "Okay, here is the thought. The next rip I get called out to seal I want to grab you two and, if it isn't Chaos, whoever the lord for that realm is, and step through."

They both choked. Stepping into wild rips was dangerous. Lava wasn't the major danger. You just never knew where you would end up. It could be the ocean, a desert, a place where magic ran wild. As best any of them had been able to explain to me, there were areas where magic was still creating, and no one had dominion over them. Tirsane, Salistra, Esmere, the others, were all powerful because they controlled so much area. I'd tried to nail Esmere down one time and as best as she could figure it was thousands of square miles. She told me she could run for three days, sleeping at night, before she hit the edges of her controlled territory. She preferred her savannahs, but she had jungles, rivers, even lakes that were part of what she kept regulated and let all the creatures live.

"Why not Chaos? And do what?" Shay squeezed out.

"See if it is easier to close from that end? I don't know. But it is literally the only thing I haven't tried. If there are any other options, I'm unaware of them. And if it is in Chaos, Carelian should be able to guide us well enough."

There was silence except for Shay shipping on his coffee.

"Kesis says yes. It should be interesting. Maybe we will find new unexplored areas," Citlali responded after a minute.

"She sounds much more enthusiastic than Carelian. I had to promise only a rip that looked like it was moderately safe," I admitted, settling back into my chair. I had chocolate with cream and sugar. I'd already had two cups of coffee and needed more than just caffeine.

"Do I want to know what he regarded as unsafe?" Shay asked, sounding wary.

"Lava, ocean, you know, deadly things."

"I am getting way too old for this stuff. You should have told me you needed a young Scott Randolph. This is not politics, this is adventuring. Why couldn't this have happened thirty years ago? That would have been right up my alley." Shay's muttering made me smile. He was still very fit and if anything, it had revitalized him, though the circles under his eyes weren't a good look.

"Okay, then I'll let you know when I grab one. Just keep clothes nearby. Usually I'm up and out in less than ten minutes," I warned. While I had zero doubt Citlali could do that, Shay might need a bit of prodding.

"Why does that feel like a disparagement directed at me?" he huffed. "I'll be there. Now go. I want to finish getting caffeinated and Sloan is making me breakfast." He hung up with that.

I laughed, said goodbye to Citlali and hung up. Then I dialed Yolanda.

"Yes, Merlin Munroe?" Her voice wasn't friendly, but neither was it rude. I'd take it.

"Call me for the next level 5 you get. I have a new option I want to try."

"Can others do it? You looked like hell Monday. I was planning on calling 911 if you fell." Her voice was sharp and direct, no sympathy, just someone dealing with resources.

"Oh, I'm getting better. I can function without a wheelchair but the walk through airports and the capitol building would have knocked me out. Mostly it was so I could talk without being beyond exhausted."

She snorted. "You should have seen the pandemonium after you left. It amused me. I'll call. It has been quiet of late, so I'm hopeful."

"Always. Thanks." I hung up and looked at Carelian, who had laid back to stretch.

"You know I'd rather spend my life hiking and exploring the world with you, right?"

He huffed and stood up. ~I chose a quean. They do not live boring lives. If I wanted something boring, I would have followed my siblings. ~ Carelian walked over and rubbed against my hand. ~That does not mean I enjoy seeing you putting yourself at risk.~

"I know. I'd rather be in the mountains hiking, too." I stared at the useless books. "I thought of something after talking to Bob," I said idly.

~Before or after you passed out from pain?~ His voice was bitter.

"Before, actually. I just didn't remember the thought until now. The gift I gave Tirsane. She said it was of a sea serpent, one so old his thoughts were uncomfortable. She had no idea how James got a hold of it. What if there is something on that one, or one of the other stones he has that contains information about Atlantis? Or maybe the Undoing."

His ears twitched back and forth in thought. ~That is possible. There are many memory stones that are only historical that people have kept as mementos. Esmere has multiples. We tend to regard them as just family history, nothing important.~ His words were slow as he thought them through.

I tamped down hard on the hope that spurted up in my chest. The odds were nothing would come of this. But if it was possible. "I'll ask Freya to send out a notice. It might trigger something."

Carelian nodded. ~You do realize no one is purposefully not helping. Or at least most of us aren't. We just don't live in the past as much as humans do. This isn't things we think of often. I have listened to my great-great *malkin*'s stories. But it never occurred to me they would be of any use in something like this. Even the old songs. They are.... ~ He trailed off, trying to explain.

I got up and kissed the top of his furry head. "I get it. They are like antique photos. You look at them and go 'oh cool' but unless something grabs you, they aren't something you pay attention to or remember. It's okay. But now that we are thinking about it, let's not let it slip." There was no time like the present, so I pinged Freya. The last time she had visited, I got her address for lack of a better word.

~Freya, do you have a minute?~

While I waited, I headed downstairs to find something to munch on. When all this was over, I was going to have to relearn how to eat. Butterball wasn't a body shape I wanted. A snicker escaped me as I headed to the kitchen. Most people didn't complain about being encouraged to eat as much as possible.

~Yes, Lord Cori,~ Freya responded into my mind. I rocked

back a bit. She didn't yell, but the power in her voice was a bit intense.

~Freya,~ I frantically wondered if she had a title I was supposed to use. Oh well, too late now. ~I had an idea about memory stones. Could you place a request to all in the realms to review all their memory stones, especially those that are older, and see if there is any mention of Atlantis or the Undoing? There might be old memories that you never think of that contain the information we need. That I need.~

There was a long pause. ~Huh. That can be done. Valkyrie don't use the memory stones. We have our scrolls and those were gone through quite thoroughly, but as for other beings, that is not always true. Many of them are regarded as ... amusements, not things with information. Yes. I will spread the word - though asking Jeorgaz might be almost faster.~

I frowned at her words, though the refrigerator took the brunt of my confusion. ~Why Jeorgaz?~

Another pause, then a tinkle of laughter washed through my mind. ~Truly, you do not know?~

~Know what?~ By this point I'd closed the refrigerator door. Nothing looked good, and I stood staring at the ceiling.

~Jeorgaz is the gossip of the familiars and the bard for most of the realms.~ The amusement in her voice grabbed my attention more than anything else.

~What? I don't understand.~

~Jeorgaz visits almost everyone. He loves to share news and tidbits and makes sure everyone knows what happens at the council meetings. That is why he is usually there, though hiding up in the gallery. He is the one that will bring issues to the lords. It was one of the reasons Brix had so many issues with his presence. I won't say he is loved by all, but he is respected and we need his chattiness.~

I just stared at the refrigerator, reassessing every interac-

tion with Jeorgaz and his desire to chat and tell me bits of information. I had thought it was just with James. ~Wait, he was a
chick because he had his burning day not long after James died.
How could he have done that?~

~That was his job, even with James. But is also part of the
reason the council had been in such a disarray. While he was a
chick, no one stepped up to take his role.~ A touch of chagrin
slipped into her voice. ~It is why Brix managed to get us to this
state. The stuff I've uncovered.~ She sighed. ~But that is not
your problem. I will put out the ask and let Jeorgaz know to
spread the word. Is there anything else?~

~No thank you.~ I had already turned to head back
upstairs, climbing the moving stairs to speed up my ascension.
She had faded from my mind by the time I hit my office. Carelian still lounging on the window seat. "Did you know Jeorgaz
was like the gossip of the realms?"

~Of course. Who else could navigate between all of them so
easily?~ He didn't even lift his head. ~Birds are chatterboxes.~

I threw a pillow at him and sighed.

In a graphic scene, Cori Munroe was caught on film attacking a dragon in China while the military let her do it all by herself. You can see the blood from the uploaded phone video as Merlin Munroe tortures the creature. Rumors are that it was later offered as a sacrifice to Empress Cixi herself. ~ Magical Daily News

---

CHAOS

The stupid phone jerked me out of my sleep at three am. It took me a second to find it. The last few days I'd almost gotten enough sleep and my hair was half an inch. I really couldn't carry off bald well.

"Yeah," I answered, knowing Yolanda was on the other end.

"You wanted a level 5. I've got one. It opened up in Peoria. It's all but engulfed a bridge."

I rubbed sleep out of my eyes even as I dragged myself out of bed. At some point I'd laid out the clothes I'd need if this happened, so I was dressing with the phone on speaker as she spoke. "What does that mean? Engulfed?"

There was a sigh on the other end, mixed with a yawn. I shared that sentiment. "The rip is right across the Illinois Bridge. Like literally, you can walk into the rip from the bridge – if you were that stupid. Since it happened in the wee hours of the morning, as far as I'm aware, no one did. But there are creatures coming out. The Illinois State police have a perimeter set up and are killing them as they come through, but this rip is huge, and it looks like there is some sort of formation on the other side? I'm not quite sure. You don't look into rips, but it looks like some rock formation is slowly forming on the other side?" She sounded unsure.

"Well, that works great for my plan. Let them know I'm coming, and I'll have guests."

"Oh Merlin. Please, no more dragons. The emails and calls I got from that one still haven't stopped." Yolanda sounded a bit panicked. I enjoyed that more than I should have.

Quit being a bitch.

I pushed down my internal thoughts and responded. "Well, it should be two humans and a fox along with Carelian. Worst case another gorgon or a unicorn," I said while trying not to laugh. "I'll be there in ten or so."

"I swear I should get hazard pay for dealing with you. You cause as much drama as you prevent. Whatever, just let me know what is going on when you can." Yolanda hung up with nothing more than that.

I took a minute to load up my backpack and get Carelian into his harness. This was one advantage of Jo and the kids being at the Tudor house—I didn't have to worry about waking them up.

"Hamiada?"

"Yes, Cori?" Her voice filled the house as I headed down the stairs. "Let Jo and Sable know when they wake up where I went, please? But don't wake them up for this. I'll have Citlali and Shay with me."

"Very well. Please do not be injured," she said with her odd cadence. "I will wait."

"Thanks." I put food and protein drinks in the bag while I made coffee. One for me, one for Shay. He would not be appreciative of this wake-up call. "You ready Carelian?" I had the address on the phone and zoomed out the map so he could see where we needed to go.

We popped into the gray crossroad, then a minute later stepped onto the bridge in Illinois, behind the cops.

"Please let Kesis know I'm here and go get Shay."

Carelian scanned the cops, who were looking at me with wide eyes and fingers clenched on weapons. ~You are not allowed to be injured.~

"I won't be. Go." I rubbed his ear as reassurance.

He stepped away, and I walked over to the cops. "Hi. I'm Merlin Munroe. I was dispatched out here to see about this rip?" I kept my voice light and lilting. They were already on edge, so me being arrogant wouldn't help.

A man with two bars pinned to his collar came over to me. In his forties, with skin the color of burnished mahogany, he had stress lines at the corner of his eyes and a grim look on his face. "You're going to close this?"

"That's the plan. What can you tell me?" I continued to keep my voice light and with a mug of coffee in each hand, I was pretty sure my frail frame and fuzzy head didn't present a threatening appearance.

He scanned me, eyes lingering on my odd tattoo. "It opened about two hours ago. We know some of these just close again without any interference, so we set up barricades and set to monitor it. The other side just ends into air. As if the bridge stops, but on this side, you can see it goes on in."

I nodded, peering at the area. It was about two hundred yards away, stretching across both sides of the bridge. This bridge had one section going north, then open air, then the next section going south. There were cops on both the north and southbound lanes about twenty strong on each side, with rifles and shotguns.

"What does the other side look like?" If Carelian was here, we could have moved over to look. I guessed I could sidestep, but that took offerings I didn't want to spend.

The man grunted, pulled out his phone, and called someone. "Paul, flip on video and show me the other side. Do a slow pan back and forth."

"Yes, sir." He held the phone out to me, and I took a look. There were only two cop cars and barricades on each side over there. I could see people far behind watching just like on this side. But he was right, the bridge just ended. It reminded me of the cartoons where they would erase part of the scenery. Everything was there, then it wasn't.

"That is oddly creepier than I expected." I handed the phone back to him.

"You're telling me. Thanks, Paul." He hung up. "Can you close it?"

"Maybe?" I hated guaranteeing anything at this point. "Right now, I'm waiting for some back up and we are going to go check it out. What can you tell me about what is coming through?"

He jerked his head to the side and moved over to one of the edges. There an animal lay, dead from gun shots, and I forced down a shudder. Most of the realm creatures were either from our various mythologies or very closely resembled animals on earth. This was not one of those instances. It looked like a wolf mixed with an iguana. All teeth, scales, and muscle. If one of those had been running at me, I'd have had a heart attack.

"Do you know if anyone tried to talk to them?"

He gave me a long side eye glance. "If screaming 'go away, get out of here' counts as talking to them, yes. Otherwise, no."

I shrugged. "Did they stop and go back in?"

"No. They attacked the cars. Luckily, no one was stupid enough to step out, so we've been killing them as they step through. I have a mage or two and they looked at the rip and let me know it was way too big for them to close."

"Yeah," I said nodding. "It's going to be a pain. I need to get closer to that."

"Why?" He didn't quite grunt the word, but it was close.

"Trying to get more information to see if we can stop these. I'm tired of applying band aids." I took a mouthful of coffee, the rich scent a nice balm to my spirit in the cool evening.

"Come on then." He spun on his heel and started toward the rip. "Men, keep your eyes open and for Merlin's sake, don't shoot us."

I fought back a snicker and followed him. We'd only made it a few steps when I felt a stab. "Wait a moment, back up is arriving." He halted to turn and look at me. I pivoted to see Kesis step out of a rip with Citlali right behind her. Citlali looked like she'd been up for hours, had taken a shower and everything. I might have hated her right then, as I was being forcefully reminded I hadn't taken the time to brush my teeth. A moment later, Carelian came out with Shay.

"Really Munroe? Three in the morning. You couldn't wait until one at a decent hour?" Shay was bitching the second he stepped out of the rip.

"Don't look at me. I had nothing to do with the timing of this, and I was woken up like you were." I handed him the coffee, which he grasped with both hands.

"Really?" The amount of sarcasm in his voice made me pause. "You were awakened by a three-hundred-pound cat standing on you and licking your nose? I'd like to point out I'm not used to opening my eyes to see a deadly predator inches from my face." He all but snarled that last point, hands white around the tumbler.

I glanced at Carelian, surprised.

~I do not weigh three hundred pounds, that would be fat. I was 185 last time I got on a scale. And it is all muscle.~ Carelian sniffed, holding his head up in the air.

"It felt like three hundred and you have horrible fish breath," Shay sniped back, but his focus had changed to the coffee.

I fought back a laugh, and took another mouthful of my coffee. Coffee breath had to be better than mouth funk. "Morning, Citlali. You two ready to see the other side?"

"Yes, this should be interesting," she said with a calm smile. "Though remember, I have roamed through the beast realms quite a bit."

"No, I want to go back to bed," Shay snapped back, but he was walking toward us and actually had clothes on to go hiking.

"Excellent. We are ready now, sir," I said, turning back to the officer.

For his part, he gazed over all of us, his attention lingering on Carelian and Kesis. "Okay. It's on your heads."

"I, for one, agree with him. Why are we doing this?" Shay managed not to whine, but it had a level of petulance to it.

"Because I have zero idea why magic is bursting out, and neither does anyone else. I mean, we know it is overloaded, but that doesn't really explain why it is ripping through or what could be done to mitigate it. This might give us some information." I narrowed my eyes at him, the cold night air and the odd level of quiet around us making my words ring louder than I would have preferred. "So, unless you have some new information for us, I don't know what else to try."

He hunched his shoulders and peered out from under his eyebrows in a glare.

"Really?" I waved my hand at him. "You're worse than me when I was nineteen."

Shay dropped the attitude and stood up. "Ouch. Fine." He rolled his eyes. "I'll go, but I want to point out I left a warm bed for this."

"And I didn't?" I moved and walked toward the rip. My left hand was still wrapped around the mug. It was one of my stainless steel ones. If needed, I could throw it. It hurt when it hit. At least according to my toes.

~I agree with Shay, we should all go back to our warm beds.~ Carelian sat and stared at the rip. ~The next one will be better.~

"Oh, why would the next one be better?"

~Because it might not be Chaos. We should not go into this one.~ His tail was lashing back and forth as he stared at the rip.

"Is there any deadly environmental danger?" I had zero desire to walk into lava or gas clouds.

~No,~ he admitted, his tail still lashing. ~But Chaos is always more unpredictable than the others.~

"We got this. Two familiars, three merlins. We can do this." I moved away from him to look at the stone that was indeed blocking the rip. It protruded out, grinding into the cement of the bridge. "What is this?"

Citlali and Shay had both come over to look at the stone with me. The two familiars were prowling back and forth, neither of them at all relaxed. That jacked my stress level and awareness up as well.

"Huh," Shay said, tilting his head. "I think I recognize this, but this rate of growth doesn't make sense." He turned around and yelled back at the cops. "What time did the rip open?"

"12:04 A.M.," someone yelled back.

Shay knelt to look at the cement. "It looks like there is a one-inch long scrape here in what, two and a half hours?" he said after glancing at this watch. For us it was almost three-thirty in the morning, but for Illinois it was only two-thirty.

"What do you mean, you recognize this?" Citlali was leaning over him, peering at the stone. "Isn't it just rock?"

"No. It's something that we barely agree on how it works. And I thought it only existed in Romania." Citlali and I were both just staring at him. "I'm a geologist, remember? It is something called trovants. It is rock that grows and even gives birth to other rocks. But it grows like an inch or two a century, not an hour." He stared at it a bit longer, then a slow smile spread across his mouth. "If this is caused by magic, I've got a paper that is going to make the rest of those stick-in-the-muds choke on their own arrogance."

In the news again today, more planar rips in Europe. A summit is being held next week to address responses to this rising threat and the OMO is expected to attend. However, no one seems to have an answer other than throwing more mages at the rips. The United States is by far the least affected mostly due to the efforts of one merlin – Corisande Munroe. ~ CNN Mage Focus

ORDER

"Oookay," I said, drawing it out. "Does it affect anything that is going on right now?"

Shay stood and shrugged. He stared at it for another minute, then drained the coffee. "Maybe, maybe not. We won't know until we get in there. You ready?" Where before he'd been reluctant, now he looked like he was about to start bouncing in place with excitement.

I gave Citlali, who'd mostly been quiet a look. She shrugged. "Might as well."

~Fine, follow me when I say it is clear. If I say stop, stop.~ Carelian's voice was more discordant, almost jangly. He stepped into the rip.

I stood there waiting, unable to breathe. When he created rips, I could see where I was going. This was like looking into a swirl of something that pulled at my heart and threatened to rend my mind.

~Enter,~ he said, and I closed my eyes and walked through. Every other rip I'd been in felt like stepping across a threshold. Sometimes into the heat or cold, but most of the time it was oddly neutral. This time it felt like what I'd imagine a sea of sticky caramel to feel like. It pushed against me, tried to pull me under, and then refused to let me move.

And that was the physical. Mentally it was like talking to Bob and Salistra, but muffled and seductive. I kept leaning forward, trying to listen to what I could almost hear, even as I pulled back because of the pain. The last step through, I stumbled, my knees threatening to buckle as I was freed from the in between.

The three of us stood there, panting and shaky, while the two familiars watched us.

~I told you this was not wise. But still, better this than Order.~

I breathed in and the scents of rich flowers, jungle, wet, and moss surrounded me to the point I almost choked on it. Shaking off my disorientation, I looked around, letting my eyes focus on something other than Kesis and Carelian. It took three passes to make sense of what my eyes told me and even then, I'm pretty sure what I saw was what my mind could create comparisons to, kind of. If you took the jungles of Hawaii, dumped them into the swamps of Louisiana, then added an active volcano and traveling boulders, you might have a general idea that wouldn't even be close to what we stood in.

Wetness seeped into my shoes as my feet steamed. "The water is hot," I said, still staring at my feet and the mud that was baking around them.

~Yes. This is a Chaos realm. Nothing is orderly.~ The sarcasm in Carelian's tone snapped me back to some logic.

"Oh. Yeah." I scrambled up to the log to where Carelian and Kesis were. The thick mud dropped off my boots with sickening plops. Citlali joined me up there, but Shay was poking at the boulders, muttering to himself.

"Are they what you thought they were?" I asked as I tried to clean the mud off my shoes.

"Yes, but maybe a new formation. This is fascinating. Is this a realm or area we can get back to? I didn't realize that the realms had geological activity." He didn't look at us as he spoke, still busy poking at the rocks.

~Possibly. It depends on how magically stable this region is. Not very would be my guess since we are here because of the rip.~ Carelian's voice was so without inflection it hurt.

Shay flinched and moved toward us. "Yes, point." He clambered up with us, looking around. "So what are we looking for, anyhow?"

I shrugged. "Not a clue. Something to show why this is ripping here?" I looked around. From this side you could see the bridge and the police cars arrayed around us. "Odd. We can see from this area but not in." Something from my physics classes tickled the back of my mind. "Is it just me, or does this kind of remind you of how collapsed stars are thought to work? Everything being a single direction?"

Citlali shrugged. "That isn't anything I have training in, but I can ask our scientists and researchers."

Shay tilted his head. "It's been a long time, but if I follow that, you are saying something exploded here and that is why it is a one-way view."

"Maybe?" I wasn't positive, but it seemed viable. A long hair-raising howl set up in the distance and we all turned. My heart pounded as we looked. "What was that?"

~Most likely more of the creatures that were killed outside. These are probably hunting grounds. I smell many small creatures. It is an area rich in creatures to eat.~

I nodded. It meant we needed to move fast. "Let me see if I can close it from this side." My magic reached out to feel along the rip. It was odd—from the other side it always felt like a zipper with teeth that needed to interlace. Here it was different. The magic pressed against it, wanting to escape, to find someplace new. The pressure of it ebbed and surged. My mind twisted, feeling it out, trying to figure it out.

"Shay, is there anything you can see that might have caused the rip? You said those stones are pretty unique." He jumped off the log, ignoring the squelch of mud as he hit.

"Let me look." He began to poke around, humming under his breath.

"Citlali, do you know anything?" The howls were getting closer.

"That there is a hunting pack headed our way and all of us except Carelian will be regarded as easy prey?" She had a knife in her hands and was facing the jungle around us.

I might have been more worried, but her wide grin told me she was looking forward to it.

"In other words, no?" I sighed and looked around. There were so many plants, rocks, moss, mud, grass, and decaying vegetation that I had zero idea what I was even looking at. But what I didn't see were any signs of an explosion in the vicinity. If there had been a disruption, I couldn't see any evidence. Maybe there wasn't anything to see? I froze, thinking. Or nothing humans could see.

"Carelian?" I asked, turning to look at him. He was focused on the trees behind us and even I could see shuffling shapes in there. An ear flicked back at me. "Can you see magic?"

This garnered a full head turn, then back to his prey. ~Not how you mean. If you are asking are their signs of an explosion that are not visible to human eyes... maybe? But it is more along the lines of gas bursting into flames when a match nears it. Glorious destruction, little evidence.~ He lowered down, only the tip of his tail twitching.

The incident he referenced was Marisol one day, back at her house in Georgia, had been talking too much when she went to ignite her gas burner. The automatic pilot light had gone out ages ago and as a Fire mage it wasn't any effort for her to start a spark. It whooshed up, creating a huge flame and singeing her eyebrows. He'd been properly impressed with the ferocity of the stove for months afterward.

"Huh. So maybe magic pools up and explodes when something ignites it," I muttered mostly to myself.

"You know that might explain this and why the stones are growing into the rip and our world," Shay said.

That shook me out of my mental wanderings. "What?"

"So, these stones. We've always thought they collected minerals from the water and it caused a swelling effect that enabled them to grow and even move to a certain extent. But, if there was an explosion of magic and it fed into these trovants even as it ripped through the fabric of reality, then that might explain everything."

"Explain everything what?" I walked down the log toward him but didn't step back into the warm mud. Hamiada was going to be upset regardless.

"Why they move and grow even on Earth. This has already grown since we've been here. It's amazing."

I'd never seen Shay this excited about anything. It was a new look.

~You need to close the rip quickly. The packs are coming, and you are not fighters.~ Carelian's voice cut into our discussion and I turned to see that he had disappeared.

He's a cat. He's hunting.

The reminder didn't stop the spurt of worry as I stared at where he'd been.

"They aren't, but Kesis and I are." Citlali turned to look at me. "You and Shay work on the rip and I'll help with the enemies incoming." As she said the words, she dropped off the log and all but vanished, Kesis right behind her.

The words of "don't go" and "be safe" caught in my throat. They would not be appreciated or wanted. Instead, I turned to Shay. "You heard them. We need to get this closed and I can't with the rocks in the way."

"Trovants," he corrected. "But I know this geological structure. I can fracture it. Once it is broken, pushing or pulling it through shouldn't be hard. You think you can close it after that?"

I checked what was blocking the rip. A bit of dirt and mud, but mostly it was the rocks, growing ever thicker. "Yes. And the faster, the better."

A howl, a hiss, and a strangled cry sounded behind me. I started to turn, needing to see what was going on.

No, focus on your job. Trust him. Trust them.

It ranked up there with some of the hardest things I'd ever done, not turning and rushing to help. The sounds of battle filled the area behind us: yelps, snarls, growls, and, most disturbing, the random laugh from Citlali.

Shay had wide eyes as he gazed behind me. "Stop it. We can't help. Start breaking and I'll start closing." He bobbed his head up and down, his face going paler, but to his credit, he turned and began to use magic at what seemed an exorbitant rate. His long braids were vaporizing as he moved.

I almost said something, but the stones that were blocking the way were splitting in half. This I could help with. The more education you got, the more finesse you had. It seemed like I could never learn enough, but brute strength I was experienced at using. With a tug on Earth, which was sluggish to respond, I rocked the ground in front of the rip and flipped the broken stones either forward onto the bridge or back away from blocking anything.

"Oh yes, magic is at play. Even where I broke pieces off of them, they are regrowing fast enough I can see it." Shay was poking at a trovant again.

"Shay, now is not the time."

"Oh, yeah." He went back to breaking. At least he was cutting them a good foot from the wall, but the sounds were getting louder.

~Cori, while this is great fun, the numbers are becoming more than we can easily handle. It might be a good idea to speed this up.~ Carelian's voice was conversational, but given how easily I'd seen him carve through things before I knew he meant it.

"You clear, Shay?" I yelled as the battle sounds were even louder and I was constantly flinching and struggling not to turn and race toward Carelian.

"I think so. Try it now," he called as he stepped back away from the tear.

I grabbed the rip and started to press it together. Oddly, when the edges got close enough, it was like a magnetic pull, and they started to snap together as I pushed. It cost me so little compared to what I'd been fighting with. With a mental snap, the gaping wound in reality disappeared and revealed more of the odd jungle and a bubbling hot spring not a hundred yards away.

"This place makes no geological sense. I love it." I'd never seen Shay with his eyes shining.

"Yep, but we aren't staying. Carelian, it's closed." I yelled the words as I turned, hunting for his ruby red coat in the jungle swamp.

~Opening now, get through it.~ A slice of pain and I glanced over my shoulder to see a long vertical rip waiting for me, the bridge on the other side.

"Not without you," I said, standing there. A roar shook the air, and I heard trees fall. "Carelian?"

Citlali came booking out of the greenery she'd disappeared in. She was spattered with blood and had a huge smile on her face, while Kesis ran beside her. "Time to go."

"Yep, I'm gone," Shay said.

I started to walk backward, unwilling to leave without Carelian.

"Cori, come on."

"No. He has to come with us."

"Cori," Citlali said, exasperated. "He'll be right behind us. Now come on."

I didn't turn around though I took a few more steps backward until I could feel it at my back. "Carelian?"

A flash of ruby red caught my eye, and I focused on the Cath racing at me at top speed. I smiled at that sight, then froze as I caught sight of what was behind him. It looked like a cross between a rhino and a bear. Teeth, horns, gleaming eyes, and a tough furry hide that I wasn't sure a bazooka would get through.

~Go! Now!~ The force of his words pushed me through the rip even as he sprang through, the tear sealing as the creature rushed us, surrounded by the same things the police had killed earlier.

I landed on my back on the bridge with Carelian standing over me panting. ~You do not listen to orders well my quean.~ He licked my cheek with a bloody tongue.

"Ewwww," I rubbed at the blood. It reeked.

~Next time, listen. I would not leave you so easily.~ He stepped off and let me get a good look. To my relief, I could only see a cut across his nose. Most of the blood seemed to be other creatures' as nothing was seeping out.

"That doesn't mean I'm ever going to leave you." I pushed myself to my feet, groaning a bit. I'd landed on some of the rock bits I'd tossed out of the way. Using his strength to steady me, I turned to see cops from both sides of the bridge staring at me. "And now I get to try to explain what happened." With a sigh, I made my way over to the man headed for me, while Shay picked up rocks, putting them in the pouch he'd made of his shirt. Citlali was checking on Kesis with that same smile on her face.

She must have felt me watching her as she looked up and grinned. "That was fun. Can we do it again?"

I just groaned and went to deal with the political issues.

THIRTY-THREE

In a twist, Cori Munroe helped save a city in Mexico. While she is jumping around the US closing rips, other countries don't have her. In a plea from one of the Mexican teams she got on a Zoom call so she could see the rip. Cori provided advice and some tips to help them get the rip closed, as well as deal with the creatures coming out of it. The question many people are still asking is: what happens when we lose her? Is this a hint of what the apocalypse will be? ~ Talking Head CNN Mage Focus

SPIRIT

I ended up dealing with Yolanda and Stephen and soothing Carelian's stress on Thursday. The two government employees—no I wasn't happy with them—demanded details about the other side of the rip and how we managed to close it. While I was completely honest with them, I might have overstated the danger to convince them that this wasn't the correct option for most rips. Carelian showing them his teeth and then stating that he had to run convinced them that wasn't a good idea, especially after I sent an image of the thing that had come for us at the last. Yolanda was green and Stephen pale. I had to fight not to smirk.

As for Carelian, that involved me going to a realm under his mother's control with a large shady tree, a natural spring, and lots of rabbits for him to chase while I didn't move. It wasn't that hard to convince me. It was quiet and gave me time to create my game plan. The next order of business was memory stones. Some were easy, some weren't, and I had more than I wanted to go through. By the time Thursday was done, Carelian was stuffed and exhausted, and I knew the only way to deal with the stones was to jump in. I'd never really cataloged them, so I'd do it as I went.

Friday morning, a large thermos of high calorie Mexican coffee, three *queso pollo* chimichangas, my water bottle, and a bag of salt & vinegar potato chips were arranged in my office.

I'd set up the big bean bag that we usually used downstairs so I could lounge in it as I accessed the memories. Plus a blanket. It was starting to warm into spring, but the house wasn't hot enough that a blanket would be too much. I still got cold easily.

I headed into the memento room with a basket and stared at the collection. Carelian had followed me in. He was still in mothering mode after the rip adventure.

"Carelian, is it possible some of the other things might be memory stones?" I looked at the collection of things and cringed.

~Nothing of organic material. No feathers, eggs, or wood can hold memories. They are too fluid. You need a stronger structure.~

That made me feel a bit better. It still seemed more than I wanted. The two remaining statues seemed to glower at me. I really needed to find another request for Tirsane and get these creepy things out of here.

"I'll just try them all, I guess." Instead of the slow methodical selection, I just grabbed everything vaguely rock or crystal like and dumped it in the basket. By the time I was done, my wicker basket was groaning and the room looked barren and somewhat creepy. I stopped as I was about to walk out, staring at the obelisk. It was what Hamiada tested me with the first time I came here.

"Hamiada?" I asked, my eyes not leaving the stone.

"Yes, Cori?" She spoke from the doorway, not entering the room. Now that I thought about it, I'd never seen her in here, though she'd been in every other room, including the bathroom while I was using the toilet. That had been an ... interesting discussion with her deciding human biology was horribly inefficient. I agreed.

"What is the obelisk? I remember melting it. But it reformed."

275

"Magic and hematite," she said with a shrug.

"Is it a memory stone?" I had looked back at it.

This time she froze, eyes locked on mine, then tilted her head inhumanly far back, staring at the ceiling. "If it is, it is from the time of the Nephilim before humans learned to make use of magic."

That bit of information let me know I absolutely was not going to check and see. "Got it. No way does it have any information about Atlantis on it."

"I would not think so. That was gone from the realms way before the Undoing," she said as she spun.

My body locked. The dryads, I'd never asked them. "Hamiada, you don't know about the Undoing, do you?"

She laughed, her mostly green teeth flashing. "No. I am a tree that has a life span of a few hundred years. Not thousands."

My eyes widened. "Are there any trees that have dryads that have been around for thousands of years?"

"I do not know. Most of us that are that old are all but petrified. We retreat to our protective trees and rarely come out. Besides, you would need one that still grew on Earth, not the realms. And I know of no seeds or saplings that survived." She frowned, as if thinking. "I will ask, but do not think I will find answers. Even if seeds or saplings lived, they would not remember what they were not there for."

I sagged. She had told me how long it took before saplings awoke. It would have been years after the devastation.

"Thank you anyhow." I trudged back to my office, Carelian silent beside me. I settled down to look at the stones I had. Most were semi-precious, a large opal, amethyst, a few moonstones, one of obsidian, a few cut gems, two geodes—uncut— three sculptures of marble or granite, two hunks of uncut ruby, and the phoenix heart. I sighed, having grabbed it with everything else.

"Here goes nothing," I muttered as Carelian flormped on the floor next to the bean bag. I grabbed the first one, the opal with the gold running down the middle, and closed my eyes. With a sigh I pushed my focus toward it, letting the memories stored inside open up. Scenes from a gorgon enclave filled my mind and I swear I saw a young Tirsane. I just let it play, doing the equivalent of fast forward looking for anything that might be worth a second glance. Luckily it was the equivalent of home movies, so I didn't see anything that I felt embarrassed on Tirsane's behalf.

When I came out of the stone, I set that aside. Request or not, that was immediately going to Tirsane. The idea of keeping it felt wrong. I randomly picked up another one, the unopened geode. I fell into the crystals that were contained in it and it was like being hit with a photo album. Lots of little snapshots. If I had grabbed a photojournalist's camera with fifty years of random shots, it might equate to this. There were pictures of creatures, odd school-like scenes, hunting, the jungles, savannas, even one or two pictures of the stars, which gave me a spurt of hope, but not much else. Even if they had been pictures of Atlantis, there wasn't anything to connect them. My head was spinning by the time I dropped it and I groaned softly.

~Are you well?~ Carelian asked in my mind, and I sighed.

"Just a headache. I found the denizen's version of a photo album. That was exhausting. And ultimately useless. I still don't even know who fed all the images in there. It could have been a human, snake, or chaos blob." I drank some of my coffee, the chocolate ice cream melted in it enhancing the richness. "Two down. Way too many to go."

~Do not overstress yourself. Some of those contain years of

information.~ Carelian warned. ~I would only do one more today.~

"Probably two, unless one of them is really long. Right now, bathroom." I struggled up out of the oh-so-comfy bag and made it to the bathroom. Then I curled right back up, warmed up a chimichanga while I made notes about the two stones I'd done so far. When that was gone, I grabbed another stone, well actually one of the marble statues. It was of a centaur holding a staff. The marble was white and grey, and the detail made me uncomfortable. It took me a minute to sink into it. Then I was there. This was a teaching stone on what I designated as home-steading skills. Magic yes, but more like how to wash, clean, build, repair. I skimmed through it and bounced out relatively quickly—only twenty minutes.

"That was interesting. I really hope I never need to learn to spin or weave, but it is interesting. It even had things about moving large stones for protective walls." I yawned and stretched.

~Are you done?~

I checked the time. It was two in the afternoon. I was headed over to the Tudor house for dinner. "I think I have time for one more."

He lifted his head to check the basket. All the chimichangas were eaten, the coffee half gone, but I hadn't opened the chips yet. ~Very well, one more.~ He licked my toe. ~You will figure it out.~

"And if I don't? What happens?" I let my head fall back on the bag. "Does everything keep breaking? I'm rather surprised the realms haven't felt anything but given that last area I get the feeling the ruptures are occurring outside areas where sentient denizens live. But what happens if they start doing it in populated areas or we fire nukes?" That was my huge worry. I didn't trust any government if they got scared enough. And while I suspected they could stop a nuke with magic, that was only if they knew it was coming and had time to think or plan.

Carelian moved enough to put his head on the bottom of the beanbag, and I rubbed his cheek against my foot. ~I do not know. But not even the seasons stay the same. You will find the right path for all of us.~

I fumbled in the basket for another stone. My fingers wrapped around something cold and faceted. "Maybe. I just, if I fail, will there be another herald?"

~Cori, do you have a moment?~ Freya's voice rang in my head before Carelian could respond.

~Yes,~ I said, blinking my eyes. Sudden exhaustion had hit me like a wall.

~I thought you should know, Brix was found dead. A memory stone was left behind.~

I jerked up, my hand squeezing hard on the next stone. ~What happened? I know phoenix's aren't immortal, but they don't just die. And there aren't that many.~ Carelian lifted his head to look at me as I had broadcast that thought.

~They are, but they can be killed.~ Her voice held an odd note of sorrow. ~As far as we can tell, Brix refused to eat or drink since the council meeting. One of my Valkyries found the body and the stone.~ She took a mental pause, and I stiffened. ~It is addressed to Humans. The amount of anger and hate in it is … uncomfortable. You are blamed for the influx of magic into the realms and how you changed everyone.~

~Changed? Tirsane mentioned that too, but I didn't force anyone to do anything.~

~No, but you are such a presence that beings, especially those of us sensitive to magic, alter our behavior to please you. Even if we are unaware of our actions. Your presence has started to create a balance that we had not realized was missing.~ Freya's words weren't exactly comforting.

~That wasn't my intent,~ I started already trying to figure out what I could do, how to make amends.

~Stop. No, you had no intentions of being anything other than what you are, the Herald of Magic. A herald announces change, ushers in those with the power to make laws, and provides the weapons needed. You are doing all of those duties, just in ways the more literal of us never thought of. Your weapons are information and love. The power to make laws is the lords of both our people. You are what you should be, Cori Munroe – the Herald of Magic.~ Her firm no nonsense tone didn't let me argue, but it still felt wrong. Brix wasn't supposed to die. The bad guys had to be defeated, right? Not just fade away or die. But I wasn't sure Brix had ever been the villain, just the victim.

~If you say so. But I don't want any more to die. There has to be an answer and I'm just too stupid to see it.~

Freya laughed. It reminded me of distant battle horns, rich and powerful. ~If there is, the rest of us are blind too. At this point we have no option but to have faith that Magic will provide the answer.~

~I hope you are right.~

~So do I.~

I would have felt better if her voice had been confident, not wistful. My eyes closed as I tried to fight back the tears, but they seeped out between my lashes. Another death I'd be laying at my feet. How did I fix this? If I was supposed to be the hero, where were the clues leading me to the answers?

Carelian licked the side of my feet and I clenched the stone hard enough it hurt. I let the exhaustion and grief pull me under and I fell into a doze.

THIRTY-FOUR

Office of the President

What exactly does Herald mean? We've had Cori Munroe under surveillance for years, but she has avoided almost all political groups. Who is calling her the Herald and what are the ramifications. Having someone with her power running around is like losing the codes to nukes. I want information and details asap. Do what you need, but we need to keep her under control or we need a solution.

Chief of Staff K. Lewis for the President

CHAOS

Wind rushed through my wings as I dove through the clear blue sky. The clouds laughed at me as I swirled around and through them. My trill filled the air, calling out my delight to all the world.

~What are you doing beloved?~ Brix's voice filled my mind, and I hummed in response. His rich voice always made me smile.

~Chasing the sun, awaiting the moon.~ I spun again, my feathers trailing magic behind me as I curved. My luminous feathers caught the light, reflecting rainbows into the clouds and off the water far below. Up here you could see until the world curved away from you and nothing existed but the eternal sky and sea. I could fly for seasons, and had many times, and still I hadn't seen all the beauty of this world.

~The sun fears your beauty and the moon longs to be as bright as you. But I have a place I believe we could call home?~ Brix's voice contained a questioning note that surprised me. Brix personified assured arrogance. What would cause this unusual tone?

Curiosity, my driving characteristic, washed through me and I tilted some feathers to change my direction. Brix's presence shone in my mind, like the stars in the unending sky. I allowed the wind to carry me closer to him as I danced across the vast expanse. The golds and reds of flame-colored feathers appeared in the distance and I soared toward my love. My tail wrapped around Brix as I spun in a dance of joy, letting our magic wash against each other until the sun changed to match the feathers of my love as it sank around the earth.

~Home? What is this home you speak of? We have roamed long. Do you wish to tie to the earth instead of soar in the sky?~ This was a new idea and often seasons passed where we only landed to pick the sweet berries or sip on water that bubbled from a hidden spring. Most of the time, we danced in the air and spent our lives following the clouds around the world. ~Why or where would you want to go? What place could've caught your imagination to the point that you would want to call it home?~ I let the wind ruffle my feathers around him as I waited for an answer.

Brix ducked under my wing, letting red feathers mix with my rainbow white as we created a painting in the sky. After a few dances in the sky, he provided an answer to my query. But words were not what I expected.

~You had mentioned a while ago about raising another clutch of eggs. Is that something you still want to do?~

In surprise, my wings faltered, and a sudden downdraft caught me unawares, and I spun in the air, looking at him, my golden eyes shining with both surprise and excitement. ~Are you serious? Is that what you wish to do? To leave our chase of the seasons and raise young once again?~

I recovered, but I allowed the Earth to pull me toward her. Brix fluttered after me, following me in a long, lazy spiral towards the waves cresting below. Before my fears could grow, or the waves reach us, Brix elaborated.

~Yes. I think it is time. Our one child was a long time ago

and I would like to try again. Maybe this time have a better relationship with any hatchlings that we are blessed with. Perhaps this time it will go better. I would love to see your eyes in a chick with my feathers.~

Joy burst through me, giving my feathers a halo of color as I spread my wings and let the wind pick me up and throw me back into the skies. Brix followed, weaving in my wake as I danced my joy around the clouds and down through the spray of the ocean.

~Yes. I would like hatchlings. Where is this place you think we could make a home of?~

~It is but a day's journey toward the rising sun. This land is full of berries, honey, thick trees, and fresh water. There are those odd things - humans? I think that is what the name was. They live there, but they are magic users. I have stopped and talked to them before. They seem friendly and we can always call magic if needed.~ His words tumbled around my brain, bringing images with them. Full dark berries, honey dripping from hives, trees with thick branches, and amusing two-legs to watch. It sounded like it might work.

~Will they hunt us?~ Most creatures worried about being prey. While we were small enough to not be much to settle a hunger, even among the other magical beings our feathers were prized.

~I think not, but our feathers are of use for trade, plus my stashes of sparkles.~

That comment almost caused a disruption in my flying. ~You would raid your collection?~ Brix collected sparkles. Anything that caught the light and shone with a hidden radiance he had collected, creating a treasure trove. When we found things we needed, we could trade for them, sometimes for much, others for little. But we had the air and the sky, we had little need for other things. Locusts were fat and tasty, fruit hung off trees, and even honey could be gained for the price of a few stings.

~For a nest with you, full of chicks, I would give them all up. You are my life, Shera. Do you not think I would do anything for you?~ The trill of honesty, love, devotion made everything sweeter.

I wrapped my wings around him, and we mated there in the boundless sky with the hope for eggs, offspring, new lives in this world. Together, we pushed our magic out into the world and we focused on celebrating life.

Days later, we floated on a warm breeze above the ocean, my tail feathers almost orange in the light of the setting sun behind me. A land mass was in front of us, lush trees, wide bays full of their little wooden floats, and the scents of honey, a sharp spice, and human waste. I sighed. Even after all this time, humans still had not managed the disposal of their refuse.

~We should teach them the spells to transform waste to plant food. This manner of disposal smells and is a waste of resources,~ I chittered, annoyed. The smell and piles could spoil a paradise, and this looked as close as I'd ever seen.

~Then why do we not? It would raise our value to them and create a working relationship that we can build over the years.~ Brix always sounded logical and calm where I went with my emotions always ready to shift with the wind. We flew closer, and I inspected the place from afar. Did I want to settle down here? Phoenix hatchlings were not like normal birds with a month or two of growth and then done. It would take them at least three years to be fully feathered and able to Ash if badly injured. It meant a safe place and the need to have food and shelter. It was unlikely we had started a family with our mating, that had just been for fun. We had a better chance of quickening life if done during times when magic surged. The longest day, the longest night, or best of all when the sun ate the moon, or the moon ate the sun. If we mated then, our children would be strong and have the opportunity to grow into amazing beings.

But first I needed a nest.

The closer we got, the more I saw. Square caves dotted the land with fires coming out of them, and lines. Everything was made up of straight lines. Rigid lines of grapes, trees, paths, even their houses were created around ungiving lines. It felt odd and somehow wrong. Few things in the world were done in harsh lines. I missed the shapes where you never knew what was next, a curve, a sharp turn, maybe a wiggling line.

My thoughts escaped me as a soft trill that Brix did not miss. ~You do not like?~

~I do not know. We must meet, talk, there are many of these humans here. If they are not friendly, I would rather the mountains, the trees and animals of the forest.~ Telling him my fears would only bring facts and figures, they were not what I wanted at this point.

~There would be less rich food, harder to raise chicks.~

There was the logic that I did not care about. ~True, but safer away from those sharp sticks they throw in the area with all too high of an ability to hit.~ I could reply with logic as well as he, but a home had very little to do with logic.

Brix did not respond, instead tilted heading toward a cave that reached far into the sky, but this one felt warmer and welcoming. There were no lines, everything was made up of curves from the roof to the sides to the holes to go in, there were gentle curves that invited magic to play. I landed on the top of the building, my talons wrapping around the frills in the covering. It was painted with blues and greens and it had looked like the ocean from above.

Beneath us was magic bubbling around, full of promise and possibilities.

~This place is rich in many things. But what about the ones that live here?~

Brix ruffled feathers and rubbed his beak along my wing. ~I have spoken to many of these humans, but there are others like us. A centaur lives on the other side and teaches many of their children. Dolphins hunt fish with them and are happy with their generosity. There are some naga in the caves below and the Aralez visit from their islands across the bay.~

I let my wings fully collapse to my side, no longer holding them ready to flee. ~That is good to know.~

~They have a person who leads the worship in magic. She is the one I have spoken with.~ Brix scanned the area while I considered those words.

~They worship Magic? Why?~

A trill of laugher filled the air, and I let myself join in, the music of our voices creating its own type of magic. Around the area there was a slowing and stopping as humans paused to listen. A few spotted us on the roof, from their pointing arms to the harsh mouth noises, but no one came rushing to chase us away. When we let the desire to sing fade, something laughter often caused, we continued to survey the area.

~I have no idea why they worship magic, but it is plentiful. Maybe they think it will teach them better ways to use it? If so, then we are here at her behest? Either way they can be foolish, it matters not to me.~

I let the words sway me. After all, if they wished to worship the moon, magic, or the distant lights in the sky, it mattered not to me.

~There. It is the woman I wished to have you meet. Will you?~ Brix's eyes held an odd mix of hope and a please.

~Why would I not? Let us speak with this female.~ I sprang into the air, my white feather reflecting rainbows as I let myself burn off a bit of energy. Then I followed him. Brix headed to a woman wearing coverings of white and brown, but there were hints of blue and red at the borders. It was not an unpleasant covering, if confusing. Humans always seemed to be covered, even when the weather did not require it.

We landed on a low wall that put us uncomfortably close to a human's grasp, but Brix did not seem concerned.

The female looked up at us and she bared her teeth suddenly. I pulled back, ready to flee, but Brix whispered in my mind. ~That is how they say welcome. Let it be.~

I forced myself to settle back down, but I managed to hit Brix with my primary wing feathers as I did so.

"Flame feather, you have returned, and you bring with you a friend of moonlight?" The voice was soft and oddly melodious, as if she sang constantly. It helped me relax a little.

~I did, Lenia. May present my mate, Shera?~ Brix tilted his head toward me and I nodded, still ready to flee. These humans could become violent in but a moment.

"Ah, I am honored. May I present my daughter, Zenobia?" She placed her hand on the child, who looked at us, eyes wide with wonder.

THIRTY-FIVE

In the sleepy town of Austell, GA the head of a local HOA woke up this morning to find his house surrounded by the endangered Sarraceniaceae plants. The head, Harold Lavik, swears it is mage Ben Griff who did this. The person in question was fined for the plants he has around his house and is an Earth Mage. He allegedly swore he'd get revenge. Right now, Harold is in violation of the HOA rules for plants, but because they are endangered plants and the state forbids any disturbance of them, even mowing the area around the plants is prohibited. ~ KWSC Local News

ORDER

I jerked up in the beanbag, something clenched tight in my hand to the point it hurt. If I'd been in a chair, I would have gotten hurt trying to spring to my feet. As it was, all I could do was look around feeling unhinged.

~Cori? What is wrong?~ Carelian asked, looking at me. ~Did you dream?~

I took a shuddering breath in and then out. "That wasn't a dream. The phoenix heart is a memory stone, of Shera..." I said, but that wasn't right. "Or me? I was Shera. I should go fly some more so I can sort out my mind." My hand trembled as I reached for my water. The longing to be in the sky, to feel the wetness of clouds against my beak was a physical desire. A few long gulps of cold water helped to center me and get me back to being Cori, a human. "That was intense."

~Odd that it pulled you in so far. What sort of memory? And why does Shera sound familiar?~ He moved around the bag, licking my cheek as I settled back down.

"She was the spouse of Brix. Her memory of Brix is of a kinder bird. Someone who didn't hate or fear humans." The depth of the betrayal Brix must have felt was registering. These weren't humans who had randomly destroyed the building he lived in, but friends? I couldn't imagine that. But the fear that spiked through me told me I needed human interaction. It would be dangerous to dive back in right now. The stone warmed in my hand as I thought about them, pushing the feeling of soaring through the air into my mind.

I lifted my watch up and had to blink a few times to figure out the time was four in the afternoon. Yeah, people. The kids should be home and isolating here was the worst thing I could do. "I'm struggling to figure out who and where I am." The world spun around me as I focused on my body. I frowned at my cup of chocolate, but I couldn't come up with a memory of me putting alcohol in it.

"Carelian? Can you ask Sable to come get me for dinner? I think I need that." I didn't move from the beanbag. My wings were still missing and their lack confused me. Was the world always this blah with colors?

He hissed and was gone. "Carelian?" He had been there, right? My bladder imposed on me its demands, and I didn't think I could empty it safely via magic right now. That meant walking. I rolled out of the beanbag, once again grateful it lay so close to the ground and began to crawl to the bathroom.

One hand, then a knee. No, the other knee.

"Cori, what's wrong?" Marisol's voice surprised me, and I almost fell over as I tried to look at her and move simultaneously. It didn't work well.

"My wings are broken? I should fly. Why can't I fly?" The words sounded wrong, and I could see my arms but shouldn't they be wings?

"Oh my. Come on, get up Cori. You need to use the bathroom?" Marisol slipped one arm around my waist and helped me stand up.

"You're strong?" It surprised me she could do that. She shouldn't be able to lift me with ease. Should she?

"No, you're light. Bathroom, then we're going to my house."

She had the stern no nonsense tone that told me fighting her would not be wise.

"Okay," I murmured as my memories fought between running on two legs and flying with wings. Before I could formulate any objection I was at Marisol's craftsman house. She wrapped me in a blanket, handed me pureed chicken soup, and a bottle of water filled with electrolytes and sugar.

"Eat, drink, then we'll talk." She watched my every move, and I didn't even think of disobeying.

My head wobbled like it wasn't attached all the way. Images of my head floating away into the clouds lasted until I had the soup gone and most of the drink. The memories were fading, and I realized Carelian had his head on my lap, tail twitching, while Marisol was in the chair across from me.

"Um, hi." I swallowed, verifying I knew where I was. "That was odd."

Marisol set down her book and looked at me. "Care to tell me what happened? If you had been one of my sons, I would have assumed you were experimenting with recreational drugs."

"Gah, no. Not right now. It's a memory stone. One I absolutely have to go back into. It is the memory of the spouse of Brix, the one who died with their chicks. I don't know how far it goes, but it's amazing what I've learned so far." I paused and thought about what I'd seen. "It at least soothed my feelings towards Brix. The love between them was borderline magical."

"Then what was all that?" Marisol waved her hand.

A shrug slipped out, because to be honest I wasn't positive what that had been. "A rebound effect, I guess. I thought I was fine, then when I moved my mind got confused as to whether I was a bird or a human. That made it very hard to function. The world didn't even look the same anymore." I sighed. "And I still need to go back. There is more. She just met Zenobia. It is the closest thing to a clue I've found."

Carelian hissed and I didn't blame him, but he didn't argue. There didn't seem to be an option.

"Not right now, you aren't, and not while you are alone," Marisol said sternly. "Tomorrow is Saturday. We will arrange with Jo and Sable for you to be watched. There is no way we can risk that again. What if I hadn't been here?"

The desire to shrug and just mutter something about figuring it out was overwhelming. But I nodded instead, still working on accepting that they loved me. "I know. I just never expected that level of disorientation. I get that everyone wants to keep me safe, but people are dying and if I am too scared to do anything, more people are going to die."

Marisol's lips thinned out as she looked down, but she didn't argue. Instead, she verified with Jo and Sable what dinner time was going to be and what she should bring. More and more, we were having big dinners together. Kris and Sanchez even asked Carelian to get them occasionally.

Kris was still upset, but he'd caught up in all his classes. I didn't know how to help him, so I didn't pry. He knew I'd drop everything for him if he asked, and right now, that was all I could I do.

We settled down for dinner. The twins were sitting on opposite ends of the table. That was odd, as they usually sat next to each other, talking and feeding their quetzo's little tidbits. The dragons were at what everyone said would be their full growth for a while. They were about two feet long, their colors vibrant, and their personalities much closer to the kids' than the formless food pits they had been. Esmere thought when the kids hit their late teens growth spurts, they might gain another foot and a few more pounds, but that was a ways off. But the twins had been growing like weeds. It seemed like every time I saw them, which was daily, they'd grown another inch. They would start first grade in September and both looked like they might be the biggest kids there.

"What is up with you two?" I had sat down in between them and looked at them one at a time.

"Magne stole the first friend I made. I am not talking to him." Jaz spat out the words, her fist tight around her fork.

"I did not. She just wanted to play trucks with us. You didn't," he protested, though he looked miserable.

"Oh? Why didn't you want to play?" I asked Jaz, flicking my attention between the two of them. Jaz might be a princess, but she did enjoy playing with cars sometimes.

"Last time Bobby dumped sand down my shirt." She wouldn't look at him or me, instead glared at her empty plate. "Kerri was playing fashion show with me, but Magne came over and asked if she wanted to play cars in the sandbox."

The trials and tribulations of a kid. It seemed so far away, but I did remember this sort of stuff.

"I was being nice. She's new." Magne was getting upset, his lower lip coming out. "You're supposed to be nice."

"But she was playing with me. You just don't want me to have friends." There were hidden sobs in the words.

"You can have friends, but can't they be my friends too?" Both of them now had bottom lips out and were staring so hard at the table I was surprised it hadn't caught fire.

"You have friends," she protested, her head jerking up. "Bobby, and the other boys. Even Laurel and Becca like to eat lunch with you. I don't have anyone." Tears were welling up on her lashes and her lip trembled.

"Oh Jaz." I scooted my chair over and wrapped an arm around her. "I don't have an answer. But I bet Kerri will play with you tomorrow and Magne can play with Bobby." I shot him a look, waiting until he looked up to darken my glare. He hunched his shoulders and nodded. "But, if she says she wants to play cars, why don't you play too? I can't promise Bobby won't dump sand on you. I can promise he will be in big trouble and Magne won't get to go over to his house for two weeks if he does."

Magne's head jerked up. "Wait, why can't I see him if he does it?"

"Because I don't want you associating with someone that would treat your sister like that? Why would you want to be friends with someone that would do that to your sister?" The crease on his forehead as he considered this heartened me. Jaz gave another sniff.

"Okay. I'll try again tomorrow."

I kissed the top of her head. "Good." I looked up as Sable walked in from the kitchen and Jo came in from the rest of the house.

Jo smiled at us and headed for Sable. "Sorry, long day at work," she said, then pulled Sable into her arms and kissed her.

The kids just rolled their eyes, all too used to the behavior by now.

"Mm, hello Jo," Sable purred back. "Your mom will be here in a minute and it's Friday."

"Yay! Beer! Anyone else want something?" Jo kissed Sable again. "I know what you want."

"Not in front of the kids," Sable said with a grin.

"I meant to drink, woman. I'm not that much of a pervert," Jo protested, laughing.

"Yes, you are," I corrected. "But no thanks. I think I'm on water today and this weekend."

Both of them stopped and glanced at me. "Something we should know?"

"Yep, but let's eat first." I waved at the set table and the kids who were perking up a bit, their pouts fading.

Fifteen minutes later, everyone settled down, plates filled with food, and we started sharing our day. Sable was working on more flow designs. Her last one had been patented. Her company gave her a nice six-figure bonus check for that, so they'd been talking about an RV or a nice vacation. As far as I knew, nothing had been decided.

Jo was still working for a local specialty machine shop, but there were plans in the works for her to open her own custom motorcycle shop, something she'd always wanted. Marisol had a date next week, and well, the kids were sniping at each other a bit more than usual and both of them seemed like they were on the verge of tears multiple times during dinner. That wasn't like them.

Maybe they were getting sick. I'd mention it later.

"So, tell us about your day and what is preventing any adult fun." Jo waggled her eyebrows at me and I rolled my eyes in response.

"I don't have adult fun, too ewwww." The three women snickered at me and I just shook my head. "No, I had an interesting experience with a memory stone." I spent a good five minutes sharing what it had been like.

"That sounds fascinating," Sable admitted. "But the aftereffects don't sound as appealing."

"I know, but I have to go back in. This time with someone around to watch me, so if anything weird happens, someone is there."

"Yes. You sure you're up for it tomorrow?" Sable had her hand entwined with Jo's on the table, a worried look on her face.

"Probably not, but going to do it anyhow. At this point, every moment is too long." Part of me wanted to rush back and do it now, but even I could admit to needing longer to recover.

THIRTY-SIX

The Secretary of State and the Senate Chair, as well as the Ambassador to the UN, met with delegates from the AIN today. We received word that four people from the AIN would be coming to meet today and here we have video of them entering the White House. At this time, no information on their names or what was discussed has been released, but this is the first confirmed meeting with the US heads of state since the 1800s. ~ CNN Mage Focus

SPIRIT

S aturday morning, I felt like the actor of a one person show with everyone else helping to manage me. The kids made sure I had their blankets to cuddle into— because they wanted me to know they would be there. Jo had cleared a space in the living room looking out the balcony in back so I could nestle into the beanbag. Sable had created a little feast for me if I needed. While Marisol positioned herself with her laptop so if I spoke or wanted to talk I could tell her. It also allowed her to monitor me.

"I think you are all overreacting. While I'm in the stone, I doubt I'll be aware of anything. It's when I come out that the issue starts." My protests fell on deaf ears, or at least hearts that cared more about my wellbeing than my protests.

"That's nice, *mi hija*. I'll be here anyway. I can ask you questions as soon as you wake up and I'll record it, just in case your brain starts to confuse the memories after you wake up." Marisol just smiled at me and sat with her own Mexican coffee.

"Okay, okay. Carelian, you're the only one I haven't heard from. Are you good with this?"

He had been sulking near the doors to the balcony and laid his ears back and hissed. ~No. This is not good. It is not something I like. But I agree it is important and even more, you would not rest if you didn't. So, you will do this and I will complain. I can not protect you in the stones, so do not get hurt.~ His tail flicked back and forth like a rattler, but his hiss had faded.

"I can get hurt in a memory stone?" That shocked me. How could you get hurt in a memory? Jo and Sable, who were lurking behind me, gave twin oofs of surprise.

~Physically, no. But there exists the possibility of psychic and emotional trauma. Remember what it felt like to fly? If Shera imprinted as deeply as I suspect she did, you will feel everything. I doubt you can do anything other than be fully immersed but remember that they are not your emotions. Not your sorrow.~

"Oh," I murmured, turning it over in my mind. Shera loved Brix with her whole heart. It had softened my attitude toward him because of the different way she saw him. "That is valid. I will try to remember." Though I had no idea how you healed from someone else's sorrow.

Jo and Sable were doing their silent talk thing when I glanced back at them. "Stop it. I'll be fine, you two. I understand grief."

With her arms crossed over her chest, Jo huffed at me. "You'd better not explode with magic again. This is new carpet and expensive."

"I love you too," I said, smirking at her.

She made faces at me until the kids, who were sitting on the couch watching all of this avidly, started giggling. I'd told them it would just look like I was asleep, but they didn't care. They were going to "guard Momma Cori" and that was all there was to it.

I made faces at everyone, took the phoenix heart and settled down, closing my eyes. I hoped it would be less immersive if I didn't fall asleep holding it. With a final mental bracing, I pushed myself into it, searching and waiting. And nothing. I kept trying, pushing, all the things that worked with all the other stones and it sat in my hand like an inanimate jewel.

"I don't understand," I said, opening my eyes to see everyone staring at me. "I can't get in. And I know there is more in there."

No one had moved in the ten minutes I'd been trying, though the twins were busy with their quetzo's. They both had found little vests from a doll set and the silly dragons loved them.

"Didn't you say Jeorgaz had wanted to talk to you about it when you first got it?" Sable said, leaning against the wall. "Why not ask him?"

"He had said something about it being used to channel energy, not being a memory stone. But I might as well." I cleared my mind. ~Jeorgaz? Are you able to come talk to us?~

I struggled out of the bag and dropped into a chair. Talking to people was easier when you didn't look like a candidate for milk and cookies.

A poof of flame. ~Cori,~ he said, looking around with wings still ready to fly away. ~This is a new place. Jo, this is your house?~

"Well, ours and Zelinka's when she matures, but yes. How are you?" Jo had her normal smile. There was something just so disarming about the bird.

~Curious as always. What prompts this? Questions? Information?~ For the first time I translated his interest not as a willingness to serve or even a need to help, but gathering gossip to spread. I wasn't sure whether to laugh or scold him.

So I ignored that aspect. "Jeorgaz, this, the phoenix's heart. What is it exactly?"

He tilted his head, his red feathers flickering around him. ~The Phoenix heart, as I said.~ He sounded confused, and I tried to put my questions into something more specific.

"Right. James said it was a way to focus magic, amplify. But what else is it? I'd just assumed it was a faceted gem, maybe embedded with magic." I was watching him carefully. Often the way his feathers reacted told me much. Other denizens' reactions weren't as easy to pin down.

~That is what it is. Not much more is known about it. As far as I know, it was found in the ocean a century ago. But James said no one was sure what type of gem it is. When faceted about twenty years ago, the notes state each section removed crumbled into dust minutes later. James said without a sample there wasn't a way to any sort of testing as to its age.~ Jeorgaz watched the Trilliant cut gem in my hand, the pink seeming to turn redder to match his feathers.

"Do you know how James got it?"

~Not really. I was his familiar, but not his equal. We were not as close as you and Carelian, though I wished for that. I spent much of my time ... elsewhere.~ That comment made me smirk, though I felt a pang in my heart for what James had discarded. There were days I disliked that man and days I felt sorry for him.

"You mean spreading gossip around the realms?" I could barely hold back my laughter at this point.

His feathers puffed up a bit. ~It is not gossip. It is information sharing. I only share facts.~ His indignant remark got a giggle out of me.

"As long as you share nothing if I ask you to keep quiet or it is a personal matter," I said, not all that worried about it. After all, most denizens regarded human issues as weird or slightly amusing.

~I would never,~ he protested. ~Why do you think so few knew what James was up to? I never spoke of it.~

I tilted my head. "Jeorgaz, did James hurt or threaten you?"

All his feathers puffed up, and I felt Carelian tense. ~Never.~ He turned his head almost upside down. ~Cori, I liked James, but he was very private. He loved knowledge for the sake of it. Was he nice? Not by your standards, but neither was he cruel. He was much more like...,~ Jeorgaz floundered for a moment searching for something. ~He liked old books. If he was a character, I would say he was Ahab in Moby Dick. Obsessed, driven, impatient. But he asked questions about things and probed. I found that way of looking at life fascinating, so I chose him. He had a very strict code of conduct, which

I found attractive, but he was not social or given much to doing anything but research and talking to me about his research.~

He sighed and it came out like a long trill. ~He was himself, flaws and all. But he shared anything that would help others. Mostly he was happy living in his world of research, buying odd items, and asking me to find information. That was primarily what I did for him, and it matched my passion to keep the beings up to date. But I also never told him about the Council or the lords. It was information I did not choose to share, and it was never where his focus was. Does that help?~ It was the most direct I'd ever heard Jeorgaz speak regarding his life before his Ashing.

Carelian spoke, surprising me for some reason. ~Cori, you are different and I received criticism in the beginning for how much I shared with you and that I brought you freely into the realms. I never cared. You are my quean and I will do what I believe is the best for you. Regardless of what others might think.~

Every time I thought I had my mind wrapped around what went on in their world, they revealed some other aspect I had not expected.

"I'm never going to understand all of this, will I?"

~We are a different culture. Give yourself a few decades to be immersed in it and maybe. For now, it doesn't matter.~ Carelian yawned, showing all his teeth. ~Get back to what we need to know now.~

I regretfully pushed aside the thoughts of how much I still underestimated and didn't understand about the realms and focused on Jeorgaz. "The stone. He got it somehow. What made him think it was a focus and why was it called the Phoenix heart?"

With a flutter of wings, he took a moment to settle down.

~It feels like magic. Can't you sense that? So it must be a focus. Many magic crystals are. What am I missing?~

"The name?" I pushed for the answer.

Jeorgaz shrugged, an odd movement on a bird. ~He said it brightened when I got near it as if it reacted to my flames, so Phoenix Heart.~ He ruffled a bit, looking at me, then everyone else. ~Why?~

I watched him, surprised that he didn't know. "Jeorgaz," I said, weighing each word as I spoke. "Were you aware this is a memory stone, specifically the memory stone of Shera, Brix's mate?"

Jeorgaz went still, every feather and flick of flame freezing. ~It is a memory stone?~ Each word was said slowly, as if being pulled out one syllable at a time.

"Yes. But I can't access it awake. I fell asleep with it in my hand and it pulled me into it, and it was as if I was Shera, not watching like the other stones I've experienced."

~A memory stone?~ He questioned again as his feathers puffed up, blown by an unseen wind.

"Yes?" I wasn't sure where this was going, but his response confused me. "What is the issue?"

He pulled all his feathers toward him and ducked his head under a wing, creating a little phoenix ball. In any other situation I might have teased him, but I could hear all of us holding our breaths, even the kids, as we watched. His bright feathers paled to a faded version of what they normally were. If he were a human, I might have said he was going into shock. "Jeorgaz?" I started to worry and even Carelian had sat up, staring at the ball of feathers.

A ruffle of the feathers and Jeorgaz pulled his head out. ~I believe you, I just had not known. How many memories must have been lost. Stupid humans, so blind, yet I didn't see either.~

The back of my skull throbbed with the beginnings of a headache. "Jeorgaz, what are you talking about?"

He inhaled and his feathers started to come back to life. ~There is a legend of a phoenix about to experience a final death.~ He gave a bitter snort. ~Which now that I think of it, Brash started that legend. I wonder if he knew.~ He shook himself. ~It doesn't matter. There is a legend that a phoenix which knows their final death is upon them can create a stone with their life in it. That the stone will be precious beyond measure, yet you will only know its worth in dreams. If I could get my hands on that phoenix ... ~ He trailed off. ~This must be what he meant. The original version would have just been a stone. Nothing obviously fancy but yet unusual. One of the reasons James bought it, and yes, I'm just now remembering, was because it was an unidentified gem. No one knew what type of mineral the stone was, and many suspected it to be a hoax created by a mage.~

Jeorgaz started to laugh. ~He used it trying to figure out what it was, and it amplified everything. Of course, it did. It was full of phoenix magic. It would have intensified everything to the same level as the amount of energy that was put into creating that. If she died when the realms were sundering, then it was created with the energy that broke apart the worlds.~

The room fell silent as we all stared at him.

"Well, fuck." Jo's voice broke the tableau, and I turned to gaze at her. She shrugged. "I guess we really need to know now, don't we?"

"That we do," I said, looking at the gem with a greater respect mingled with overwhelming sadness.

CHAPTER

THIRTY-SEVEN

The best selling book series "Adventures of Montana Smith – Rip Explorer" has just been optioned for a movie. The thriller series follows one Montana Smith as he dives into portals and rips to explore new places and find artifacts that were stolen by monsters. It is on book nine of the series and routinely lands on number one on the best-selling lists. We can't wait to see which adventure will hit the big screen. ~ CNN Entertainment news.

CHAOS

We let it be until Monday. We hadn't wanted to pursue it after that bombshell and I'd asked Jeorgaz to see if he could find the child of Brix and Shera. There was no reason that a phoenix couldn't still be alive. We would have done it that night, but another level five rip appeared, and I went with Carelian to close it. Luckily, this one was a Spirit rip and Carelian pulled me to the other side. Once I created a dam in the river, it closed without extreme effort. I let Tirsane know, and she created a prettier reservoir than the dam I'd made.

Sunday night I was tired, even though my offerings had been much less than usual. I knew I could tell people the trick of getting to the other side to close rips, but Carelian pointed out it would possibly result in a lot of dead mages, even those with familiars. The intelligence range for familiars, after I forced Carelian to explain, seemed to go from him—higher than human intelligence—to Dahli, who struck me as about the average six-year-old. Just more excitable. He'd admitted it was usually the more adventurous beings that became familiars, which didn't always mean the most intelligent, just more willing to take risks.

I cuddled him close Sunday night and fell asleep to his purrs, my anchor to the world.

"You sure about this, Cori?" Jo asked, sitting on the bed next to me the next night.

I nodded even as I snuggled down into my bed. "Yep. I need to see the rest of the story and perhaps get some answers. I just don't know how many nights this is going to take. Or worse, if the parts I need were in the parts removed."

We both looked at the beautiful gem, but every cut meant

knowledge lost. All I could do was hope it wasn't the parts I really needed.

"Hamiada?" Jo said, looking back at the door. "You sure you're okay to watch her?" Jo and Sable both needed to work the next day. Marisol admitted she'd fall asleep, and the twins were kids with school in the morning.

"Yes. If she is distressed, I will get you," Hamiada reaffirmed. "I have little need of sleep. She will be guarded."

Jo sighed, then stared at me. "You'd better not get hurt and not get up fast in the morning until you're sure you don't have wings."

"Yes, ma'am," I said with a laugh. "I'll be good. Now go. You have work tomorrow and I have a mystery to dig into."

Jo huffed at me, then kissed my forehead and left. I heard the door open and close. My eyes locked on Hamiada. "I'll be fine."

"Of course you will." She gazed at me with an inhuman blankness. "You are the Herald. How could you not be okay?"

I choked thinking about how awful I looked right now. I might not have been a particularly vain person, but I'd preferred having hair and some weight on my bones. "How could I not?" I responded, managing to keep the smile on my face. "Okay, I'm headed to sleep," I said, holding up the stone clutched in my hand. "Let's see what Shera has to show me."

Hamiada bobbed then faded away. Carelian hmphed. ~I would never allow anything to happen to my quean.~

"I know." I rubbed his sides, amused that I was stuck reassuring everyone I'd be fine. The mix of humor, love, and wonder lashed at me as I curled around my living pillow and settled myself for sleep. Sleep came easily, and I slipped into the darkness.

My wings tucked tight into me as I streaked down from the skies to the white structure that opened to the sun. The building my nest was in. It stood tall into the sky but possessed many openings for light and breezes to slip in. They used the open room of gray stone bricks for rituals and quiet communing with magic. There were circles laying out the places of magic, the different branches. Hot springs kept the entire area under this portion of the land warm, which was also why the crops were so rich and abundant.

The bunch of dried seaweed in my beak would work well with our nest. I admired it as I flew toward where Brix was working on creating a home for our chicks. Nest was a misnomer for the work of art that lay before me. We took the materials and used magic and fire and light to warp and change them, creating a structure that looked more like a multilayer basket than a nest like a bird would make. The green of the seaweed would add splashes of color against the red and beige.

It had three spaces. One that would be big enough for me to slip into and settle over eggs, pushing my magic into them. Another that we stored food for the time when I couldn't go far from my eggs, and a third open area that we would rest in.

~My light, you have returned,~ Brix's voice said in my mind as I landed on the open area.

~Always. Though I feel the time is drawing near. Not as soon as we had supposed, but still. The nest should be done in the next moon.~ The magical time when I would be fertile was approaching. Phoenixes took longer to hatch and mature than most, though not as long as dragons, but easily approaching a cycle of the sun before they could fly. We needed to surround the eggs in magic and let them develop in their own time.

~Yes, the shortest day is coming fast. That day and not the longest?~ Brix asked as he plucked the seaweed from my beak and applied it to the walls as a design.

~Yes, the shortest. By the longest day they should be ready to hatch and meet their parents.~ I felt magic hum in my mind and body. We had delayed building as I made sure this was as good of a place as Brix implied. It had taken multiple cycles of the seasons before I agreed with him. The land was rich and fruitful; the people accepting and welcoming, and those that served magic were strong and true. They were even entertaining for limited beings. A shudder rushed through me as I imagined being unable to fly.

~Then I look forward to our family,~ Brix preened my feathers, pulling me back to the work at hand.

"Blessings of the light on you," a rich voice called out from the open area below us.

I pushed my silly mate away and looked down to see Zenobia moving into the area carrying offerings for Magic. In the cycles we had been here, she had grown strong and true, her magic full and rich. On the shortest day she would take over the mantle of guide from her mother.

~Magic favors you,~ I replied.

"It is fun. How goes the building of your house?" She seemed interested, and I trilled in amusement.

I jerked as my life skipped and jerked. With a shudder, I watched Zenobia in all white, kneel before their altar to Magic. The mantle of herald cloaked her, and Brix and I trilled in surprise and celebration. That had not been expected and I watched the girl child, woman now, flare with pride and arrogance as her magic swelled. Amusement filled me as I leaned into Brix.

~She is a dragon with her power, hoarding and guarding. If she had wings, she'd make one to rival the others.~

Brix nibbled my neck feathers. ~Yes. But now I think the skies are calling us. Magic is swirling. Can you feel the call?~

I opened my wings, letting the magic from below swirl up and wash over me. I felt it kindling in my body. Instead of answering him, I launched into the sky, letting Brix chase me through the clouds, rolling with him as the light wrapped around us and magic filtered through.

My memories stuttered, and I sat in front of Zenobia, my eggs heavy in me. She was staring up at the sky, her magic buzzing like angry insects seeking to hurt and destroy.

~I do not understand your anger,~ I said, watching her. These last few months, her magic and rage keep rising. ~You are chosen by Magic to be her witness. Your people love you. Why is there anger?~ In this place, with abundant food, pleasant weather, I did not understand what drove her rage.

"You don't see?" She waved her hands around. "All they do is want, want, want. Zenie do this, Zenie do that. They expect me to be their servant because of Magic's choice. What about what I want?"

Her anger at her role surprised me. ~Is that not the goal? To be a servant of the people?~

"Like you are a servant of Brix? I notice you are the one staying here, while he galivants around. Does that not anger you?" Her spite made me coo in sorrow for her own chains.

~No. This was planned and hoped for. I could be out flying, seeking food and other things. But staying here is safer for me and it lets me give more magic and nutrients to the eggs I will lay. And soon enough I will fly again.~

Her hand twitched, brushing away my words. "You don't have age or pressure creeping up on you. Or a mother that expects children or men that expect you to be honored with their attention."

I tilted my head, having no basis for understanding. Brix was my joy, and I still felt honored to have won such a creature.

~I do not understand. Do you not wish to have children?~

The snarl that rippled over her face changed it from what most of the humans called pretty, to an expression worthy of a dragon's rage. "And destroy my body? My eldest sister died giving birth, and her husband, the man that swore she was the love of his life, had another in her bed in three moons. I will not do that. I need more magic, more power, more something to let them know I am their better."

~I hope you find what you need, Zenobia.~ My words were sorrowful. But then I wasn't human. They had strange rules that made no sense. My opinion wasn't worth much.

"Oh, I think I've found it," she said, her smile harder than made me comfortable. "But like all things, it will take a bit of work."

My trill filled the air. That was a truism, no matter what species you were. ~True. I wish you well in your endeavors.~

She smiled and for a moment I wondered if she had dragon in her background. With a shiver, I pushed it off and launched into the air. Brix and I made our home ready for the eggs. He roamed far, tasting the magic, while I stayed here, exchanging the occasional feather for a treat.

Our eggs were laid and I hovered over them most of the time, but Brix gave me breaks and I found myself following Zenobia. Not any reason really, just she was one of the few on the island whose travels were not completely predictable. She wandered the hills and the trees, then went into the caverns. One day I followed her there, more out of my curiosity than anything. She wove under where the air all but rippled in heat and I thought how much Brix would enjoy a bath down here in this hot air. I made a mental note to create a bath for him as a present once the chicks hatched.

I hid in the shadows, muting my colors to let me blend with the walls. It was like playing find with others. It had been a while, but it seemed my skills had not faded. There in the warmth of the caverns she had created an altar with each of the magics inscribed on it. The liquid rock down here all but bubbled with magic and I could feel it as almost a living being as Zenobia set offerings down in front of each of the symbols, channeling want and need into them. I watched for a moment as she pled for power and strength I did not understand. She was the Herald. What more could she want? After a bit I left, but the strange altar with the sigils of magic burning with the light of magic disturbed me.

Brix was trilling when I landed at home. ~They are rocking,~ he said, and all thoughts of the caverns and Zenobia vanished as I focused on the new lives awaiting to meet their parents. It took many days, but finally the hatching of the eggs happened on the longest day of the summer. I found it only appropriate for that to match the long path from the shortest day of the year to now. I had been trilling to my chicks when I felt Magic scream.

My mind skittered, and Zenobia smiled at me. "Shera, Brix, may I have a feather from each of you? A tail? I have honeycomb to trade." Her smile was warm, beguiling, the eggs inside of me not heavy yet. Honeycomb sounded so good.

~Yes. Honeycomb would be good. Brix?~ He laughed at me, but we willingly parted with a tail feather.

Time swerved on me again. The chicks hatched at the height of the sun, three beautiful younglings. Only time would tell their abilities, but already one was of each of the magic streams. Spirit, Order, and Chaos. Brix watched while I got some fresh air. Zenobia sat in the sun, a pile of fruit on her lap. The rich berries called to me, and I winged my way to her.

"Ah, Shera. Are your chicks well?"

~Yesss, strong. One of each magic. They will be powerful, I can feel it.~

She smiled, her teeth too sharp, but I feared it not. "I am working on a project for this evening, the shortest night. I will trade you berries for some of each shell. A bag full enough for all of you."

I brightened at that. The idea of a long flight had not excited me and a bag of berries was a good trade for something that I would have disposed of soon enough. I returned with shells and left with berries on that day of birth.

The sun was high, my chicks fed, Brix left, at my urging, to go stretch his wings and find some cactus fruit I craved. I crooned to the chicks, this their first day of life as the sun sank into the ocean. Magic changed.

I shrieked as I burst out of our little home, trusting it to protect my chicks, and I looked around as the world rippled. It came from the caverns. I dove through the walls wondering if the volcano had decided to rupture its container. Already I tried to figure out how to move my house. I could take things with me when I traveled to other places. But the magic lands were few and far away and I'd never brought anything bigger than a melon with me before. My chicks were not even a day old yet. Could they survive? Did I have enough time for Brix to get back to help me? He had jumped far away to get me a treat. I burst into the cavern where Zenobia stood, pulling in magic like I'd never seen, feeding into the volcano whose long dormant arms the country nestled in. She had offerings for each of the magics and she pulled, feeding them into something that wasn't powerful enough to hold that amount of magic. The realm, this realm, started to fracture as she pulled in more magic.

~What are you doing?~ I cried, fear for my chicks, this land, magic all warring with one another.

"I will ensure I am powerful enough that they can't trap me in their traditions and how women act. I will have enough power to make my own way. Magic will ensure it." She dumped power into a crystal the color of the fire below and it glowed with pent up energy.

~Magic won't work like that,~ I cried out, fear making my heart race.

"I'll make it. I'll make it give me the power or I'll sunder it altogether." Her voice rang with madness, and I spun, flying toward my chicks. But Magic broke and bucked beneath me. It twisted into shapes that could not exist and rather than wholeness, it shattered, driving pieces of reality away. I dove into my nest, my chicks alive and crying out in fear.

~Brix!~ I screamed, but I knew he could never return that fast. There was nothing to do but protect my chicks. I pulled on my magic and wrapped it around us in a crystal shell, but it wasn't enough.

Magic pushed against me and into everything I was, would be, and had been. With a whoosh it pulled into me, including my children, my love, everything that could have been crystalizing. The happy chirps of my children, becoming a part of eternity without pain or fear, were a balm to my soul as I quit existing, becoming of Magic.

THIRTY-EIGHT

There are few hereditary familiars, the two most famous being the Phoenix of Paris and the Dragon of China. But the Dragon, whose name is Tiantang, is also where the choice of emperor lies. Earlier when the Dragon was injured, the question of who would choose the next ruler arose, creating disquiet in many quarters. While the creature might be immortal, it is obviously not invulnerable. ~ CNN Talking Head

ORDER

"Cori? Are you awake? Can you hear me?" A woman's voice sounded far away and very near simultaneously. I blinked my eyes, or tried to. They seemed to be glued together. "Wait a minute," she said. Something cool and damp scraped against my face and eyes multiple times. "Try now."

My eyes opened, and I stared at gray flatness. Where was the sky? Was that color from clouds?

~Cori, look at me.~ The voice was everywhere, but nowhere. I forced my head to move, though it was stiff and unwieldy, it flopped over to the other side where a huge cat lay staring at me. I squawked and tried to fly away, my limbs thrashing against fabric that entangled me.

~Peace, my quean. You are safe and human.~ Amused worry filled my mind, and I stilled, the sharp teeth taking up all my attention. But memory filtered in, and the life of a bird became more of a story, not reality.

"Carelian?" My voice croaked as if I had been silent for eons.

~Excellent. Now turn the other way and tell me who that is.~

I obeyed more because I had nothing better to do than fear. The lack of fear made me realize I didn't fear a cat with teeth big enough to make a snack out of me. A woman sat on the other side, looking worried and relieved. Familiar features and face. "Marisol?"

A smile spread across her face and her body sagged as if the supports holding her upright were severed. "You were starting to worry us. How are you doing?"

I wiggled my claws. No, that wasn't right. Toes. I had toes. I lived here. Hamiada. "Wasn't Hamiada going to watch me?" That was right, wasn't it?

More stress faded at those words. "She did but after eight hours and you were still asleep, I came to watch over you."

"She was well. Her focus was not stressed," Hamiada said, stepping into view with gray-green moss covering the bark of her arms and torso. "Were you?" Her head tilted the slightest bit toward Carelian.

~Not overly stressed. Though my concern was rising—twelve hours is a long time. Cori, can you stand?~ He stretched with a head splitting yawn and the avian part of me squawked and tried to fly again. This time, only my legs twitched.

"Yeah. Pee sounds good. Then coffee?" The fog that clouded my brain was thicker than normal, but I felt it would be easier to clear if I had some caffeine.

"After I get you downstairs. The last thing we need you to do is try to fly down the stairs and break your leg, or worse." Marisol replicated her actions from the other day and had me downstairs eating and drinking before I had full command of my senses. She made me calorie laden Mexican coffee. That combined with a protein filled omelet helped to push the confusion away.

Cries of "Momma Cori" and pounding footsteps heralded the arrival of the twins and soon enough I had two limpets on my sides, each squeezing me like they hadn't seen me in months. "Did you go see the story again?" Jaz asked as she pulled back to look at me.

"I did. Though I'm still thinking about what it meant." I leaned down to whisper to both of them, "Flying is really neat."

They giggled as their dragons zoomed through the house, flying above them with a freedom that I wanted to join.

"It was worth it?" Jo asked, coming in, dropping a kiss on my head, then her mother's cheek.

"I think so. But I really need to let it settle in. The transition back to this world is the most disorienting aspect of it." I drank more coffee and thought I might remember how to walk without assistance at this point.

"Excellent. Well, we came by to check on you, and waited until now only because Hamiada assured us that Marisol had come over." Sable squeezed me tight as the kids detached to race into the sunroom. "We are headed out grocery shopping and then if the kids behave, we'll take them out to pizza. Do you want to come with us?"

"Hmmm," a day out with them sounded good. "Check with me after the shopping and I'll see how steady I am at that point. But if I think I'm up to it, absolutely."

"Deal." Ten minutes later, they headed out in their SUV for groceries while Marisol chivied me into the sunroom. I sat pulling the memories into my mind. There were parts that struck me looking at it now like a movie, though I did wish I could somehow rewind and zoom into the memories. The white grey stones and circles that seemed to be a theme. The caverns, the volcano in the distance. Even the trees that I'd never seen on Earth all resonated, but I couldn't place them.

I shared images with Carelian, asking his opinion. ~Strange temple, but then humans always worship oddly. It does have the same feel as other places I've been in. The room in Japan and the palace in China.~

"True." They had the same stark smooth rooms with the symbols on the floors. "Okay I need to get back into my body." I stepped outside, and as it was almost seventy degrees, the temperature was comfortable. I went to the little lawn area near the fountain and moved through some yoga, needing to get my mind and body synced back up. Nothing fast or strenuous, but I was aching by the time I finished. Overall, I felt better and more human, literally.

The strident tone from the phone grabbed me, and I sighed.

I pulled my cardigan back on and walked in as I answered the unwelcome call. "Morning, Yolanda."

"Cori. I have a rip. We've not seen one in a week, but this one..." Yolanda trailed off with a sigh. "This one is just huge, big enough that we can't close it. I'm hoping you'll be able to. I've had two groups try. They get a portion closed, then run out of offerings and it slowly opens back up."

I fought back a yawn. I wasn't tired, just exhausted. "Nothing is keeping it open?"

"Nothing obvious," she replied.

"Get me the info, I'll get there but it doesn't sound like it is an absolute emergency." I was stretching as I spoke. I needed another hour to make sure I was really human and not a bird. "And there are no sharp drops or anything near it, are there?" I had this sudden vision of me jumping off, expecting to fly. The vision of me plummeting to my death made me swallow hard.

"Umm no sharp drops. Yeah. We've been trying for a few hours, but it is blocking a major highway. It's in Atlanta at the 75 and 285 merger."

"Oh," I said perking up. It had been a while since I'd been back in Georgia. "Top or bottom?"

"Ummm, it says near Cumberland?"

"Top. That makes it easier. Get me who I should contact, and I'll head that way. But let them know it will still be about an hour." I walked toward the door, still swaying a bit. There wasn't a tail there to move to alter my direction. Humans were designed weird.

"Got it. Headed your way." I could hear her typing as she talked.

I hung up and moved through the house. "You hear that?" I called out to Carelian.

~I did. Though I am not sure that I approve of you leaving

319

now. But if you keep moving you should be fine shortly.~ He had risen from the floor, stretching himself.

"Yeah, let me get my clothes changed, get you in your harness and get my bag ready, then we'll head that way." I spoke as I was walking toward the stairs.

"I heard that, young lady. Where are you going?" Marisol stuck her head out of the kitchen looking at me.

"Atlanta, huge rip."

Marisol blew air out, lifting her bangs up a bit. "And they need you?"

"This one is just huge. I'll be careful. But let Jo and Sable know?" I sighed. Getting pizza with the kids had sounded fun, if exhausting.

"And I'll make you some energy bombs." She turned her formidable attention on Carelian. "You ping me if anything goes wrong. She pushes herself too hard."

~Yes, she does and I will. But this sounds safe even to me. I feel motion and being Cori will help her more than sitting here.~ Carelian rubbed by me as he headed to the stairs.

I rolled my eyes in loving amusement. What would I do without these people in my life? Twenty minutes later, I was indeed moving slow but at least I wasn't looking for my wings any longer. Carelian was pulling me through to the crossroads with my backpack stuffed with emergency supplies.

"She said it was near Cumberland Mall. You remember that?"

~Of course. The all you could eat Mongolian grill was there. We should have lunch there before we return.~ He opened a portal, and I could see the lights flashing and the gash against the sky.

"That looks like the place." We stepped out, and I started walking over to the cops that had everything blocked.

"Sorry, this is a restricted area. Stay back." A young officer, his uniform almost squeaky new said with authority.

I smiled and tapped the side of my head, highlighting my tattoos. "Merlin Cori Munroe. They sent me to try to close this portal? I'm looking for Captain Jennings." I'd learned to keep it simple.

"One minute, ma'am." He turned to speak into his hand-held radio. I tuned it out as I looked at the rip. It was indeed huge. I was standing on the ramp from 285 to 75 North, and the gash blocked out all of 75 North and 285. The roads just disappeared into the open space. If there had been lava or water pouring out the damage would have been extensive. Instead, it was just emptiness.

"Carelian, where is that pointing to?" I couldn't look long as the seams of the portal pulled and taunted, but I knew he could withstand it better. I turned to look at him, only to see his ears pulled back and a snarl on his face. "What?"

~I will get Esmere, she needs to see this.~ His tail lashed back and forth as he continued to emit a low growl.

"Let me get up close first, so hopefully the huge Cath showing up won't spook anyone."

He just nodded, and I turned to the young officer. "Well?"

"The Captain is coming," he said, nodding behind him. A large woman with obvious Samoan heritage was stalking toward me. While not frowning she had the don't mess with me vibe clear in her every motion.

"You the help?" she snapped out, giving me and Carelian both once overs.

For some reason her tone caught me wrong. "Help? I am here to assist you, but I'm a merlin, not the help."

She blinked at me and then sighed. "Agreed. My apologies. There is a bit of angst over this." She waved her hands, and I focused on the sea of cars around us. I glanced at my watch, and saw it was eleven in the morning.

"Wait, this has been open for hours. Did this happen during rush hour?" I had a lot more sympathy for her. Atlanta traffic was notorious in the first place, but if this had happened during rush hours, she was probably getting yelled at by everyone that knew her name.

"Yes. The only thing that saved this from being a bigger issue is it started small enough that cars stopped before they went into it. As it is, I have two cars that had damage as they clipped the edges, one heart attack from having to slam on the brakes to avoid going into that, but otherwise it is just there and cutting off everything."

I let loose a long sigh. "I'm very glad no one went in. Let me get closer and I'll see if I can shut it."

She nodded and waved me under the police tape, and I followed her past where they had their cars acting as a barricade. "On the other side everything just ends into blue sky and if you touch it, it zaps back like static electricity. Fried a few phones."

Every one of these seemed to be different than the last. "Okay. I'm looking." I felt around it, and it was just a rip, sitting there. It resisted me closing it, but not that hard.

"Carelian, where does this go to?" He still stared at it, his fur standing on end and his ears laid back. His snarl had every cop in the area backing away with their hands on their weapons.

~It is to the realm created to contain the excess magic. It burst. The outpouring of magic is keeping it open. Esmere is coming now.~ His words matched the slice of pain as Esmere stepped out. Her reaction was exactly the same .

~This should not happen,~ she snarled, and I flinched a bit as the words sliced into me.

"Softer, please. I get that. But how do I close it?" I looked around at all the people with magic spilling over them. The odds were everyone in the right age range would emerge, probably a few outside of the normal range. There was that much magic spilling out, something I could sense after they pointed it out to me. I pulled out my phone, sending Stephen a message and asking him to give the OMO a heads up.

~We wait. When the magic has completed flowing, then we can close it. It should end soon.~ She sat down, tail twitching. ~But this means our solution isn't one. This has to stop soon.~

I rubbed my eyes, the image of a temple with gray floors dedicated to magic floating in my mind.

Much to everyone's annoyance I couldn't close it until three p.m. By then the Governor had declared it a work from home day as the major arteries were impassable. Esmere went back to the realms to talk to Freya and Tirsane. I expected a council summons in the near future. For my part, I headed home and caught up with Sable and Jo. Closing the rip hadn't been that expensive once the magic quit flowing. I'd only needed to use the two weeks growth on my skull to close it. But the ramifications were exhausting.

I pushed everything away and enjoyed pizza and games with the kids. We got a few stares, but for me being able to be out with them and enjoy living made it worth it.

Our favorite Merlin, Cori Munroe, has now been spotted in China and France. Our girl sure gets around. If anyone has pictures, be sure to upload them for a chance to be our "Cori Candid" of the day. But this does raise other questions: with her jet-setting around the globe, is she at risk of bringing infections home or worse bugs that shouldn't be here? We all love Carelian, but he is an animal. What if a new type of tick or another parasite hitches a ride home on him? ~ CNN Mage Focus

SPIRIT

T he next day I was having an early lunch, and I felt like myself, though there were still the occasional twitches. My phone rang, not the discordant noise that was Yolanda, so I answered it. Yolanda I might have hung up on. I didn't feel up to dealing with any more drama that morning. "This is Cori," I said not looking at the phone. My sandwich called my name, but I drank some iced tea waiting.

"Good afternoon, Cori." Citlali's voice came through and I relaxed a bit, but still resisted the sandwich. Crunching in someone's ear wasn't good manners—-and I liked Citlali.

"Afternoon. Has the Council meeting been called already?" I kind of thought I'd have received notice via Esmere or Freya, but what did I know?

"Council meeting? Not that I know of. Is there one?" She sounded confused, which made me more confused.

"Probably soon. So, if you aren't calling about that, what's up?" I pulled out a pickle that was sticking out of the sandwich and nibbled on it.

"The elders wanted to know if you would come meet with them today. They would like some feedback."

I stopped nibbling. "Wait, the AIN elders want to meet with me?"

"Yes, then dinner with my family afterward?" There was a hint of hope in her voice along with an undercurrent of worry.

"Sure. Give me an hour? I need to eat and change clothes." I'd slipped back into lounge clothes and wasn't going anywhere in those. And I'd eat my sandwich first, it was an excellent sandwich.

"Will do. I'll be there at 1:10 PM your time?"

I glanced at my watch. "Yep, sounds good." She hung up, and I focused on food. While the rift hadn't exhausted me, I was still trying to put on weight and build energy. Then I got ready to visit the AIN with excitement rippling through me. I hadn't heard of anyone who had been in the AIN ever. The AIN provided fodder for constant tabloid discussions, but I thought I'd heard news of some recent talks with various governments. I took a minute to call the news article up on my phone and sure enough, there had been three sets of delegates in the last six months talking to different governments about lowering the barrier.

That barrier had been there for centuries already, but it was different from the one James had discovered. The one Hishatio had desperately desired. Maybe I'd find out how they created the barrier. Anything for a bit more knowledge that might hold the key to everything.

I dressed in my normal outfit, just in case I ended up running for my life. While I knew Carelian wouldn't wear his harness there, it got shoved in my backpack, just in case we needed it. Ready to go, I headed back downstairs just as Kesis pinged me.

~May we step in?~

"Hamiada, incoming." She and Carelian communicated, but I tried to let her know when others were coming. At least those not family.

A moment later, Kesis and Citlali stepped out into the little square in the corner.

"Afternoon. What's the occasion?" Looking at Citlali, I felt a bit underdressed, but I let it be. She was wearing a long broom-stick skirt in shades of blue, with a tunic in cream with embroidery running along the bottom hem and the neckline. Her various types of long braids fell to her waist. She still had on her belt, holding knives and a pouch, and her ever present moccasin boots.

"Changes are coming, and they would like a friend to talk to first."

Her voice remained noncommittal, and I rolled my eyes. "Political ambush?"

"Yep," she said with a shrug.

I just shook my head. "Oh well, I'm getting good at those, but are you sure you don't want Stephen? Regardless of what the magic council thinks, I really don't have any political power."

"I know, they know, but your name has come up multiple times and they would like the input." She shrugged, and I looked at Kesis.

"Should I be worried?"

Carelian's ears flipped forward at that also, his focus sharpening.

~No. They only want to talk, I swear to that.~ Kesis took my question seriously, and I didn't know if that made me feel reassured or not.

"Let's go," I said, trying to pass by my own worries.

A rip opened, by Kesis I assumed, and I stepped into a courtyard that was open and airy. The sky above was the same as I'd seen at home, though at the moment it gleamed pale blue and had cotton ball clouds floating through it.

"At least there is sky here," I commented as she waved toward a door at the other end of the courtyard. The sun shone down making the plants all but shimmer.

"I know. That weird diffuse light in the realms is insane. I have zero idea if the creatures there even have circadian rhythms, or how they function without solar radiation," she commented, her voice sparking in interest.

"Oh, the realms have the radiation. I tested it once with solar panels. It's just very diffuse and low. So think constant cloudy day without rain levels." I looked around as I spoke. The courtyard possessed plants in raised garden beds, an apricot tree with a bench around it, and a small pond that had creatures in it based on the splashing and canted ears from both familiars. But why were the walls green? And were they fuzzy?

"Huh. That is interesting. The beast lands aren't much better, but the light is brighter and there seem to be seasons that mimic our own." She led me through the door and into an open area with a large table at one end and a woman working at the other end, putting things in huge filing cabinets that took up most of the room. A door stood on the opposite side of us leading outside.

"You don't have computers?" I asked, looking at all the filing cabinets.

"We do, but so much of the records were in paper, we are still working on transcribing all of them into electronic media. That is what she is working on. As the team completes each cabinet, someone will go through and check the data, then we will recycle the files. It's an ongoing project." Citlali waved me toward the table. "They should be here shortly."

I headed over to it, amused and somewhat appreciative that there were low ottoman-like seats for familiars as well. I settled myself in a chair that was against the wall so I could watch people come in. Carelian stepped onto the low seat next to me on my right and curled up, his body fitting on the wide upholstered ottoman.

~I approve of this. Much better than human chairs.~

I scratched his ears and watched.

It took a minute, but the other set of doors opened, and people streamed in. The only things I could see they had in common were all of them but one was at least one to two decades older than me and most of their hair was in the wild mix of braids like Citlali had. That and none of them seemed happy to be here.

Joy. I'm not that bad. Why can't someone besides my family ever seem happy to see me?

There were seven individuals and six of them settled on the side opposite me, while Citlali finally settled down at the right end of the table, leaving the seventh person to sit at the left end of the table.

"Hi," I said, trying to project something other than exhausted victim. "I'm Cori Munroe. Citlali said you wanted to speak to me?"

"We are the Elders of Beast Lands or what we call the Nation. We will introduce ourselves and the area we have responsibility for." The one who spoke was male with all the various braids but had a flat grim look on his face and his hair was white with no grey left in it. "I am Elder Wya and I am responsible for the smooth communication and governing within the Nation."

The next one spoke, a male in his seventies, with turquoise at his throat, wrists, and braided in his hair. "I am Shaman Vohkinne, responsible for status of healthcare in the nation and elder care." All of them spoke English but with enough of an accent that I had to focus to pay attention to the words, not the sound.

A woman spoke next. "I am Chief Hausis, responsible for the land and foods grown there." Mentally I dubbed her secretary of agriculture. She had her braids twisted around her head like a crown, showing off feathers and ribbons that were twined within.

The next person, a woman bigger than any I'd ever seen, not fat, but height and muscle, spoke with a voice that made me ache to hear her singing jazz. "I am Elder Zitkala, and my responsibilities lay in technology research and implementation."

I blinked at that and wanted to pepper her with questions, but I stayed silent to let them finish their introductions.

"Shaman Kinta, and I am happy you are here. My responsibilities lie in education and family." He smiled, but as his head turned toward me, I saw sightless blue eyes. He was tiny, my size now, with his white hair in a jumble of braids twisted in a bun on his head. A large hummingbird sat on his head next to his bun head cocked. Then his eyes turned and his smiled inched up a bit.

Huh, seeing-eye bird. That's new.

"Chief Espowyes, military and diplomacy. You are welcomed." His voice sounded like gravel, and he gave me a sharp nod that exposed scars on his throat and chin. But he sounded more inviting than the rest of them.

I turned to the last person, the one that didn't fit the general theme of everyone else. Round braids festooned with feathers and beads gleamed in the jet-black hair and the person was pretty. I couldn't say if they were male or female, just that they were healthy and oddly attractive with white teeth and green eyes that sparkled. "Cori Munroe, you are welcomed. I am Dakota, Spirit Talker. I am the Voice of the Nation." The capitalizations were heard in the title.

"Hi everyone," I tried to smile, but the formality caused a frisson of nerves to run down my spine. "So, what is this about?"

Elder Wya spoke, his flat voice neither welcoming nor aggressive, his dark eyes locked on me. "Citlali has kept us informed of the council and the issues you are facing. We have been seeing rips in our lands as well, but we work together better and as the Beast realm, as the council calls it, works in harmony with us, we have been able to close these breeches without excessive damage. We wish to know what the ultimate goal is for you, regardless of the council."

I slanted a look toward Citlali. She lifted her shoulders in a tiny shrug.

"I just want to stop it and try to get things back to the way they were. But I don't know what I need to do."

They nodded as if this didn't surprise them.

"Do you think if we dropped the borders around the nation it would help?" the raspy voice of Chief Espowyes said.

I blinked in shock and Carelian stiffened next to me. "Do you believe they are a part of what is causing this? I don't understand how your borders work to even begin to answer that."

There were quick glances between the members and Wya gave a sharp nod.

"That would be my cue," Dakota said with a smile. "Short answer, I don't think so. Long answer, we need to take them down in the next few years, but the rips might force our hand sooner and we'd rather do it at an auspicious time than have the choice taken from us."

CHAPTER
FORTY

The Phoenix of Paris spotted at the scene of a rip. Reports say the phoenix, which has always been attached to a family of bakers, was seen in full flame blocking creatures from coming out of the rip. It stayed there for an hour protecting the city until mages could get the rip closed. Then it vanished. The family the phoenix resides with has declined all requests for comments. ~ CNN Mage Focus

CHAOS

"I don't understand," I admitted, wondering once again how I got into the middle of all of this. "How is your wall created?"

Dakota smiled. "You have created a pocket realm, correct?"

"Yes," I said, shifting in my seat. "I had no choice. A pocket realm seemed the only possibility to contain a nuclear device." That didn't seem to come as a surprise to them, as no one reacted.

Dakota continued. "The border, which blocks off ten sections of this planet, is essentially a series of thin pocket realms with pathways between them and they all link to the Beast realm."

I blinked at that. It seemed so easy and hard simultaneously. "What exactly is the Beast realm?" I fought with myself to not ask questions nonstop. Sticking to the things I needed to know and understand were the best options. If the least satisfying.

"When Magic washed over us, it gave us an option. There were many creatures that time and man were destroying, and there were many mystical creatures that felt trapped in the sunless lands. We agreed to share our lands with them and they the realms with us. So we created the Nations. They are all the creatures that wish to live as creatures and those that Magic grabbed to protect. Here we have many of the animals extinct in the rest of the world and those that are of magic but not like your spirit animal or Kinta's M'mi."

"I'll take your word for it, but aren't animals from magic all sentient?" I would never understand how Esmere and Carelian could eat something that could talk to you, one more of the many agree to disagree topics.

"Yes," Dakota said with a smile. "Which is why when they

slay us, they have the right to dine on our bodies as much as we on theirs."

"If the next words out of your mouth are 'hot sauce solves everything', I'm done." There was no way I could handle an entire culture with the same attitude toward food as Carelian.

They stared at me. Citlali started snickering first, then Dakota. Zitkala and Wya fought smiles as the others sighed and just looked exasperated.

"That is a conversation many of us have had with our spirit animals. Your confusion is understood and shared." Dakota's lips twitched. "It is still an ongoing and cherished argument."

I snorted a bit at "cherished", but let it go. "So, what exactly do you want from me?"

Zitkala in her rich deep voice, responded. "Do you think we should pull down our walls now or wait until something forces them down? We need an outsider's perspective."

My eyes widened as I stared at them. "You understand I am not in the government and I'm only aware of a small fraction of the world at large, right?"

Why me?

Shaman Vohkinne nodded. "We know. But for all the people we have in the outside world, they are either tourists or they are limited to experiencing a tiny part of the world. You have seen multiple governments from the inside and have dealt with a council full of beings that have only a passing familiarity with humanity, and yet you are respected by all. We understand your answer will only be your opinion, but what and how you say it will give us much to think about." His turquoise caught the light as he spoke and even though this group of people didn't seem welcoming, I didn't get resentment from them.

I leaned back in the chair and reached out to pet Carelian as I pondered my response. They let me think, not giving any signs of being impatient while I processed my answer. At that moment I really wanted some ice cream-laden coffee so I could sip while I tried to think.

"This is just me, but I think you should wait." I could see the question in their eyes, so I tried to explain my thoughts. "Right now, everyone is on edge with the rips. They would love to blame someone and if you are right about all the areas you block off, when they fall, it might cause people to blame you. Or give them convenient scapegoats. Not to mention that your people, society, don't wear tattoos. It will cause a lot of strife and pressure from other governments and the OMO. I would wait until either the rips force down your walls, which makes you look like victims, or there is a resolution for the rips, one way or the other. But absolutely start talking to the governments because.... " I trailed off then shrugged. I might as well offer everything versus offering nothing. "Governments are the worst of humanity. They want power and control, and they will want so badly to control you. If you aren't already viewed as equals by the time the walls come down, there will be a feeding frenzy to control you."

A ripple of reactions went through the table and some of them glanced at Dakota, who just kept a pleasant smile.

Finally Elder Wya spoke, his voice soft, though his face could have been carved in wood. "That is in accordance with some of our thoughts. The tattoos were not something we had considered. The braids are not enough?"

"Braids?" I said dumbly, then I actually looked at all of them and the fact that Dakota only had one braid. "Wait, those say what type of mage you are?"

Citlali looked at me this time, surprise on her face. "You did not know this?"

I threw my hands up to shoulder height in exasperation.

"How would I know this? Mages braid their hair constantly. Why would I assign any value to braids?"

Shaman Kinta, his mouth and eyes smiling as he faced my direction with his blank eyes, said, "I suppose that is unreasonable of us. The joy of inherent cultural understandings. Spirit is a round four strand braid, while Order is the five strand, and Chaos is a fishtail braid." I turned and looked at them all with eyes that saw what I'd missed before.

"How do you tell strength?" That confused me, as I still didn't see any indications implying levels of power.

Kinta shrugged. "We don't. It makes no difference what level you are capable of. All Merlins can access something in every branch, and their strengths are mostly immaterial."

"And you don't worry about people braiding their hair to appear to be other than what they are?" I pressed, now just more curious about the cultural aspects.

"No?" Kinta sounded confused. "Why would you pretend to be a Spirit mage if you were an Order mage?"

I could only answer with a shrug. "I mean I guess that doesn't matter, but what about those without magic pretending to have magic? Or people with magic pretending to not have it? That can get you in big trouble with the draft."

"Ah," Kinta said, and I saw Chief Espowyes clench his hands, then relax them as if giving in to a situation he hadn't wanted but was letting it go. "That would be the second aspect, then."

"What?" I looked between all of them, but they had the best poker faces. Only Citlali's face seemed to be reactive.

"The Nation doesn't have any members that aren't mages. We are all part of magic and Earth." Dakota dropped this bombshell on me, and I just stared at them, trying to process that.

"Huh. Okay. I mean I don't suppose it changes anything. So

what now?" I refused to ask about those incapable of using magic and the Tirsane thing. I'd had enough bombshells for one day and part of me still fretted over being imprisoned under a roof, unable to see the open sky. The last thing I needed was dropping anything new on them, though the odds were Citlali had passed on that information as well.

These bird reactions need to fade and fast.

Elder Wya nodded, his eyes still hard, but the corners of his mouth softened as he watched me. "That was the extent of our needs. We wanted to see if you were who both Amadahy and Citlali were saying. And they were correct. Enjoy your visit to our lands, though we request lines of communication stay open? We have others who live in the outside world, but we sometimes need a true outsider perspective."

"Sure. Citlali's got my number. You can call. Just remember, I'm not anyone with power in our governments. I might be able to talk to a few people, but most won't listen to me or if they do their power is limited." I wanted to make sure they realized that. Even being friends with Cixi didn't actually let me do anything besides ask a favor and those were prickly in politics. Besides, I hated the idea of using a friend.

"That is understood. We thank you for your time," Chief Espowyes said in his gruff voice. With that he rose and a moment later the rest of them did as well. The final person to leave was Dakota, who nodded at me with a smile, then headed out the door. Citlali sat at the end of the table, watching me.

"So what next?" I asked as I noted the expressions ripple across her face.

She shook her head in bemusement. "If you had bet me, I would have said you'd tell them to tear them down now, before the rips did it accidentally because ripping off the bandage would be easier and would divert attention from you and the rips."

I huffed out a chortle. "Honestly didn't even think about that. It would definitely get people off my back—think we can call them back and change the answer?" I was smiling as I said it. "Until the various governments realized I'd been talking to the AIN. At that point, I might never get out of a locked cell." I paused, suddenly unsure. "They do know not to bandy my name about, correct? I mean, I'm not even sure of the legality of this." I waved my hand to encompass everything as I searched through my memory, trying to find anything about talking to AIN members.

Citlali waved her hand dismissively. "It won't go anywhere. Mostly you will be mentioned in our internal meetings. There are multiple city-state chiefs who will be interested in hearing about this. But these plans have been in motion for a few years. This is just more data for them." She pushed up from the table and I followed her movements.

Carelian, who had been quiet the entire conversation, jumped off as she led us outside. Stress that had been lurking in my shoulders faded as I saw the open sky above us.

"I was thinking I could give you a tour of this city, then dinner?" Citlali said with a question in her voice.

I checked my watch, almost three in the afternoon. She'd mentioned the dinner with family when she called. "That sounds good. I left text messages telling everyone where I was."

A smile softened her normally stern visage. "Excellent. Let me show you Bassée." She led me out of the courtyard we stepped into and onto the street outside. In most cities I'd been in, you had sidewalks, roads, and tall buildings with lots of little alleyways. At best, in small town America, you would have cute buildings, wider alleys, and usually a max of three stories tall for the buildings. If you went to New York City, you couldn't see the sky unless you looked straight up in many parts of the city.

This was different. We walked down a sidewalk of green moss, while vehicles without tires used a road made of dark blue flowers. There were buildings with windows and doors, but the walls were green, the roofs glinted in the light. There were bikes everywhere, and they had their own path that was made of tiny stones in a clear substance.

"So why green walls? And you have hover cars?" Shock rippled through me as I watched a car zoom by. The rest of the area reminded me of future concept sketches for cities of the future.

"The walls are moss, and they regulate the temperature, collect water, and filter it back into storage tanks. We have solar generators on the tops of most buildings. We don't run electricity anywhere. Everyone produces their own." Citlali pointed around the paths. "They are a type of hover cars. We have magnets buried under the streets and the vehicles run on them. It took us five years to create linking interchanges between the city-states. The bike paths are from plastic we collect from your world. We melt it, mix in debris from building and pour it out. It makes a very strong, flexible, and resilient path. Everyone has been enjoying the low cost for that."

She talked as she walked through, pointing at things. The AIN wasn't a mystical city full of tech so far advanced it seemed like magic, but they obviously prioritized nature much more than we did. Everywhere sprouted trees, little open spaces. I saw deer jumping through undergrowth in small wild lots that had bike paths through them. No building was over three stories, and all of them crawled with life. As we walked, she talked about this city and why she lived here. Carelian followed, not saying much, but his nose twitched constantly. I just didn't know if that was in a good or a bad away.

"I actually have an apartment in one of the bachelor apartment buildings. It is filled mostly with single adults who have jobs that keep them busy with little time for family or maintaining a residence. It would seem horribly small to you. My apartment has a bedroom, a small kitchen and living area, then a toilet only restroom. Each floor has communal showers. It's more efficient and lets us have nice large tubs for soaking." She gave me a wicked grin at that implying more than soaking went on.

"I'm not sure what I expected, but this is fascinating." My head was swiveling constantly, trying to take everything in. It felt like a radically different culture and one that I rather enjoyed. "The moss. Do you think that is something Hamiada could use? The summers can get a bit much."

Citlali shrugged. "I'm not sure, but I could get the information on them and give it to you, then she can decide." She walked ahead, aiming toward a neighborhood set off to the side.

I ducked my head to keep my grin unseen. The amount of delight that filled me when others treated the sentients in my life as people never got old.

CHAPTER
FORTY-ONE

This Day In Magical History: Today in 1956, Air Hedge Mage (Dolores McGuffin) attempted a DIY air balloon ride for her daughter's birthday party. During her test run, something reportedly went awry and the party-goers lost sight of her above the clouds. The where-abouts and/or remains of the, locally known as, Balloon Girl have never been discovered.

ORDER

American cities tended toward grid layouts. Instead, the Nation, or at least this city, created theirs in spirals and circles. The businesses were all in the center of a circle, with everything easily accessible. Then you went out to more of the manufacturing, though I didn't see any big shops, but lots of little ones. I saw at least five different cloth manufacturers, two clothiers, then a custom makeup shop, and a store with a name I couldn't pronounce that had in English below it "Grafts".

"What is Grafts?" I asked as we walked.

Citlali glanced over to see the store I pointed at. "Ah, that is for plants, so you can graft different types onto your orchard."

"Personal orchard?" That idea made me think back over what I'd been seeing. I started looking at the houses more carefully. Most of them blended into the land, with parts of it under the ground, and all of them had neat garden areas staked out full of plants in a tumultuous burst of vines, leaves, and fruit.

"Most people have a tree or two that is theirs, but we also have neighborhood orchards that everyone shares. Most families have gardens, and we raise a significant portion of our own food, though a few things have changed over the years. Hothouses, freeze drying, canning, processing of animals, all things that people want and complain about at the same time." She flashed me a grin as she turned down a street where if I hadn't seen a house being built, I would have just assumed this entire area was gardens.

"And the bachelor apartments?" I asked looking around. It was too quiet, especially compared to my area. There were no sounds of cars or heavy equipment and no kids running around. "And where are the kids?" The temperature hovered around eighty degrees, so no reason not to have kids around.

"Bachelors don't have individual ones, though there is a

hydroponic for vegetables so you can grab fresh food--usually carrots, squash, tomatoes, peppers, those sorts of vegetables. That is part of your rent, someone else maintaining the building garden. As for the kids, school or jobs right now," she said. "But they should get out soon. Get ready to be swarmed if they see you. You will be fascinating to them. Carelian might get mauled to death. They know any creature they see here is a familiar and the majority of ours love attention."

~Yes,~ Kesis chimed in. ~They do scritches and pets. You will enjoy.~

Carelian tilted his ears forward as we moved past the school, but no swarms of children came out to assault us.

We kept walking, with me looking at everything and Carelian and Kesis apparently in a conversation from the low mental hum that was just out of my hearing. Citlali angled toward a large plot with trees laid out in front, with rows of corn and beans in between. "This is my family's. They have a large area because they've been here a while and provide a lot of extra food to the store."

~They will like both of you.~ Kesis seemed relaxed as did Carelian, so I pushed down any worry I might have had.

There were so many implications with that statement that I wanted to follow up to, instead I followed her as we walked down a path made up of the same materials the bike path had been, to a wall that was about seven feet high. Citlali pulled the wooden gate open and waved me in. We walked into another courtyard, though this pond was more of a water feature with the stream running over a large area with several deep pools and trees and seats in the area.

"This is gorgeous. Do all the houses have this?"

Citlali shrugged. "Many. It's easier to keep a healthy fish garden in an enclosed area. Makes maintaining and verifying the fish are okay easier. I think my mother said we were having mammoth for dinner. A hunter found a wounded one and most of the town got a share."

"A mammoth?" I said slowly unsure I'd heard correctly. "Aren't they extinct?"

"On Earth, not in the realms. It's where a lot of your mythical creatures exist." She walked up to the wall that held a large wooden door and pulled it open. "Come on in." She glanced back at Carelian who was peering over the pond with ears pricked forward and a tail that had gone still. "Carelian you even so much as wound one of my mother's fish and she'll have your hide on the wall."

I followed, wondering how cave-like the house would feel. Instead, a bright airy space with diffuse light coming down from sky lights greeted me. The area we walked into was a large open area with a fireplace in the middle of a circle of chairs. Right now, it had obviously been closed down for the summer, and instead a wooden platform set on it with a cherry tomato plant on it. To the right was the kitchen area, or at least I assumed that. A large round table with what reminded me of a Korean BBQ grill in the middle sat in one area. Behind that I saw a wall of cupboards with a sink and a metal contraption that I assumed was a refrigerator.

To the left was a hallway with a woven stretch of fabric blocking any further view.

"Tusa, we're here," she called out. Citlali turned her attention to me. "Do you need anything?"

"Bathroom?" It had been a while, and I drank a lot of water and protein drinks lately.

She nodded to the wall directly in front of us with three doors. "Use the one with the moon on it," she said as she moved over to the kitchen. "You need something to drink?"

"Water, please?" I headed to the bathroom. This, at least, was normal: a toilet and a sink. I used the small facilities and came back out to see Citlali talking to another woman. This woman was rounder than Citlali with only fishtail braids in her dark hair that was just showing hints of silver. Carelian was sprawled out in a patch of sunlight.

Citlali looked up and saw me coming out. "Tusa, meet Cori Munroe. Cori this is my sister Tusa. She's already met Carelian."

Tusa smiled at me, her eyes the same brown as Citlali. "Welcome be to my home, Cori Munroe."

I nodded, unsure of the social niceties. "Thank you for having me."

She gave me a long look, then nodded. "You indeed have been using too much magic for too long. Dinner will be good for you. And you," she turned her attention to Citlali, "have you forgotten so much about having guests?"

Citlali sighed. "No, I was going to get her some water, but you showed up first." It had the sound of a long-standing tease between the two of them, so I didn't worry about it.

"I see," Tusa said, arching a brow as Citlali laughed and headed over to the kitchen. "Come sit, Cori. Tell me about your world. I have so many questions. I'm waiting for the others to get here, so we have time."

She pulled me over to the low chairs circling the quiescent firepit and peppered me with questions about the rest of the world. Tusa was funny, smart, and eager to hear about my world. We talked as the familiars either slept or entertained themselves, sometimes the difference was hard to know. Tusa knew some aspects about the outside world already and about others had no clue. The inconsistent knowledge struck me as odd.

A small bell rang, and she looked up. "Ah, the others are here. Citlali, will you go harvest three beefsteak tomatoes, four zucchini, and some spinach?" She stood as she talked and headed into the kitchen. "The mammoth has been marinating, so a quick salad, and zucchini to roast and that should be a satisfying dinner."

I had managed to stand before the door opened and in walked John Taliance in his sheriff uniform and Sergeant Amy Johnson, also in uniform.

His eyes caught me, and a slow smile creased his face. "Merlin Munroe. Nice to see you again."

I inclined my head to him. "Thank you for your help in getting the AIN to talk to me." I'd known Citlali was his aunt, but this put all the pieces in place more firmly.

"Meh. It wasn't that hard once they decided to listen. That group is a bit hard-headed at times," he said dismissively, heading into the kitchen. He wrapped his arms around Tusa and dropped a kiss on the top of her head. She laughed and hugged him back as Citlali slipped out the door with a pair of shears and a basket in her hand.

Everyone made Carelian and me just rest. The organized chaos was entertaining as the four of them worked together to make food. Amy was obviously a long-time friend, though I still wasn't sure if she and John were in a relationship outside of friends. It didn't matter, I was just curious.

Fifteen minutes later, they pulled me over to the round table and set me down and pulled up two ottomans for Carelian and Kesis. The grill was going and circled by a wide section that then turned around it. It made it easier to share and get the various items to grill without having to ask anyone to pass what ever caught your eye.

By this time, I was starving, so we spent the first fifteen minutes putting strips of marinated mammoth on the grill along with strips of seasoned zucchini. The fresh salad had a green herbal dressing to go with that just made me want to coat everything with it.

"I take it you aren't estranged from the AIN," I said when the first rush of eating was done, watching John closely.

"Nah. My superiors think they kicked me out because I have no magic and it never occurred to them to ask questions. It's a risk, as if I ever get tested it could cause issues." He shrugged. "But since I don't use magic the way most OMO mages do, it is unlikely."

"And Amy?" I turned my gaze to her.

For her part, she just grinned at me. "I'm cover, a friend, and who am I to turn down mammoth for dinner?"

That part I had to agree with. The mammoth was rich, flavorful, and Carelian had eaten so much his stomach distended as he laid on the floor with Kesis in much the same condition.

"So, if the council has you, why are they asking my opinion? Wouldn't yours be more nuanced?" This was what was bugging me. Why ask me when they had no idea who I really was as a person?

"Oh it is, but I'm a low person on the totem pole in a very rural area. I'm male, I'm not a mage, and I'm not dealing with rips. I told them to get more info. We all know the walls need to come down in the next few years, but the opportunities to leverage what is going on now can't be overstated. Besides all of our spirit animals like you, even the ones that firmly believe Carelian would eat them given half a chance."

~Would not. Have decided I am on a fish and mammoth only diet. Never again shall I mess with fur or small bones.~ Carelian's murmured words made me laugh and glance over at him.

"You mean until tomorrow when you're hungry and there is a rustle in the leaves," I said.

~Or until then.~ His agreement made us laugh.

"I still just find it disconcerting. Why not someone in the

government or, heck, run an online poll?" I shrugged, both amused and fretful. "My answers could be incorrect and if you make a mistake because I thought something was the right thing to do?" I trailed off on a question.

Tusa snorted. "If we do something because of your advice, that is on us. We have information, the odds are yours is one of the least biased we have available. Like I said, we are working on how to integrate and retain sovereignty, but that is a problem for the elders, not us. Berry crumble?"

I spent the rest of the evening talking to Citlali's family. Tusa was John's mother. Citlali had an interesting family. Tusa and Citlali's parents lived in the Australia pocket, working on creating sustainable gardens and water sources with a vastly different climate, soil, and wildlife. All of them were extremely against anything besides native plants, so it was taking a bit of work to get a sustainable solution in a limited area, and worse, make sure it could survive the walls falling. They had secondary learning but in a completely different structure than our schools. And everyone, as in all of them, had magic at magician level minimum. Which is why they all wore braids, except someone like John, who purposefully cut them off to infiltrate American society. I felt like I'd had dinner with spies or adventurers. Though they seemed to react the same way to my stories.

By the time we left, it felt like I had another family. Carelian brought me home and I crashed after letting everyone know I was home safe—we'd left my cell phone at the house just in case I was being tracked. But it added one more group depending on me, and I fell asleep thinking of Magic compacting everything I had ever been, could be, to a stone the size of my palm.

FORTY-TWO

More and more cases of dementia are arising among the elderly mage population. This is requiring drastic measures for those with mild dementia. Oddly the same effect that pulls the magic for those who are damaged or mentally disabled will pull it from these mages, but only when they are beyond any further aid. Those are rendered 'normal'. But those with mild dementia are kept constantly drugged and most offerings are removed, no matter how dehumanizing it might be. We know this isn't the correct option for our elderly, but without research and funding any other options remain undiscovered. ~CNN Mage Focus

SPIRIT

The next few weeks were quiet, the sort of quiet that convinced you maybe the monster under the bed had gone to sleep. I knew better. Possibilities loomed over me like a thundercloud created from fear and worry. I'd checked and Tirsane wasn't overloaded with magic yet, and the lords said they had fixed why the realm ruptured. Their random noncommittal comments about discussing it at the next council meeting told me something had gone wrong, and they'd fixed it.

Esmere hadn't given Carelian any other information, which either meant she didn't know or had decided the information had zero imperative value to me. With her you never knew. The kids were in their last few weeks of school. Next year they would be in first grade. Time seemed to fly by and they were growing just as fast. Part of me missed the simplicity of them as babies. My breasts and body did not. It had taken a full six months after breast feeding to get my breasts back to a normal size. I was more than happy to be done with aching breasts and waking up in the middle of the night for feedings.

Yet my mood was melancholy as I thought about how fast everything was changing. I pushed off the mood with a shake of my head and picked up the next set of notes from the scholars in the Library. They had had almost five full months and while it would take years to read everything in there, the volunteers had skimmed through an astounding amount. But while the kernels of information they had pried out contained fascinating stories, tidbits, and hints, none of it shed any more light on the problem. My stress only continued to rise as nothing came forth. Even asking about the Phoenix Heart gained only vague rumors of a life not lived and transformative possibilities.

Jeorgaz let me know that if Brash was still alive, no one knew where. I thanked him for his time, gave him a few tidbits to share with others, and tried to make myself believe all the silence meant good things. It didn't work. In an effort to distract myself I called Indira. Big sister, mentor, friend. I hadn't talked to her in over a month.

"Hello?" she answered in a distracted tone.

"Morning, Indira," I said, my smile clear in my voice.

"Cori. How are you doing? It seems ages since I last saw you." Indira's voice wrapped around me like a hug, and I settled down in the club chair, staring out the windows but not really seeing the outside.

"Eh. I've put on a few pounds, so that helps. Though I miss having hair. I never realized how much hair kept your head warm." I rubbed my bare head as I said that, the stubble velvet soft.

Her laughter bubbled through the phone, and I realized I needed to find time to hang with her. "I can see that. Hopefully that issue will be gone soon. Any word on an ultimate solution?"

"Not yet. There are a few things that are falling into place, though that doesn't mean solutions. An instruction guide to this whole herald thing would have been nice," I said with a wry tone. "Trying to figure this out is worse than putting a puzzle together with the backside up."

"Have you done that before?" Her voice laughed.

"No. But it feels like that. What have you been up to?" I wanted to get the conversation off of me. I was tired of being the one everyone worried about. "Are you still doing custom chip designs?"

"Not right now. I'm assigned to one of the emergency response teams. I'm getting better at closing rips even if Spirit mages still tend to be better at it. My team responds to most of them in the DC area. If nothing else, I've been stretching myself in ways I haven't for years. But I'll admit I keep hoping this will all go away soon. I'm getting too old for this sort of adventure."

Indira was in her fifties, I knew, but she could easily pass as being in her late thirties. Her skin had no wrinkles and her style seemed ageless.

"Tell me about it. I'm years younger than you and I'm exhausted."

"You are burning yourself out. I am trying not to do that. Mostly, I just would like Stephen to retire." She paused for a second, then said in a hushed tone. "Can I tell you a secret? You can't tell anyone."

"Sure, one minute, though." I set the phone down and called out. "Hamiada, please don't listen to this conversation for the next fifteen minutes."

Her disembodied voice drifted down. "Very well. I shall go and tend to Zilenka."

I waited a minute and picked up the phone again. "Go for it."

She cleared her throat, then said quietly. "As soon as this is done and Stephen retires, I'm going to ask him to marry me."

The squee sat in the back of my mind and I had to struggle not to let it out. "Really? That's great. And totally leads to the next thing. Want to go shopping when this is over? I need some new clothes and I want something that isn't so oriented to dealing with drama. Something that will help me feel better as I gain some weight."

"Yes! I need a dress to propose in. I want him so stunned when he looks at me, he's going to be thanking his magic for delivering me into his life."

I giggled at the imagery, and we kept talking for a few minutes until she got called to respond to a small rip in the area. We said our goodbyes, and I took a minute to close my eyes and think how lucky I was to have her in my life.

"We need to have our friends over more," I said, mostly the Carelian. "Oh, and you can't mention anything either."

~Marriage is a weird human formality. Mate, enjoy mating, then when you no longer enjoy it, move on.~ He lay on the window seat, the sun heating his body.

"Easy for you to say. Do you even know your father?"

He flicked an ear at me. ~I am aware of his existence and who he is. He and *malkin* agreed only for the duration of her pregnancy and once we could walk, he left. He is a traveler of the realms and did not wish to stay as a father, but *malkin* admired his skill with Spirit.~

That was the first I'd heard of a Cath not being of Chaos. "He was Spirit then?"

~Yes. He was born there, as an experiment, and it seemed to influence his magic. But he felt it set him too far apart from the other Cath. Hence his desire to travel.~

"Do you hate him for leaving your mom?"

Carelian chuffed out a laugh in my mind at that. ~Esmere chose him because he would not interfere in her life. We are not human, do not expect human emotions. He was an excellent specimen and provided strong magic and genes for us. What more do you expect?~

I opened my mouth to argue about providing and caring for your children when a voice rang in my mind. ~Earth Lord Munroe, your debt is being called in by the family of Graphine. Your attention is required.~

The voice was unfamiliar and the name "Graphine" meant nothing to me.

~Who is this and what debt?~ I double checked my arm, but the three sections of the horn were still empty, the base one filled. The snake and cat whisker lay unmoving on my arm, though that passiveness didn't make me feel secure.

~I apologize Earth Lord. I am Order Lord Ilian. Per instructions from Salistra, the villagers that were traumatized due to your actions have called in the debt you owe them.~ The cool, precise voice awoke images that I'd avoided over the years. Parents of children terrified because I had attacked, thinking I was saving them. Even now, I winced at the thought of what I'd done. Stupidity didn't begin to cover it.

~Ah. Yes. What is the need?~ I answered as soon as the memories hit.

~A rip appeared in their village and several children tumbled out into your world. They are requesting you retrieve their offspring and close the rip.~

The second the word rip echoed through my mind, I was up out of my office and headed into my room to change clothes. The last month had helped, and I felt like I could handle most things.

~Can you give Carelian your location so he can get us there?~ I pulled up my pants and buttoned them while I waited.

~Of course. They do need assistance.~ Her quiet voice didn't make me feel any better.

~I'll be there in ten minutes or less.~ I mixed my assurance with a dash of hope that I could get out the door and there in less.

~I shall let them know.~ She disappeared from my mind, and I finished with my shoes.

~Harness, I may need it for multiple reasons.~ Carelian said from my side.

Without responding, I had him in it with all the various pouches secured. I grabbed my bag and headed to the kitchen, calling Marisol as I went. In a minute I'd given her the rundown of what was happening and where I was going. I grabbed water and food and looked at Carelian.

"You know where we are going?"

~Yes. You ready?~

I did a quick double check of everything and nodded. A moment later we stepped into a small village. Thatched roofs, a central well, and low fields greeted us as we walked into the middle of it. Quaint described it, as well as low tech, but looking at the denizens that were headed our way, it didn't need to be more. I saw gorgons, gryphons, a few Cath, and some Chitterians. I tried to figure out how this disparate group all worked together, but the rip gaping across the middle of the area grabbed the majority of my attention.

It wasn't as big as some, but it distorted the ground and the area below it.

Two gorgons slithered straight to me followed by a large Chitterian.

"You are the Earth Lord? The one that owes my family?" one of the gorgons demanded. She was about my height, darker skin than Tirsane, and had five thick snakes on her head.

"Yes. Can you tell me what happened?" I didn't waste time with anything else, as I could see glimpses of road and grass through the moving rip.

The children were playing in the square while we were working," she said, waving at the rip. "Before we could pull them away, a few tumbled in."

~Watchers went after too many breaths,~ the Chitterian said. ~No return with hatchlings. Not safe.~

It took me a few seconds to parse out the Chitterian meaning. But then I followed up. "How many of what species?" I knew I needed to go get them asap, but I couldn't take the risk of missing any. Maybe luck would be on my side and the place on Earth was in a peaceful pastoral area. Even as the hope ran through me, I knew it was a false one. If it was rural or quiet, they would have pulled the children back already.

"Three gorgons, a gryphon, and two older Chitterians," one of the gorgons responded promptly. "The gorgons are mine and my sister's. The gryphon parents are not back yet from hunting."

~Watchers younglings not hatchlings. They jump. Not wait. No word. Worry.~ The Chitterian was about three feet tall and a dark green with brown strips and ten legs. The legs in question were tapping restlessly, expressing the worry involved with the words.

"You can't talk to them?" My voice was sharp as I didn't know if that had other ramifications.

~Realms apart. Too young, too unfocused.~

I nodded, figuring teenagers, scattered attention, and they should have called for backup. That much I could handle. The big question would be—what were the humans doing?

"Thank you. I'm headed to see if I can get them back here. As soon as that is done, I'll close the rip."

Multiple heads or tails or legs bounced up and down in agreement. I turned my attention to Carelian. "Do I step through or hold on to you to go through?"

He stared for a minute, his fur a bit more puffed up than usual, tail lashing. ~Hold on to me and close your eyes.~

We moved over the rip, I wrapped my fingers around the loop in his harness, and we stepped through from the realm to Paris.

FORTY-THREE

EMERGENCY ALERT – This is not a test. We have spotted a rip with creatures emerging in the immediate vicinity. All residents should return to their homes and lock their doors. Do not attempt to interact with these creatures, they are considered extremely dangerous. Do not call 911 to report sightings. The correct authority is being contacted. Repeat this is an emergency alert. ~ Emergency Broadcast System

CHAOS

Noise, a chilly wind, and the smell of something burning assaulted me as I opened my eyes. My first breath turned into a cough as I inhaled smoke. I coughed as I looked around and tried to get a handle on what was going on.

~Down,~ Carelian barked and next thing I knew, I was on the ground with something flying over us spewing smoke.

I fought to breathe between the Cath on my chest and how hard I'd hit the ground. I lay there breathing and listening. The chaotic mass created enough confusion that I couldn't make anything out, but knowing someone was throwing smoke grenades was not a positive sign.

"Let up. Need see," I wheezed out, pushing at his body.

He snarled, but slowly moved off of me and I clambered back up to my feet. The Eiffel tower was behind me. The admissions building for the tour should have been right behind me, but the rip wavered instead, creating a gaping ripple of magical danger. Around me were various police cars, their lights spinning, and sirens screaming. More and more police were lining up in riot gear, and I could hear and see more vehicles coming.

The tower straddled a paved area with green space on either side. I had stepped out right underneath the tower facing a long green field, kinda like the water feature at the Washington Monument, but with grass. Cops were converging from everywhere, people running and screaming behind them, and a thousand people with phones out filming it all.

"Where are they, Carelian? We need to find three gorgons and a gryphon, plus two teenaged Chitterians." I scanned the area, wishing the families had provided me pictures, so I had some idea how large the gorgons were or what colors the gryphon sported. Screams came from my right that had a certain high pitch to them I recognized. The pitch of a scream when you saw monsters, versus random danger, excitement, or anger contained a sharper more panic-stricken note. Less horror, more denial. It said way too much about my life that I could tell the difference in screams.

I spun to my right, searching for the source of the sound.

~There, near the support,~ Carelian said even as he bounded away from me. I locked on to the area he was talking about, and I saw it. A head of snakes, a pretty face, and people cowering while others were oddly stiff. A police officer was lifting a gun pointing it at her.

"No!" The snarl came out without conscious thought. I grabbed earth and yanked it up, creating a wall between the cop and the gorgon. Carelian was already there, weaving around her as she looked around wildly at the humans freaking out. "Get her out of here," I shouted as I looked for the other one and wings. A gryphon shouldn't be that hard to find? They were a winged creature and the panic surrounding them would be noticeable. Right?

A slash of pain along with hissing told me Carelian had opened a rip, but I didn't have time to look, still straining to see the missing others. Movement ahead in the green space, a flash of white caught my attention. A swarm of police, all in riot gear, were circling something, shields up, batons out, but above their heads I caught another glimpse of white feathers.

Wings!

"Carelian, headed to grab the gryphon," I yelled, figuring he would hear me or find me. His response consisted of a snarl of annoyance. I ignored it, trying to shove through the crowd. There were too many people. "I need you!"

In a flash the huge red Cath was beside me, his hackles raised and tail lashing. When all fluffed up, he appeared to be larger than a tiger, and his snarl cut through the noise around us. Until more people started screaming and trying to run away, while others were trying to get away from something else.

He pushed ahead of me, snarling the entire time, creating a path as people fell over themselves trying to get out of his way. Light flashed and I could hear the fake shutter sound from cameras. The newspapers were going to have a field day. I kept trying to get to the gryphon before the police did something irreversible, but too many people were between me and the circle around what I assumed was the gryphon was getting smaller.

"I don't have time for this." A quick check verified there were no cars coming down this road. The press of people ensured even if a car had wanted to get through, they couldn't have managed. I pulled on magic and sent a KO spell in an arc in front of me and people collapsed as I short circuited their bio-electric systems. It created a fan of people collapsed on the ground in front of me, which meant I couldn't get through without risking grievous injuries to others. "Argh!"

Another pull of earth, and I lifted a path for me, causing bodies to tumble to the side. A quick check verified no one looked hurt, then Carelian and I jumped up on the path I'd created racing toward the circle of police. A hawkish scream ripped through the air, making people cover their ears.

" S'il bouge, tire dessus," a voice boomed.

~Cori, they are saying they will shoot anyone that moves,~ Carelian's voice was tight and harsh in my mind.

"That isn't happening," I said, mostly to myself as I ran to the group, already exhausted. I was too worn down to do this and I could feel my legs trembling as we raced toward the circle of cops. I started shouting when I was ten feet away. "Stop this. I'll send him home!"

Two of the men turned, their weapons up, pointing at me. I only had a few seconds to decide. In the US, attacking a cop was almost an automatic death sentence. But I wasn't in the US. With a heave of magic, that physically hurt, I hurled out another KO at everyone in the vicinity, pushing it hard and using up the majority of my new grown hair.

They collapsed like broken dolls, including the gryphon. It was a male about the size of Carelian, but that meant too big for me to push. I'd have to be creative.

"Get an opening as close to the ground as possible. I'm going to flip him in." I looked around and then pulled two belts off of cops and linked them together. Then I folded the gryphons' wings down and belted them. The last thing I needed in all of this was to hurt a kid and have the denizens pissed at me. A vague hush spread behind me, but I ignored it.

~Ready?~ Carelian stood next to me, still puffed up.

"Yes," I said as I stood and used Move Earth to pull up the gryphon. Carelian opening a long low rip and I used the mound to tilt him into the hole. He rolled in ungraciously, but his wings were secured against damage. "You did warn them he was coming, right?"

~No. They can figure it out,~ he spat back as the rip sealed. ~It is my quean they are putting in danger since they can't teach their children how to avoid rips.~ He sounded pissed and scared and I turned to see what he was looking at as a spreading quiet grew. The hush was explained as hundreds of people were staring at me and then at the two huge spiders on the side of the Eiffel Tower.

"Oh. Huh." I said as hundreds of phones were being held up and pointed in my direction. "We really need to take care of that and get out of here."

~That might be a wise choice.~ His words were polite, barely, and I flinched at his stress. But right then soothing him was stupid because this wasn't good.

We took off toward the tower, this time the conscious

people getting out of the way and the phones going the entire way. As we raced back the way we'd come I heard the roar of vehicles approaching at great speed. I glanced down the road in front of the tower and flinched. A mix of Army and police vehicles raced toward the tower and I already had cops drawing their guns at me as I ran from the pile of fallen officers.

"Merlin's balls. This is going to suck." I readied my responses. I knew I could stop bullets, but I only had so much energy. We had almost made it to the towers when one of the Chitterians moved, and people began to scream. Before I could react, the police had pivoted and bullets ricocheted off the metal as they scurried higher.

"No!" I screamed the words as I dug a scalpel out of my pocket. With the ease of long practice, I had the protective lid off and the blade sliding through my skin, blood gushing out. I created a shield of dust, hair, anything that floated around. Then I heard the screams as a bullet bounced off and hit someone. I kept running.

Another scream, this one sibilant, and I spun looking for it. There to my left stood a small gorgon, her tan skin blending into the brown of the metal. People had pieces of signs, their purses, and I saw a few mages getting ready to attack her.

At this point if screaming would have helped I would have been screaming myself hoarse. As it was, I struggled to keep the shield up as I yelled to Carelian. "Grab the gorgon. I'll hold them off for another minute."

He snarled but pivoted and raced to the child, bowling over people without caring about them and I heard more than one person scream as he shouldered them out of the way. The girl was trying to stone people and kept focusing on the mages. Her beauty flared into something almost sublime, then it would fade. The people would freeze for a moment, then shake their heads, their fear ratcheted so high they had formed a mob.

I felt the portal open behind her, seeing the dark slash as Carelian leaped and both of them disappeared into another realm. It sealed and I sagged. All I had were two Chitterians to worry about. More and more people were yelling and pointing at me, though that had been present since the second I stepped out of the tear. But now they had me and the creatures that came out of their nightmares to focus on.

The shield I'd erected was above me. It prevented bullets from hitting the spiders, it didn't stop anyone from coming after me. And at this point everyone had realized I was involved with what to their eyes were monsters. At least five cops were rushing my direction. I looked around; the blood coming out of my cut spurting with each twist of my arm as I tried to get a plan in place.

I gave up and KO'd the first group running at me. Keeping up a shield and sending out a wide KO stressed me, and the shield wavered. When they realized that distracting me would make the shield drop, I saw them move the guns to point at me.

When did my life become this?

I reached for the elements again, the easiest to control right now with my mind scrambling. I pulled on Air creating hurricane force winds to whip around me. When the flimsy snack building under the leg started to wobble, I lowered the strength, keeping myself in the eye of the storm. More and more the responders were pointing at me and talking on their radios or phones. I had to figure this out fast.

A slash of pain and then a warm furry body was helping to support me. Even though I tried to stay in the center the wind was still strong. "Carelian," I had to yell over the screaming of the wind. "Can you get them to come down here so we can leave?"

If I had known their names or something, I could have tried to mindspeak them, but I didn't and I doubted they knew who I was. His tail lashed back and forth across my leg as he stared up. ~They are coming. But you'll need to drop the winds.~

I sighed but did so, heading to where they would arrive. Their multiple legs made quick work of the distance and the few people remaining fled as they came down, heading toward us.

"Come on, we'll get you home," I called out as Carelian created a rip to their home. They raced toward us and the gate to home. I peered around at the devastation I'd caused. Lots of people still unconscious, torn up ground, raging cops, and was the tower tilting? That last bit of earth I'd pulled up and lifted one edge of it. That wasn't good.

I turned to head in, when pain lanced through my body, and I cried out as it felt like a red-hot needle went through my shoulder.

~CORI!~ The words were a roar in my head. Long, multi-jointed, fuzzy legs grabbed me and pulled and the noise, shouting, gun shots, sirens, all disappeared as I was yanked to the other side of the rip. I lay on the ground and sobbed as my body convulsed in pain.

CHAPTER

FORTY-FOUR

Breaking news, lead Rogue Mage Hunter, Archmage Michelle Lupian Saldua, has executed Dennis Stricfield. In a showdown distressingly similar to the events that formed the basis of the movie and the career of Scott Randolph, Dennis was executed in a mall where he shopped for clothes in a disguise. Archmage Saldua severed his spinal cord with a break pattern. The rogue dropped and no one else was put in danger. ~CNN Mage Focus

ORDER

The tumultuous attention of the village I lay in the middle of was a mix of joy and horror as children raced to their parents, and beings raced to help me. I just lay there trying to breathe and any movement hurt so much I wanted to throw up. Laying still and breathing sounded like an excellent idea.

~Tirsane is coming. Esmere is coming. I am going to get Jo as soon as *malkin* is here.~ Carelian whispered the words in my mind, his tongue scratchy against my face, his body all but vibrating with stress.

"Uh huh," I murmured, not willing to react any more than that.

~Carelian, what happened?~ Esmere's voice was a hiss in my mind, and I retched, then cried out and tried to stop the cycle of pain-driven retching, which caused yet more pain.

~Shot, but children rescued. We need human hands to get the bullet out.~ He paused for a long moment. ~Tirsane would be helpful.~

All of this went on around me, but I could barely concentrate. Labor had been hard, even painful, but this? Every move set off new burning pain, and I kept swallowing down my bile. Every time I opened my eyes there was a new being staring down at me. Ones I didn't know. I closed my eyes again.

~I will call Tirsane. Cori is a lord, a herald, this is not a favor, this is saving ourselves.~ Esmere's words were sharp.

~Do that. I must get Jo.~ A slash of pain and I cried out, reaching for Carelian, and only causing more pain.

Did he leave me?

Tears flowed down my face from the pain and the thought he was gone. I couldn't live without him.

~Hush little one. He will be back. Trusted human hands are better for this. Tirsane is coming.~ Esmere lay next to me, and a purr rumbled from her. Deeper and throatier than Carelian, it vibrated my body, but the sensation was soothing, not painful.

"Promise?" I croaked out, wanting nothing more than to close my eyes and just quit. But I had promised to close the rift. I needed to. My mind locked on that. "Rift, close."

~Cori, no, you are weak and hurt.~ Esmere sounded alarmed. That made no sense. I closed rifts all the time.

"Will close. No more danger," I whispered. I had so much blood to offer, it coated everything, it coated me. Why? Why was there so much blood? I hadn't cut myself that badly, had I? The world wavered as I moved, and I convulsed as the pain radiating from my upper body made everything spin. "I'll just lay here. No stand," I said, my eyes closed as the whirling world made vomiting even harder to resist. I reached out and took all that blood, so much blood, and offered it to magic. Magic inhaled it, taking it all and the rift snapped shut. My head lolled toward Esmere. "See, closed?"

~Silly child. Tirsane could have closed it. Multiples working together could have closed it. Though it might make your wound easier to deal with. But we need that bullet out.~

Bullet. Why would a bullet be here? Denizens didn't have guns. Humans had guns. Oh, guns.

"Oh. Shot? I'm shot?"

~Yes, and if I could rend the being that did this to you limb from limb, I would. Then I would roast them with some of the hot sauce my son likes so much.~ Esmere snarled in my mind.

I giggled, whimpered, then giggled again—this time not letting my body move—at the idea of Esmere roasting someone over a fire while basting the dead body with hot sauce. It wasn't cannibalism if they weren't human, right?

Two slashes of pain, then my Carelian was next to me, licking my face. ~We are back, I have Jo and Sable.~

"You didn't leave?" I asked, trying to lift my arm to touch him.

~Not even Magic will stop me from being with you always,~ he replied.

"Cori, what the fuck? You're shot. What happened?" Jo leaned over, peering at me as her hand touched my forehead, then moved to my shoulder.

"Police shot me. I'm in trouble. But couldn't let them hurt the kids. Paris is going to be so mad." The words barely made sense in my own mind, but before I could explain Jo poked at my shoulder and I cried out.

"Let me bite her. It will remove the pain, numb the area, and help her body to restore blood," Tirsane said, and I saw her briefly before I closed my eyes. "Cori? Can you hear me?"

I opened my eyes again, my hand on Carelian's body where he lay next to me. "Hi, Tirsane. Where's Sable?"

"I'm here, love. Let's get you fixed up," Sable said, appearing in my field of vision. "While Cori would be better at this, given her training, I can tell the bullet didn't go all the way through, but I think it's almost out the other side. I'll need a scalpel." Sable sounded calm. My partners were the best.

"Her pocket. We'll need to roll her," Jo responded, just as controlled.

"Tirsane you first, this is going to hurt as soon as we move her," Sable said, her voice smooth, but the hand that touched my face was trembling. Silly, I would be fine. How couldn't I be? They were here to help me.

"Cori, my snakes are going to bite you. Twice now, and twice after we have the bullet out." Tirsane moved very close to my face, her endless eyes searching mine. I saw the snakes bouncing up and down, agitated, darting out to lick me in quick little snake kisses.

"Okay, bite away." I cut myself with scalpels all the time.

How bad could a bite hurt? A scream ripped out of me as two sets of pain lanced me right where it already hurt the most. I clamped my mouth shut and fought back the sobs. I hated crying. It never solved anything.

"I know, little one, but breathe in and out three times. Then the pain should subside," she said as she gave me a soft touch to my nose. "In, out," her voice pulled me with it, and I breathed, in, out. "Again." In, out.

The pain, which had been lava battering at my walls, cooled, pulled away, and I took in a breath that while it hurt, it only hurt. Hurt I could handle. With one more in and out cycle, my fourth, I opened my eyes, the pain no longer pulling at, pushing at everything. Though there existed a slight fuzziness at the edges of my mind that said drugs, but I could handle that.

Esmere was on my left side, Carelian on my right. Jo on my left side near my head while Sable mirrored her on my right. Tirsane bent over me from above. Everyone stared at me.

"Ow."

Jo snorted. "That's one way to put it. Anything else hurt beside the bullet in your shoulder?"

"Right now, nothing hurts. That part is rather nice," I retorted, but I wasn't stupid enough to try to sit up or even move.

"Answer the question," Jo scolded, but the worry in her tone overlaid everything.

I closed my eyes, running a scan, wiggling toes, tightening muscles. "No," I said after a minute. "Just that. How bad is it?"

"It's not good." She paused, a heavy sigh slipping out. "I really should take you to the hospital," Jo said, her voice slow.

"Let's not. If our friends will help, let's do that first," I said quickly. The last thing I wanted was all the police reports that went with a gunshot.

"The bullet didn't go all the way through. I'll need you to move your arm, so I can cut it out," she warned. I felt Sable's hand tighten on mine.

"It's okay. Tirsane has the good drugs. It doesn't hurt." I could feel my smile was a bit loopy but that was okay.

Jo dug one of the sterile scalpels out of my pants pocket and had me sit up.

I turned my head to see the hole in my shoulder. "Ouch. And nothing broke?"

With gentle hands, Jo manipulated it. "Not that I can see. It looks like it hit and lodged under the scapula. I'll need you to lift your arm so I can pull it out."

My head tilted in acquiescence or the happy drugs, either way it didn't matter. Jo had never been an EMT, but both her and Sable earned their First Aid certs and Basic Life Saving. And I knew if my life was at risk, she would have knocked me out to take me to the doctor. It was the oddest feeling, the blade sliding into my flesh, yet no pain. I could feel the pressure and the sensation of my flesh being pulled apart, and I knew I should be screaming in pain.

"Tirsane, if you sold your venom, you'd be a millionaire. This is amazing."

She watched from a distance, an odd look on her face. "I will take that under advisement." Her eyes darkened as Jo pulled something from my shoulder. "This is normal to the way humans fight?"

"Very," I said dryly as Jo wiped the area clear, first with alcohol, then water. "I'm lucky they weren't using bigger caliber bullets or that it didn't hit someplace more fragile than my shoulder. If this had hit my heart, my head, my stomach, I'd probably die."

The village, who apparently had been listening to us

intently, went silent as this information disseminated through them.

"That is more than terrifying. I kept thinking you were overstating the weapons. After all, I can call storms and earthquakes," she said slowly. "The last time I truly fought either with or against man, you were still using swords and bows."

"Yeah, that's the problem. For most mages it takes a minute to figure out what they want to do, show it to Magic, pay the price, then do the spell. I'm good in that I have done it enough it takes me seconds, ten to fifteen. A decent shot can fire a gun in under five seconds."

"Oh," Tirsane all but whispered, arms crossed over her breasts, hugging herself tightly.

"All done. Esmere, Carelian, you're up, you too, Tirsane. Cori, more bites and licks." Jo had her voice artificially bright, and I glared at her from the side.

"You're enjoying the pain a bit too much," I accused.

"What pain? You can't feel any," she said back with a smile. She and Sable held me while Carelian licked the front wound and Esmere on the back while Tirsane had a snake bite me on each side.

"That venom should promote healing and clotting, as well as keep it pain free for the next day or so. Though if she moves it because it doesn't hurt, she might make it worse. Usually, we tie up wounds to remind ourselves that we are injured." She had pulled back to watch me.

"Days? Wow, yeah, you could create a thriving business selling snake venom," Sable said as I was buffeted between two huge Cath, their rough tongues dragging across my skin. I'd whine, but I knew the roughness would fade in hours and the saliva would make me heal much faster.

"Thank you," I said when everyone was done, and they had helped me to my feet. My head was a bit spinny, and all I wanted was a very, very long nap. The gorgon that had claimed one of the children approached, giving a nod of respect to Tirsane as she did so.

"Earth Lord?" Her voice was hesitant, and the baby gorgon was right behind her clinging to the tail tip.

"Hey. Is everyone okay? I forgot to ask." I waved at my shoulder. "That distracted me more than it should have. They are okay, right?"

The gorgon glanced at my shoulder then back to me. "Yes, they are well. Scared, which I figure will wear off and soon they will boast of their big adventure." The bit of humor at that statement faded, and she cleared her throat. "We did not realize you would be in danger. We knew you were of the Earth and figured as a lord worst case, it might cost you some trinkets to get them back. We did not know we were sending you to battle. Our gratitude is more than we can express. We declare all debts to us cleared."

An odd pulse of magic ran through me. I forced myself to straighten, and I nodded. "You are welcome. I acknowledge the clearance of a debt."

She sagged in relief, and I wrinkled my brow but it was too much effort to deal with. They slithered off as Tirsane and Esmere seemed exasperated with me.

"What?" I demanded. At this point while I didn't hurt, exhaustion flowed from the bottom of my feet to the top of my skull. Hunger gnawed at me. Food, bath, and bed sounded delightful.

"Nothing. Continue being you, it is a refreshing change," Tirsane said. "Go home. I will alert Freya to this matter."

I nodded, and Jo and Sable wrapped arms around me. "Home?"

"Yes, home."

Carelian opened the way, and we stepped into the house,

with me weaving a bit. I shook my head, trying to get the pounding and echoes of sirens to stop.

Jo and Sable were staring at the front door. "Cori, why are the cops here?"

"Not a clue. I didn't do anything in the United States," I protested as Jo went to answer the door.

FORTY-FIVE

Given the attacks we have been facing lately, a new class called 'Magical Protection' is being instituted in all state universities. This class will provide instruction and techniques for offensive and defensive use of magical abilities. This has always been reserved for those mages that enter the military, but given the current situation we feel the general public needs to know these techniques. It will be open to anyone who wishes to take it, free of charge. ~ Chancellor of University of California system

SPIRIT

S able supported me, with an arm around my waist, while Jo headed to answer the door. I pulled my phone out of my pocket now that I had a signal again, and the messages and voicemail notifications exploded.

"Yes?" Jo said after she got the door opened up.

I looked up as the person at the door started talking. "I'm here to pick up Cori Munroe on order of the State Department." The voice sounded vaguely familiar.

"And you are?" Jo sounded as exasperated as I felt. Today just wasn't going to end, was it?

"Grab me food, water, and protein drinks and stuff them in the backpack. I have a feeling I won't be sleeping in my bed," I said in a low voice to Sable. She nodded, grabbing my backpack, leaving me leaning against the stairway railing.

"FBI Agent Jake Arnold. I'm here to take Cori Munroe in for questioning," he stated, but I saw him watching me. I stood in a straight line from the front door, so I couldn't hide or pretend I wasn't there.

"Identification?" Jo kept her voice cool, using her body to block him from coming in, her own tattoo easily seen in the afternoon sun.

Rather than arguing, he reached into his pocket and pulled out his ID and badge and handed it to her. She made a show of looking at it, then nodded. "Looks legit. Do you have a warrant?"

Jake cleared his throat. "The Secretary of State has requested we collect her for questions regarding her actions in France a few hours ago."

Hours?

I glanced at my watch, surprised. Apparently, the whole mess with me getting hurt and then moderately healed took more time than I thought. I'd left about noon my time and my watch told me it was pushing four in the afternoon.

"And she is supposed to be able to get from France to New York in a few hours?" Jo asked archly, both pretending I wasn't standing in the hallway. And that my penchant for traveling impossible amounts didn't exist.

"We did point that out to them, but the response boiled down to go wait for her until she shows up," he said with an apologetic air.

"Ah. I see." She looked at him for a minute, then called over her shoulder. "Are you here?"

"Yeah. Agent, can you let me go pee first and change clothes?" I asked as I could still hear Sable in the kitchen getting me what I'd need.

Jo moved enough that the agent could walk in and look at me. "No offense, ma'am, but while I would advise bringing some clothes with you, I wouldn't change. The way you look right now might help your case."

I sighed. "Give me a minute." I detoured to the hall bathroom and looked at the person in the mirror. She had grass and dirt covering her, blood soaked her shirt. The gaping hole in the front provided testament that she'd been shot. Across her face and arms were scratches either from Carelian or the flying debris. Then bright red puncture marks on her neck where Tirsane's snake bit her. All in all, the woman in the mirror looked like a refugee from a war.

"What have you been doing, woman? You can't keep this going too much longer," I asked.

The stranger in the mirror didn't answer, so I used the bathroom, washed my face and rinsed out my mouth. With luck, Tirsane's bites lasted as long as she said they would, or I'd be in trouble soon.

I came back out to find Sable, Hamiada, Marisol, the kids,

and Carelian all glaring at the FBI Agent. Honestly the kids looked like they were about to tear him limb from limb, Carelian just looked annoyed.

"You can't take our Momma Cori. She's hurt. She needs sleep and us p'tecting her," Jaz insisted. Azul fluttered above her, darting over to me as I stepped out.

~Hurt, hurt? No hurt?~

I lifted my right arm and ran a finger down the quetzo's belly. "I'll be fine. Tirsane and Esmere helped." The quetzo's were in awe of Tirsane and very respectful of Esmere. Her teaching them how to properly speak had sunk in hard, making her someone they did not want to piss off.

"I still don't understand why she has to go," Marisol insisted, arms crossed, as Hamiada fretted behind her. "Cori, you look awful," she burst out as I stepped back into the hall.

"I'm okay. Jo and Sable were wonderful. They should have been doctors."

Matching expressions of revulsion met that statement, and I laughed, cringing as I did so. "Can you grab me a change of clothes, including underwear, and then I'll be ready to go. Agent, are we staying local?"

"No ma'am. They want you in DC post haste." He nodded. "Director Alixant said he'd meet you there." If anyone had asked for a poster boy of being in an uncomfortable situation, Jake Arnold was their mascot.

"I see. Did they say anything else?"

"No, ma'am, just requested your presence for questioning and talk of an international incident." He shrugged, and I had sympathy for his role as the errand boy. I'd behave no matter how much I wanted to sleep.

Sable headed upstairs while I got hugs from the kids, worried looks from Marisol and Hamiada. Jo pulled me into a hug and held me there until Sable got back and joined it.

"I swear Cori, you are going to give me more gray hair than the twins," Jo muttered into my hair.

"Ditto," Sable said kissing my temple. "Are you sure you have to go?"

"Yeah," I said without elaborating. I didn't know if I'd be coming home. Some of my actions in France carried the death penalty in the United States. A lot would depend on politics, something I didn't like at the best of times. And if they wanted to appease France or not.

"We'll be waiting," Jo assured me. One last round of hugs and kisses, then Jo helped me to the agent's car. They got me into the back seat and Carelian jumped in on the other side. He lay across the seats, his head on my lap.

A minute later, the agent pulled out and headed to the airport. "There's a plane waiting for us, ma'am."

"I figured. I'm just going to close my eyes." He nodded in response, and I petted Carelian, trying not to fall asleep. My body didn't hurt exactly, but I could tell I'd been injured. The venom kept the pain at bay and the saliva from the cats had healed the wound to the point it looked like it had happened a day ago, not hours.

~Don't fight them if they come for me,~ I said in my mind to Carelian bracing myself for the response.

~I will never let them get near you. We can live with Esmere or some of the other villages. Tirsane has an entire city in her caverns. Many would find room for us, support us.~ His voice was calm, but his tense muscles and flicking tail indicated his pose was an act.

~And our family? We can't pull the houses with us. You know if I fight, Tirsane and the others can't help. I broke the laws. I won't risk the lives of anyone else.~ The weight of exhaustion pushed against me like a suit of lead threatening to put me into the ground, never letting me rise.

A soft growl was the only response I got.

~I know. Carelian, we've always known this was a risk. I'm only surprised I've made it this long. There's a reason most old mages are quiet people that never use magic. I just don't know what to do about the rips that are still occurring. If I'm executed, run home. Make sure that Jo and Sable and the kids have the life they deserve.~

~You deserve that life too. We need to be doing Search and Rescue, getting fat, playing with children and grandchildren. We have other options.~ His voice almost begged me to run, to create the life we deserved.

I hummed without answering and let the weariness take me. At this point, what else could I do. A soft burn on my arm cut through the haze of exhaustion and I glanced down. Three of the four sections of the arm glowed with a silver ink, leaving one empty. Another favor done for Salistra. I stared at it frowning as the number felt wrong. Oh well, I'd deal with it later.

The car slowing at the airport woke me, and they had to help me stagger up the stairs to the plane. There were five armed agents there and none of them were as nice as Agent Arnold had been.

"That cat makes one move and I'll put a bullet in it," one of them warned as Carelian came up the stairs behind me.

I pushed myself up from the plane seat I was leaning on. My legs trembled and my head felt light. "You lift your gun to him, and I'll evaporate all the blood in your body before your finger has time to pull the trigger." He blanched at my promise. The rest of them, including the flight crew stepped back, giving me space. I nodded and settled down in the seat they gestured at. Carelian lay on the floor, my feet resting on his back. He wasn't letting me out of his sight, no matter how much he disliked the airplanes.

~Evaporated blood? That is new. But leaves the flesh a bit too dry to be palatable. I wonder if that would make it like unseasoned jerky? I think if you kill them just boil their organs. It would cook them nicely, and I do enjoy cooked heart.~

~You are incorrigible,~ I said, my eyes closed as I listened to them moving around me. ~Just warn me if I need to do something drastic.~

~They are all cowed and sitting far away from you. You would think in this world they would know better than to threaten mages.~ He sounded disgusted with them all.

~Most people fear death more than I do. At this point....~ I trailed off.

~I know, my quean. But soon you will solve the problem and will be able to enjoy the rest you deserve.~ He licked my right hand and then lay quietly as the plane took off. I let myself sleep again, too tired to do much else.

The Regan airport was a reverse of the previous, but now my escort consisted of ten agents, half of which were mages. They were all grim looks and long hair that didn't look like they used magic at all. My own bias was sneaking up on me as I let them usher me into a car. I sat in the back of a Suburban with a row of seats to myself and Carelian, while an agent sat behind me. Probably with a gun drawn ready to shoot me. I didn't care, I just closed my eyes and dozed. This time they took me to the FBI headquarters.

Stephen was waiting there as they pulled me, gently, out of the car. Carelian had snarled a warning anytime anyone got too close, was rude, or even looked darkly at me. I ignored them all.

"Cori, are you okay? What happened?" His hand reached out to touch the hole in my shirt. "Do we need to get a doctor here? Are you still bleeding?"

"Gunshot. No, mostly healed." I pulled open the shirt to show him the healing wound. "How much further do we have?

I'm about out of energy." I hated to admit it, but just standing took more concentration than I liked to admit, and I didn't know what I was going to do when it all went away. Hitting the ground would just hurt me more. Besides, Esmere would never let me live it down if I tore open the wound.

"Sit here." He pointed at a chair in the hall we were walking through. "You," he jerked his head at an agent. "Go find a wheelchair. Either security or the medical response team should have one."

"Sir, we've been instructed to make sure she doesn't escape or talk to anyone," one of them protested.

"And I'm a director and I don't care. If she wanted to kill us all, we'd already be dead. Go," his voice snapped out, and the agent blanched, turning and taking off at a run to get me a wheelchair.

He sat down next to me, the ring of agents somewhere between an honor guard and an escort to my death expanding outward a bit.

"What happened?" He looked at me with drawn brows and I wanted to sob.

I groaned. "Can we wait? I suspect I'm going to be telling this multiple times over the next few days and right now I don't have the energy to hash it out. It was a debt called in, and let's leave it at that for now?" I held my arm out and he saw the new sections of horn filled in.

"Ah, interesting. They won't be ready to meet you immediately, and technically the US Marshals should be babysitting you. Yolanda and I threw our weight around and got modified custody of you. But it's still limited as to what we can do. That means no one else will be able to see you and they are going to treat you like a prisoner." He kept his voice low, but it was still audible to anyone in the hall. "You've worked with us and put your life on the line too much for us to do anything else. Some of us understand you're a hero."

I glanced at him, unsure if the words were for me or our listeners. "Don't worry about it. I'll be fine," I managed. If I didn't believe I would survive, I'd never make it through the next round of political theater. He fell silent as an agent came back with the wheelchair and they continued to take me to my prison.

CHAPTER

FORTY-SIX

When the government built the FBI headquarters, they included state-of-the-art Mage Restraining Cells. The argument with Hoover was that any mage that had a death wish could escape any arrangement. These were to remind them they were prisoners and make it as difficult as possible for them to escape but making them suffer would just encourage them to flee at the first opportunity, even knowing escapees would be shot on sight. They set the cells up as tiny bedrooms with a half bath, just to make it not too overwhelming. However, Hoover also installed a sniper hole, just in case they tried to run. ~ History of Magic

CHAOS

Stephen pushed me down a bewildering number of halls, elevators, and past offices and conference rooms, before showing up in a room with one way in and out, a desk on the same wall as the door, and a series of cells. They were better than jail cells in that they had a bed, a sink, a toilet with a half partition, and a small desk with an office chair. Yet, it remained a cell. The cells lined the wall along three sides, creating a U shape, with solid cement ceilings above, and only the desk and one door out. There were no windows or any other obvious means of escape. Though nothing would have stopped me from sidestepping away.

"Really?" I gave Stephen a look, ignoring the other agents.

"Technically, you are in custody, though not under arrest. And while I could justify keeping you in an office closer to where I'm sure they'll have the investigative hearing, given the blood, the exhaustion, the bald scalp, I figured you would prefer to get a nap while you could."

I sagged in relief. Sleep sounded exquisite. All I could do was hope the pain killing venom would still work by the time the senate or congress or the cabinet called me. Whomever wanted to lecture me this time.

~Yes. You must sleep. The healing is going well, but it still takes days,~ Carelian said, his tone brooking no argument.

Not only did I have zero desire to argue, but they were also correct. It took five minutes to get me in the cell, curl up on the surprisingly comfortable bed, with Carelian on the floor next to me. Then darkness swamped me like a rogue wave, and I submitted with relief.

~Cori, they demand to see you.~

Carelian's voice wormed through my brain, forcing me to surface from the depths of sleep I'd been in. Gray floors and an altar swam through my brain as I opened my eyes to cement ceilings. I groaned. I ached, but it didn't actively hurt. However, I could feel the pain hiding behind everything and suspected in a bit I'd either need another bite or I'd be screaming.

A few dry swallows and my mouth started working, so I sat up, turning to look outside my cell. Stephen leaned in the doorway, giving me time to reboot my brain. "Yeah," I croaked as I winced with every move. The only place I should be right now is in a bathtub.

They will kill you. Don't let them kill you.

The mantra rattled through my brain as I struggled to stand up. Carelian was near me, letting me use him as a steadying force.

"They want to talk to you. You sure you don't want to clean up?" He looked at me, a frown and drawn brows creasing his face.

"Oh no. I want them to see exactly what the consequences are. I don't know if it will help, but I can hope. Though I'll need to eat something on the way." According to my watch it was eight am. Which meant I'd slept through the night. Which meant I was going on 36 hours of no shower or clean clothes. Whatever, maybe they'd think twice about pushing me.

"I have a breakfast burrito here," he said turning to pick up three foil wrapped items. "The cafeteria isn't half bad."

He watched me with worried eyes. I ignored him and

fumbled in my pack for a protein drink—warm, blech—and then I reached for the burrito. I felt sticky, my mouth tasted horrible, and the low-level headache didn't help. Carelian stayed silent, which worried me, but now wasn't the time to ask questions. That and I figured he had to be as exhausted as I was.

More and more people appeared in the halls as Stephen and the quartet of agents got me in a car and then headed to wherever we were meeting the committee.

"Do you have any idea-" I said, but Stephen shook his head in a sharp jerky motion glancing at the other two agents in back with us. He had circles under his eyes bigger than mine and grooves along his mouth proving he'd probably been up all night. I sighed and ate the second burrito, giving Carelian a nibble.

~You hungry?~ I asked, worried. I couldn't remember the last time he ate.

~No. Stephen brought me food earlier, two pounds of grilled chicken with hot sauce. Not as good as feasting on your challengers, but it will suffice for now.~ He lay at my feet in the large suburban SUV.

I managed to muffle my laugh and concentrated on water and food. "Any chance of coffee? I'm kinda dying." That comment, I figured, was safe.

"No, detainee-" one of the agents started to snap at me. Stephen cut him off.

"Yes, Merlin Munroe. I will make sure you get a large coffee with sugar and cream." He glared at the other agent, and they backed off.

"How long?" I asked to give myself some options.

"Another fifteen, depending on traffic," the driver answered.

I hummed to myself and munched on the next burrito. I

was pretty sure there should be some hard-boiled eggs somewhere in my bag if I needed more, but right now I was fine. Carelian's harness was in there as we'd taken it off in the village. Part of me thought of putting it back on him. Maybe the simple version. I'd keep his bowl and treats with me. People were going to be antsy enough as it was, I didn't need to make it worse.

"Cori?" I looked up to see Stephen peering at me. I hummed an encouraging sound, my mouth full. He frowned, glanced at the others, then looked at Carelian. I sighed.

~Yes, Stephen?~ I sent mentally, getting what he wanted. It took energy to do this, but he was right here, so it wasn't too draining.

~Thank you. I'm trusting you're okay, but they are going to be out for more blood. What are you going to do? What exactly happened and why?~ He looked out the car window, focused on the scenery for all the other agents could tell.

I provided a simplified rundown of the situation and what had happened. He shot a brief look at me, and I tugged up my sleeve, revealing the altered tattoo.

~Well, that is better and worse than I feared. Good part, Paris. Bad part, you.~

~Yeah, my reputation is getting ahead of me again. But we as a race need to quit attacking beings just because they are different. If some of them ever truly grew mad at us, we would be in big trouble.~

~Why do you say that?~

~Dragons don't care about our stupid rules, and I'm not sure anything less than a very high caliber bullet could touch Zmaug and that is only if she didn't know it was coming. They are magic users too. If I can create a shield, so can she. You've become used to Tirsane. Do you remember the SEC game? At that point, she and the others were terrifying. She is a friend, but she's still a demigod and for the most part, she finds humans boring. If she or Bob decided they wanted to play with us?~

Stephen swallowed, and made a show of looking at his phone. ~We would be fucked.~

I said nothing else. My toes petted Carelian, who wasn't purring. His awareness was too high, and I didn't blame him. I'd have much rather been at home and eating a meal with my family, not in a car headed to an inquisition. Swallowing a mournful sigh, I consoled myself that Stephen had made sure he had food. It would help with his temper, if not mine. I finished the last bite just as we were pulling around. Already reporters mobbed the area.

"Is there any place else that isn't reporter filled?" I asked hopefully.

"No ma'am. This is the best place."

They got me out and into a wheelchair, which was becoming too common in my life, amid shouts of "Cori, what did you do?" "Cori, how many did you kill?" "Whose side are you on? The monsters'?"

I ignored all of it but took a minute to get the harness on Carelian before I was wheeled inside, my best friend walking beside me.

~Remember, no killing anyone,~ I said mentally, as my fingers stroked his back, our version of hand holding.

~Then they had better ensure to not make any threatening moves toward you,~ he replied back, unconcerned.

My mental cringe to his response had my stress ratcheting up. I started scoping out who had weapons and reviewing the law in my head. Just how much trouble would I be in for this?

It took another twenty minutes before I found out the level of heat coming down on me. The same jerk who'd run my other hearing sat as the chairman and the person running the show and the truth teller looked familiar.

"Senator John Williams, you have the floor," the man at the front said.

"Merlin Munroe, what exactly do you have to say for yourself?" His demand over reading glasses brought to mind images of an overbearing teacher.

They set me up similarly as last time, at a table with the wheelchair, but this time I was alone, well mostly. Carelian wasn't hiding. He was on a chair next to me, peering around at everyone. It amused me how many people flinched as his gaze raked over them. And I didn't see all my fans in the gallery.

"In regards to?" I asked mildly. Stephen had followed through, and I had a large coffee loaded with sugar and creamer. And it was hot, which helped a lot. They kept these places too cold.

"Really? You are going to play stupid? Fine, this," he snapped at me and pressed a remote. A screen slid down at one side and taped images of me knocking people out, lifting the ground, Carelian grabbing a gorgon and disappearing, and then the Chitterians catching me. That part was new to me. I'd been unable to remember anything after the spike of pain that slammed into me.

I looked at him and shrugged. "What about it?"

"Who are you to interfere in other nations' activities? You jump in and hurt people to rescue monsters? You attack the officers of the law doing their duty! And then you disappear leaving a mess behind. France has been on the phone with the Secretary of State non-stop demanding your extradition." He delivered each word like an attack, and I couldn't help but flinch at the last part. Extradition would be bad.

"There were children in danger. Just because they weren't human children does not mean they weren't in danger. I was obligated to help them." I shrugged and sipped on my coffee, trying to act nonchalant. The only positive part of his rant had been the "injured" comment, not dead. That meant I hadn't killed anyone.

"Children—you mean monsters," he scoffed. "You act like they had parents that were worried about them."

My head snapped up as rage flushed through me and I glared at him. "No, I mean children. Anyone that has a familiar will tell you that even though they aren't human, they are sentient beings. Which means the denizens that live in the realms are just as capable of loving their children as we are, and they do. So yes, they were children and if you can't see that, you're a moron." My temper was rising again, but I didn't care.

"Fine, they were children. That doesn't justify you attacking officers of the law," he snapped back at me, and my magic urged me to react.

I pushed it down and looked at him. "And to them, we are the monsters. We were the ones threatening their children. No one was seriously hurt. They didn't come after you. They had children get lost by falling through a rip. Something we know happens on our side as well. I will not apologize for rescuing them from their monsters." I gave the panel a bitter smile. "After all, humanity has a much better track record of hurting others in larger numbers than they ever have."

He glared, but before he could open his mouth, someone else spoke. A woman, though from my seat I couldn't see her name tag. She at least smiled and nodded at me, though that didn't mean I trusted her.

"Do you realize France is calling for your head? You damaged the Eiffel Tower when you called Earth under it. Bent the girders holding it up. What should we tell them?" It sounded like an honest question and one I didn't have an answer for.

"Oops?" No one laughed, and I sighed. "Tell them in the heat of the moment while in a frantic effort to save children, the placement of the earth I called to protect both myself and the children was detrimental to the tower. However, unless they would be just as upset if it had been human children I was rescuing, their complaints have no weight."

One corner of the woman's mouth tilted up in a smirk as she nodded to me. "I will relay the message, but should we give you over to them?"

I shrugged, trying to be nonchalant. "Did my damage fall under anything that creates a valid extradition charge?"

"No," she said, just as amused as I was.

"Then my preference would be no extradition and remember that I am not covered by French law, only American." My pulse was slowing down, but from how hard the Senator was fuming I knew I wasn't in the clear.

The committee looked like they might have argued further, when both on the panel and in the chamber, phones started going off with alarm sirens. It took a minute as various people pulled out their devices, staring at them.

A moment later, a man in military undress uniform strode out onto the floor. "At this time, we are asking you to disperse. We need to get the elected officials to safety. Please make sure you follow the guides toward the shelters in the basement." His voice was crisp and no nonsense as others streamed after him, headed to the officials.

Senators reacted immediately, grabbing their belongings in their hands and racing toward the exits while military and security waved them down halls. I wheeled my chair around to find Stephen headed for me in his brisk take no prisoners walk.

"What is going on?" I called out to Stephen. I needed people to get out of the way before I could move the chair. The wheelchair was too bulky. If I tried to walk, I'd just be knocked over, too risky. The last thing I needed was more injuries.

Stephen had made it to me. "Rip in DC, come on, let's get out of here." He grabbed the chair and wheeled me back the way we came.

FORTY-SEVEN

Attention MC Fans, the government is attacking her again. This time they are trying to keep it as a private hearing, not open to the public. We have an insider who is willing to live stream it on our private website. Please remember to show up so we can make sure we know exactly what the government thinks they can do to our Marvelous Cori. ~ Email from the Marvelous Cori Fan Group

ORDER

We pushed against the flow of the crowd with the entourage I always seemed to have lately. As we moved through the halls, we garnered more than a few looks, but the agents could quell any curiosity with a glance. I needed to learn that skill.

"What can you tell me about the rip?" I asked as we fought to get out of the main traffic.

"Not much. Creatures coming out, but they either aren't sentient, or they aren't responding to our attempts at communication. Either option could be accurate." There was an odd tightness to his voice I didn't understand.

"What aren't you telling me?" I kept trying to look back at him and see his face, but the angle made it difficult to see more than his nostrils flaring down at me. Carelian loped alongside us, doing more to scatter people out of our way than the other agents managed to do.

"Indira was called in. She should get there shortly," he admitted as we turned a corner.

"And where are we going?" I asked, already knowing the answer. I could see it in the tightness of his shoulders and the other agents.

"Taking you back to detainment, and then I'm headed that way to see if I can help." He didn't look down at me, just locked his eyes straight ahead, pushing me.

"No." I let the word slip out. "Get me out there. You need me there and I can help."

"No time, so it isn't anything to worry about. It would take us thirty minutes to drive there, and that is assuming traffic doesn't lock up." He growled as his feet moved faster and my wheelchair bounced more.

"Then there is no reason for you to go, or you let us go and Carelian can get us there in a minute." I almost fell out of the chair, he stopped so fast. "You can do that? Take me there now?"

~Yes,~ Carelian affirmed. ~Show me where.~

Stephen took a second to pull us out of the flow of frantic people and pulled up his phone. "Here, at this section of the Washington Mall, it's at the base of the Lincoln Memorial."

"Sir, we can't do that. She's being detained," one of the agents protested.

Stephen didn't even bother to look at the agent as he responded. "Don't care. You don't like it, report me. But we're going to help protect people. Remember the oath we swore? 'Defend the Constitution against all enemies, foreign and domestic'? If we let the rips continue, we won't have a country left to defend and she is our biggest weapon." The last words were bitter as he turned my existence into a tool, but I understood where he was coming from.

"Sir," one protested but another raised his hand.

"I think they need us to help with the evacuation. Director Alixant can handle one woman from here." The agent nodded at me with a twitch of his head, then he and the others left. Stephen's shoulders sagged a bit, and I made a mental promise to not cost him his job if I could avoid it.

I took a deep breath and stood up. "Let's go, Carelian." It was an order and an act of faith. He'd never let me down and never would. He flicked an ear at me, but the rip opened. We stepped into the crossroads and the rip closed behind us. The empty grayness of the area, along with the quiet, let me breathe for a moment, some of my stress sloughing off.

~Stay,~ he growled at both of us as he opened up a rip. He jumped through and I obediently waited.

"Aren't you going to go?" Stephen demanded.

"Not until he says I can. He's my partner. I'll wait until he says it is safe to go." I cast a look up at Stephen. "He'll let us know."

As if in response to my words, Carelian spoke in our minds. ~Come.~

I stepped into the bedlam that was a rip scene. The clothes I wore were still the same from the day before, stained, sweaty, and I probably stank. Not that my nose was working at this point. Which meant I fit right in with the chaos. Everyone was yelling, running away from things that chased them, sirens wailed, and the rip hung right above the ground.

"Have you figured out what has come out?" I reached out to pet Carelian. I should have made him put his harness on, but we didn't have time.

~The rift opened into a breeding area of rous. They are savage, aggressive, with bites that can kill.~

"What are they?" Stephen asked, patting himself and going white. "No gun. Forgot they require me to lock it up."

I gave him a side-long glance. "You're a mage. Use magic. What do they look like, Carelian?"

~Large, angry rodents. They are quite tasty when roasted.~ His tail lashed back and forth as he crouched, his ears pricking one way, then another.

"Can you tell where Indira is?" Stephen asked.

~Maybe,~ Carelian replied after a second. ~We go this way. The rip needs to close. Rous are mindless but will keep attacking until there is nothing left to attack.~

"So, kill quickly. Got it." I pulled up my fast kills, usually causing blood to boil or freeze, or easiest, burn out their lungs. I put action to words as we talked, dropping two of them as we followed Carelian. They were like gigantic rats. Closer to the size of large dogs. I could see why Carelian would enjoy chasing them, but people in general were running around like idiots.

Including the cops. They shouldn't be causing this much drama for enormous rats.

There were so many days I wished Laurel was here. She just handled the weird better than most.

"Let me see if I can close it," I said as Carelian headed toward a cluster of trees. "But I'll need to focus. I can't close the rip and walk at the same time."

~I think we have time-the rous are annoying, but not particularly deadly in these numbers.~ Something about his words made me freeze, or maybe it was the confusion in the tone.

"Carelian, what's wrong?" I hurried to catch up with them.

~There is too much panic for rous. Why are people screaming and dropping? They are deadly once you've been injured, not before.~ His head moved back and forth on a swivel, as if trying to track something.

"Worry about it later. Get me to Indira first." Stephen's voice was tight and worried, and I couldn't blame him. The place just radiated chaos, and at this point, people should be a bit more blasé about rips. What was going on?

Another piercing scream filled the air ahead of us, full of agony and disbelief. We automatically swiveled toward the sound.

~Wait here. Do Not Move!~ His imperative rooted my feet to the ground and Stephen wasn't much better.

"Carelian, what's wrong?" I called as he raced over to the woman that had just collapsed.

~Voids take them,~ he hissed in my brain, a harsh sound that rattled through my mind. I flinched, as did Stephen. Carelian pivoted the way only a Cath could, and between one leap and the next was racing toward us. ~Asclepius vipers are attacking people. They kill with a single bite.~ He ran right up to us, spinning around, looking for danger. ~Cori, close it now, then kill them all.~

I needed to ask questions. That name sounded familiar, but not as something I associated with deadly. But if he wanted me to focus on this, I would. I turned and looked at the rip, seeking its magic, its power. It wasn't a huge rip, but it opened into an active area of the Spirit realm, which surprised me. Whatever, I grabbed and tried to pull it closed. And ran out of offerings.

"Fuck," I muttered. I fumbled in my pants, but they'd taken all my scalpels. Too big of a risk. "Carelian, I need blood, now."

He leaped over to me, razor sharp claws snicking out, and with surgical precision drew a deep cut down my extended arm. I sucked in a breath, but the pain was familiar by this point making it easy to ignore. I grabbed the blood, offering it to Magic. She grabbed it with an odd level of greed and the rip snapped shut.

I sagged a bit as the blood vaporized, leaving my arm clean, but more blood welling up. "Done. Now what?"

~You must kill all the snakes. Healers in your Ancient Greece once used their venom. It was a humane way to kill those they could not save. But these snakes haven't been milked in centuries. When they bite, their venom races through your system, shutting down all your organs. Past the bite, there is no pain, just death. And before you ask, no. There is no way to save someone once the venom enters their bloodstream.~

The amount of fear and stress in his words had me focusing. Trying to figure out how to find and kill so many creatures. I didn't practice killing beings and the Soul Grab would only work on sentient beings.

"I need an example to figure out how to isolate them," I said, trying to figure out how to nail down what I needed.

~One moment. Again, do not move.~ He was gone before I finished processing the words.

"Cori, I need to find Indira. Something is wrong."

The tension in his voice had me staring at him, but Stephen peered off in the distance toward a stand of trees. I gave my head a shake. "I know you need to find her. But give me a minute. I'm working as fast as I can."

He glanced at me, but before he could say whatever his eyes heralded, Carelian came bounding back, a hissing snake in his teeth. ~This is what you must kill. Quickly.~

I looked at the snake. A dark brown snake with green and red diamonds alternating down its back, with a viper head and a thick sinuous body. It hissed and thrashed as it tried to bite Carelian. He held it firm in his teeth, holding right behind the skull.

I pulled on Pattern Match, pulled its pattern, and then just liquified its brain with a pulse of Pattern Break. The snake went limp midway through a hiss.

"That is disturbing," Stephen muttered, looking at the snake that Carelian spat out. It fell to the ground in a pile of lifeless coils.

~Now do it for all of them.~

I queried, and Magic responded as if waiting for my request. The price made me wince, but I could and would pay it. Snakes infested the area where the rip had been. A quick flex of my arm refreshed the blood flow, and I offered it up. Magic grabbed, a bit reluctant this time, and I felt a smidge of guilt. By my best guess, I was killing over two hundred of these snakes, which in many ways were innocent victims.

But I didn't see any other option. A push, a price, and I had killed hundreds of beings whose only crime had been to be dangerous. "They're dead," I muttered, my energy sagging.

"Good, where's Indira?" Stephen stared at Carelian as if willing him to come up with the answer.

~This way,~ he said, bounding away. Stephen raced after

him. I hobbled. The energy I needed to run didn't exist. Part of me wanted to crumple to the ground, but the fear in Stephen's voice had infected me.

~Cori, she was bit,~ Carelian's words rung in my head like a bell and gave me a burst of energy from somewhere.

"Indira?" Stephen's voice rang up ahead, fear and anger as I saw his figure drop to the ground and pull a limp form into his arms.

I moved faster, trying to get to them. But something told me it didn't matter, it was already too late. Stephen had Indira wrapped in his arms, her bright green blouse garish against his tan suit jacket. He didn't let go as her body racked with shivers.

"You came," she whispered, her eyes locked on his face.

"I always will," he said just as quietly. His eyes darted over toward me. "Fix her," he hissed. "She can't die."

"I don't know how," I stuttered. Her body stopped shivering, and I reached over to grab her hand. The long flexible fingers were clammy and stiff. "Carelian, what do I do?" My heart begged for an answer that would give me something to stop this.

~Mourn her,~ he said privately to me. He walked over and curled up around her, purring as he gave his warmth to her. Publicly he said, ~Stephen, love her. Not even Tirsane can save her. These snakes were meant to provide a quick death. There is no way to stop the process.~

"No! I don't accept that. Cori, you're the most powerful mage that has ever been. Heal her!" His words were a demand, a plea, a soul screaming for salvation.

I reached in, pulling on the lessons I'd learned so long ago. If anyone could do it, it was me. My magic dove into her body and I offered recklessly, the blood that seeped from my wound vaporizing before it touched the air.

"Stephen, marry me?" Indira said quietly, her voice so soft that I had to strain to hear her.

"Forever and always," he said, leaning down to press his lips against her. "I was waiting to ask."

"So was I. I waited too long. I'll always love you," Indira managed, each syllable coming out softer and softer.

"Cori?" His voice broke as he begged and I reached, I offered, and I tried. I repaired her organs, replenished her blood cells, bolstered the synaptic processes. And nothing I did was enough. Her body failed faster than I could repair it. She wasn't hurting, her body just shut down as the magic venom raced through and everything just stopped in its wake.

"I love you," Indira whispered and closed her eyes, her body sagging as her life fled the venom that had taken everything she was.

"Indira? Indira?" Stephen shook her lightly and Carelian quit purring, instead he wrapped around her, giving what comfort he could to the body that had seconds before been someone we loved and the man who still loved her.

"INDIRA! NOOOO!" His grief shattered the air, and his magic did more than that.

FORTY-EIGHT

Rips of magic cross the globe, something we could have prevented if we had shunned magic from the beginning. Humans were not meant to play with the power of the gods. As you wail and mourn those who have died, remember it is your fault. If we had shunned that which was not ours to meddle in, our world would still be hale and whole. Eat the regret you sowed and know the blame rests on your shoulders. ~ Final blog on the Freedom from Magic Website

SPIRIT

His magic snapped out. Though a merlin, his primary branch was Order. Stephen's strengths lay in Pattern, Earth, and Air. Wind picked up as the ground beneath us began to shake.

It was known that a grieving mage was the most dangerous creature, topped only by a scared mother who was a mage. Trees began to topple as the earth shook harder and I saw cracks starting to run across the ground as his magic lashed out his grief.

I wanted to sob, scream out my own loss, but fear of losing him too drove me into action. If he continued, the responders would have no option but to kill him. His blind fury made him deadly. Already people were headed this way.

"Carelian, open a portal. We need to get him out of here," I screamed over the sound of the rising wind.

The Cath nodded at me, his ears down and whiskers flat against his face. A portal opened behind where Stephen still clutched Indira's limp body to him. I lifted the ground beneath them and tumbled them in, the sudden motion disrupting his anger. I dove in after them, Carelian following as he snapped it shut behind us. My ass hit cold gray stone and I blinked to find ourselves in the council chambers.

There wasn't time for much more than a surprised "huh" to cross my mind before Stephen was on his feet raging at me.

"This is all your fault. If you'd figured this out, done your fucking job, she wouldn't be dead."

Every word hit me with the force of a knife to the gut and I fought not to cry out at the emotional pain. Carelian growled but Stephen didn't notice, advancing on me with grief-fueled rage in his eyes.

"Stephen, I'm sorry. I'm so sorry." My voice broke on the

words, and I fought to remain standing as my own grief and sorrow threatened to undo me.

"Sorry? SORRY? That doesn't change anything!" His eyes were dilated wide with rage and grief. "If you'd figured it out. You were smart! WHY DID YOU LET THIS HAPPEN?!" Every word was punctuated by the ground rocking, throwing me and Carelian to the ground, even as he pulled more to him, protecting Indira's body as he cracked open the council floor.

"I'm sorry," I sobbed out and I hit him with the strongest KO I had, pulling blood out of the still bleeding wound. Stephen collapsed with a muffled groan and lay in a heap on the split council floor.

I collapsed next to him sobbing, raging, screaming. "WHY? Why her? You want me to fix this? Show me how to fucking fix this!" I started sobbing, holding my hands over my face, as I faced the loss of Indira and probably Stephen's friendship. He'd never care about me again, how could he? He was right. If I'd figured this out, Indira wouldn't be dead. Tears streamed down my face, each one draining me of moisture and energy that I really couldn't afford to lose, and I didn't care.

Tears, grief, rage all poured out of me in a stream and Magic didn't care. Time froze as I raged against the unfairness of the universe. Why set me to an impossible task? Just show me how to fix it. I'd do anything, anything, to stop this madness.

~Cori?~ Carelian's voice nudged against my mind. I ignored him. ~Cori, look,~ he insisted, nudging me with his nose.

"At what? My dead friend? The friend that now hates me? What am I supposed to look at?" I didn't bother to lift my head from my hands, my face buried in an attempt to avoid the consequences of my failure.

~Cori, look,~ Carelian insisted. He shoulder bumped me, throwing me off balance. I fell onto my side and glared at him.

"What? What is so important that I can't grieve?" I all but

shouted the words, wanting someone to understand my anger, fear, sorrow.

~There is a staircase to caverns,~ he said simply, turning to look at one of the huge cracks in the floor.

I followed his gaze to catch my breath as the gaping wound in the council chamber, slashing through the ring of the chairperson, revealed a set of worn stairs leading down.

Familiar worn stairs.

A familiar stone.

Light that burst out from memories that had never been mine.

"Could it?" My tears still ran down my face, but slowed as I blinked and tried to focus on what I was seeing. I leaned forward on my hands, peering down the sloping stairs that glowed with an eerie light. Stairs no one had ever mentioned or even hinted at.

"I have to go," I said as I forced myself up on wobbly legs. With effort I managed to stay standing, the backpack a lead weight on my body and soul.

~I will come with you,~ Carelian said, pushing up against me.

"No," the words were out of my mouth without a thought.

He snarled back at me, his face too close, and I realized I'd tilted down to him. With a force of will and desperation I yanked myself back up to standing, letting the pack act as an anchor and balance.

"Carelian, you have to stay here. You need to make sure Stephen doesn't awake and cause issues. You need to explain if anyone comes. You're the only one I'd trust to do this."

He didn't back down, a long hiss and lashing tailing proving he didn't buy it. So, I went for the metaphorical jugular.

"And if something happens to me, you are the only being

that can take care of Jo and Sable, not to mention the twins. Carelian, you have to be there for them."

If anything, his snarling hiss got louder, but his tail dropped between his legs and he crouched down next to the limp body of Stephen.

~If you die...~ He trailed off, unable to finish the sentence.

"If I die, I will know you love me and will make sure our family never has to fear anything."

He whined, a long low sound that brought tears to my eyes and I closed them to fight the emotions it elicited. "But I will be back. I will," I assured him.

I knew I was probably lying. But he needed to believe me, at least right now.

~Go. Scream for me and I will come. Not even the gods shall stop me.~ His voice held absolute certainty. I didn't push.

"I will," I said and in the same breath I turned and headed down the stairs.

In the memories, Shera had flown down them—I had to walk. The cool walls let me lean against them for support and every five steps I had to stop and convince myself I could do this. There weren't any other options that I knew of, though I had zero idea what this entailed.

The stairs twisted and kept sloping down, but they grew warmer rather than cooler. Evidence as to the existence of the volcano. Just when I was sure I'd have to sit down and rest, my legs were shaking and vision had gotten blurry, the stairs stopped at the entrance of a large room with an altar at the end.

Working on lowering my heart rate and breathing I leaned against the doorway and examined the room. It didn't strike me as a place for traps or hidden objects. But I knew it held the answers to the puzzle I'd been fighting to find for so long. With shaking legs, I moved further in until I stood in the center of the chamber. Remnants of memories showed me what Shera had seen versus what I saw now, and it was almost an exact match. An altar lay in front of me, with three chalices standing above each of the classes of magic.

Each goblet was the same shape, a large bulbous bowl tapering down to a stem that was simple then a wide base, ensuring it would not tilt easily. But there the similarities ended. Order was silver and shiny with diamonds surrounding the base of the goblet. Chaos swirled with rainbows, cycling through all the colors then fading to black before starting over. Spirit looked like opal, milky, soft, pastels creating an elegant fragile thing. Above each of them Magic swirled and pooled and somehow became liquid dripping drop by drop past sigils and runes into each chalice, leaving it brimming with magic.

Images of Zenobia in those final moments, bolstered by Shera and pulled to me by Soul, the imprint of the last actions here. I watched as she called on magic and then dumped the liquid over her, bathing in the magic of each realm. At first, she glowed and her smile was radiant, and then it faded away, her hands clutching at her body as magic ate into her, dissolving her. I watched her scream as Magic lashed out, the power exploding from her as she vanished into nothingness and the entire cavern vibrated.

"That obviously wasn't the way to do it." I muttered. I looked at it trying to figure out what in the world I could do.

~Carelian, is Stephen still unconscious?~ I asked, not taking my eyes off the alluring goblets.

~Yes. Is everything okay?~ His response was instant, and I felt better, though to feel good I'd need a shower and clean clothes.

~Maybe? I'm not in danger.~ I stared at the goblets. "Screw this, I'm the herald but that doesn't mean I need to do it blind. ~Tirsane, Salistra, Bob? I found the key, but I don't know what to do. Can you come here? I'm at the council chambers. Hurry.~

I sent to all of them and tried to brace myself for responses from Salistra and Bob.

The sensation of a questioning sound caressed my mind, then short responses of "Yes" that didn't hurt too much. I walked around the altar, not touching anything, just looking. It was made of the same stone as the floor and whoever had carved or raised it had been much better with Calling Earth than I. I'd never thought about raising carved stone. Might be a fun idea for later, if there was a later.

Magic in tangible form was odd and creepy yet I wanted to touch it, bath in it. The imprints of the past managed to kill that desire without much effort. A silver chime echoed down the hallway of stairs.

~The lords are here, they say you summoned them,~ Carelian told me as the chime continued getting closer.

~Thank you.~ I sent back and turned to watch as Tirsane slithered out, followed by Salistra whose every step chimed like a bell with her silver hoofs against stone floor. Then Bob, his oozing shapeless form puddling at the bottom of the stairs.

"You found it?" Tirsane said looking around, her snakes tight against her head.

"I guess. I know this is where Zenobia severed everything, though I'm not sure how. I don't know what I'm supposed to do next." I waved my arm to encompass everything.

~You look ill. Why are you ill?~ Salistra's sharp voice sliced through my mind and I shuddered at the slash of pain.

"Rescuing children from your village from a rip and then I've been using too much magic. She doesn't do anything for free."

Salistra froze, teeth bared at me. For a long moment she just stared at me, but I felt like she was looking through me, not at me. ~Ah. The debt. I see. You have repaid most of your transgressions. Only one left.~

I shivered at those words but tried not to let it show. Instead, I changed the subject. "Any clue what I need to do?"

Tirsane had moved over to Spirit and stared at the chalice full of liquid magic. She slowly lifted her right hand and touched her index finger to the liquid. Her body went rigid, and all her snakes went limp.

"Tirsane?" I said starting to move toward her, but she lifted her left hand holding it out to me.

"Pax. I am ... okay. Salistra, Bob. Will you see if you learn what I just learned?"

Salistra moved over and dipped her horn in the liquid of Order, while Bob dipped a pseudo pod into Chaos. They both changed as they stood there, then pulled back, looking at each other. I sensed a fast and furious conversation that I was not invited to. If the words from Bob and Salistra didn't hurt so bad, I might have been more offended.

"So, it is agreed," Tirsane said aloud, and I jerked my attention back to the three Lords. The other two nodded and then they all looked at me. I took an involuntary step back. This wouldn't be good.

"What is agreed?" I looked between the three of them.

"You must choose," Tirsane said. She must have seen the incomprehension on my face because she continued after a moment. "Magic is at a crossroads. You must decide which magic survives." Her voice was suspiciously flat as she said that.

"What do you mean survive?"

~She means, herald, that you will decide which of our realms continue in conjunction with earth.~ The amount of contempt in Salistra's voice slashed as deep as her words. ~I am tempted to call in my final debt and demand you choose order.~

Tirsane's snakes started hissing. "And I am the godmother of her child." Her voice icy.

~Did I not send the Cath to her?~ Bobs voice as always was the worst and I couldn't contain a low grunt of pain.

I lifted up my hand silencing all of them. "Fuck that shit. I'm not letting anyone die or disappear."

Tirsane's voice, so full of sorrow that I almost cried, responded. "You must choose a chalice and drink from it. Then that realm will merge with Earth."

"That makes zero sense, but I'm still not choosing," I snarled at them. "I have to drink, right? Then magic will do whatever shit she wants to do? And the rips will stop?"

"Essentially," Tirsane said.

"Did you know this is where it would all end?" I stared at each of them, anger bubbling up in me.

"No. Not until I touched Magic. You can see for yourself." She waved at the chalices.

I moved over, fear and anger lending me energy. Leaning one hip on the altar, I placed my right middle finger in Spirit, my left in Chaos. Knowledge filled me, whispers of healing, togetherness, and the urge to drink my fill. I yanked my fingers out and glared at the altar.

"See? You must choose." Tirsane's voice forced me to turn around, to push the urges out of my mind. "Cori, it is okay. You are the herald. This is what Magic wanted." Salistra didn't say anything but the sharp chime of her hoof striking the floor declared her anger and concern.

"You are all overly melodramatic. I don't pull that shit. I need to drink, fine. But I'm not choosing," I snarled back. I slipped off my pack, my knees almost buckling as the weight left me. I dug inside for Carelian's bowl—a bit of Cath saliva wouldn't hurt me, at this point I was pretty sure I had him in every cell of my being.

~What are you doing herald?~ Salistra's voice cut like an epee into my mind, but I ignored her. I set the bowl on the altar and carefully picked up sprit, pouring the liquid into the bowl. The bowl I used for him was an old mixing bowl so it had measurement lines. I poured a cup of each chalice into the bowl. The cavern seemed to quake as if waiting. Once I had three cups in there I dug into my pack and pulled out a bottle of water and added a cup. Picking it up carefully I held out the bowl to the three lords.

"All realms and earth, equal amounts of what allows life and magic. To Magic." I didn't tell Carelian what I was doing, I just picked up the bowl and began to drink. The question was would I live to ever see him again? I'd seen what happened to Zenobia. I just hoped the pain wouldn't be too bad.

Flavors I couldn't place swirled past my tongue. Some I chased after, sweet and delicious, others I shied from, dark and bitter. But I drank, feeling the magic well and bubble, but I kept drinking. The last drops passed my lips and I pulled the bowl away from my mouth with a gasp. My head was spinning with new sensations. "It is done. I choose everyone." The words sounded like a gasp as I felt magic surging.

~I love you,~ I sent to everyone with the image of Zenobia dissolving fresh in my mind.

The lords stared at me with horror or surprise, a horse and a blob weren't very emotive.

"What have you done?" Tirsane whispered.

I didn't have a chance to answer as Magic extracted her price. She pulled it out of me, shredding me from the inside out. My knees gave, but I didn't even notice the pain of the impact as the rest of me screamed. Then it reversed and from each chalice a stream of magic bubbled up and flowed like a river toward me. About a foot from my body, they blended into a fire hose of magic that impacted into me.

"Cori!" Tirsane cried out and she headed over to me. At the same time, Carelian's voice echoed in my mind, ~CORI~. I couldn't respond, couldn't think, couldn't breathe, all I could do was experience agony.

Tirsane's hand touched me, and where her hand rested pain stopped. "Oh," her voice was soft, so soft only my need to focus on anything other than the pain let me hear it. Then her voice whispered to me. "Cori, I regret I will not be able to fulfill the final favors I owe you." Then in a louder, much clearer voice, she stated, "I accept the price. I will pay the price for Spirit." She moved and stepped into the flow from the Spirit chalice.

The pain ebbed, and I turned my head to look at Tirsane whose hand had slid until she just touched the fingers of my right hand. Her body arched back, and her mouth gaped open in a scream. Her snakes had all attacked her, biting hard, pumping venom into her body. I knew they were attempting to lower her pain. A wiggling in my arm grabbed my attention, not pain but so uncomfortable it still registered. The snake that had been my tattoo wiggled out of my skin and slithered up my arm to Tirsane's hand, then continued up until it joined its brethren, teeth sinking into her neck.

"Nooo," I stuttered, but the howling of magic swallowed my protest.

~Really? Really?~ Salistra's sharp tone cut through, offering a different flavor of agony and I clung to it. ~I will not be less than you. Cori Munroe, your debt to me is declared paid in full.~ Her horn sliced across my arm, a ribbon of liquid fire, but a scratch compared to everything else I experienced. ~I accept. Order's price shall be mine!~ Her words were a roar of defiance, and the pain level dropped as Salistra screamed standing in the flow from Order

I knelt on the ground, tears streaking my face, drool dripping out of my gaping mouth as swallowing was past my abilities. At this point I just sobbed as I tried to remember how to breathe.

Let the pain end. Please?

~Then Chaos shall be no less. Thank you, Herald, for your courage. I accept the price for Chaos.~ Bob's words tore through me, but I had no breath left to scream. Black tar surrounded me, and the pain dropped from incapacitating to agonizing. Bob moved into the flow, his being flaring white as magic impacted, then filtered through his substance.

Standing between me and the magic, it changed, becoming less and more at the same time. The three lords shimmered and sparkled while they screamed in my mind and in my ears, the same agony they were sparing me from. Somehow, the magic became calmer, less aggressive as it filled me to bursting. But it wasn't enough, it wasn't enough to change everything.

"Carelian," I called out, my voice inaudible over their screams. I tried again. ~Carelian?~

~Yes?~ His voice instant in my mind.

~It isn't enough.~ I tried not to sob as pain washed me, but it was so much less than it had been. And that was the problem. ~I need the phoenix stone. Now.~

He didn't argue. I don't know if I would have had the strength to convince him. A minute later, he placed the cold stone in my hand.

"Thank you," I sobbed out.

This has to work, it has to.

Carelian curled up around me, supporting me. ~I will never leave you, my quean.~

I took solace in his warm fur and solid weight as I raised the phoenix stone into the stream of magic. For one blissful second the pain stopped and I began to sag as the feeling of being torn apart vanished. The stream went from a solid stream of grey blue into a rainbow kaleidoscope of colors. It flared up, then raced forward to impact me.

It filled every corner and I knew I was screaming but I couldn't hear it, it wasn't recognizable as human as the magic washed through me and changed me. Every cell felt like it was full to bursting. I felt like it had to leave me, and I let go of everything. I gave myself over to Magic.

The last sight I saw was magic bursting from me, hitting the walls, the earth shook, and something popped deep in my soul. The light and pressure lasted an eternity yet only a few seconds, then everything went dark.

Around the world, all the rips have snapped shut. There are reports that the permanent rips at Area 51 are gone. A worldwide quake caused damage across the globe, but not insurmountable damage. Reports are still coming back on the death toll, but it seems minimal as few buildings were destroyed. Geologists say having a global 6-point earthquake isn't possible, yet that is what has been seen. GPS is going haywire, and all the governments are refusing to comment. Oddly, the only information we have is from a few familiars who have stated, "The world and realms are together again. All thank the Herald." ~ CNN Anchor

CHAOS

"Cori?~ A wet nose and tongue brushed at my cheek, and I opened my eyes. Carelian's emerald orbs stared back at me. ~Are you okay?~ He kept licking me, on parts that should have had clothes between his tongue and my skin.

I lay on my back in the cavern, the roughhewn stone above me. Groaning, I pushed myself up to a seated position and waited for the world to stop spinning. The walls still looked the same. The bowl I'd used sat untouched on the shattered altar and all my clothes were gone, remnants of fabric lay on the floor next to me. An image of the three lords dissolving into nothing jerked my spine rigid as I turned, seeking them. But nothing remained, not even dust, to show where they had been.

I wanted to cry, but I couldn't process this all yet. Instead, I stared at my arm, trying to figure out why they looked wrong. My arms were thin, but the skin intact with my offering wound completely healed. But it still looked wrong.

"Cori?" Stephen's voice came from behind and to my left. I leaned my head back to look at him out of the corner of my eyes. He stood in the chamber, eyes wide, lines on his face from tears and stress. He came forward, pulling off his shirt. "Can you stand?"

"I think so?" Leaning on Carelian, I staggered to my feet, a breeze brushing against my naked body. Another glance and I realized why my body looked so funny. I had a slight glow and my tattoos from the lords were gone. I touched my arm where the snake, horn, and whiskers had existed. Now only pale, glowing skin existed. Stephen slipped his shirt on me. It hit me about mid-thigh. It gave me some modesty, but it barely registered.

"What happened?" we asked each other at the same time. A soft laugh escaped.

"I'm not sure. The world shook and the best thing I can say is it felt like something snapped back in place. If you've ever had a dislocated joint and it pops back into place. That was what it felt like. The world snapped back into place." His voice was hoarse. "But I know Indira is still gone." The grief was at the forefront, not the rage.

"I know. I'm sorry. I couldn't save her." Tears welled back up as I tried to swallow them down.

"It wasn't your fault. I shouldn't have blamed you, I just..." he trailed off, waving his hand in the air, avoiding looking me in the eyes.

"Yeah. I get it. I'm not sure what happened, but ...But..." The lump formed larger and harder. I forced another swallow, wanting to gag at what I needed to say. "Tirsane, Salistra, and Bob are gone. They offered themselves to magic. They saved my life by their death."

"I don't understand," Stephen said softly as he wrapped his right arm around me on my left, Carelian by my right side. Together we walked to the stairs, then climbed them at a glacial pace as I explained what had happened. I had no injuries, but exhaustion soaked me, like my blood had turned to dust. Even the pumping of my heart and breathing seemed a laborious effort. Carelian held me up, his tail lashing, and I knew I needed to ask him what he'd seen, but for the moment the stairs were all I could focus on.

We stepped up into the broken chamber and I froze, my eyes locked on the shadows slicing away from the open wall. The wall looking onto a lawn where Zmaug would sit. The green lawn that glowed in direct sunlight.

"Is that sunlight?" My words sounded echoey to my ears and the possibility I might still be in a dream or memory occurred to me. "Or am I seeing things?"

~It is sun.~ Carelian sounded just as shocked as I felt and the three of us moved out onto the grass and looked up. Above us a blue sky with white clouds and a yellow sun shone down. In all the time I'd ever been to the realms, it had always been a diffuse light, never anything direct, but now the sun warmed my skin.

"Can you get your mother?" I wanted to say and Tirsane, but I knew that wasn't possible. Not anymore.

~Yes,~ he said in a soft whisper, as shocked as I was.

"Let me sit," I told Stephen, as my legs were already threatening to buckle. "Carelian, can you check on Jo and Sable? The kids? Kris, Charles? Everyone? Are they okay?" Even saying that threatened tears, there were too many beings that weren't okay and Indira and Tirsane were at the top of that list.

~I will check. Esmere said she would come.~ He sat down next to me, letting me use him as a pillow as I stared up at the impossibility of a sky.

"Huh. My cellphone works," Stephen muttered. He'd sank down next to me. I blinked at him but didn't know what to say. Cellphones didn't work in the realms.

~Everyone is fine, but the news is exploding. Wait, what?~ Carelian jerked up a bit. His head tilting.

"Carelian?" I touched him. Breath caught in my throat as I waited for another attack. I couldn't handle any more, I couldn't. So many dead. Beings I loved. I couldn't lose anyone else.

~Esmere says she can't come. The realms are gone. There is no way to move through the realms.~

I stared at him, unsure of what he meant. "The realms are gone, but she's okay?" I needed reassurance that she was fine.

~She is fine. There was a huge quake, then the realm jolted, and they were somewhere else. She says everyone is staring at the sun and marveling at the feeling of it on their skins.~

Stephen spoke in a distracted voice. "The news is going crazy. They say new land has appeared and the GPS is inaccurate across the world." He kept flipping through this phone.

"Any rips?" That was my priority still.

"Not in the last hour, but we've had longer lulls. The question is where are we?"

"No clue. Can you go get my pack? I need food and water, then maybe my brain will start working." I was staring at the trees, trees I'd never seen on Earth before, but then maybe I just didn't recognize them.

"Yeah, give me a minute," he said as he got up. My phone had been in my pocket when I went into the cavern. I assumed it had been fried or disintegrated with my clothes. I leaned back against Carelian, enjoying the warmth of the sun. We lay there just enjoying being alive for a minute.

"Do you think I did it? That is what Magic wanted?" I asked quietly, staring at a cloud drifting across the sky.

~I am unsure. But the world feels different. In a way I can not put to words,~ he replied just as softly in my mind.

Stephen came back carrying my pack, and we dug into the water and food in there. I felt better after I'd eaten and drank. The change of clothes consisted of underwear, a tank top, and leggings. I slipped into them with relief, then handed Stephen his shirt. The glow was fading, but I still felt off balance as if something was missing from me.

"Now what?" I asked. Though a large part of me would have been more than willing to just lay here for a week. It was a pleasant area.

"We probably need to go back and face the music, or at least deal with the ramifications." Stephen heaved a sigh. "Do you think sidestep still works? Can you do that?"

"Probably. That was always easy for me, just easier to let Carelian do the hard work. Let me check the cost." If it was as low as usual, I could do it with a simple offering of a nail. It would hurt, but they grew back. I didn't feel like I could lose more blood right now.

I reached for magic, picturing our entry point in Hamiada's house and.... Nothing. That shook me out of my lethargy a bit. I sat up and reached again. Magic did not respond. I fell back to something that was simple and easy: fire. Just a simple flame on my palm. Again, Magic didn't seem to hear me.

"Stephen? Can you do magic?" I asked, unsure of anything at that moment.

"Me?" I nodded at him. "Um...." He looked at the water we'd been drinking and nothing happened. "Okay, that's odd. Let me try this." This time the earth rose and created a little table. His head tilted, and he focused on something for a minute. I could see and feel things happening, but I wasn't sure what was going on.

"That is.... odd. I have access to Order - all of it. And if I had to guess, I'm strong in all classes, but... the others are gone. Spirit and Chaos aren't there for me to use." He said each word as if feeling it out. "I've never had access to Transform, and now I do."

"Okay," I said slowly as I thought.

"Cori," he snapped, his voice urgent. "Look at me."

Surprised, I turned to look at him. He'd been on my left side. Now he reached out, grabbing my chin between his thumb and forefinger and turned my face all the way so my right temple was facing him. He let go and ran a finger over my temple. "Your tattoo is gone. There is nothing there. Not even scars."

My fingers trembled as I lifted my hand, running it over the marks that had defined me for so long. I'd always been able to just barely feel them, but now the skin felt smooth and unmarred. "I don't have any magic?" It was a question.

Carelian rumbled a distressed sound. ~I do not know. Esmere will need to look at you. I do not know how to travel without the realms, neither does she. Sidestepping was a human thing.~

Stephen frowned. "I thought you could travel to the house directly?"

A tail snapped in response. ~Yes, but I still stepped through the realms. If I knew where I was going, I didn't need to stop at the crossroads. But even that isn't working. I have zero access to the realms as a whole, so I can't open anything.~

The words changed my world view. I tried to talk to Carelian mentally, but they were just thoughts in my head. "I can't talk to you via mindspeak anymore." My heart rate climbed. "Am I going to lose you? If I'm not a mage, I don't need a focus. Carelian, will I lose you?" My voice hit a high note as I began to shake, everything crashing in on me.

First Indira, then Tirsane, Salistra, and Bob. Now if I lost him?

Nausea rose in my gorge, and I fought to not throw up what I'd just managed to get down.

~Cori. You will never lose me. Ever. You are my quean, mage or not. You are mine.~ His strong fierce voice pounded in my head, and I forced myself to breathe in and out in a slow steady manner. ~Magic doesn't matter to me. You are my quean.~

I kept breathing even as I leaned back on him. "Can you get us home, Stephen? I don't know how."

"I'll figure it out. You did good Cori," he said, his voice reassuring if as broken as my heart felt. There in the sun on a strange piece of land, I laid down my head on Carelian's warm body and closed my eyes. My family was okay. Carelian was okay. With a little sleep, I could figure out the rest. I let exhaustion pull me down into a deep slumber.

EPILOGUE

A memorial for those lost because of the rips has been slated to be installed in DC. They have contacted the renowned sculptor Merlin Jackson Vinci to create the artwork. The names of those lost will be engraved into the art. The first round of sketches is due in three months where the committee will vote on them. The final three sketches are scheduled to be presented in a public voting system. Their intention is to honor those lost while celebrating the new status quo of magic in our lives. ~ Talking Head on CNN

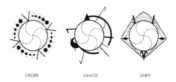

ORDER   CHAOS   SPIRIT

I t took two days for us to get off that piece of land. We explored the area, but it was bigger than we could walk. The FBI was able to pinpoint our location and a US Naval ship picked us up and took us to Australia, the closest point of land. One long flight later, though we both got first class, we returned home to a world that seemed more alien than the realms.

I spent two weeks in meetings with the OMO, the Senate, the President, the UN, and even all the governors of the states. We went through my memories of Shera and what we faced now.

There had once been a theory that the moon had been part of Earth because a geologist felt like we had been bigger once. He wasn't wrong, but we'd become smaller not millions of years ago, but about five to six thousand years ago. It turned out when Zenobia separated the realms, she'd ripped the Earth apart. This was where so many of the flood and world ending stories came from as the Earth tried to reassemble itself. This time, it had been the opposite. While there were worldwide earthquakes, everything kind of fit in and the death toll had only been in the thousands, not billions. Which allowed me to sleep at night. But it had stopped all the rips, though now all of us were in the same place.

They were still mapping everything and trying to figure out

the ramifications. It took a month for the satellites to remap everything. It turned out that the Earth added something like a thousand miles at the equator. Clashes were occurring between the new areas and the existing countries. The denizens were fiercely defending their borders, and our world watched all of it with a mixed sense of horror and fascination. The oceans had merged with the seas in the realms. That meant some of the monsters we'd talked about in our legends showed up. Those creatures were in an all-out war with our navies. The majority were not sentient, so it made it easier to agree to hunt them, but they weren't easy prey.

It turned out Atlantis had existed in the North Atlantic Ocean about nine hundred miles from the Strait of Gibraltar. The buildings that had once existed were at the same level as our ancient ruins. Atlantis was the size of Maryland and contained at least thirty-five thousand square miles of untouched land. Several sentient denizens elected to move there. The United Nations declared it sovereign territory of the magical beings, mainly because Zmaug made it crystal clear that if they didn't, every airplane in the world would become fair game and the dragons had no issues eating humans.

The dragons' favorite areas were parts of South America and Africa, and no one even blinked at their claiming of the areas. Luckily for everyone involved, the lands they loved were inhospitable for humans, to say the least.

The AIN still had their walls. The denizens could still create pocket realms, but most of them had collapsed. Hamiada's grove materialized in the middle of our street, the land itself shifting and moving. Now instead of a street with four houses on it, it was a grove with a road circling it with driveways to each house. This had happened around the world with various degrees of acceptance from the residents already there.

Then there was the issue with magic. Everyone was a mage.

But there were no more merlins. Everyone had full access to one of the branches, Spirit, Order, Chaos, but that was it. The big change was how much power they had. It was as if Magic had paid attention to the problems of humans. Those with limited understanding, the disabled, the damaged, they never rose past hedgemage. They could do simple magics at high prices. The more you studied, the greater your understanding of the mysteries of the universe, the stronger your magic. Someone at archmage levels had strong's in everything.

The drama that change caused fueled laughter and nightmares. Laws across the globe were being rewritten, people lost their elected positions, Freedom from Magic completely collapsed. Mages still emerged at the end of puberty for the majority of people. The OMO had a field day with retesting, new tattoos, and new ways of measuring abilities.

And I was the only adult they could find that had zero magic. I still didn't know if that was a blessing or a curse.

The crossroads was gone, so teleporting or sidestepping was the only option left, which annoyed Esmere to no end. But all Spirit Mages had the ability, which meant all the Spirit denizens also had that ability. Stenia, Tirsane's sister, agreed to bring Esmere to see us after everything settled down and I was home.

~Cori?~ Esmere's voice pinged in my mind, and I smiled, rising from my chair in my study.

"Up here, Esmere."

Soft thumps as Esmere came bounding up the stairs and into the study. Amber eyes in emerald fur raked over me, and the tension dropped out of her.

~You look much better than last I saw you.~ She rubbed her face against me, her tail relaxed as a purr rumbled out of her body.

"Two months of no magic, getting regular meals, and sleep

helped. Carelian has been making sure no one stressed me too much." I rubbed her ears, just as glad to see her. Of all the things I missed about magic, it was the inability to see people that affected me the most. But there wasn't an easy way to travel globally right now. I foresaw a few more years of turmoil before we gained a new equilibrium. I still didn't know how I felt about not being in the middle of it.

~Excellent. Are you up to visitors?~ she asked, eyes closed, leaning into my attentions.

"Besides you? Sure?" I didn't know who else would visit me. The publicity of me being the only adult without magic after being the most powerful had created an odd backlash. Now everyone felt sorry for me, and I'd been receiving presents from all over the world, though not from my fan club thankfully. Even Cixi had sent me a present via post and Tiantang had told me of his frustration to be unable to come see me, but he wasn't of Spirit so that option wasn't available. They had released me from my draft as I wasn't eligible, though they looked very annoyed at being unable to charge me with anything, but the laws weren't written for my situation - they never were.

~Come. We are in the back.~ It was almost August, and the days were hot and muggy, but Hamiada now claimed the entire street as her grove. It let her control the temperature to a certain extent and no one could get near her that wasn't approved. That ability helped shelter me from all the attention and even death threats. Lots of people were not happy about the changes and my participation in it had been widely advertised.

Stephen had retired the moment we returned. The second they let him go, he'd claimed Indira's body and disappeared. He'd sent me an email letting me know he wasn't mad, but he couldn't return. I replied, letting him know he always had family here.

All these thoughts went through my mind as I headed downstairs and out through the sunroom where I stopped in surprise, Carelian at my back. There were a cluster of beings on my lawn. Hamiada watched them warily from the edge of the house, her dark brown skin and thick bark telling me she was uncomfortable.

I recognized Freya and Frej, Shiarissa, Zmaug, and others. In fact, if I thought about it, the council of lords stood on my back lawn. Even Shay and Citlali were there, though I'd talked to them regularly over the last two months since phones still worked fine. Citlali was well on her way to being a good friend and Kesis could sidestep, dragging Citlali with her.

"Hi?" I said, unaccountably nervous. Carelian crowded closer to me and his weight and heat against my leg let me center myself. For the first time, the fact that I had no magic slammed in on me. I was more helpless than most.

Freya stepped forward to meet me. "Cori, you are looking well," she said with a smile. "We had been worried seeing the images of you that were shared among us."

I ran my hands over my head, a bit self-conscious. My hair was almost two inches long, and I'd put on some weight, though I was taking it slow to make sure I gained muscle, not fat. "Thank you. So, I have to ask, what brought everyone here?"

~We have a request to ask of you,~ Zmaug said in her normal blunt way. ~We do not feel anyone else would be as suited as you.~

There was a general murmur of agreement, and I sighed. "I'm not a mage. Definitely not a merlin. Almost anyone on Earth would be more suited to anything you might need."

"Not this," Citlali said. "They asked us, and we agreed you are the one person who would excel in this task."

"I'm missing something," I said. "Let's sit and you can talk to me."

It took a few minutes to get everyone situated, with Hamiada making chairs out of the soil. I did love her comfortable creations, though I grabbed a blanket. There were more insects on Earth than had existed in her glade.

Once everyone was settled, even Zmaug looked comfortable, I waved my hand. "Okay, spill. What is this all about?"

"You know about the lands and the rearranging of territories on Earth," Freya started, watching me closely.

"Yes. I've been following that." I managed to close my mouth and not say anything else no matter how much I wanted to either apologize or assure them I had no idea what would happen.

"We are being approached by multiple governments all over the world. Everyone has different demands or questions or offers, and we are struggling to make sense of them all. Tirsane had always been the best at doing that and we miss her."

A pang stabbed through my heart, and I bowed my head. "Yes, I miss her as well."

Freya nodded. "We are working on creating an actual government, though it is challenging, but we do not have the time to work through creation slowly and situations are heating up in some areas. Others are quiet for now. In many ways, the US and China have been the most lenient. We are not as fortunate in other areas."

That information did not surprise me. An entire section of Africa had reappeared. That was Esmere's domain. It turned out Madagascar wasn't an island, but the land between it and the continent had been in the realms. Numerous large islands near Australia, Fiji, and Japan appeared, throwing off politics in those areas. Huge sections of land in the middle of Asia, South America (primarily along the mountains) and Central America appeared complete with the beings that thought they had first say. Too many humans disagreed, thinking they could claim those new resources. The denizens were not shy about making sure they paid for their arrogance.

"Okay, but that doesn't explain why you are here talking to me. I only have some friends in a few governments, not any real influence." I really hoped they didn't think I could swoop in and save them, because I couldn't.

"That is true. But you have something that almost everyone else lacks," Freya said with a subdued smile.

I just arched a brow, waiting. The smirks on Citlali's and Shay's faces didn't make me feel better.

"You are recognized and respected worldwide. Everyone has heard the story of what you did. The sacrifices you made. You are regarded as someone with honor, someone others respect."

I could feel my cheeks flushing, but I watched them waiting for the shoe to drop.

~Why are humans so wrapped up in politics?~ Zmaug grumbled. ~We wish for you to be the ambassador for the denizens of the realms to the human governments. They will listen to you, your focus can translate any language, and we will provide an aid from Spirit for transportation and truth sensing. Will you save us once again?~

Sharp whispers and hissing and multiple deadly glares were directed at Zmaug, but she ignored all of that, instead choosing to watch me.

"Me? Your ambassador?" That wasn't something I'd expected. And the note of pleading in Zmaugs' voice took me back. I'd never heard anything even close to that in her tone.

"Zmaug is accurate, Cori." Citlali moved to the front, Kesis at her side. "They are being hounded and need someone who will advocate for them. I can't think of anyone better than you."

"Ambassador?" I repeated, but this time weighing it out. "Carelian?" I asked, turned to look at him.

~It would show people how strong my quean is, and if we have an aide from Spirit we could do the Search and Rescue once you are stronger. They could take us anywhere.~ His voice was quiet, whispering only in my mind. He needed to stretch himself, but the inability to get away from civilization was gnawing at him.

My hand found his head, and I rubbed it, understanding. "I'm not going to say yes right now, but I'm not saying no. Who would our aide be and when would this start? I need at least another month or so to recover." That couldn't be skipped. I needed to work out and eat and get back into shape. At least I could walk between our houses now.

~That would be me, if you would have me.~ Jeorgaz popped in front of me with a flash of fire. ~I've always traveled via side-stepping, and I can sense lies. It would honor me to work with Herald Cori.~

I snorted. "I'm not Herald Cori anymore. Would you be able to keep secret anything to do with my job?" Jeorgaz loved to gossip so that was a valid concern.

~Of course.~ He puffed up in indignation, then subsided. ~Besides, many are discovering the magic of the internet and phones. I am not as needed as before.~ Jeorgaz landed on a perch Hamiada pulled out for him, his feathers shining and flickering with flames. ~And you will always be Herald Cori to us. You sacrificed everything for everyone.~

I shrugged, focusing on the denizens watching me. "You trust me to make decisions for all of you? That is what I would be doing. Binding you to agreements with my word. Signing treaties, forging alliances." The idea terrified and thrilled me. It sounded exciting and so rife with pitfalls.

"Yes." Freya was confident and I saw no doubt in anyone.

"You have always been honest and done what you could for the best of everyone. We have no doubts you will do what is best for us, not humans."

I laughed and shook my head. "Then yes, I will do this - but not for a few months."

The tension faded from Freya. "That is fine. We need to finalize our government and our leadership. When that is done, we will let you know, but for now we can let other nations know we have an ambassador—Cori Munroe." There was a muted cheer, and I just shook my head. So much for my life of peace and boredom, but then my luck always was twisted.

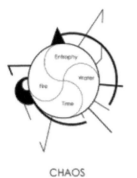

CHAOS

Chaos:

- Entropy
- Fire
- Water
- Time

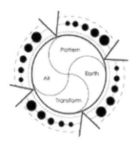

ORDER

Order:

- Pattern
- Air
- Earth
- Transform

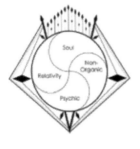

SPIRIT

Spirit:

- Soul
- Relativity
- Non-Organic
- Psychic

AUTHORS NOTES

Well... it's done. That was the last of Cori's story, I think. I know I have some novellas about life with Carelian and I can't say she won't show up in other stories down the road, but now she is the only person on Earth with no magic.

A few things slipped in but people won't realize this until decades have passed - things like no more disabled children, no more dementia, lots of cancers will fade away, little things. All the damage that crept in without magic to renew cells and ensure health.

But there will be more stories in the Ternion universe.

Currently I'm working on a Mage Hunter book and I have another trilogy set in the late 1800s/early 1900s I'm looking forward to. I'm also working on an epic fantasy that I hope you love.

Other than that, all I can do is promise more stories.

See you on the next newsletter.

Mel

Remember you can sign up for my newsletter at www.badashpublishing.com/newsletter

ABOUT THE AUTHOR

Tired of stories that didn't fill her needs, Mel Todd decided to share the weird worlds that occupy her mind. Action, magic, sci-fi, and more, her stories have it all. You can follow her on Facebook at - https://www.facebook.com/badashbooks/ You can also sign up for her newsletter and follow her blog at https://www.badashpublishing.com Author of over 44 stories, you should check out her other worlds. You never know what might grab you.

f facebook.com/MelTodd.Author

instagram.com/BadAshBooks

Made in the USA
Middletown, DE
23 March 2024

51963376R00245